Acclaim for Ha Jin's

Nanjing Requiem

"*Nanjing Requiem* is both plainspoken and revelatory, the saddest of Ha Jin's novels. After this past decade of armed conflict, which has put millions of civilians at risk, his reminder of the human costs of war is also, unfortunately, timely." —*The Boston Globe*

"An affecting, insightful portrait." —*The Oregonian*

"[Minnie's] humanizing voice and struggling perspective personalize the story and provide an element of reasonableness and decency amid so much savagery. . . . Harrowing." —*The Wall Street Journal*

"[Ha Jin's] sparse prose can achieve a masterful precision. . . . Demonstrates how humans cope when forced together in wartime. . . . Testament to the bravery of women in the most horrifying of circumstances." —*The Independent* (UK)

"Exquisitely painful. . . . Creates an unforgettable impression." —*St. Louis Post-Dispatch*

"Haunting. . . . He has honed a distinctively dry, laconic prose style." —*Financial Times*

HA JIN

Nanjing Requiem

Ha Jin's previous books include the internationally best-selling *Waiting*, which won the PEN/Faulkner Award and the National Book Award; *War Trash*, which won the PEN/Faulkner Award; the story collections *Under the Red Flag*, which won the Flannery O'Connor Award for Short Fiction, and *Ocean of Words*, which won the PEN/Hemingway Award; and three books of poetry.

INTERNATIONAL

ALSO BY HA JIN

Nanjing Requiem

HA JIN

Nanjing Requiem

VINTAGE INTERNATIONAL
Vintage Books
A Division of Random House, Inc.
New York

Vintage ISBN: 978-0-307-74373-2

Book design by Iris Weinstein

www.vintagebooks.com

For Lisha, who also gave birth to this book

CONTENTS

ONE

The Fall of the Capital

FINALLY BAN BEGAN TO TALK. For a whole evening we sat in the dining room listening to the boy. He said, "That afternoon when Principal Vautrin told me to go tell Mr. Rabe about the random arrests in our camp, I ran to the Safety Zone Committee's headquarters. As I was reaching that house, two Japanese soldiers stopped me, one pointing his bayonet at my tummy and the other sticking his gun against my back. They ripped off my Red Cross armband and hit me in the face with their fists. Then they took me away to White Cloud Shrine. There's a pond inside the temple, and a lot of carp and bass lived in the water. The monks were all gone except for two old ones who'd been shot dead and dumped into a latrine. The Japanese wanted to catch the fish but didn't have a net. An officer emptied his pistol into the pond but didn't hit any fish. Then another one began throwing grenades into the water. In a flash big bass and carp surfaced, all knocked out and belly-up. The Japs poked us four Chinese with bayonets, and ordered us to undress and get into the water to bring out the fish. I couldn't swim and was scared, but I had to jump into the pond. The water was freezing cold. Luckily, it was just waist-deep. We brought all the half-dead fish to the bank, and the Japanese smashed their heads with rifle butts, strung them through the gills with hemp ropes, and tied them to shoulder poles. Together we carried the fish to their billets. They were large fish, each weighing at least fifteen pounds.

"The soldiers had fried fish for dinner but didn't give us anything to eat. Instead, they made us pick up horse droppings left by their cavalry with our bare hands. At dusk they took us to an ammo dump to load a truck. More Chinese were there working for them, eleven in total. We carried boxes of bullets onto the truck. When the loading was done, three fellows and I were ordered to go with the truck to Hsia Gwan. I was shocked to see so many houses burned down in that area. Lots of buildings were still burning, and the flames snapped and howled like a rushing wind. The electric poles along the way were blazing like huge torches. Only the Yangtze Hotel and a church stood undamaged. We stopped at a little slope and unloaded the truck. Near the riverbank a large crowd had gathered, more than a thousand people. Some of them were Chinese soldiers and some were civilians, including women and kids. A couple of men in the crowd raised white flags, and a white sheet was dangling from a tree. Beyond the people, three tanks with their turrets like large upside-down basins were standing on the embankment, their guns pointing at the crowd. Near us some Japanese soldiers were sitting around a battle flag planted in the ground, drinking rice wine from a large keg wrapped in straw matting. An officer came over and barked out some orders, but the soldiers at the heavy machine guns did nothing and just looked at one another. The officer got furious. He drew his sword and hit a soldier with the back of it. *Thwack, thwack, thwack.* Then his eyes fell on us Chinese coolies squatting close by. Raising his sword, he gave a loud cry, charged at the tallest one among us, and slashed off his head. Two squirts of blood shot into the air more than three feet high and the man fell over without a whimper. We all dropped to our knees and banged our heads on the ground, begging for mercy. I peed my pants.

"The soldiers at the machine guns were flabbergasted. Then one of the guns began firing, and the other two followed. In a flash the machine guns posted at other spots started shooting too. So did the tanks. The crowd was swirling around, crying and falling, but the people were trapped. Every bullet cut down several of them. In less than ten minutes they were all mowed down. Then groups of soldiers carrying fixed bayonets went over to finish off those who were still breathing. I was so horrified that I couldn't stop trembling and crying. One fellow worker grabbed hold of my hair and shook me, saying, 'Don't make so much noise—it will draw attention.' That stopped me.

"We returned with the truck to carry loot for the soldiers, mainly furniture. They didn't keep all the stuff and threw lots of things into the big bonfire in front of their regimental headquarters. Over the fire were pigs and sheep and quarters of a buffalo skewed with long steel bars, and a couple of boiling cauldrons. The air was full of the smell of roasted meat. That night they locked us in a room and gave us each a ball of rice and a cup of water. The next two days they took us to the area east of the Central University to carry loot for them again. They stripped every house of its valuables and then torched it. One soldier carried a safe cracker, but most times they didn't use the tool and just blew the safes open with hand grenades fixed to their bottoms, where the iron was thinner. They were very fond of wrist-watches and jewelry—those were what they were after. One of them, a young fellow, even took a baby carriage. I couldn't stop wondering what he'd do with that. He was too young to have kids.

"Afterward, they whisked six of us out farther east to Jurong Town, and we worked there for a whole day, moving artillery rounds and shell casings. In the evening they released us and said we could go home. Dog-tired, we slowly started trekking home in the dark. The first night we covered only ten miles. Along the way every pond and creek had dead bodies in it, humans and animals, and the water had changed color. When we were thirsty, we had no choice but to drink the foul water. Oh, I still can smell the stink of the decaying corpses. Some of them had eyeballs sticking two or three inches out of their faces, probably due to the gas built up inside them. We once came across a young woman's body with one foot missing, dark blood still oozing out of the stump; on her other foot was a small purple shoe— she had bound feet. Some women were naked from the waist down, stabbed to death after the Japs had raped them. My legs would keep on shaking whenever we passed a pile of corpses.

"Again and again we were stopped by Japanese soldiers. Lucky for us, the officer who had released us wrote a note, so the guards along the way didn't arrest us and allowed us to come back to Nanjing. One of the fellows, dehydrated from diarrhea, couldn't walk anymore. We could do nothing but leave him behind on the roadside. He must be dead now. Not far from where we left him, we stumbled into a little boy, two or three years old, sitting at a deserted bus stop and crying from hunger pangs. I gave him a piece of pancake, but before he could eat it, four Japs came and prodded him with their boots. One of them pulled out his dick and started peeing into the boy's mouth.

The boy was crying louder and louder while the Japs cracked up. We dared not watch for long, so we moved on. I'm sure the other three Japs did the same to the boy. He'd be lucky if they didn't kill him.

"Oh, human lives suddenly became worthless, dead bodies everywhere, some with their bellies cut open, intestines spilled out, and some half burned with gasoline. The Japs killed so many people that they polluted streams, ponds, and wells everywhere, and they themselves couldn't find clean water to drink anymore. Even the rice they ate was reddish because they had to use bloody water to cook it. Once a Japanese messman gave us some bowls of rice, and after I ate it, I had the taste of blood in my mouth for hours. To tell the truth, I never thought I would make it back and see you folks again. Now my pulse still gallops in the middle of the night."

While Ban was speaking, I jotted down what he said.

I

MORNING, ANLING," Minnie greeted me as I was approaching the Central Building, the largest one at Jinling Women's College. Together we headed for President Wu's quarters in the Southern Hill Residence, where we were scheduled for breakfast. The late November air was frosty, and I could see wisps of breath hanging around people's faces when we passed them. A skein of mallards was drifting north, squawking loudly, their wings paddling like tiny oars. Then the whole flock became invisible in the livid sky. The mountainous clouds looked heavy with rain, which meant that no Japanese bombers would come today. So in spite of the cold and damp weather, people would say "Such a nice day" when they met. Overcast skies put everyone in a better mood.

Dr. Wu had been sorting and packing the school's papers because she was planning to take some of them away with her. A number of our Chinese faculty members had also been preparing to leave. Many staffers had nowhere to go, yet they too were busy, hiding away food and valuables. Minnie hadn't packed a thing. As the dean of the college, she wanted to remain behind. She told me, "If I lose anything, I might lose all."

Dr. Wu was waiting for us, in cheerful spirits. On the table were toasted slices of baguette, a bar of butter in a dish, a sauceboat of jam, and a jar of mayonnaise. At the sight of the Western breakfast, Minnie's eyes twinkled. She said, "Wow, I've been eating rice porridge and salted peanuts every morning for weeks. Where did you get these?"

"Madame Chiang gave them to me yesterday," Dr. Wu answered, adjusting her eyeglasses with her fingertips. She often went to see the first lady, as both of them had been educated in the United States—Madame Chiang had gone to Wellesley and Dr. Wu had earned her PhD in entomology from the University of Michigan.

She'd been an executive member of the Women's War Relief Association headed by Madame Chiang and had held many meetings and rallies to garner support for our army and to solicit donations for orphanages and refugees. Dr. Wu was a minor celebrity, the first Chinese woman who had earned a doctorate in the United States. She was one of the first five graduates of Jinling and had succeeded Mrs. Dennison as its president in 1928, when our government stipulated that all foreign colleges and universities in China must be headed by Chinese citizens. "Sit down. Let's eat while we talk," Dr. Wu told us. She was wearing a black silk tunic with a brass button like a huge coin at its neck. Despite being in her late thirties, she looked youthful, with bright vivid eyes and high cheekbones, probably because she wasn't married and had never been burdened with children and housework.

I poured boiled water from a thermos into three mugs to dissolve the powdered milk and then handed Dr. Wu and Minnie each a mug.

"Thanks," Minnie said, spreading the toast thinly with both jam and mayonnaise. She took a bite. "Hmm, what a treat! I wish there were eggs scrambled with ham, cheese, and mushrooms," she said in her slightly accented Mandarin. "How I miss a hearty Midwestern breakfast."

"Me too," Dr. Wu said. "I miss bacon."

We all laughed. I took a sip of the hot milk, which tasted rich and sweetish. I wished I could save my mug for Fanfan, my two-year-old grandson.

Our school's board of founders in New York had just instructed Dr. Wu to join the Jinling group that had recently moved to Chengdu, in western China, while Minnie Vautrin, as she herself had requested, was to stay behind in Nanjing as the head of our college for the time being. Dr. Wu had asked me, and I had agreed, to remain here and help Minnie run the school. The three of us still needed to make plans for safeguarding the campus. The valuables in our vault would be packed in a huge portmanteau to be delivered to the U.S. embassy. We dreaded being looted by Chinese troops, who were notorious for their unruliness, especially when they were frustrated and desperate.

"The embassy is going to evacuate onto the *Panay*, I'm told," Minnie said, referring to a U.S. gunboat.

"That's all right." Dr. Wu sloshed her milk and took a mouthful. "It will be safer to put our stuff in their charge."

"Where should we hide our cash?" I asked.

We all believed that soon no bank would be open in town and there would be widespread shortages. Dr. Wu smiled and suggested that we leave one hundred yuan in the vault and hide the rest, more than four thousand in total, in different places known only to Minnie and me. Minnie asked me, "Isn't Mrs. Dennison's silver in the vault too?"

"Yes, what should we do about that?" I said.

"Is it an expensive set?" asked Dr. Wu.

"I don't know."

"It's her wedding silver," Minnie replied, "a fancy set, probably worth four hundred yuan."

"Pack it into the portmanteau," said the president.

Minnie briefed us about the work that the International Committee for the Nanjing Safety Zone had been doing. That relief association had just been established by some foreigners who were remaining behind despite their embassies' urging them to leave. The Safety Zone would be a neutral district in the center of Nanjing, in an area of about two and a half square miles, where foreign embassies, consulates, and some mission schools were located; it was meant to provide sanctuary for noncombatants. The city officials supported the foreigners' effort and had given them eighty thousand yuan in cash and forty-five tons of rice and flour to set up camps for refugees. Thank heaven the rice crop was good in the Yangtze Valley this year. So there was plenty of rice in the city, but trucks were at a premium and often commandeered by the military, and so were unavailable for transporting the promised rations into the neutral zone. Some departing troops would have burned hundreds of tons of rice stored near the riverside in Hsia Gwan if the Safety Zone Committee had not intervened. Generalissimo Chiang had personally offered a hundred thousand yuan to the committee as well, though to date only forty thousand had been delivered. The Japanese authorities, whom the committee had contacted by way of the U.S. embassy, did not respond directly to the proposal concerning the neutral zone but stated that the Imperial Army would "try to respect the district as far as consistent with military necessity."

The Safety Zone Committee was composed of fifteen men—Americans and Europeans, most of them missionaries, as well as some businessmen and academics. It was chaired by John Rabe, a fifty-five-year-old German and the representative of the Nanjing office of Siemens, the company that had built our city's telephone system, maintained the turbines of our power plant, and supplied modern equipment for our hospitals. Rabe also ran a small German school, which he would open, together with his home, to the refugees. There were no women on the Safety Zone Committee, because it was understood that its members might have to run unimaginable risks, including confronting the soldiers in person. Two American women, however, were actively involved in the relief work: Minnie Vautrin and Holly Thornton, a widow of forty who was now a naturalized Chinese citizen. Holly, a friend of mine, was a part-time English broadcaster. Both Minnie and Holly were on the Nanjing International Red Cross Committee, which was headed by Reverend John Magee. Some of the American men were on both the Safety Zone Committee and the Red Cross Committee.

Having heard Minnie's report about the relief work and the prospect of using Jinling as a refugee camp for women and children, Dr. Wu lowered her head, her hair short like an overgrown crew cut and her eyes dim and watery. She turned pensive for a moment, then said to Minnie, "Do whatever you feel is appropriate and necessary. I can't stop thinking about how badly the foreigners were treated here ten years ago. Now, only a group of foreigners can help the refugees. What a shame."

Dr. Wu was referring to the attacks by the Chinese army on foreigners in 1927. In March of that year, the troops had gone on a rampage, plundering, burning, and destroying foreign schools and residences. It was believed that the Communists had instigated the violence to frame Chiang Kai-shek and damage his relations with the West. Some soldiers beat up foreigners and assaulted women. A platoon broke into Jinling and carried off several microscopes from a biology laboratory and some staffers' personal belongings. At Nan-jing University six foreign men were shot dead. I remembered how some missionaries had climbed down the city wall and scrambled onto American and British gunboats, which had been laying down a barrage inside the city to keep the Chinese troops from approaching a group of foreigners trapped on a hill. Eventually all the Westerners fled Nanjing, and Minnie and our other foreign faculty members went to Tsingtao and dared not come back to teach. It looked as if that was the end of their mission work here, but some of them returned six months later. Minnie was the very first to come back, eager to complete the construction of a dorm building and the rose garden.

2

MINNIE HAD GONE to the U.S. embassy to deliver the portmanteau when Searle Bates arrived on a bicycle to inspect our camp in preparation for relief work and to collect the Red Cross flags made by some women from the Jinling neighborhood. He was wearing a gabardine coat and work boots, which made him appear more imposing. He was somewhat slight in build, around five foot nine, and nearsighted. He told me that there were plans for nineteen other refugee camps in the Safety Zone, but there was only one other besides our college that would admit women and children exclusively, the one at Nanjing University's dormitories. Searle also delivered some letters and a bundle of the *North China Daily News*, a British newspaper some of our faculty members had subscribed to. Since August, when the Japanese began attacking Shanghai, the paper had always arrived in batches, usually two weeks late.

Searle was a history professor at Nanjing University, most of whose staff had just fled inland with the national government. He had a PhD in Chinese history from Yale and spoke Chinese, Japanese, and Russian. My husband had worked with him before the war, so I had known him for years and liked him. I walked with him through the halls, from which we had cleared all the furniture to make room for refugees. I told him that we expected to receive twenty-seven hundred people maximum, figured on the basis of sixteen square feet per person (each refugee would have a two-by-eight-foot space), but we'd feel more comfortable with two thousand. He nodded, smiling, while his craggy face wrinkled a little, a pair of delicate glasses on his bulky nose. He jotted down the numbers in a notebook, his Parker fountain pen shiny in his sinewy hand. As we were crossing the quadrangle, he tilted his head toward the thirty-foot U.S. flag we had spread in its center to indicate to Japanese bombers that this was American property.

"That's impressive," he said.

"Gosh, it took us more than a month to make it," I told him. "It's hard to find a capable tailor nowadays. At first the man mistakenly placed the stars in the upper right corner of the flag, and he had a lot of trouble getting them to the left."

Searle chuckled. "What a pretty haven you have here." He clucked his tongue. Jinling College was known for its lovely campus, planted with many kinds of trees and flowers. Every fall there'd been a flower show here, but not this year.

Suddenly the air-raid sirens went off, wailing like a mourning crowd. People began running for shelter. "We'd better go underground," I said, and pointed at the chapel, which had a basement.

Searle shook his head. "I won't bother with it until I see bombs falling."

I tugged at his sleeve. "Come. Consider this part of your inspection. You should see our air-raid shelter, shouldn't you?"

"It's a false alarm."

There had been so many wrong warnings lately that people tended to ignore the first signal. But at this point the second siren—shorter but more rapid—began howling, meaning you must take cover. More people were hustling away. As Searle and I were going out the front entrance of our college, explosions thundered in the residential area about a mile away to the east, near West Flower Gate, in the old Manchu city now inhabited by the poor. Pillars of whitish smoke were rising over there while a couple of antiaircraft guns roared, shells bursting in the air like black blossoms.

"Let's get into that," I said, leading Searle to a dugout nearby. A hail of flak fragments was rustling through the treetops and pelting the roofs. A handful landed at our feet, raising dust.

Inside the cellar some women held babies in their arms, with toddlers sitting next to them. A mother yelled at her children to stop them from peeking out. Two old men seated on folding stools were battling over a chessboard in a corner lit by a bean oil lamp as if this were their regular haunt and they'd been at the game for hours. A smell like deep-fried fish hung in the air.

When Searle and I sat down, I told him about the women seated around us: "They're so used to the raids now. In the beginning they wouldn't dare to let out a peep in here, believing the planes had a device that could detect conversations down below."

Searle chortled, then said, "It's despicable to keep bombing the residential areas. I'm going to file a complaint with the Japanese embassy."

"Those pilots must enjoy dumping bombs on civilians," I said. "The bastards, they should know this is a war crime."

"If Japan loses this war, some of them will be brought to trial, I'm sure."

Uncertain about the outcome of the war, I didn't say another word. I turned to watch an old woman stitching a cloth sole with an awl and a flaxen thread, a piece of adhesive tape wrapped around the tip of her forefinger.

A minute later Searle remarked, "So only the old, the young, and women are here."

I didn't respond, knowing that some foreigners had their doubts about the Chinese, especially the elite and the educated among us. Most of those people were gone. But why would so many of them flee upriver with the national government or to the other interior regions? Why wouldn't they join the army, if not to fight in the trenches, then at least to help bolster the troops' morale or to look after the wounded and the sick? This war seemed to be fought by only the poor and the weak. That point neither my husband nor I could dispute. These days I hadn't been able to drive out of my mind the vision of recruits I often encountered in town. Many of them were merely teenage boys from the countryside, emaciated and illiterate, who could hardly fend for themselves. They were sent to the front as nothing but cannon fodder.

After the all-clear siren, Searle rode away, and I headed for the Administration Building. As I approached it, I saw Minnie talking with Big Liu at the entrance. Liu was six foot two and hulking like a basketball player retired long ago. I went over and greeted them.

Big Liu was asking permission for his family to move to our campus. Minnie had been studying classical Chinese with him since last spring and trusted him, so she granted his request. I was glad, because Big Liu was levelheaded and resourceful, knew English, and had taught Chinese to foreigners for many years. It would be good to have him around.

"Thank you, Miss Vautrin," Big Liu said in a ringing voice.

"Just call me Minnie," she reminded him.

"Minnie," he said with a straight face.

We all laughed. Most people in Nanjing called Minnie "Principal Vautrin," a form of address that seemed to discomfit her a little, though she wouldn't object if a stranger called her that.

Then Minnie hit upon an idea, and blinking her large brown eyes, she said to Big Liu, "Why don't you work for us? Our secretary, Mr. Kong, went back to his home village and left hundreds of letters unanswered."

"You want me to be on your staff?" Big Liu asked.

"Yes, to be our Chinese secretary."

"For real?"

"She's in charge now," I told him.

"Yes, I just offered you the job." As Minnie was speaking, I heard a thrill in her voice. Evidently she took great pride in her new role.

"Wonderful! I'm delighted, delighted." Big Liu's rugged face lit up.

Big Liu, who'd been looking for work in vain, had a teenage daughter and small son to support. He would start the following Monday, with a monthly salary of twenty-five yuan for the time being. That was plenty, compared to the other staffers, since we had all taken a sixty percent pay cut. Minnie now was making fifty yuan a month while I was making thirty. She suggested that Big Liu's family live at East Court, a group of houses set around a courtyard in the southeast part of campus. It was Minnie, as a construction supervisor a decade ago, who had designed that servants' residence, which had been built so well that later some Chinese faculty members complained that those quarters were superior to their own. My family was also living at East Court, so the Lius would be our neighbors.

As the three of us were talking, our business manager, Luhai Bai, appeared and waved at Minnie. Despite that impressive title, Luhai mainly handled external business dealings, because it was I who managed most of the logistics on campus. The young man, limping slightly, hurried up to us, a little out of breath. He said, "Madame Chiang has sent us her piano and Victrola."

"Oh, as gifts?" Minnie asked.

"Yes."

"Where are they?" I said.

"Some men are unloading them in front of the Music Hall."

"Let's go have a look," said Minnie.

As the four of us headed to that building, which also housed the chapel, I realized that Madame Chiang must be evacuating. This upset me, because it confirmed the rumor about the Chiangs' secret departure. I wondered if Dr. Wu had known all along about their plan to leave. Would the generalissimo's withdrawal affect the defending troops? Wouldn't the soldiers feel deserted? On second thought, I realized that it would be unreasonable to expect the generalissimo to remain on the battle line. If he were killed or captured, it would be catastrophic.

In front of the Music Hall stood a six-wheeled truck and five soldiers smoking self-rolled cigarettes, their overcoats piled on the ground. The piano, a Baldwin, had already been unloaded. Its finish was dull and it looked well used, but the Victrola was spanking new, in an oxhide case and accompanied by a gleaming brass horn and two boxes of records. Minnie lifted the piano's keyboard cover and tickled out a couple of random notes. "Sounds powerful. This behemoth is what we need for the chapel service," she said, then motioned to the men. "Please carry it in and put it next to the organ."

We were glad about the gifts, but I couldn't think of anyone on campus able to play the piano. Not a single person among us could do that. My friend Holly was a musician, but she was occupied with the radio station. Even Minnie couldn't punch out a tune. She often said that all her life she had wished she could play an instrument, ideally the cello—as a child, how she had envied the children who could take art and music lessons after school. She seemed to still suffer from the privation in her girlhood (she'd lost her mother at six, and even before her teens had to keep house for her father, a blacksmith in Secor, Illinois), as though this were an illness she couldn't get over. That's why, whenever possible, she'd have the underprivileged children in the Jinling neighborhood learn something more than read-ing, arithmetic, and practical skills, even if it was just a song or a ball game. I admired her for that, for her large heart, which set her apart from the other foreign women on the faculty.

I told Luhai to give the five soldiers each a pack of Red Chamber, the Chinese brand name of Old Mill at the time. These young men might go to the front at any moment, so I wanted to make them happy.

"We're just out of cigarettes," Luhai said.

"Go to my home and ask Yaoping for five packs," I told him.

Minnie said, "Yes, tell Mr. Gao that the boss needs them."

They laughed, assuming that I ruled the roost at home, which was not true. I love and respect my husband and never impose my wishes on him. It was my job at the college that required me to stay on top of many things and gave others the impression of my being bossy. I told Luhai, "Let Yaoping know we'll give them back to him as soon as we get a carton."

Luhai was happy to fetch the cigarettes.

3

A**S USUAL,** Yaoping started his morning with a pipe, a cup of aster tea, and the local newspaper *The Purple Mountain Evening News*, which in early December was still full of wedding announcements—parents were anxious to marry off their daughters, assuming that the grooms, and their families, might be able to protect the brides when the Japanese came. Our daughter, Liya, had been up since six thirty and was busy cooking breakfast in the kitchen, while her son, Fanfan, was still sleeping in bed. She was four months pregnant, but her belly wasn't showing yet and her movements were still nimble. Her father hoped she'd give us a granddaughter, while I preferred another boy. I liked girls, but they would suffer more than boys in this world and needed more protection. As a parent you would worry about them constantly. Yaoping, a quiet man, had been a history lecturer at Nanjing University, but he hadn't left for Sichuan with the rest of his school, reluctant to be separated from us. In addition, he had low blood pressure, dizzy spells, and arthritis, and he needed to be taken care of, so he couldn't make the long trek to the interior province. Besides, we felt that we would be safer together at Jinling College, an American school less likely to be attacked by the Japanese soldiers. But my son-in-law, Liya's husband, had departed with the Nationalist army, in which he served as an intelligence officer.

As soon as I washed up, I went to see Dr. Wu, who was leaving today. She and I were both from Wuchang, Hubei Province, and I had been working for her ever since she became the college's president.

The campus was deserted. In early September, when school was supposed to start, only two girls had returned, and a month later they both had left. Then some of our faculty members departed for Wuchang, where they resumed teaching a small group of students. Some of our foreign teachers were still in Shanghai after the summer. Dr. Wu was leaving to join another group of our staff and faculty, mainly Chinese, together with some twenty students, who were on their way to Sichuan, where the national government and many universities were to be relocated. At the sight of me, she said, "Anling, I'm leaving the college in your hands. Help Minnie take care of everything here."

"I'll do my best," I said.

"Write to me as often as you can." Her face puckered a little as she spoke, as if in a vain attempt to smile.

It was understood that I'd be her unofficial proxy here, because there'd be things that Minnie, as a foreigner, couldn't handle. As we were speaking, Minnie showed up, panting slightly and her cheeks pinkish, glowing with health. She hugged Dr. Wu and Miss Fan, the petite accountant, saying we would see them again soon. The porters had already loaded the luggage. Without delay we set out for the front entrance of campus, where the truck was waiting.

Minnie and I didn't go to Hsia Gwan with them, knowing they would tarry hours there before the boat cast off. For the whole morning we were anxious, and not until it began drizzling in the afternoon did we feel relieved, because the rain could deter the Japanese bombers. The boat also carried four hundred boxes of art treasures from the Palace Museum, so it might have been dangerous for Dr. Wu and Miss Fan to be on board. By the next morning they would pass Wuhu. Beyond that small city the enemy planes would be less likely to attack them.

The previous evening Miss Fan had told Minnie and me the combination to the college's vault, and we took out the cash and hid it in different buildings.

I WAS PLEASED that Holly had just joined our staff and stayed with us after her radio station had been dissolved. She was the only foreigner besides Minnie on campus and could play the piano and organ. This meant that our chapel service could resume as before. Holly was so energetic that she also took part in charity work outside our college. Lately she'd been going to Hsia Gwan to help wounded soldiers in the evenings. Sometimes I went with her, bringing along a couple of newly made garments and bedding. I had trained in a missionary hospital to be a nurse—that's why I could speak English and would also help out at the school's infirmary whenever they needed me.

On the evening of December 7, Holly drove Minnie and me to Hsia Gwan in her De Soto coupe. Minnie was shocked and also disturbed, as we had been on our first visit there, by the sight of more than three hundred soldiers lying about in the train station. Most of the men suffered from gunshot wounds, and many had lost limbs. The waiting hall brought to mind a temporary morgue, though moaning kept rising in there and some men cursed their superiors. One man raved "Kill, kill!" while flailing his arms. Most of the wounded were barefoot, which made me wonder who had stripped them of their footwear. Maybe they hadn't worn real shoes to begin with, since a lot of the troops from the southern provinces had gone to the front wearing only straw sandals.

The three of us began distributing the half-dozen thin quilts we'd brought along. For the moaning ones we could hardly do a thing aside from saying they'd be shipped to the hospital soon. In a corner a man with a wound in the shoulder lay on a string stretcher gazing at Minnie and me. He smiled and said quietly with a Hunan accent, "Don't let them take me away."

"You want to stay here?" Minnie asked.

"I'm so tired, still drenched. They carried me through driving rain for three days, all the way from Danyang. So many men died on the road. I have to rest some before going to the hospital."

I saw a small puddle on the terrazzo floor under his stretcher and realized he must have wet the cotton quilt underneath him. "I'll be back in a second." I stepped away and looked around for some dry bedclothes but couldn't find any. Outside a storage room filled with undelivered parcels, I came across two used hemp sacks and, ignoring who might own them, brought them back. Minnie and I pulled the man's stretcher a few steps away, placed the sacks beside it, and helped him move onto the makeshift bedding.

"Thank you, thank you," the man kept saying as Minnie spread the soiled quilt on the stretcher to dry. "It's so kind of you," he added, and closed his eyes, as if about to fall asleep.

Minnie wordlessly adjusted his leg while I moved the stretcher alongside him so that he could get on it again once the thin quilt dried a bit. Before we could turn away, he opened his eyes. "I met another good-hearted foreigner," he breathed, as if he couldn't see that I had a Chinese face. Then his voice became a little louder. "A Canadian doctor dressed my wound every other day in Danyang. Every time I was in such pain that I yelped like mad, but he never lost his temper and always patted my forehead to calm me down. Once he wiped my face with a warm towel. Before I left, I told him that if I were younger, I would've wanted to have him as my godfather. Such a good man."

I realized that this young fellow might be a Christian. Touching his forehead, Minnie said, "God will help you get well soon."

I couldn't say a word. As we stepped away, I wondered how we could console these men without lying to them. Most of them, infested with lice and fleas and depleted of strength, would soon join the yellow soil of China. An upsurge of sadness constricted my chest. Suddenly tearful and stuffy-nosed, I rushed out of the waiting hall to compose myself in the chilly air. Why would God let our land go through such horrendous destruction? Why did these innocent men have to suffer like this? When would God ever show his wrath against the violent aggressors? Those questions, usually lurking in the back of my mind, again cropped up and bewildered me.

Minnie came out and joined me. "This is awful, awful," she said with a sob in her voice, her cheeks tear-stained. "I never thought it could be so bad." Her brown hair was tousled a little and her lips twisted as if she were chewing something. In silence I patted her shoulder.

We went back in a few minutes later. A young man, actually a teenager, howled in a childlike voice, "Take me home! I want to see my mom and dad before I die." His eyes were injured, and his entire face was bandaged save for his mouth.

Minnie touched his head and said, "They're going to send you home soon."

"Don't lie to me! Liar, liar, all of you are liars."

She turned away while I went to help Holly fill canteens with boiled water that had cooled down. At the far end of the hall, John

Magee, the kindhearted minister, was praying. He came here every night to direct a team of young volunteers trying to help these men, and also to administer the last rites for the dying ones.

"Anling." Minnie beckoned to me from behind a high-backed bench.

I put down the canteen I was filling, went over, and saw, lying on the floor, a man whose right leg had been shot off close to the hip. He was motionless, his gaping wound emitting a foul odor. Minnie whispered to me, "Do you think he's still alive?"

As I was wondering, his hand twitched as if stung by something. "Apparently he is," I said.

I bent down to observe his wound. The flesh had begun to rot; it was whitish and oozing pus. Thanks to the cold weather there were few flies, yet I saw four or five tiny maggots wiggling on the edge of the decayed flesh. The stench from the stump was so overpowering that I had to hold my breath. Obviously these men had been left like this for days.

"Do they have a list of their names?" Minnie asked.

"I'm not sure," I said, surprised by the question.

"I'm wondering if there'll be a cemetery for these poor men who have sacrificed everything for China." Minnie turned tearful again.

Deep inside, I knew there might be no list of their names at all. Everything was in such disarray that their superiors wouldn't bother about these useless men anymore. After they died, who'd be able to tell where their bodies were? Perhaps their parents would receive a "lost in battle" notice. These country lads seemed to have been sent into this world only to suffer and to be used—the spans of their lives depended on how much they could endure.

The more we observed the one-legged man, the more grief-stricken we became. Minnie went up to Holly and asked almost crossly, "Why can't they cleanse and dress his wound?" She pointed at the man behind the bench.

"They have no medicine here, not even rubbing alcohol or iodine solution," Holly said.

I was afraid that Minnie might fly off the handle. As I feared, she stepped across to a young woman in a white gown and said, "Look, I know the man over there might be a hopeless case, but why not dress his wound and let him die like a human being?"

"We don't have any bandages," the woman answered. "We're here just to feed them and give them water."

"So your job is to prolong their agony?"

"I wish I could do more, Principal Vautrin." The young thing forced a smile, her face careworn and haggard.

"Minnie, it's not her fault," I said.

As I pulled her away, Minnie admitted, "You're right. She's not even a nurse and must be a volunteer like us."

"At most she's a nurse's aide," I replied.

"If only our students were still around. Then we could bring over two or three classes. Some of the well-heeled students would donate medicines and bandages for sure."

"They would," I said.

I debated whether I should wipe the man's wound—to get rid of the maggots at least—but I was uncertain whether that would increase his pain. Without any medicine, it might make his wound more infected, so instead I found a newspaper and spread it over his stump.

We left the train station after ten p.m. All the way back, Minnie was withdrawn while Holly and I were talking about the collapse of the Chinese lines. Evidently Nanjing would fall in a matter of days. We were sure there would be more wounded men and refugees pouring into town.

As we approached our campus, Minnie said, "I must take a shower to get rid of the awful smell."

"I guess you won't stop thinking about those dying men for a while," I said.

"Are you a worm inside me, Anling?" Minnie asked, using the Chinese expression. "How can you read my mind?"

Holly chortled, then said, "We may not be able to visit them again."

Indeed, we would be too occupied in the forthcoming days to go to the train station again.

4

THE BORDERS of the Safety Zone had all been marked by Red Cross flags, though the Chinese army had been building batteries and defense works inside the southern part of the zone. John Rabe had to wrangle with Colonel Huang, an aide-de-camp to Generalissimo Chiang, to get the troops out of the neutral district. The young officer believed that the very sight of the Safety Zone would demoralize the soldiers who "must defend the city to the last drop of blood." No matter how Rabe argued that from the military point of view it was absurd to set up defenses here, the colonel wouldn't be persuaded—yet he took off with the general staff a few days later. Rabe joked afterward, "It's so easy to resolve to fight with others' blood."

Before the generalissimo departed, he'd had another forty thousand yuan of the promised cash delivered to the Safety Zone Committee with a letter thanking the Westerners for their relief work. Some of the foreigners believed that the Chinese army was just putting up a show to save face, but Rabe didn't think so. He was fearful that General Tang Sheng-chi, Chiang's rival of a sort, who had only reluctantly assumed the role of the commander of the Nanjing defense, might sacrifice everything, including the lives of tens of thousands of civilians. Two days earlier the general had had dozens of boats burned to demonstrate that his troops would stand their ground, fighting with their backs to the river.

Rabe protested again to the officers in charge of the artillery units placed inside the Safety Zone and even threatened to resign his chairmanship and dissolve the Safety Zone Committee if the military personnel remained there, because that would give the Japanese a pretext to attack and eliminate the zone. General Tang assigned Colonel Long to work with Rabe, and together they managed to remove the troops. At the news of their withdrawal, we breathed a sigh of relief—our effort to set up refugee camps might not be wasted.

On Wednesday afternoon, December 8, Minnie held a neighborhood meeting, and more than a hundred people attended it, mostly women. Usually such a gathering in the chapel would draw a larger crowd because food was offered afterward, mainly bread and light pastries. Today the attendees were not interested in loaves and fishes; instead, they were eager to find out how soon they could come to Jinling at the time of crisis. For many of them, our college was the only sanctuary they could imagine. Miss Lou, an evangelical worker in the neighborhood, was present at the meeting. The previous day Minnie had allowed this middle-aged woman with intense eyes and a slightly sunken mouth to move into the Practice Hall and take charge of the refugees to be housed there. Miss Lou had no official affiliation with our college, but she was one of the few locals we could depend on. This little woman knew which people in the neighborhood were really destitute, so whenever we wanted to distribute charity, we'd go to her for assistance.

"Principal Vautrin, can I bring my dad with me when I come?" a slope-shouldered woman asked. "He's bedridden and I can't leave him behind."

"Well, we will open our camp only to women and children," Minnie answered.

A few men booed. One of them complained, "You can't reject us like this, Principal Vautrin! This is unfair."

I turned around to scowl at those men, some of whom were ne'er-do-wells, playing chess, cards, and mah-jongg day and night. Some had even snuck onto our campus to pilfer things.

Minnie waved for them to stop. As the hall quieted down, she resumed: "Ours is a women's college, so it would be inappropriate for us to accommodate men." She turned to a group of women. "Your menfolk can go to the other camps that take in families."

"Why separate us?" a female voice asked.

"You won't be separated for long," Minnie said. "We're talking about a matter of life or death while you're still thinking about how to stay comfortably with your man."

That cracked up the audience. We all knew that this woman had no children; she had been nicknamed the Barren One. She dropped her eyes, her cheeks crimson.

"Where are those camps that also accept men?" another female voice asked.

Minnie replied, "Wutaishan Primary School, the old Communications Ministry, Nanjing University's Library, the military chemical shops—practically all the other camps admit families except for the one at the university's dorms."

"They're too far away," an old woman cried.

My temper was simmering. As I was wondering whether to say something to those selfish people, Miss Lou stood up and turned around to face them, her deep-set eyes steady behind her thick glasses. "Let's remember who we are," she said. "Jinling College is under no obligation whatsoever to accommodate any of us, but it offers to shelter us from the Eastern devils. We ought to appreciate what Principal Vautrin and her colleagues have been doing for us."

"Shut up, little toady!" a male voice shouted from the back.

I stood and began to speak. "This is a chapel, not a cheap tavern where you can swear at will. So stop name-calling or make an exit. As for the men here, don't you feel ashamed to compete with women and kids for safety? If you cannot fight the enemy and protect your families with arms, at least you should have the decency to leave them in more capable hands, while you look for refuge for yourselves elsewhere."

That silenced the crowd, and for a moment the hall was so quiet that the distant artillery fire suddenly seemed to rumble louder and closer. After Miss Lou and I had sat down, Minnie continued, "We welcome all women and children, but we will do our best to shelter young women and girls first. That's to say we encourage older women to stay home if they already live within the Safety Zone."

"How about boys?" a woman asked from the back.

"Good question," Minnie said. "Boys under thirteen will be admitted."

"My fourteen-year-old is still a little kid," a mother cried.

"But there're fourteen-year-olds who are almost grown. We have to save room for girls and young women. In your son's case, you should say he's thirteen."

That brought out peals of laughter.

"When can we come?" the same woman asked.

"When it's no longer safe to stay home. Bring only your bedding, a change of clothes, and some money. No chests or boxes, please."

At the meeting's end, Miss Lou, the zealous little woman, read Psalm 70 loudly. She cried out the refrain in a shrill voice: "Make haste to help me, O God." Then we all stood up and sang the chorus from the hymn "Rock of Ages, Cleft for Me." I'd bet that only a few of the attendees knew the words by heart; nevertheless, we all sang with abandon, some holding large hymnals with both hands, and our voices were earnest and strong.

THAT EVENING we received the first group of refugees. Most of them had come from the countryside, and some had trekked all the way from Wuxi, a city more than a hundred miles to the east. The Japanese had not only plundered their villages and towns but also seized young men and women, so people had abandoned their homes and fled to Nanjing, or had tried to cross the Yangtze to reach Pukou, unaware that the Japanese had just captured that area outside Nanjing to cut the retreat route of the Chinese army. The Japanese torched most houses along the way, destroyed whatever they couldn't use, and had felled thickets and forests within a quarter mile of the railroads to prevent their supply trains from being ambushed. To defend the capital, the Chinese army was also razing civilian homes, especially in the Jurong area; it ordered people to leave their villages and then burned their houses to clear all possible obstructions to its cannons. This created more refugees, and now crowds of them swarmed at the city gates, waiting to be let in.

A woman with salt-and-pepper hair collapsed in front of us, sitting on a boulder and weeping while relating her story. "My daughter and I came to town to sell taros," she sobbed, "but there was such a big crowd gathering outside Guanghua Gate that I lost her. I thought she'd get through the gate anyway and we could meet inside the city wall, but after I came in, the gate was suddenly closed 'cause the Japs

began shelling that area. I waited inside the wall for the whole afternoon and couldn't go out to look for her. Our home's already gone,
and she wouldn't know where to go. Oh, my poor child, she's just
eleven."

Some families came intact, but the men had to go elsewhere to
find shelter for themselves. Most of them were willing to do so,
grateful that their wives and children were in safe hands. A sleepy-
eyed man went up to Minnie and implored her to give his family a little food because they had no money. She told him, "Don't worry. We
won't let them starve."

Word had it that the camps that accepted men as well were filling
rapidly. We had not expected to receive refugees so soon, and now,
on the evening of December 8, more than a hundred were already
here. Minnie told ruddy-faced Luhai to set up a soup kitchen that
would open the next morning.

5

I T WAS EERILY QUIET the next morning, and for hours few gun-
shots were heard. The cannonade in the east, south, and west had
ceased too. We couldn't help but wonder if the Japanese had entered
Nanjing. That seemed unlikely, since the Chinese troops were still
holding their positions. As Minnie and I were discussing the influx of
refugees, Old Liao, our gardener, came and handed Minnie a leaflet.
He was her longtime friend. Minnie had hired him from Hefei eighteen years ago when she came to Jinling to become its acting president—in place of Mrs. Dennison, who had gone back to the States
for fund-raising for a year—because she wanted to create a beautiful
campus. "I found this on the west hill this morning," Liao said in a
husky voice, pointing at the sheet, and smiled as if it were just a regular day for him. "There're lots of them in the bushes. A Japanese
plane must've dropped them. I don't know what it's about but
thought you might want to take a look."

Minnie skimmed it, then handed it to me. The leaflet bore words
from General Matsui, the commander in chief of the Japanese Central China Expeditionary Forces. He demanded that the Chinese
side capitulate without delay, declaring, "This is the best way to protect the innocent civilians and the cultural relics in the ancient capital." So we must all lay down our weapons and open the city gates to
welcome the Imperial Army. The decree continued: "It is our policy
to deal harshly with those who resist and to be kind and generous to
noncombatants and the Chinese soldiers who entertain no hostility
to our invincible force. Therefore, I order you to surrender within
twenty-four hours, by 6:00 p.m., December 9. Otherwise, all the hor-
rors of war will be unleashed on you mercilessly."

There were fewer than ten hours left before the zero hour. Minnie
told Liao, "This is an order from Iwane Matsui, the top Japanese
general."

"Never heard of him. What's he want?"

"He demands that the Chinese surrender the city to him. What do you think we should do?"

"Well"—Old Liao scratched the back of his round head—"I don't know. I hope he'll leave people in peace."

His answer seemed to amuse Minnie. Unlike the other staffers, Old Liao was untroubled by the coming of the Japanese, though his daughter had left with his grandchildren. We knew he was a timid man, and all he cared about was growing flowers and vegetables. War was simply beyond his ken. Yet Minnie had deep affection for this old gardener, who had a marvelous green thumb—whatever he touched would turn pretty and luxuriant in due time. As he slouched away trailing the grassy smell that always clung to him, I turned his answer over in my head. Maybe he was right to a degree—the common people would have to live, so whoever the ruler was, insofar as he did not interrupt their livelihood, they could accept him. But I stifled this thought, because all the recent Japanese atrocities spoke against such a possibility.

The leaflet from General Matsui might explain the quiet of this morning—the invading force must have been waiting for our side to respond to the ultimatum. I told Minnie this, and she agreed. Lewis Smythe confirmed our hunch when he came later that morning to inspect our medical clinic. Our telephone was already out of service, so he had to come in person. Lewis was surprised that Jinling had so far admitted only three hundred refugees, but he praised our careful planning and also told us that the four Britons and the Danish man on the Safety Zone Committee had just left Nanjing. We shouldn't worry, though, he assured us, because more people, especially the locals, had begun participating in the relief work.

Lewis was a sociologist from Chicago teaching at Nanjing University and was also a missionary. He was rather sensitive and frail but always spoke eloquently. Even when conversing with people, he'd speak as if he were giving a lecture, with his hand gesticulating vividly. These days Lewis seemed quite spirited, as if the impending siege had charged him with vim and vigor; he even confessed to Minnie that he enjoyed "all the activities." I guess he had never found his life so active and purposeful—above all, so intense.

Minnie invited him to a late lunch in the main dormitory, and I joined them. The food was plain: rice, sautéed mustard greens, and salted mackerel. Lewis, like Minnie, was one of the few foreigners who liked Chinese food. This was an advantage, since all stores had disappeared in town and foreign groceries were impossible to come by; what's more, it was believed that eating the local food every day could build up one's immunity to diseases, such as dysentery and malaria. Lewis told us that his effort to organize the ambulance service had collapsed, because the military commandeered automobiles at will. At the moment, he had only two vans that ran. As the secretary of the Safety Zone Committee, he was swamped with work, running around to make sure that basic medical services would be available in every camp.

While we were eating, Lewis talked about a truce that he and some other members of the Safety Zone Committee had attempted to arrange. The previous day they had proposed a three-day cease-fire, during which the Imperial Army would remain in its positions while the Chinese troops withdrew from the city, so that the Japanese could march in peacefully. In spite of General Tang's belligerence in public, he was actually anxious to secure the truce. He asked the Safety Zone Committee to send a radiogram to both Generalissimo Chiang and Tokyo through the U.S. embassy, which was on the *Panay* now. Searle Bates and Plumer Mills, a board member of the Northern Presbyterian Mission in Nanjing, set out with one of General Tang's aides for the American gunboat anchored upriver a little off Hsia Gwan. The message about the cease-fire was dispatched, and both General Tang and the Safety Zone Committee were waiting restlessly, but Chiang Kai-shek had replied earlier this morning: "Out of the question."

"Foolish and crazy," Lewis said about Chiang's rejection. "He simply would not consider how many lives a truce would save. Now the city is doomed." Lewis sighed, his mustache twitching as he chewed. He wore wire-rimmed glasses, the small lenses barely covering his lackluster eyes.

"He must have meant to save face," Minnie said. I knew she liked Generalissimo Chiang, who was a Christian and had once come to Jinling's commencement. I remembered that occasion, when he'd said he converted because the burden on his shoulders was so heavy that he needed God's succor. I lifted the porcelain teapot and refilled everyone's cup.

"Thanks," Lewis said. "When a city and tens of thousands of lives are at stake, it is insane to worry about one's own face."

"The poor soldiers—they'll all be trapped like rats," said Minnie.

"Chiang Kai-shek should not have attempted to defend this place to begin with. The only explanation for this imbecility is that he desires to get rid of his rivals in the military."

All of us knew of his eagerness to diminish his rival General Tang. Chiang's German advisers had exhorted him not to defend our capital. The terrain around the city was like a sack, its mouth at Hsia Gwan, abutting the south bank of the Yangtze. If the Japanese forces, about 100,000 men in total, attacked from both east and west along the river, they could seize the docks in Hsia Gwan and completely cut the withdrawal route of the thirteen divisions and fifteen regiments defending our capital, about 150,000 men, who could then be squeezed into the "sack" demarcated by the city walls. From a military point of view, it was self-destructive to defend such a place.

Minnie asked Lewis, "So this morning's peace is just the eye of the hurricane?"

"The Japanese will resume attacking any minute."

The artillery bombardment of the downtown area started that evening. Huge shells landed near New Crossroads, the center of the city. Then explosions burst out in various places. Time and again shells fell in the Safety Zone, into which the civilians were flocking. All the streets leading to the neutral district were thronged with people carrying their possessions by whatever means they had—wheelbarrows, rickshaws, bicycles, even baby carriages, anything with a wheel on it. Many men bore their things with shoulder poles, and some had bedrolls on their backs. Women held babies, clothes bundles, thermoses. Some old people, too feeble to walk, were carried in large bamboo baskets by pairs of men with long poles. We heard that the camp at the Bible Teachers Training School was already filled to capacity with fifteen hundred people, yet they continued receiving new arrivals. By contrast, Jinling had admitted nearly seven hundred. Numerous families came, but we were adamant about taking in only women and children. Many women, reluctant to be separated from their menfolk, left for the camps that accepted families. Some men cursed Big Liu, Miss Lou, Holly, and me at the front entrance, and one even threw mud on our college's sign and the steel-barred gate.

Throughout the night refugees kept streaming in. As the other camps were already full, all men now were willing to leave their families at Jinling and seek shelter for themselves elsewhere. Our college was said to be the safest place for women and children, so more and more of them were coming. Our staff, overwhelmed, was aided by dozens of refugee women who offered to help. There were so many arriving that by noon the next day the Faculty House was full, and the Central Building and the Practice Hall were also filling up. Some people, once admitted, wouldn't go to any of the buildings, instead taking bricks from a construction site nearby to set up their own nests on the sports ground. These rectangular shelters were like giant cooking ranges, covered with pieces of bamboo matting supported by thin beams, which were mostly whittled branches.

In the south machine guns had been chattering without cease since daybreak; in the northeast, where a battle was raging, Purple Mountain was in flames. The smoke often obscured the sun. Time and again bombs exploded somewhere outside the Safety Zone. Japanese bombers were appearing without any alarm being sounded, though once in a while a flak battery or two still fired at them. Whenever a plane flew over our campus, most people would run for cover, but some from the countryside had the false notion that the Safety Zone was bombproof, and they'd stay in the open to watch the planes bombing or strafing something. Luhai and Big Liu had to yell to disperse them into the trenches and dugouts.

All day long, the mother who'd lost her eleven-year-old daughter two days earlier stood behind our college's front gate, staring at the crowds in hopes of spotting her child. She kept asking people if they'd seen a little girl with bobbed hair and dimpled cheeks. No one had. Miss Lou took a bowl of rice porridge to the woman, who ate it without a word. I thought of having her brought into the campus but decided to let her continue grieving where she was.

6

THE NEXT DAY heavy artillery pounded the city without letup. On campus our staff was unsettled but kept working. Long sheds were being put up between the two northern dormitory buildings, and under them we let vendors sell food to the refugees. Steamed rice was five cents a bowl and *shaobing*, wheaten cakes no longer dotted with sesame seeds, were also five cents apiece; no one was allowed to buy more than two of each. The local Red Cross had promised to open a porridge plant here, but it had not materialized yet. Some people, without any food or money on them, had to go hungry. By noon on December 11 we had admitted about two thousand refugees, and so far had been able to accommodate them.

While I was serving hot water with a wooden ladle to the exhausted newcomers, John Magee arrived. I let a staffer take over the work and went up to the reverend. "I just came from downtown," he said to Minnie and me. "It's horrible out there, dozens of bodies lying in front of Fu Chang Hotel and the Capital Theater. A teahouse got hit, and some legs and arms were hanging in the air, tangled in the electric wires and treetops. The Japanese will be coming in at any moment."

"You mean the Chinese troops just gave up resisting?" Minnie spoke with sudden anger, her eyes ablaze.

"I'm not sure," Magee said. "Some of them had appeared in the Safety Zone, looting stores for food and supplies."

"They just disbanded?" I asked, enraged too as I remembered the suburban villages they had burned in the name of defending the city.

"It's hard to tell," Magee replied. "Some of them are still fighting."

He told us that a good part of Hsia Gwan was on fire. The Communications Ministry building, which had cost two million yuan to construct and, with its magnificent ceremonial hall, was the finest in the capital, had been gutted and torched. The Chinese army was

destroying whatever they couldn't take with them. They had set fire
to many houses and buildings, including the generalissimo's summer
headquarters, the Military Academy, the Modern Chemical Warfare
School, the agricultural research laboratories, the Railway Ministry,
the Police Training School—all were burning. Probably it was their
way of venting their rage, since by now they knew that Chiang Kai-
shek and all the generals were gone.

As John Magee was speaking, a stooped man wearing a felt hat
with earflaps and holding a walking stick turned up, leading a small
girl with his other hand. "Please let us in?" the man asked in a listless
voice.

"This place is only for women and children," Minnie said.

The man smiled, his eyes gleaming. He straightened up and said
in a bright female voice, "I am a woman. Look." She took off her hat,
pulled a bandanna out of her pocket, and wiped her face to get rid of
the dirt and tobacco tar. We could now see that she was quite young,
in her mid-twenties. Although her angular face was still streaked, her
neck seemed longer now and her supple back gave her a willowy
figure.

We let her and the little girl in.

"What's your name?" I asked.

"Yanying," she said. "This is my kid sister, Yanping." She threw her
arm around the girl.

Yanying told us, "Our town was burned by the Japs. They took lots
of women and men. Our neighbors Aunt Gong and her daughter-in-
law were tortured to death in their home. My dad told us to run. Our
brother was too scared to travel in broad daylight, so my sis and I
came without him."

Minnie sent them to Holly in the Central Building. Then George
Fitch appeared, wearing a corduroy coat and smoking a cigarette with
a holder that resembled a small curved pipe. He looked exhausted,
his hair messy and his amber eyes damp. Fitch was the head of the
YMCA in Nanjing and the administrative director of the Safety Zone
Committee; he had been born in Suzhou and spoke the local dialect
so well that some Chinese mistook him for a Uighur. He told us that
hundreds of Chinese soldiers had gone to the University Hospital

camp to surrender. Many men dropped their weapons and begged the staff to let them in; otherwise they'd break into the buildings. He was sure that more soldiers, thousands of them, would come into the Safety Zone for protection, and this might get the committee into serious trouble with the victorious Japanese, so Magee and Fitch wasted no time and set off together for the hospital camp. Viewed from the rear, spindly Fitch seemed more stooped today, while Magee was stalwart with a sturdy back. Minnie said to me, "I hope no Chinese soldiers come to Jinling for refuge."

"There won't be any room left for them anyway," I said.

That evening three buildings on campus were already filled, while the others continued taking in new arrivals. The Arts Building, the last one in reserve, was just opened. The Red Cross still hadn't set up the porridge plant. The soup kitchen we had put together two days ago could meet only a fraction of the need. Minnie had proposed that we assemble the porridge plant by ourselves, but the local Red Cross people, who controlled the staffing of the kitchens and the distribution of some rations, insisted that they build the porridge plant. Apparently there was money to be made in this. Infuriated by their concern with profit under such circumstances, Minnie again sent Luhai to the local Red Cross headquarters to ask for permission.

THE NEXT MORNING it was quiet, as though the battle was over. We wondered if the Japanese had breached the city walls and gained full control of Nanjing. Word got around that the Chinese defense had collapsed after Japanese units had scaled the city walls and then dynamited them open in places. Soldiers swarmed in, shouting "Banzai!" and waving battle flags, but met little resistance. Big Liu said he'd seen the streets in the Aihui Middle School area littered with bodies, mostly civilians and some children—other than that, the downtown looked deserted.

For the whole morning Minnie scratched the nape of her neck continually. She felt itchy and sticky all over. She'd slept with her clothes on several nights in a row and hadn't taken a shower since her visit to the wounded soldiers at the train station five days before. She hadn't been able to sleep for two hours straight without being woken by gunfire or emergencies she had to cope with in person. Whenever she was too tired to continue, she'd take a catnap, and luckily she'd always been able to fall asleep the moment her head touched a pillow. If the battle was over today, she said she'd draw a hot bath and sleep for more than ten hours.

I was a light sleeper and had spent most of the night at the gatehouse and in different buildings. Thank God I was in good health and needed only three or four hours of sleep a day; still, I had underslept. Sometimes when I was too exhausted to continue working, I'd go into a storage room in the Practice Hall and doze off in there. These days my head was numb, my eyeballs ached, and my steps were unsteady, but I had to be around the camp. There were so many things I had to handle. My husband and daughter joked that I had become "homeless," but they could manage without my help.

Late in the afternoon Minnie wanted to go to the riverside to look at the situation. Big Liu offered to accompany her, yet she told him, "No, you'd better stay." Holly volunteered to go with her too, but Minnie said, "You should be around in case of emergency. Let Anling keep me company. No troops will hurt two old women." In fact, I was fifty, one year younger than Minnie, but she looked like she was in her early forties, while my hair was streaked with gray, though I hadn't lost my figure yet.

So I set out with her in a jeep, a jalopy given to us by Reverend Magee. Minnie was driving, which impressed every one of us, because she seemed clumsy with her hands and, unlike Holly, was not the kind of woman who could handle a car nimbly.

"Let's hope this car won't break down," said Minnie. Indeed, the jeep was rattling like crazy.

"I wish I could drive," I said.

"I'll teach you to drive when the war is over."

"Hope I won't be too old to learn by then."

"Come on, don't be such a pessimist."

"Okay, I might take you up on that."

We dropped into the headquarters of the Safety Zone Committee and found John Rabe, Searle Bates, and Eduard Sperling there. They looked glum and told us that the Chinese army had been withdrawing. In fact, just three hours earlier, Sperling, a German insurance broker, had returned from the Japanese lines, where he had offered to negotiate a cease-fire on behalf of the Chinese army. But General Asaka, Emperor Hirohito's uncle, had rejected the proposal, saying he meant to teach China a bloody lesson. He intended to "soak Nanjing in a bloodbath," so that the Chinese could all see what an incompetent leader Chiang Kai-shek was.

More appalling was the story Rabe told us. The previous day, General Tang had received Generalissimo Chiang's order that he organize a retreat immediately. Tang's troops were already in the thick of battle, so it was impossible to withdraw them. If he carried out the order, it would amount to abandoning his army. He contacted the generalissimo's headquarters to double-check with Chiang, who was adamant and reiterated the message, dictating that he must execute the retreat to preserve his army and cross the river without delay. Tang couldn't even pass the order on to some of his troops. Besides having lost their communications equipment, some of the divisions had come from remote regions, such as Guangdong, Sichuan, and Guizhou, and spoke different dialects, so they couldn't communicate with one another or relay instructions. Worse still, earlier that morning the Japanese fleet was steaming upriver. The Chinese army's route of retreat would be completely cut off soon, since we had no warships to repulse the enemy's navy. Desperate, General Tang approached the Safety Zone Committee and pleaded with the foreigners to intervene on China's behalf for a three-day cease-fire. Eduard Sperling started out early in the afternoon, trudging west toward the Japanese position and raising a flag made from a white sheet and inscribed TRUCE & PEACE! in Japanese by Cola, a yellow-eyed young Russian man. Sperling carried the weight of our capital on his roundish shoulders in hopes of preventing further bloodshed.

General Asaka, the button-nosed prince wearing a patch of mustache that made him look like he had a harelip, received Sperling and spat in his face. He drew his sword halfway and barked, "Tell the Chinese that they have brought death on themselves. It's too late for them to employ a peace broker like you. If they want peace, hand Sheng-chi Tang over to me first."

"Please inform General Matsui of our request," Sperling pleaded again.

"I am the commander here. Tell Sheng-chi Tang that we won't spare even a chicken or dog in Nanjing."

So Sperling returned to report back to General Tang. The emissary was in such a hurry that he sprained his ankle and had to use a stick to walk. By this time, some of the defending troops must have heard of the withdrawal order and had begun pulling out, but many units were isolated, fighting blindly with their flanks open, doomed to annihilation.

A prolonged silence followed Rabe's account of the failed effort for a cease-fire. I wanted to weep but took hold of myself, covering my face with one hand. I could hardly breathe.

"An army in flight collapses like a landslide," Searle said to Minnie, using the Chinese idiom.

"Chiang Kai-shek should be held accountable for this catastrophe," she huffed.

"Yes, he should be court-martialed," said Sperling.

"The problem is that he's the judge in his own court," Rabe added in a bantering tone, fingering the strap of his binoculars. In spite of his attempt at levity, he sounded grim.

Searle had to leave for the temporary hospital established the week before at the Ministry of Foreign Affairs. The city government had given the International Red Cross Committee, of which both Searle and Minnie were members, fifty thousand yuan for setting up hospitals, but even with such generous funding there was no way to staff them. Searle had yet to figure out how to get hold of some medical personnel and couldn't stop grumbling about the Chinese doctors who had fled. At the moment only one surgeon, Robert Wilson, a recent graduate of Harvard Medical School, remained in town, and he'd been working around the clock at the Nanjing University Hospital. Minnie and I went out with Searle and then headed for our jeep. The two of us got in the car and pulled onto Shanghai Road, driving northeast.

The moment we turned left onto Zhongshan Road, which led to Yijiang Gate, the route to Hsia Gwan and the wharves, we were

struck by a horrific sight. The entire city was fleeing toward the
waterside. Every street we passed was strewn with uniforms shed by
our soldiers. Both sides of the road were lined with burned vehicles, artillery pieces accompanied by boxes of shells, and heavy machine guns still tied to dead donkeys. A pack of mules stood loaded
with parts of an antiaircraft gun and ammunition, too confused to
move. A roan horse, still saddled, was neighing toward the clouds as
though it were being attacked by some invisible beasts of prey. The
soldiers were swarming north, mostly empty-handed but some still
wearing enamel rice bowls on their belts. The street was littered
with helmets, rifles, pistols, canteens, Czech machine guns, knap-
sacks, swords, grenades, overcoats, boots, small mortars, flamethrow-
ers, short spades, and pickaxes. Beside a brass bugle lay a pig's head,
its snout pointing skyward but both ears missing. As we were
approaching the International Club, the street was so jammed with
overturned automobiles, three-wheeled motorcycles, animal-drawn
carts, and electric poles and tangled wires that it was impossible to
drive farther. So we decided to walk. We veered right, pulled into the
compound of the German embassy, and parked our jeep there with
permission from Georg Rosen, the hot-tempered secretary of political affairs and one of the three German diplomats remaining behind.
Unlike his colleagues, Rosen was half Jewish and not allowed to wear
a swastika.

Minnie and I headed north on foot to see whether our army still
controlled its route of retreat. The Metropolitan Hotel appeared,
swathed in smoke and flames. The instant we passed it, a squad of
soldiers ran up to us, still bearing arms. The nine men, all wearing
straw sandals, stopped in front of us, dropped their rifles, and, with
hands clasped before their chests, begged Minnie to accept their
capitulation as though she were a conqueror as well. Their leader, his
face tear-stained, pleaded with Minnie, "Auntie, please save us!"

That flustered her, and I intervened, telling her, "They must think
every foreigner has access to sanctuary. Poor fellows, all abandoned
by their officers." As I was speaking, tears streamed down my face. I
was so sad that I doubled over sobbing.

Patting my head, Minnie said to the men in Mandarin, "We are not entitled to accept your weapons. If you want to stay in town, go to the Safety Zone, where you can find protection."

The men waggled their heads as if they were too frightened to move back in that direction. They did an about-face and ran away, leaving their guns behind. Minnie picked up a rifle, which was quite new; its stock bore these characters: "This embodies your people's blood and sweat." Those words were instructions from the generalissimo, engraved on many weapons in the Nationalist army. Minnie, her thick eyebrows knotted, dropped the gun and sighed.

Still wiping my eyes, I told her, "In this country a peasant's lifetime's earnings can buy only a rifle. Imagine all the equipment they have abandoned—what a horrendous waste."

"Yes. Lewis said he had seen some heavy cannons left on the outskirts of the city that had never been fired."

We continued toward the gate. It was gut-wrenching to see the entire area destroyed, most of the buildings and houses burned down and some still smoldering. After passing the British embassy, with Yijiang Gate already in view, we were too exhausted to push farther and realized that it would be impossible to get beyond the city wall to see what it was like on the riverside, so we stopped. In the distance, on both sides of the gate, blocked by sandbags and machine guns, strings of men were scaling the fifty-foot-high wall with ropes, fire hoses, and connected ladders. The top of the wall and the two-story pavilion on it were dotted and blurred against the smoky sunset by the scramblers. From the way the crowds were moving, we could tell that the piers must still be in Chinese hands. We turned back and headed for the German embassy.

Dusk was falling and a few bats were flitting around, zigzagging like ghostly butterflies. We had to slog against the crowds; Minnie was ahead of me, jostling and shouting, "Let us pass! Let us pass!" People were so desperate that some cursed us for moving against the human torrents. Suddenly automobiles began honking and guards, waving Mauser pistols but dressed in civvies, shouted, "Make way! Make way!"

Those unable to move fast enough were shoved aside by the guards. Following them came two long cars. "Look, General Tang!"

Minnie told me, pointing at the lean-faced man in the back of the second Buick. The general hung his head as if nodding off.

As we were observing the commander of the Nanjing defense, a half brick hit his car, followed by a voice yelling, "Bastard, fuck your ancestors up to eight generations!"

The brick left only a powdery spot on the side window, and without a word the guards glared at the swearing man, then went ahead to clear the obstacles. A few minutes later we lost sight of the two sedans after they made a left turn. General Tang must have had his own way to cross the river when it was dark.

7

ARTILLERY POUNDED the southern and western parts of the city throughout the night of December 12. After two a.m. I returned to the inner room in the president's office to steal a moment of sleep. Bursts of machine-gun fire broke out now and again. With my coat on, I dozed off in an armchair. In a semiconscious state, I saw Chinese soldiers scrambling onto junks, sampans, and rafts on the Yangtze while Japanese planes were strafing them. Some of the boats caught fire and some were overturned, dumping thousands of men into the roiling water. Some of them were dog-paddling and some clinging to boards and poles, while others sank, screaming for help.

Then an explosion woke me. "What a catastrophe," I muttered, shaking my head. I sat up, fumbling my feet into my shoes. I reached out for the floor lamp, then realized there was no electricity anymore—our college had a generator, but it hadn't started producing power yet. Tears blurred my eyes as I stood and made for the door.

While I was plodding to the front gate, the eastern sky was already aglow with rust-colored clouds, and all was quiet on campus. Luhai greeted me and said that groups of Chinese soldiers had passed by, some begging for civilian clothes. The men at the gate had given them whatever they could spare.

Along the front wall were clumps of uniforms tossed over by the soldiers, and there were also some rifles, daggers, and cartridge belts. We gathered the clothes and set fire to the pile. As for the weapons, I told Luhai to drop them into the pond behind the Library Building.

When it was light, scores of neighbors appeared at the front entrance, begging the guards to let them in. Minnie went over and told them through the steel bars of the gate that since their homes were already within the Safety Zone, they would be safe and should give the space to the refugees who had no place to stay. The neighbors groused some more, then left unhappy. A few men who had offered to work started swearing, because we could use only two of them as water carriers. Jinling had its own well for tap water, but drinking water had to be delivered to the people who stayed in the open. By now the camp was full, with more than twenty-five hundred refugees.

On December 13, the day that the Japanese took full control of the city, the porridge plant, a doorless shanty about seventy feet long, was finally set up beside the sports ground. It sold porridge to those who could afford it, at three cents a bowl, but it also gave free meals to those without money. The refugees went to the food stands building by building, one group after another. Even so, at mealtimes, crowds swarmed there with bowls and mess tins in their hands. That outraged me, and I couldn't help yelling at them. Breakfast lasted more than three hours, until half past ten. After that, the kitchen staff could take a breather for two hours and then would serve porridge again in the midafternoon. They provided two meals a day for the camp.

When breakfast was under way, many women washed laundry and toilet buckets at the four ponds on campus, mothers now and then calling to their children. A bunch of boys ran around as if eager to explore this new place, a few small girls following them. For the rest of the morning the camp was quiet, but around noon a clamor broke out at the front gate. "Japs, Japs are coming!" a boy hollered. Minnie and I went over and saw an officer slapping Luhai, and a soldier, rope in his hands, about to tie him up.

"Stop! Stop!" Minnie shouted, and hurried up to them. "He's our employee."

The squat lieutenant turned to her in amazement, saying something none of us could understand. He then motioned dismissively to the soldier behind him, and the man let Luhai go.

As the platoon of soldiers was moving away, a voice called out, "Save me, please!"

We rushed over and recognized Hu, the janitor of the Library

Building, his arms clutched by two soldiers, one of them carrying Hu's new serge parka in the crook of his elbow. Minnie grasped Hu's belt from behind and forced the two soldiers to stop in their tracks. "He works for us," she shouted at the stocky officer. "Coolie, coolie, you understand?" Her brown eyes were smoldering with rage. "You cannot arrest people without any charge."

The officer looked at the Red Cross badge on her chest as though unable to make head or tail of it. Then he waved at the two soldiers, who released Hu.

"Save me too, Principal Vautrin!" another voice cried. That was from a boy named Fanshu, who was also being dragged away. He was struggling to break loose while still holding a basketball under his arm.

We ran toward Fanshu, but a soldier spun around and held out his rifle, its bayonet pointed at Minnie. She had no choice but to stand there watching them pull the boy away, together with three other Chinese men we didn't know, though one of them looked strong, like a soldier. Fanshu worked for an old American couple who had just left town. He was supposed to stay and watch over their property, but he had snuck here to play basketball. He was merely fourteen, though tall and big for his age, so the Japanese caught him as a potential soldier.

"Thank you for rescuing me, Principal," Hu said, bowing to Minnie and showing his splotched scalp. "I spent a whole year's savings on that parka they robbed me of."

"Damn them!" Minnie stamped the ground, puffs of dust jumping up around her feet. "Ban, Ban, where are you?"

"Here, I'm here." Ban, a skinny boy of fifteen, who was our messenger, came over.

"Go tell Mr. Rabe that the Japanese took people from our college."

"I don't speak foreign words, Principal."

"Mr. Han, his secretary, knows English. Let him translate for you. Ask them to come and help us stop the soldiers."

Ban broke into a trot, sticking out his elbows as he ran, his police boots too big for him. He was short for his age, about five foot one. I wondered if it was wise to send him on the errand, but I didn't share my misgivings. Even if Rabe was notified, what could he do? Such random arrests must have been happening everywhere in the city.

Around two p.m. Rulian arrived; she was nicknamed Lady Fowler thanks to her love of Emily Brontë and because she kept our domestic fowls. She panted, "Some Japs are on the hill." She pointed at a hillside to the west, beyond our Poultry Experiment Center, which was in her charge.

"Do you think they'll break into the fowl house?" Minnie asked her.

"Sure they will."

"Let's go have a look," I said.

Minnie had to remain at the front gate, so Luhai, Holly, and I hastened west with Rulian. I looked askance at the young woman; she was wearing a countrywoman's dark blue jacket, her smooth face smeared with soot. She was thirty-one and comely, but had deliberately made herself look dirty and diseased. She even walked slightly bandy-legged to reduce her height. Yet there was no way she could conceal her prettiness altogether. I wanted to tease her by saying she couldn't possibly rusticate herself so rapidly, but I refrained.

Chickens, ducks, and geese were squawking like mad in the poultry center. We entered the enclosure and saw two soldiers there, one gripping a goose by the neck, the bird treading the air in silence, and the other man chasing a long-tailed rooster. He tripped and almost fell in an attempt to catch the cock, which landed on top of a shelf, shaking its red and black feathers while peering at him with one eye. The man cursed the rooster and spat on the ground.

"Hey, hey," Holly shouted, "they're not for food!"

The soldiers stopped and came up to us. The taller one pointed at a hen and rapped out some Japanese words none of us could comprehend. Then the shorter one said in Mandarin, "Eat . . . chicken . . . meat."

"No, no," I said, glad he knew some Chinese. "These are for experiments, not like the birds raised by your mothers. Don't eat poison, all right? If you eat any of them, you will bleed from every orifice."

"Poison?" the man asked, then mumbled something to his comrade. They both looked puzzled.

"Yes." Rulian pointed at a line of brown bottles along the wall, containing herbs and medicines for poultry diseases.

The short man again spoke to his comrade, who then dropped the goose and kicked a terra-cotta water bowl. Together they strode out, blustering as if cursing their rotten luck.

The four of us smiled, because the fowls were all healthy. "My goodness, 'you will bleed from every orifice,'" Holly said to me. "You must've scared the heck out of them."

Rulian giggled. Without delay we went back to the camp, where rice porridge was being doled out to the refugees for the afternoon meal.

Ban hadn't returned yet, and Minnie was worried. The headquarters of the Safety Zone was just a stone's throw away, and he should have come back long ago. We couldn't help but wonder if he had run into trouble. The boy was an orphan, whose keep in a nearby orphanage had been paid by our college for years before we hired him, so he was more than just an employee to us.

After the refugees had finished their meal, we went to the dining hall to have supper. Most of us hadn't eaten anything since the morning. Minnie and Holly collapsed onto chairs, saying they preferred a nap to food. They closed their eyes, ready to drop off.

"Please, you ought to eat to keep going," I said, placing a bowl of porridge in front of Minnie. I moved a plate of fried soybeans closer. As I was getting another bowl for Holly, Luhai rushed in.

"Minnie," he said, "some Japanese broke into the house where we store our rations."

"Did they take the rice?" she asked.

"I'm not sure."

"What did they tell you?" I said.

"They just punched me." While speaking, he rubbed his bruised cheek.

The three of us went out with Luhai. The house in question was across the street from the front gate, and the rice was actually not ours. It was the Red Cross workers manning the porridge plant who'd left the ninety sacks in there, about twenty thousand pounds of rice. If the Japanese took the grain, the refugees here would starve.

Approaching the house, we saw a lamp wavering at its entrance. A soldier barred our way, shouting in stiff Mandarin, "Stop! Stop there!"

"This is our college's house!" Minnie cried back, and tried to push in. Then a young officer with a short beard came out of the room that held the rations. Minnie fluttered a small U.S. flag at him and said, "The rice is American property. You can't have it! Get your men out of here. Are you in charge?"

The officer didn't understand her; he turned around and said something to the men behind him. Two of them came up and shoved the four of us away. Then the officer pulled out his Yamato sword, cutting the air right and left while screaming as if he were performing onstage. The blade whirred and whistled. Frightened, none of us dared step closer again.

Without delay we went down Ninghai Road to the Safety Zone headquarters, which was just steps away. John Rabe was there alone, wearing a steel helmet like an officer. On his desk were some old issues of *Ostasiatischer Lloyd*, a small German-language newspaper published in Shanghai. Minnie asked him if Ban had come to inform him of a random arrest at our college. "I didn't see him," Rabe said, puzzled and wringing his plump fingers.

"Oh God, I hope he didn't fall into Japanese hands!" Minnie said.

"He didn't show up here at all?" I asked Rabe.

"No. I've been here since nine a.m."

"I should never have sent him out," said Minnie.

Holly described the rice situation. Rabe replied, "Maybe I should go and talk to them. Let's hope we still can reason with those hoodlums."

As Rabe stood up, ready to head out, the telephone rang and he picked it up. I was amazed that his phone still worked. The call was from Rosen at the German embassy; he said that squads of Japanese soldiers were at Rabe's home and his German school, about to break into the compounds. Some of them were brandishing torches and threatening to toss them onto the properties if the gates remained shut. Rabe's home and the small school sheltered hundreds of his Chinese friends, neighbors, and servants' families in addition to many refugees, so he had to run.

Before leaving, Rabe called over Cola, the Russian who knew some Japanese. Young Cola wrote a short official letter for us to take back so we could show it to the soldiers occupying the house where the rice was stored the first thing the next morning.

Cola had grown up in Siberia, where his ancestors had done business with the Chinese, Koreans, and Japanese for generations. He had lived in our city for almost a decade, and children called him "the yellow-haired Russian." He told us that the Japanese had arrested thousands of men suspected of being stragglers and deserters from the Chinese army and had raped hundreds of women in the southern and eastern sections of the city, where streets were strewn with dead bodies. There were also Japanese "fire squads" torching houses and buildings in different areas. Worst of all, some soldiers killed the women they raped to avoid being identified by them to the military police later on; in fact, there were very few policemen in town at the moment. Reports of atrocities within the Safety Zone had come nonstop for a whole day, but Rabe had been unable to contact the top officers of the invading force. We could only hope that the military would soon be able to control the soldiers who were running amok.

"I don't think those brutes would kill and rape without their officers' consent," Holly said.

"The army certainly hasn't bothered to rein them in," Cola agreed.

"Who could have imagined such brutalities?" Minnie said.

"What should we do?" Holly asked.

"Nothing I can think of." Cola shrugged.

When we returned to campus, we saw dozens of women sitting back to back in the front yard, along the cypress hedges. The buildings were already too packed to take in any more people, but more continued flocking to the camp. Agitated by the disappearance of Ban and wanting to pray for him, Minnie said good night to us and headed back to her apartment.

8

I T WAS MILD and sunny the next morning. Watching the refugees
in the quad, I was grateful for the warm weather, which felt like
October. This would make the uprooted people less miserable on the
road or in the wilderness, since they had nothing to protect themselves from the elements. Never had I imagined that our fortified
capital could be smashed so easily, like a ceramic vat hit by a mallet.
In the north, artillery fire surged and ebbed, rumbling amid smoky
and blazing clouds. There was still fighting in the Hsia Gwan area,
and the Japanese warships were shelling the remaining Chinese
troops and sinking boats and rafts that attempted to cross the river.
Around Jinling, rifles crackled from time to time.

Early in the afternoon Holly and I went out to the Drum Tower
area, a short walk to the northeast. She had not returned home three
nights in a row and was afraid that her house might have been plundered, though she had thumbtacked an American flag to the front
door and sealed it with a poster from the U.S. embassy. As we walked
along Shanghai Road, many Japanese flags were flying from the
houses and buildings, flapping like laundry. A few banners made of
white cloth even declared, LONG LIVE THE EMPEROR!

"Those people will do anything to save their skin," Holly grunted.

"They must be terrified," I said.

"I'm a Chinese citizen too, but I won't say a good word about the
Japanese brutes."

"You have a foreign face, Holly. To tell the truth, I wouldn't dare to
step off campus without your company."

We turned into the small alley alongside the eastern border of the
Safety Zone. Seven or eight houses on the street had been razed, set
on fire after being looted. Holly's home was among them, and her car
was gone too. A young man, bayoneted twice in the chest, lay dead
on his side below the brick wall of her yard, his back naked, his hair

scorched, and the exposed side of his face eaten by dogs. He looked like a stranger to Holly. "Savages, worse than beasts!" she cursed the soldiers, and broke into tears, wiping her face with the end of her scarf.

"Holly, I'm sorry," I murmured, and wrapped my arm around her.

The neighborhood was very quiet; you couldn't hear any noise, not even the tiny chirps made by the sparrows that used to live in many of the roofs. Then a Siamese cat jumped out of a coal shack in the next-door neighbor's yard and meowed forlornly, as though starved. Brushing away her tears, Holly said, "I guess this is it. Now I have no place to go."

"You can always stay with us," I said. That was hardly an invitation, since she was already indispensable to our school. She wasn't just the only other foreigner on campus but was also, as a musician, needed for the chapel services. Besides, she'd been helping our nurse care for the sick and the women expecting or in labor.

When we returned to the campus, about four hundred men, women, and children were at the front gate, begging Luhai and Miss Lou to let them in. All the women wore white terry cloth over their hair; apparently they were from the countryside. A few old men were sucking on long pipes. I was somewhat surprised, because by now we were known as a camp for only women and children, and most men wouldn't come to seek refuge anymore.

Minnie said to the villagers, "We accept only women and kids."

"Please, we can't go elsewhere," a thirtyish man begged.

"Most of the other camps take in families. You should try them," I told him.

"We dare not walk anywhere," an older man said, donning a skull-cap, the type called a melon-rind cap. "If the Japanese devils see us, they'll kill us and grab our wives and daughters."

A girl in her mid-teens shuffled over, wearing a pair of bandages on her forehead like two miniature crosses standing together, one taller than the other. "Please let me in, Aunties," she wailed to Holly and me as we were still standing outside the gate. "I'm the only one left in my family." She burst into tears.

"What happened?" I asked.

"Some Japs broke into the deserted building where we stayed last night, and they cut down my dad and brothers. Then they stripped my mom and me and started torturing us. I screamed, so they punched me again and again until I lost my voice and blacked out. When I came to, I saw my mom's body in the room. She couldn't take it anymore and hit her head on the doorjamb and killed herself."

Minnie had come out of the gate by now. I realized that the girl had been raped and told her, "You must get treated. I'll get someone to take you to the University Hospital."

"I can't walk anymore. If not for these good-hearted folks, I couldn't have made it here."

"Then you can come in," I said.

After telling a staffer to take the girl to our infirmary, Minnie decided to lead the rest of them to the university camp. Holly offered to go along, but Minnie told her to stay because John Magee had just left and we needed at least one foreigner on campus to deter the soldiers.

Nanjing University was about a fifteen-minute walk from our college, and Minnie led the crowd away with a small U.S. flag in her hand, while I brought up the rear, bearing a Red Cross flag. Passing the closed American embassy, we saw two Japanese soldiers coming from the opposite direction and hee-hawing while prodding a reedy boy ahead of them with rifles. The teenager pushed a barrow that had a large wooden wheel ringed with steel. It was loaded with booty—a stack of dried salt fish, a bundle of potato noodles, a jar of duck eggs still in brine, a wall clock, and a trussed pregnant sheep, still bleating. The soldiers each had about a dozen silver bracelets, watches, and gold rings affixed to their belts. All the women in the procession lowered their heads until the soldiers passed.

When we arrived at the university, we found George Fitch, who had been managing the large camp there with Searle, squatting under a bulky linden, his head in both hands. "Hey, George, what's the matter?" Minnie asked.

He raised his bony face, his eyes watery and somewhat bloodshot. "The Japanese took away two hundred men just now," he told her.

"Were they surrendered soldiers?"

"No, many of them were civilians."

"They just took whoever they wanted?"

"They ordered them to undress and checked their shoulders and hands. If there was a mark like something left by a knapsack or a rifle, they took the man. But most of the poor fellows were coolies who had to work with tools and carry stuff around, and of course they had marks on their shoulders and calluses on their hands. The Japanese arrested practically all the young men. There was no way to reason with them. Oh, Minnie, this is horrible, as if we still live in the Dark Ages."

"What are they going to do to them?"

"Finish them off, I'm sure."

"I guess they just want to kill to terrify the Chinese."

"Also to wipe out all the able-bodied males." He sniveled and blew his nose into a piece of straw paper.

Minnie said, "Maybe we shouldn't have offered protection to those Chinese soldiers in the first place. Some of them were reluctant to give us their weapons, but we were so foolish that we promised them more than we can deliver."

"I've thought about that too. With firearms they could at least have defended themselves."

As we were speaking, a group of Japanese soldiers emerged, two of them dragging a scrawny man onto the lawn. I recognized Chang, who used to be a librarian at the university and now worked in the refugee camp as a file clerk. They meant to take him away, but he refused to go with them.

We all stood up to watch. The leader of this group, a lieutenant, ordered a new recruit to stab Chang. The young soldier hesitated, but the officer barked out orders again. The man charged at Chang, whose cotton-padded overcoat was so thick that the bayonet didn't go through. Realizing they meant to kill him, Minnie and George hustled toward them to intervene. I followed, but the soldiers blocked us. Then, to our astonishment, Chang undid his buttons and dropped his coat on the ground, facing his attacker with just his thin jacket on, his sparse goatee wet with snot. The lieutenant again yelled at the young man, who rushed toward Chang with a wild shriek and stabbed him through. The clerk's legs buckled, but his eyes were still fixed on his killer. Then he fell, blood pooling around him.

We were so stunned that for a while nobody could move or say a word. Then the troops marched away, and people gathered around Chang, who was breathing his last. "Revenge, revenge," he mouthed.

He died within a few minutes. I had known this wispy moonfaced librarian by sight and heard he had a fiery temper, but I'd never thought much of him.

Having left the four hundred refugees with George Fitch, Minnie and I headed back. She panted a little as she walked, her gait ponderous but steady.

"I wonder why God let this happen to us Chinese," I said. "What did we do to deserve this? Why doesn't God punish those heartless men?" Just that morning I'd heard that a nephew of mine, my cousin's seventeen-year-old son, had been seized by the Japanese the night before. His parents were distraught but dared not go out and look for him.

"God works in his own ways, hard for us to fathom," Minnie said, but not convincingly.

Our ancient city, noted for its beauty and cultural splendor, had become hell overnight, as if forsaken by God. I couldn't stop wondering whether there'd be retribution in store for the ruthless soldiers and their families. No one could brutalize others like this with impunity in the long run, I was sure.

That night, Searle Bates and Plumer Mills slept in our main dormitory and the Arts Building, respectively, while Lewis Smythe kept Luhai company at our gatehouse. Before turning in, the husky Plumer wept and cursed again, his heavy-jawed face scrunched and his hair damp with sweat. He suffered from pain in his chest caused by being hit twice by the Japanese with rifle butts that morning when he had attempted in vain to prevent them from taking thirteen hundred Chinese soldiers out of the police headquarters. A group of American missionaries had disarmed those men and promised them personal safety, but all the poor fellows had been dragged away and executed in the afternoon. Fifty policemen guarding the Safety Zone were also rounded up and shot for letting the Chinese soldiers enter the neutral district. With the three American men in our camp we felt a little more secure. Minnie stayed with Miss Lou in the Practice Hall, which was more than two hundred yards away from the nearest building, tucked in the southeast corner of campus, while I was in charge of the main dormitory. The college's two policemen still patrolled, but in plainclothes. In addition, an old watchman, lantern in hand, would make rounds throughout the night.

THE NEXT DAY the Japanese went on looting, burning, arresting men, and attacking women in town. Luckily, it was uneventful at Jinling, except that early in the morning a soldier came from the house across from the front gate with four coolies and dropped two sacks of rice with loud thumps. We were pleased that the Japanese had finally let our camp use the grain and didn't sell the rice back to us. Some soldiers had seized rations from the camp in Magee's charge and then sold them back to the porridge plant there "at a discount"— wheat flour was two yuan for a fifty-pound bag and rice five yuan for a two-hundred-pound sack.

Since daybreak, more refugees had been coming to Jinling. Although the buildings were all packed, we still accepted the new arrivals, now that they wanted nothing but a place to stay. Most of them just lounged on the lawns or the sports ground. Looking at the refugees around her, Minnie said she was even more convinced that she'd made the right decision to remain behind. I felt the same. Again the Lord's words rose in my mind: "Thine is the power and the glory." That seemed to have new meaning to me now, like a promise.

I recited that line, and Minnie nodded solemnly in agreement.

Around midafternoon, Rulian came and reported that some soldiers had gone into the South Hill Residence. Minnie, Big Liu, and I set out at once for that manor, taking the path that cut a diagonal through a bamboo grove. The second we stepped into the building, we heard laughter from the dining room on the left. Three Japanese were sitting at a table drinking apple juice and spooning compote directly from an eight-pound can. Beyond them the door of the pantry was open, the padlock smashed. Minnie went up to them and shouted, "You can't do this!"

They all stood up and made for the door, holding the juice bottles and two large floral-cloth parcels, seemingly frightened. Once out of the building, they veered east and dashed away, their calves wrapped in leggings.

As I wondered what was inside the two parcels, Minnie said, "They seem like young boys who know they did something wrong."

"Some of the Japanese are quite young indeed," Big Liu said, and pushed up his glasses with his knuckle. He looked frazzled; he suffered from insomnia these days and often complained of a headache.

"Do you think they were hungry?" I asked both of them.

"They could be," he answered.

"I wouldn't mind if they came just to eat and drink something, but they must let us know in advance," Minnie said.

Big Liu shook his bushy head and spoke as if to himself. "They really love American party food."

Minnie chuckled. I liked Big Liu for his sense of humor as well as for his levelheadedness. Sometimes when he said something funny, he himself didn't realize it—which made it more deadpan. We went upstairs and found the door of a small storage room ajar. Inside, half a dozen suitcases were cut open or unzipped, all ransacked, women's clothing scattered around. One of the bags belonged to Mrs. Dennison and another to Donna Thayer, a biology teacher who was in Shanghai at the moment. There was no way to find out what had been stolen, so we closed the suitcases and placed them next to four intact ones sitting behind a tall bookshelf loaded with pinkish toilet tissue. There we saw Dr. Wu's varnished pigskin chest opened and gutted, but again we couldn't tell what had been taken.

When we were back at the quadrangle, Minnie saw John Magee speaking to Luhai. Suddenly a burst of gunfire came from the southwest, and everybody stopped to listen until the fusillade subsided.

We went up to Magee and Luhai. The reverend said to Minnie, "I just heard that the *Panay* was sunk by Japanese warplanes."

"Good Lord, what about the people on the boat?" she asked.

"Three were killed and more than forty wounded—most of the casualties were sailors."

"The staff of the embassy is okay?"

"Apparently so. They were rescued."

My mind began spinning, because Jinling's portmanteau containing papers, foreign currencies, and Mrs. Dennison's wedding silver had been aboard the gunboat. I hoped that the trunk was safe and still in the care of the embassy's staff. If the silverware was lost, Mrs. Dennison might go bonkers. She disliked Minnie, though she was decent to me, mainly because Dr. Wu kept me under her wing. From her first days at Jinling, Minnie must have known that the founding president viewed her as a rival, perhaps because Minnie was bold enough to assume the acting presidency, which no one else dared take, and also because her ability as a leader might pose a threat to the old woman, who demanded loyalty only to herself from the faculty, staff, and even students. Yet Minnie and I agreed that Mrs. Dennison had always regarded Jinling as her home and had dedicated herself to the college. It was this devotion that united the two of them.

ABOUT TEN O'CLOCK the next morning, more than a company of Japanese troops came to search for Chinese soldiers. Minnie told the commander, a tall man with hollow cheeks, that this camp sheltered only women and children. The head officer, who must have been a colonel and was accompanied by two bodyguards and an adjutant, wouldn't listen and declared that the Safety Zone Committee had broken its promise to provide sanctuary only for noncombatants, so now the Imperial Army was entitled to weed out all the hostile remnants. True enough—in its original proposal, the committee had claimed that the area would be "kept from the presence of armed men and from the passage of soldiers in any capacity." But when the letter for the Japanese authorities was composed, none of the committee members had been able to imagine such a turn of events: thousands of Chinese soldiers would come and implore them to save their lives. The foreigners accepted them after collecting their weapons, assuming that the Japanese would follow the common practice in war of treating the capitulated men with basic humanity. Now, in the name of eliminating the former soldiers, the conquerors began to seize whomever they suspected might be a potential fighter.

The search started with the Science Building, and the Japanese wanted to go through every room. If a door was locked and the key was not available right away, a soldier carrying a hefty ax would smash the lock. My heart was hammering as we followed them around. In the second-floor office of the Geography Department were stored six hundred cotton-padded garments for the Chinese troops, made by the neighborhood women the previous fall. Minnie and I had decided to keep them because we believed that the refugees might need winter clothes. Now those jackets and pants could be criminal evidence. How should we explain if they were discovered? Could we say that the Chinese army had forced us to make them? If the Japanese found the clothes, I'd have to step up and invent an excuse before Minnie could respond. She was such a poor liar that they would see through her.

Fortunately, the officer did not insist on searching the room containing the clothes first when Minnie offered to take the men directly to the attic, which sheltered two hundred women and children. The refugees up there seemed to have distracted the soldiers, since on their way down they forgot to go left and search the offices on the second floor.

As we came out of the building, one soldier grabbed hold of a water carrier we'd just hired. The poor man was too petrified to holler for help; his buckets were overturned and his shoulder pole smudged with mud. The soldier slapped him across the face and sneered in Mandarin, "Serviceman, huh?"

"No, no," Minnie intervened. "He's a coolie, our waterman. Damn it, he's already over forty, how can he be a soldier?"

A junior officer ripped open the man's collar to look at his left shoulder. Luckily no mark was on it, and they let him go. The fellow was so shaken that he tore away without a word, leaving behind the buckets, the carrying pole, and the two buttons from his jacket, all dropped in the wet mud.

Minnie and I followed the Japanese. As we were approaching the front entrance, a small group of soldiers appeared, pulling away a young boy, the repairman Tong's nephew, who had often come to campus to do odd jobs. Minnie hurried over and blocked their way.

"He's our errand boy, not a soldier," she cried, having hit upon the job title for him on the spur of the moment.

The interpreter, a soft-faced Chinese man in a trench coat, told the Japanese what she had said. One of them stepped over and shoved Minnie in the chest with his fist. The tall officer shouted something at him, and the man yelped "*Hai!*" and stood at attention. So the boy ran away to join his uncle. The officer scribbled a note and handed it to Minnie. The interpreter told her, "You can show this to other groups if they come in to search again." She thanked the officer, then seemed to flinch suddenly. She turned and whispered to me, "There're machine guns everywhere." Her chin pointed at the front entrance.

I looked and caught sight of six of them propped on both sides of the front wall. I shivered as I realized that the Japanese had meant to shoot if a commotion took place here.

After the officer and his entourage had gone out the front gate, we saw a squad of soldiers passing by with four Chinese men strung together by iron wire around their upper arms. One of them wasn't wearing pants, his legs spattered with blood. We went over to the entrance to take a closer look but weren't able to tell if the captives were former soldiers, although the youngest of them couldn't have been older than sixteen. The group proceeded in single file toward the hillside in the west, and ten minutes later came a volley of gunfire—all those men were executed.

"They shot people like that—without a trial or any evidence of crime?" Minnie said.

I realized that the Japanese felt justified in treating us in any way they wanted. A lot of people must have expected this would happen. That must be why they had scrambled away before the Japanese arrived.

More refugees had been let in. By now Jinling held more than four thousand. The newcomers recounted horrifying stories: Plundering, rape, bloodshed, and arson had taken place everywhere in the city and its suburbs in the past three days. Some girls who hadn't reached their teens yet had been snatched away from their parents. In the east and south dark smoke kept rising—thousands of houses and stores had been torched to get rid of the evidence of pillage. Some soldiers would rob pedestrians of whatever they had on them: money, food, cigarettes, coats, fountain pens, even hats and gloves. An old woman told us, "A Jap yanked my brass thimble off my finger. He must've thought it was a ring or something. I showed him it was just for sewing, but he couldn't understand. Such a half-wit, he almost broke my finger." One of our janitors, a man with a catlike face named Jian Ding, sat on his heels and wouldn't stop weeping, no matter how people tried to console him, because his fifteen-year-old son had been taken that morning.

That evening, on the way to the Safety Zone's headquarters, Minnie and I saw a stake-bed truck with double tires rumbling by. It carried a dozen or so teenage girls, who called out, "Help us! Save our lives!" One of them wore an eyeshade. Some had blackened faces and cropped hair, which still hadn't been able to disguise them from the soldiers.

We froze in our tracks, watching the vehicle until it disappeared. I closed my eyes, my eyeballs aching, while Minnie pressed the sides of her neck with both hands and groaned, "God, when will you show your anger?"

We went to see Rabe to find out if he'd heard about Ban. He had no news for us.

9

O N THE MORNING of December 17, small groups of Japanese soldiers popped up on different parts of the campus, grabbing women and girls. There'd been more than thirty rape cases in our camp. Emergencies had sprung up continually, forcing Minnie and me to run around together to confront the soldiers. By now we had admitted more than six thousand refugees. All the buildings were packed, and most classrooms brought to mind train stations crowded with stranded passengers, while the people in the open were noisy, especially the children, milling around like at a temple fair. We were worried about how to maintain sanitation and feed so many. The porridge plant was totally inadequate.

Minnie had persuaded Searle to open another dormitory at Nanjing University for newcomers and to ensure that a foreign man would stay there at night. Between four and six that afternoon, she and I led two large groups of women and children there; we also had a seventeen-year-old girl sent to Dr. Wilson—this young wife, five months pregnant, had been raped by a bunch of soldiers and had miscarried. A donkey cart shipped her to the hospital, followed by her shrieking mother-in-law.

When we returned from our second trip to Searle's new camp, we found Holly chatting with Miss Lou at the door of the main dormitory. We joined them and entered the dining hall in that building. Supper was dough-drop soup with soybean sprouts in it. Most of the staff had not eaten anything since breakfast, as we often skipped meals during the day. On the table were cruets of soy sauce, rice vinegar, and oil thick with chili flakes. While we were eating, a boy rushed in and panted, "Principal Vautrin, lots of Japs are on campus, beating up people."

"Where are they exactly?" Minnie asked.

"On their way to the dorms in the north."

We all put down our bowls and went out. It was getting dark, and the air was smoky—some houses nearby must have been burning. A flock of rooks cawed lustily in treetops, while women's and children's shrieks were rising from the west and north. *Bang, bang, bang, bang!* Three Japanese were pounding the front door of the Central Building with their fists. Minnie went up to them, but before she could say a word, a bespectacled soldier said to us in broken Mandarin, "Open this."

"I have no key," Minnie told him.

"Soldiers in there, enemy of Japan."

"No soldiers, only women and children."

Minnie produced the note written by the officer the day before, but the man glanced at it, then tore it three times and dropped the pieces to the ground. He turned to speak to the other two men. One of them came up and slapped Minnie, Holly, and me while yelling something we couldn't understand. He then shoved Miss Lou and nearly sent her to the ground. Holly muttered in English, "Bastard!" Her eyes were teary and her bulky nose twitched. A pink-fingered handprint surfaced on her left cheek.

"Open this," the man wearing glasses insisted.

At this point rectangular-faced Rong, the assistant business manager, arrived. With my ear still buzzing and hot from the slap, I asked him, "Do you have the key?"

He shook his creased forehead. "I don't. Usually we don't lock this door from outside."

Minnie said to the soldiers, "We really don't have the key."

The man blinked behind his glasses and ordered Rong in a cry, "Open it!"

"I don't know how."

At that, the soldier punched Rong in the face. The other two began beating and kicking him too. One of them kept smirking while he slapped Rong, as if having some fun with him. Then he raised his rifle, the bayonet pointed at Rong's throat.

"Stop, stop!" Minnie said. "All right, let's use the other door." She pointed at the side of the building, then led them away to that entrance. We followed them. I glanced at Rong, who was trembling and swallowing, his swollen eyes almost sealed.

To our bafflement, once the three soldiers entered the building, they looked through a few rooms perfunctorily and didn't even bother to go up to the top floor. Within five minutes the search was done. As we stepped out the side door, we saw another two soldiers pulling three Chinese men away, their hands tied behind their backs. I recognized the captives, who were all our employees. Minnie rushed over and said, "They work for us."

"Chinese soldiers, enemy of Japan," one of the captors declared.

"No, no, they're gardeners and coolies," she countered, and then pointed at Jian Ding. "He's our janitor and just lost his fifteen-year-old son to your Imperial Army."

That didn't help matters. The soldiers continued dragging the men away. Wide-framed Ding somehow made no protest, as if he didn't care where they were taking him.

The bespectacled soldier motioned for us to follow them, and together we headed to the front entrance, beyond which human shadows were moving.

Outside the gate, I saw more than forty Chinese kneeling on the side of the street, a few weeping. Rulian and Luhai were among them, though Luhai was on his feet, speaking and gesticulating to a soldier. Two squads of Japanese stood around, most of them toting rifles and one holding a bloody-tongued German shepherd on a leash. A cross-eyed sergeant came over and demanded, "Who is the head of this place?" His interpreter translated the question.

"I'm in charge." Minnie stepped forward.

As they were speaking, more of our staffers were escorted over and made to kneel down. Three soldiers came up to us and grabbed Rong, Miss Lou, and me, dragged us to the crowd, and forced us to our knees. Why are they rounding us up? I wondered. Are they taking over the school? What are they going to do to us and to the refugees? Where are Yaoping, Liya, and Fanfan? A wave of dizziness came over me, and I nearly keeled over; I grasped Miss Lou's arm to steady myself.

The sergeant asked Minnie to identify all the employees among us. She named several and told him their duties. As she continued, she stalled time and again; apparently she couldn't remember the names of all these people, especially the part-timers hired in the past few days. One of the servants, young and straight-shouldered, was quite burly. Minnie stopped in front of him, unable to come up with his name. If the man had already given the soldiers his name, she mustn't name him randomly. As she was deciding, they took him to the other side of the street and made him kneel down.

"His name is Ban!" Minnie cried at the sergeant. That was a smart choice—surely nobody among us had the same name as our disappeared messenger boy.

Luhai said, "He's our coal carrier."

"Shut up!" The sergeant punched him in the chest. Then two soldiers clutched Luhai's arms, dragged him away, and forced him to his knees next to the "coal carrier."

At this point a jeep pulled over. Off jumped three Americans: Lewis Smythe, George Fitch, and Plumer Mills, the vice chairman of the Safety Zone Committee. At once the troops surrounded the new arrivals, lined them up, and began searching them for pistols, which none of them had.

When the search was finished, George said, "*Wir sind Missionare,*" to which the sergeant didn't respond. George said again, "*Nous sommes tous americains.*"

"*Oui, je sais.*" The sergeant chortled, his squinty eyes blinking.

The two of them carried on an exchange in broken French for a few moments, but George didn't look pleased. Meanwhile, a pair of flashlights kept shining at the other foreigners' faces, forcing them to shut their eyes. George told his American colleagues, "They want us all to leave right away."

Then more than ten soldiers rushed up and pushed the Americans into the jeep. Two men clutched Minnie's arms and forced her into the passenger seat, but she scrambled out, throwing up her hand and shouting at the sergeant, "Damn it, this is my home! I have nowhere to go."

"Me either!" Holly cried out, gripping the top of the tailgate and refusing to get in the car. "My house was burned down by your Imperial Army, and I've become a refugee, still waiting for you to make reparations." Her eyes widened fiercely and her face flushed with rage.

George interpreted their words loudly to the sergeant, who then ordered all the foreign men to leave at once.

Several rifles were trained on the three men, who climbed into the jeep. Lewis waved to assure us that everything would be all right. Slowly they pulled away.

The sergeant cupped his hands around his mouth and shouted at George's back, *"Au revoir!"*

Two of his men yipped delightedly.

As soon as the vehicle disappeared, women's cries and muffled screams came from inside the wall. Through the gate I saw some Japanese hauling people toward our campus's side exit. The small ironclad gate there was always locked, so it must have been forced open. I looked around and caught sight of machine guns posted at the windows across the street. For some reason the soldiers at the front entrance suddenly withdrew, taking with them only Luhai and the hefty "coal carrier," and then trucks started revving their engines beyond the southern wall—*kakh-kakh-kakh-kakh.* I realized that the Japanese had held all the responsible staff here while other soldiers were seizing people inside the campus. Out of the corner of my eye I saw a machine gun still propped there, and I dared not move a muscle, my heart beating in my throat.

We were still kneeling, some sobbing. For a long time no one stirred. I glanced at Minnie and Holly, whose heads sagged, their eyes nailed to the ground.

Then Big Liu ran over, shouting, "Minnie, Minnie, they took some people from East Court."

"Who are the people?" She got up to her feet.

"I can't say for sure."

At that, I jumped up and raced away, my head in a whirl. Some people followed me while I was running and running, my steps as unsteady as if I were treading clouds. I hoped nothing had happened to my family.

Everything was topsy-turvy in my home, tables and chairs over-

turned and the floors scattered with utensils, books, shoes, table-
ware, and laundered clothes. All the paintings were gone from the
walls, and nobody was there. "Oh, I'm sorry, Anling," Minnie said.
Her voice suggested she assumed that all my family had been taken.

In spite of my fitful sobs, I told myself that Liya was coolheaded,
and they might still be somewhere on campus. It never pays to get
upset ahead of time.

I didn't see any trace of struggle—nothing was smashed or
crushed—so there was a possibility that my family had escaped
abduction. But where were they?

Then my husband and Liya, with Fanfan in her arms, appeared
in the doorway. "Mom" was all she could say. Her oval face was
ghastly pale and her eyes flared. Her bangs and brow were wet with
perspiration.

"They almost caught us," Yaoping told me, shaking his grizzled
head.

"Thank God you're safe," Minnie said.

Liya told us that the instant they heard the commotion on campus,
they slipped out of East Court and ran into a ditch behind an apartment house under construction, hiding among the refugees there. I
closed my eyes, held my hands together, and said, "Lord, thank you
so much for returning my family to me!"

Then Big Liu's wife came and wailed, "They took Meiyan, our
daughter!" The small, round-faced woman pressed her right flank
with her hand as though in severe pain. Her husband was behind her,
wordless and in shock, his lumpy face bathed in tears and sweat.

The girl was fifteen and used to be a good helper in the kindergarten. We had no idea how to console her parents. If only we hadn't
been held at bay by the soldiers and had been able to stay on the
campus to stop the abductors. Now what could we say to Big Liu and
his wife? I glanced at Minnie, who seemed to be struggling with the
same question but couldn't find words. No matter what, she must say
something.

Finally she announced: "I'll go to the Japanese embassy first thing
tomorrow morning. They must return our people immediately."

No one responded.

I left with Minnie to look at the other parts of campus and to make sure that the south exit was locked again. At the Central Building we ran into Rulian and two women staffers. They told us that in total twelve girls had been taken, and all the refugees in the building were terrified. I noticed Yanying, the young woman who had arrived a week ago in disguise as an old man, patting her little sister Yanping's back and whispering to the girl. The child couldn't stop crying, probably because what had just happened reminded her of the havoc back home. Around us, several voices were cursing and wailing. Minnie and I couldn't stop our tears either. What's worse, we didn't even know most of the names of the abducted girls.

Half an hour later we went to the Practice Hall. To our amazement, we found Miss Lou talking with Luhai. "Thank God you're back, Luhai!" Minnie cried. "How did you manage to escape?"

"I told an old interpreter that my wife was giving birth and I showed him I had a crippled leg. They saw me walk with a limp, so they checked my knee and let me go after the interpreter spoke with an officer. I owe my life to that old gentleman."

"What happened to the other fellow, the 'coal carrier'?"

"They kept him."

Despite Luhai's steady voice, I could see that he was shaken, his forehead bruised and his lips livid. Together the four of us went to the gatehouse, then to the cottage nearby where his family lived. Seeing him, his wife wept with joy and said, "I thought they were gonna kill you. Thank heaven you're back!"

Before Miss Lou left, we prayed together for the safety of the twelve girls and for the life of "the coal carrier." How earnest our voices were, and how we longed for a miracle.

After that, Minnie and I went to the front entrance. We stayed in the gatehouse that night, catnapping in rattan chairs in case the soldiers came again. A voice kept rising in my mind: "Lord, when will you hearken to our prayers? When will you show your wrath?" From time to time I woke up and heard Minnie muttering "Beasts! Beasts!"

AT THE CRACK OF DAWN the blast of an automobile horn shook me awake. I sat up with a start, my heart palpitating, and I heard a truck moaning away. Minnie got up too. We went out and saw Luhai hurrying over. Together we turned to the main entrance. Some women were shaking the gate and shouting, "Open it, please let us in!"

To our surprise, we found six girls, all carried off by the Japanese the previous night, standing there, their hair mussed and their faces tear-smeared. Luhai unbolted the small side gate at once. "Come in!" Minnie said, and beckoned them. She held the shoulder of Meiyan, Big Liu's strapping daughter, and told her, "Your parents were devastated when they found you were gone. Thank goodness you're back."

The bespectacled girl nodded without speaking. Minnie asked them how they'd been mistreated. They all said that the Japanese had slapped them, pinched their faces, and pulled their hair, but had not molested them otherwise. By that, they meant they hadn't been raped, as most local girls wouldn't use the word "rape" bluntly. Minnie was glad to hear that. "What a miracle!" she said, and must have attributed this to our earnest prayers the night before.

I could not believe that the Japanese would let these young girls return without doing something terrible to them, but I kept mum, not wanting to deflate Minnie's elation. There'd been so many heartbreaking happenings these days that she deserved to be happy for a moment.

Meiyan told the people gathering in her parents' apartment that the Japanese had sent the other six girls, the better-looking ones, to a hotel where some officers stayed, while the remaining six of them had been put on the truck and sent back. We'd heard that yesterday many high-ranking officers were in town for the victory ceremony.

10

T**HAT MORNING** Liya didn't get up early as she usually did; she said she had cramps in her abdomen. I felt her forehead and body—she was burning hot. As I carried a mug of tea to her, she said her pajamas were wet. I took a look and found blood and bits of dead tissue in the discharge. She'd miscarried! I told Yaoping to heat a pot of water while I helped Liya undress.

"When did the cramps start?" I asked her.

"Last night."

"Why didn't you let your dad know?"

"I thought I'd be all right after a night of sleep. Is the baby gone, Mom?"

"Looks like it. You must've run too hard yesterday evening and hurt yourself."

"I feel like hell." She sobbed, her eyes shut. "The Japs killed my baby, and I must even the score with them."

"Hush, let's worry about how to make you get well soon." I felt like crying too, but choked the tears back by squeezing my eyes.

"I don't want to live any more."

"Stop that nonsense. We need you."

While Liya was rambling and writhing in pain, I continued working on her. I wrapped the bloody mess in rags and washed and wiped her with a hand towel. I wondered whether the dead fetus had all come out or whether she might need curetting or some other treatment. Under normal circumstances we could have sent for a specialized nurse, but all the OB clinics were closed. I told Yaoping to leave Fanfan with our neighbor and then carry Liya to our school's infirmary on the back of his Flying Pony bicycle. As father and daughter started out, I followed them, holding Liya's shoulder with one hand to keep her steady.

The nurse examined her and said that the miscarriage looked complete. Even if Liya needed a curettage, the nurse couldn't help her, never having performed that procedure before. What Liya must do was rest in bed for at least two weeks, as it was generally believed that a miscarriage weakened a woman more than an actual birth, and she should avoid spicy, pickled, and cold food. She must abstain from sex for a whole month. I almost yelled at the nurse, who didn't know that my son-in-law wasn't home, to shut up. Liya needed to eat something nutritious, such as eggs, warm milk, chicken, seafood, pork tripe and liver, fresh fruits. Where on earth could we get any of those now?

Somehow I'd kept a small bag of millet and a bottle of brown sugar in my office. I gave those to Yaoping and told him to cook millet porridge and mix in some sugar for Liya. He should also bake some dried anchovies for her and make sure she ate regularly. After putting her to bed, I returned to the refugee camp.

MINNIE ASKED Big Liu to go to the Japanese embassy with her to protest the abduction of the girls. At first, he was reluctant, his eyes blazing behind his glasses. I urged him to keep her company and he agreed. He had a dignified bearing and was tactful in dealing with people, so she might feel more confident if he went with her.

Outside the front gate scores of old women were gathering and begging to be admitted into the camp. The moment Minnie and Big Liu appeared, the crowd calmed down a bit. Minnie came up to Holly and me. We'd been speaking to some older women from the neighborhood, trying to persuade them to go back home so as to save room, if there was any left here, for young women and children.

"But I have no place to go," a sixtyish woman cried at me.

"Damn it," another voice shouted. "The Japs assault old women too! Old crones are also humans."

Minnie told us, "Let them in. But make it clear that they can stay only in the open air."

"We have more than seven thousand already," Holly said. "If we take them all, there won't be an empty spot left on campus."

"We have no choice now."

As we began admitting the new arrivals, Minnie and Big Liu started out for the Japanese embassy, a twenty-minute walk. I had gone to that shabby two-story building four years ago, together with my son, Haowen, who had applied for a long-term residency visa for his studies in Japan. He had enrolled in Nippon Medical School two years before and wanted to become a doctor. He was still in Tokyo, though we hadn't heard from him for more than seven months. Ever since the outbreak of the war, his letters had stopped. Both his father and I were worried about him, but we couldn't say this to others, especially to our Chinese colleagues. We only hoped he was well and safe. My husband had studied Asian history in Japan and could speak Japanese, but rarely would he use the language. Nobody at Jinling knew about our family's current connection with Japan except for Dr. Wu, but I was certain that she'd keep this confidential as long as I remained loyal to her.

Around noon, Minnie and Big Liu returned in a car. On their way, they had stopped at the closed U.S. embassy, and a Chinese secretary, who had been paid to stay behind with a couple of local staffers to look after the premises, had assigned a Cadillac to take Minnie and Big Liu to the Japanese embassy so they could arrive in style—the secretary had said that the Japanese were highly sensitive to pomp, so Minnie, as the head of an American college, should impress them with something grand, and therefore a sizable sedan was a necessity for their visit. Seeing the midnight blue car crawling to a halt outside the main entrance, I handed a staffer the half bucket of boiled yams I'd been giving away to starving kids, stepped closer to the gate, and watched Minnie and Big Liu get out of the vehicle.

Minnie gave the Chinese chauffeur a silver yuan, but the man pushed it back and said, "I can't take money from you, Principal Vautrin."

"Why not?"

"We're all beholden to you. If not for you foreigners who stayed behind and set up the refugee zone, all the Chinese here would've been wiped out. If not killed by the Japanese, many would've starved to death. Miss Hua, please don't tip me." He called Minnie by her Chinese name, Hua Chuan, the phonetic translation of Vautrin. He adjusted his duckbill cap to cover his teary eyes and slouched away, still waving his hand as though to shield his contorted face. He climbed into the car, its fender planted with a U.S. flag, and drove away.

When they had come into campus, Minnie said to Big Liu, "I didn't expect to see a sympathetic Japanese official today."

"I still hate their guts," he grunted.

This sounded out of character, because Big Liu was kindhearted and had once even argued with us that Abraham shouldn't have attempted to sacrifice his son Isaac to God, saying that at least he, Liu, would never harm a child, never mind butchering one. Intuitively I knew something must have happened to his daughter. Maybe the soldiers had molested her. Minnie asked him, "Why do you hate the Japanese so much? Doesn't God teach us to love our enemies and even do good to them?"

"That I cannot follow."

"Don't you Chinese say 'repay kindness for injury'?"

"Then what can we repay for kindness? Good and evil must be rewarded differently."

Minnie didn't respond and seemed amazed by his argument. I mulled over his notion and felt he might have a point.

Later Minnie told me about their visit to the Japanese embassy. She said, "Vice-Consul Tanaka agreed to assign some policemen to guard our campus. He seemed quite sympathetic."

"What else did he do?" I asked.

"He sighed and shook his head while listening to me describe the rapes and abductions in our camp. Obviously he was upset and said that Tokyo might soon issue orders to stop those violent soldiers. He told us that General Matsui reprimanded some officers for not keeping discipline among their men, but Tanaka wouldn't say anything in detail about this."

"That's classified information, huh?" I snorted.

"Apparently so."

Minnie seemed perplexed by my sudden temper, and I did not tell her about Liya's miscarriage, not wanting to give her more bad news.

LEWIS SMYTHE CAME to our camp the next day and told us more about General Matsui's frustration. Lewis and Tanaka knew each

other well by now. In the beginning, the vice-consul could not
believe the atrocities that the Safety Zone Committee had reported
to the Japanese embassy every day, sometimes twice a day, but then
one afternoon he saw with his own eyes a soldier shoot an old fabric
seller who refused to surrender a silver cigarette case to him. Tanaka
disclosed to Lewis that General Matsui had wept at the small welcome reception attended by some twenty senior officers and three
officials from the embassy. The commander in chief reproved some
of the generals and colonels for ruining the Imperial Army's reputation. "There will be retribution, terrible retribution, do you understand?" he cried out, banging the table with his fist. "I issued orders
that no rape or arson or murder of civilians would be tolerated in
Nanjing, but you didn't control your men. At one stroke, everything
was lost."

After the meeting, Tanaka overheard some of the officers in the
men's room say about the top commander, "What an old fogy!" and
"He's too senile, too softheaded now. He should never have re-
emerged from retirement." A colonel at a urinal added, "It's easy for
him to play the Buddha. If we forbade our men to have their way
with the Chinese, how could we reward them?"

Tanaka had also told Lewis that the military executed Chinese
POWs partly because they had no food to feed so many of them, and
they were also unwilling to take the trouble to guard them. If that
was the reason, why did they round them up in the first place? Why
did they shoot so many men who had never joined the army? Why
did they kill so many young boys? They meant to destroy China's
potential for resistance and to terrify us into obedience.

On the morning of December 20, the despicable behavior of the
Japanese soldiers continued. Luhai found Minnie and me in the
president's office and said two soldiers had just entered the Faculty
House. That was north of the Central Building, only steps away.
Together Minnie and I ran over. Climbing the stairs, we heard a
female voice screaming. Before Room 218 stood a wiry soldier with
his arms crossed, the muzzle of his rifle leaning against his flank. The
cries came from inside the room, so Minnie pushed the man aside
and went in. I followed, as did three older refugee women, all some-

what stout. There on the floor a soldier was wiggling and moaning atop a girl, whose head was rocking from side to side while blood dribbled out of her nose.

"Get off her!" Minnie rushed up and pulled the man by the collar of his jacket. He was stunned and slowly picked himself up, his breath reeking of alcohol and his sallow cheeks puffed. He forgot to pull up his pants; his member was swaying and dripping semen. The girl, eyes shut, began groaning in pain, a blood vessel on her neck pulsating.

I tugged at the end of the man's belt, which restored some presence of mind to him. He held up his pants and reeled away, but before reaching the door, he whirled back and stretched out his hand to Minnie, grinning while mumbling, *"Arigato, arigato."* She looked puzzled while I wondered why he thanked her. She glared at him with flaming eyes, but he showed no remorse, as if raping a girl was just a small faux pas. Then he offered me his hand, which I didn't touch either. At this point his comrade came in and dragged him and his rifle out of the room, leaving behind on the floor a silver liquor flask.

"The other bastard raped her too," a woman told us.

"Get a basin of water for her," Minnie said, her eyebrows jumping.

"Some of you stay with her today and don't leave her alone," I said.

A few women nodded agreement. I picked up the silver flask as a piece of evidence, which we would present to the Japanese embassy.

As two women were helping the girl into her clothes, Rulian came in and said to us, "Some Japanese broke into the northwest dorm."

"Damn them! Where's Holly?" Minnie asked.

"She's in the Library Building. Some soldiers turned up there too."

The northwest dormitory was behind the Faculty House. When we got there, we saw two soldiers sitting in the dining room, gobbling chocolate chip cookies with a can of condensed milk, which they'd opened with a bayonet. The kitchen door had been knocked off its hinges and was lying on the floor. At the sight of us, the men lurched up and hurried out, one holding the box of cookies and the other the open can. They both wore ropes on their belts for tying up people or animals.

Nobody had said a word during the confrontation. But the soldiers' actions made me wonder if they were short on rations and hungry. Otherwise, why would they steal all kinds of food from the civilians, even a baked sweet potato and a handful of peanuts? Several times on the streets we had run into soldiers carrying geese, ducks, chickens, and even piglets tied to the tips of their rifles, some of the pigs with their innards ripped out. I hoped that the Western reporters (five or six of them were stranded here and managed to send out articles about the atrocities to *The New York Times, The Chicago Daily News,* and the Associated Press) would take photos of those savages and of the streets dotted with the bodies of civilians, their faces already black.

AROUND THREE O'CLOCK the next afternoon, a major, lanky and with a bristly mustache, came with six men to inspect our refugee camp. Minnie took them through the buildings slowly, and I knew she hoped that some soldiers would appear so the officer could witness the unruliness of the Japanese troops. We went through the Arts Building, which housed more than eight hundred refugees, then entered the Central Building, which was in Holly's charge and held more than a thousand. The moment we left that place and were about to cross the quadrangle, Luhai hobbled over (these days he often exaggerated his limp) and said that some soldiers were attacking women in the south dormitory. Minnie invited the officer to come with us, and he agreed. We set off while he and his men followed us, striding south; his hands were clasped behind his back.

In the entryway of the dorm building we heard some Japanese yelling and laughing upstairs. We hastened our steps and bumped into a group at the landing. At the sight of Minnie and the officer behind us, two soldiers let go of the four women they were dragging down the stairs and bolted out of the building. One woman, both hands still gripping the tusk-smooth banister, begged, "Principal Vautrin, please help us! They beat us and forced us to undress in front of kids. Two of them are still up there torturing others."

"We'll talk about this later," Minnie said, and hurried up to the second floor, where a male voice yelped.

Walking down the hallway, we saw a soldier standing at the door of a room like a sentry, holding his rifle with one hand, its butt resting on the floor. The man was about to stop us but caught sight of the officer and his retinue, so he thought better of it. We brushed past him, entered the room, and saw a young woman lying naked on a piece of green tarp, crying and twisting, while a soldier with a full beard was thrusting his hand between her legs and making happy noises. A bayonet stood beside her head. We rushed over and were aghast to find the man's entire hand buried in the woman's vagina, beneath which was a puddle of blood and urine. Minnie yelled, "Get off her, you beast! Don't you have a mother or sister?"

Startled, the man pulled out his hand and rose to his feet, still smiling with his lips quivering. The woman, moaning in agony, closed her eyes and turned her head to the wall, a small birthmark below her right ear. Her body reminded me of a large piece of meat ready for cutting, except for the spasms that jolted her every two or three seconds.

When the major came in, Minnie shouted at him, "Look at what your man did to her!" She pointed at the woman on the floor. I was so enraged that for a moment my vision blurred.

The officer stepped over and looked at the woman's mutilated body. He then turned to the perpetrator and slapped him across the face while yelling something. The bearded soldier stood straight, sweating all over but not daring to wipe his face with his hands, from one of which drops of bloody liquid dripped onto the floor. Then, to our bewilderment, he muttered something apologetically, sidled away to grab his rifle, which was leaning against the wall, and ambled to the door. Before he could get out, a junior officer called to him and handed him his bayonet. Meanwhile, a middle-aged woman covered the victim with a tattered blanket.

Is that all? I wondered. They let him get away like that?

"Why did you let him go?" Minnie asked the officers.

The interpreter, also an officer, told her, "Our commander scolded him. You saw, he also punished him."

"But no more punishment?" she said. "How come you didn't even take down his name?"

"There'll be more disciplinary action, of course."

"How can you identify the man?"

"We know him. Not many men wear a beard like that. He's nicknamed Obstetrician." The interpreter grinned at us lasciviously, displaying his buckteeth. I throttled my impulse to spit in his face, and averted my eyes to suppress my tears and revulsion.

The mutilated woman groaned again, holding her sides with both hands. Minnie told three women to accompany her to the infirmary. Then she furiously said to the major, "I'm going to file a protest with your embassy." We all knew they had let the perpetrator go.

The officer nodded without a word, his face dark and slightly lopsided. He waved at his men, and they followed him out of the room.

That evening, twenty-five policemen were sent over by the Japanese embassy. Their leader handed Minnie a letter from Vice-Consul Tanaka, which said that Jinling must treat these men well, providing for them charcoal fires, hot tea, and refreshments throughout the night. Minnie sighed. Where on earth could we get those things? Besides, we didn't need so many policemen. Four would be enough to keep the marauding soldiers away. Looking at these men, some of whom seemed quite rough and could easily frighten the women and children, we wondered if they were real police. Probably they were just a bunch of regular troops assigned to the embassy for guard duty. We had no option but to accept them.

By now the camp had more than eight thousand refugees, and it seemed certain that more would come.

Early on the morning of December 22, Miss Lou informed us that the policemen from the embassy had assaulted two girls in the Practice Hall the night before. Five of them had dragged the girls out of the building and raped them beyond an oval flowerbed encircled with serrated bricks. We were shocked and outraged, but we were caught and couldn't see a way out. We needed the police to deter the soldiers and had to handle this matter discreetly; nevertheless, Minnie would protest to Tanaka. By now more than seventy women and girls had been raped in our camp alone, and Minnie had submitted a report on those cases to both the Japanese embassy and the Safety Zone Committee.

Around ten a.m., Minnie and Big Liu again went to the U.S. embassy to ask to be driven to the Japanese embassy, where they would present another protest. But they didn't find Tanaka there and left word with Consul-General Katsuo Okazaki that we didn't need so many policemen—six would be enough. Okazaki, who was also the diplomatic adviser to General Matsui, promised Minnie he'd pass both the message and the protest letter on to the vice-consul, though he was in a hurry to catch the train to Shanghai, where he'd been residing since last fall.

This time the Cadillac didn't send Minnie and Big Liu back to our college, because the chauffeur feared that the Japanese might take away the car. Any vehicle driven by a Chinese without a foreigner in it was subject to confiscation. So Minnie and Big Liu walked back from the U.S. embassy, which was less than a mile from Jinling.

I was outside the front entrance bandaging a woman's neck when Minnie and Big Liu returned. The woman had been stabbed seven times by two soldiers but was still breathing. I planted a Red Cross flag on the horse cart on which she was lying before it set off for the

University Hospital. Minnie told me that they'd seen more destruction in town, that Chef Wang at the U.S. embassy had lost his father to a knot of soldiers who had also plundered the old man's small collection of antique coins. Minnie went on, "Who could imagine such atrocities! I'm wondering if there's a home in this city that hasn't been looted."

"We shall settle accounts with them someday," Liu said through his teeth.

Never had I seen him so full of hatred. I didn't know how to respond.

Minnie wondered if we should drop in to see John Rabe at the Safety Zone Committee's headquarters and find out if there was news about Ban and the six girls taken five days before. We headed for 5 Ninghai Road, which was nearby, a grand templelike house with wide windows and glazed roof tiles, owned by the former foreign minister Chun Chang and now used as the main office of the Safety Zone Committee.

We found Rabe sobbing at his desk, his bald head in both hands. He was a cheerful man who loved jokes and wisecracks, and I had never expected to see him so distraught.

"What's the trouble, John?" Minnie asked, and sat down.

"Oh, damn the Japs, they killed my workers. They lied to me and promised to give them good pay, so I went and found fifty-four men for them."

"How many did they kill?"

"Forty-three."

We were stunned, knowing that Rabe had agreed to help the Japanese restore the city's power service and had drummed up some experienced electricians and engineers for them. Those men worked day and night, repaired the turbines, and got the facilities running again. Once the electricity was back, the Japanese tied up most of them, dragged them to the riverside, and shot them, claiming that they had served the Chinese government.

"Don't they need the experienced hands to maintain the power supply?" Minnie asked Rabe.

"That's what I thought too, so I promised my workers personal safety plus good pay. Now how can I face their parents, their widows and children? People will believe I sold the men for some favors from the Japanese. Damn the Japs, they've lost their minds and simply can't stop killing."

Rabe hadn't heard anything about Ban and the six girls. On his desk lay a swastika flag beside a typewriter, on which was an unfinished letter. Whenever Rabe went out to confront the Japanese, he'd carry the flag and sometimes flutter it at the soldiers committing crimes. He would cry "*Deutsch*" and "Hitler," but even that failed to serve as a deterrent. Rabe had telegraphed the Führer before the fall of our city, imploring him to intervene on behalf of the Chinese. He even bragged to the Americans, "Just one word from Hitler and the Japanese will behave." But so far the supreme leader had not responded to his request.

"My worst fear," Rabe told us, "is that if one Chinese man in the Safety Zone kills a Japanese soldier for violating his wife or daughter, then the entire neutral district will be bathed in blood. That would end all our relief efforts."

"I'm worried about that too," Minnie agreed.

Thank God no Chinese man here had been bold enough to do that. Part of the reason for this was that no Japanese soldier would rape alone but would always be covered by at least one other man. They would loot in groups as well.

On our way back to Jinling, Big Liu said to Minnie, "The Japs kill, rape, and burn just because they can." Again his eyes glowed as if he were crazed.

I knew that his daughter Meiyan must have been harmed, but in Minnie's presence I didn't say anything. She still believed that our prayers had worked a miracle—six of the girls had returned unharmed.

THAT EVENING the same twenty-five policemen came to our camp again. We were unsure if the consul-general had passed our message on to Tanaka. Minnie talked with Holly and me, and we all thought it wise to accommodate the police, whose presence here would at least keep the soldiers away. Minnie managed to persuade the policemen to stay outside the campus. From now on, a potbelly stove would be fired for them in the house across the street from the front entrance, and there was also tea, sunflower seeds, and bean-jam pies made by our college's kitchen. These things seemed to please the policemen some. Maybe they wouldn't sneak into campus to molest women again. Minnie believed that Tanaka had rebuked them.

By December 23 the camp had ten thousand refugees. In fact, we'd lost count, unable to keep track of the traffic anymore, so the number could have been larger. The Arts Building alone housed more than a thousand now. When Rulian said that the attic of that building held about three hundred people, Minnie got apprehensive but didn't insist on calculating the numbers, since there were also people who would leave without notifying us. When it rained or snowed all the refugees crowded indoors, and many had no place to lie down at night, so they just sat on the stairs and in the corridors. During the daytime a lot of them lounged outside, content to take a spot somewhere. Minnie used to live in a three-room apartment, but now she had only one room and let the other two rooms be used by tens of women with small children. She told me that sometimes in the middle of the night she was awakened by crying babies and got annoyed, but as far as I could see, she would always greet the mothers pleasantly the next morning.

Our greatest difficulty was feeding so many refugees. There was never enough rice. To make matters worse, some people would get two helpings while others had nothing to eat for a whole day. When the porridge stands opened, many women would swarm over—pushing and elbowing others, they wouldn't bother to stand in line. For days Holly, Miss Lou, and I, together with some young staffers, had tried teaching the refugees to form lines at mealtimes. We had made some progress in this, having assigned many young refugee women to take charge of lining up others outside the porridge plant.

Tickets for free food were issued to those who had no money, and more than sixty percent of the refugees received free meals. Still, some didn't have the strength to reach the porridge cauldrons. Our staff sewed red tags on their sleeves so they could go to the heads of the lines when the afternoon meal was served. In this way they could at least have one meal a day.

12

To everyone's surprise, Ban, the messenger boy, returned early on the morning of December 24. I took him back to his quarters at East Court. Minnie joined me to find out what had happened to him. But Ban, seated at a table in the room that he shared with three others, wouldn't talk. He'd lost a good deal of weight and looked skeletal, his eyes sluggish and his nose clogged. Bundled in a threadbare overcoat cinched around the waist by a straw rope, he was more like a scarecrow, and time and again he convulsed with wheezing coughs. "Please give me some solid food!" he begged. "I'm still starving."

We had given him only some porridge for fear of hurting his stomach. I said, "You must eat liquid food for a day before you can have anything solid."

He didn't seem to recognize some of us, though he knew me for sure. He just looked at everyone with large dazed eyes. Minnie touched his forehead, which was damp with sweat. "He must be running a temperature," she said.

"He must've gone through a lot," I added.

"Let him rest well and don't assign him any work for the time being," Minnie told me, then turned to Ban. "You're home now. Let us know if you need anything, all right?"

The boy grinned without a word, but as Minnie and I were leaving, he lifted his hand and waved. That was something he wouldn't have done before.

We went to the main office to make plans for Christmas. As we were talking and Minnie was jotting down our ideas on a notepad, a group of Japanese soldiers headed by a colonel appeared. She let them into the office and asked a servant to serve tea. A scrawny teenage boy, hired temporarily as a messenger, told me that there were at least a hundred soldiers outside the front gate. I whispered to Minnie, "Lots of them are on campus now."

Why had so many of them come today? I pulled the errand boy aside and told him to run to the Central Building and the dormitories to inform the staffers about the soldiers' presence—they must make sure that young women and girls all kept a low profile. The boy set out straightaway.

As soon as the Japanese delegation sat down, the chunky-faced colonel introduced himself as a vice chief of the Logistics Department of the Sixth Division, commanded by Tani Hisao, the ruthless general we Chinese called Tiger Hisao. The colonel said they needed our cooperation. A Chinese interpreter, a fat man in his mid-forties, was translating for him, while three junior officers sipped tea. Minnie said, "I'll be glad to help if what you want is reasonable."

The officer cackled and continued, "We intend to keep better discipline among our men. After the fall of Nanjing, our troops became unruly for a short while, mainly because the soldiers had lost many comrades in the battle on Purple Mountain and couldn't stop carrying out vengeance. Now that they've calmed down, it's time to establish order and peace in this city. We're going to start the entertainment business and need some women."

When the interpreter finished translating, Minnie said firmly, "We don't have that kind of women here."

"According to our information," the colonel continued, "there are some streetwalkers in your camp. We came to collect them and will give them licenses so they can entertain men and also make a living."

"I'm not aware of any prostitutes among the refugees."

"We can recognize them easily. Don't worry about that. Besides, don't you think this will be an effective way to protect good and honest women like this one?" He pointed at me. That set my heart pounding. "Truth be told," he went on, "our soldiers are all strong young fellows and need women to release their tension, so to set up a professional service will be the ultimate solution. Don't you think?" His cat eyes crinkled into a smile.

To my surprise, the heavy-lidded interpreter paused after rendering the officer's words, then added, "Miss Vautrin, this is an order. It's no use to argue." He coughed, touching his mouth with the back of his hand.

I was worried but dared not put in a word. Did they really intend to open brothels by hiring some women? I'd heard of that sort of service organized by the Japanese military, but how could they decide who was a hooker? On second thought, I remembered seeing several painted faces among the refugees, especially two women who always jostled for position at a porridge stand or cut in line, and who still glossed their lips, penciled their eyebrows, and powdered their cheeks every day. Worse, their perfume smelled like rotten vegetables. Those two in their garish satin robes might even be willing to return to their former walk of life if they could make money.

The colonel was waiting. What should Minnie say? She looked at me inquiringly, but I lowered my eyes, at a loss about what to do. Could these men really distinguish prostitutes from other women? What if they made a mistake or took some innocent ones on purpose?

Finally Minnie said, "I don't know how you can figure out who did that type of work before."

The officer gave a barking laugh. "Don't worry about that. We're experienced in this matter and can identify them pretty accurately."

"How many women do you plan to have for your entertainment business?"

"Many, the more the better, but one hundred from your camp."

"I don't think there are that many former prostitutes here."

"We insist, because we know how to identify them."

"On one condition, though—the women must be willing to continue to do the work."

"Of course, they'll be well paid besides."

"In that case you can pick them."

Suddenly a female voice shrieked outside, then screams and shouts came from every direction. While we were talking, the troops had broken into the camp to seize women. Minnie and I both realized in horror that the colonel had been detaining her while his men were at the devil's work. How could we stop them? The door was blocked by two junior officers, one of them with a face scarred by shrapnel.

Minnie stood up, went to the window, and looked outside. I stepped across the room to join her. We could see the soldiers hauling away young women, all of whom seemed to have fine figures and relatively good looks. Some were crying and struggling to break loose, while one with an angular face hugged the foreleg of a stone lion in front of the Arts Building, screaming and refusing to let go. A soldier punched her in the gut twice, knocking her off the stone animal, and pulled her away. A little girl with two tiny brushes of hair behind her ears followed them, hollering madly, but two older women restrained her. I recognized the young woman, Yanying, and her little sister, Yanping.

Minnie spun around and sputtered to the colonel, "This is abduction. I'm going to protest to your superiors."

He smirked contemptuously, one side of his mouth tilting up. He said, "As you wish." With a toss of his head and a sweep of the kid gloves in his hand, he strutted out of the office, followed by his underlings. The interpreter waved at Minnie, shaking his double chin and unable to say a word as he turned toward the door.

Minnie slumped in an armchair and cried, "What should we do, Anling?"

I didn't know what to say. She went on, "Oh, I should never have let them pick the women. This is terrible, terrible!"

"They'd already started grabbing them before you gave permission," I said.

"That's not an excuse. How could I be so stupid?"

"Whether you allowed them or not, they were going to take some women. Everybody could see that."

"Oh, what should I do?"

"It's not your fault. Come on, Minnie, you mustn't talk like this now. We must find out what happened to the camp." Without waiting for her response, I rushed out to check with our staffers in various buildings.

This time we'd lost twenty-one young women.

ALTHOUGH MINNIE JOINED Lewis, Searle, and Plumer for the Christmas dinner, she was in no mood for the holiday. Old Liao had brought over a miniature fir and set it up in her room. Minnie liked the sight of the tree, the lit candles under it, and the Nativity scene arranged by the gardener, yet it didn't cheer her up. She said she felt drained and powerless in her limbs. At the sight of her, a group of girls asked if the Japanese would come for the other seventy-nine "prostitutes" to make up the number, one hundred, as they had mentioned. She cried out, "Over my dead body they will!" Still, the girls looked unconvinced and frightened, and people wouldn't stop talking about the women just abducted by the Japanese.

After the holiday Minnie took to her bed for three days, suffering from a sore throat and inflamed eyes. A bone-deep fatigue had sunk into her. She was so weak that she couldn't even hold a pen. Yet she wanted to write a letter to the Japanese embassy on behalf of several women whose family members had been seized by the soldiers. She had promised to intercede for them, though she told me that she wouldn't be much help.

13

FIVE DAYS after Christmas, Minnie went to the Japanese embassy and delivered the letter. As soon as she came back, Cola, the Russian man, arrived with two blind girls, one eight and the other ten, both wearing tattered robes and boots too large for them. The younger one held a bamboo flute while the older one carried an *erhu,* a two-stringed violin. They had performed with a small band at teahouses and open-air theaters to eke out a living since coming to the city the previous summer, but the other musicians in the band had fled and left them behind. Cola chanced on them outside Zhong Hua Girls' School, took them in for a few days, and found boots and woolen socks for their bare feet. He thought that our camp might be more suitable for them, so he brought them to Minnie, who had no choice but to accept them.

Cola often said he didn't like the Chinese because some business-men had cheated him, but he'd told the other foreigners that he might be more helpful here once the city fell. On top of that, he owned an auto-repair business, which was booming even now. He used to believe that the Japanese, or the Greeks of Asia, as they called themselves, should rule China because he thought they could make this country a better place for business. Yet he was horrified by the soldiers' brutalities and joined the Safety Zone Committee to help the refugees. He could serve as an interpreter since he knew some Japanese.

"Thank you, Miss Vautrin. There's no way I can keep them," he said in Mandarin, and pushed the two bony girls toward Minnie's desk a little. "Only you can give them a home."

"Jinling has been ruined by the Japanese too." Minnie turned to the girls and held their small chapped hands, saying, "You're safe here. Don't be afraid."

She then told me to give them the special room in the main dormitory, but I had to attend to a young mother in labor, so Holly led them out of the office, holding their hands as the three of them walked away.

AT LAST Ban began to talk. In the evening about twenty people gathered in the dining room to listen to him. He ate normally now, but he still wouldn't move around campus and slept a lot during the day.

He said, "That afternoon when Principal Vautrin told me to go tell Mr. Rabe about the random arrest in our camp, I ran to the Safety Zone Committee's headquarters. As I was reaching that house, two Japanese soldiers stopped me, one pointing his bayonet at my tummy and the other sticking his gun against my back. They ripped off my Red Cross armband and hit me in the face with their fists. Then they took me away to White Cloud Shrine. . . ."

Three evenings in a row he told his story to different groups of people. Sometimes, while speaking, Ban would break down, weeping wretchedly and flailing his thin arms. He would also tremble from time to time as though someone were about to strike him. We decocted some medicinal soup for him every day, made of dried tuckahoe, wolfberries, mums, and other herbs, to help him sleep well and to restore his wits.

He got better a few weeks later but still dared not step out of the compound of our college. Minnie told Luhai to assign him only domestic chores.

TWO

The Goddess of Mercy

14

NUMEROUS REFUGEE WOMEN had come and implored us to intervene on their behalf to get their menfolk back from the Japanese military, assuming they were still alive. A few even blamed Jinling for shutting out their husbands and sons—as a result, the Japanese had seized them. One woman condemned us for barring her fifteen-year-old son from the camp and told others, "See, he was made to fall into the Japs' hands." Words like those unsettled Minnie, who confessed to me that we shouldn't have set the age limit at thirteen. If we'd known that the Japanese would arrest all the young males, of course we'd have raised the entry age to fifteen for boys.

I told Minnie not to be troubled by the women's grumbles. Whenever I heard them complain, I'd say to their faces, "Look, I'm sorry about your loss, but we let in ten thousand of you, five times more than we planned originally. What else do you expect us to do? If we'd taken in more boys, some girls and women would have been kept out." That shut them up.

I advised Minnie never to show her regret in front of the complainers or they would persist with unreasonable demands. Still, some of the refugee women were so wretched and piteous, unable to survive without their menfolk, that Minnie started preparing a petition. She assigned Big Liu to interview them to gather the needed information. Whenever she had a free moment, she'd drop by his office, which was one of the two inner rooms in the president' office, and listen to the petitioners' stories. Their voices, once you'd heard them, would go on ringing in your ears for a long time: "They took my three sons and my husband, and I was too frightened to beg them." "He was my only son, and I hope he's still alive and knows how to get back." "My two grandsons were taken, the only farmhands in our family." "I have four small children left and also my mother-in-law. I can only beg on the streets." "My two sons never came back from their business trip, and one of their wives was killed by the soldiers. If they don't come back, I won't live anymore."

I was not in favor of a petition. I said, "Minnie, the Japanese always finish off the men they seize. We know that's a fact. What's the sense of begging for mercy from those beasts? It's like asking a tiger for its skin. We'd better concentrate on the matters at hand."

In spite of my reservations, I told some women to register their losses with Big Liu as a record. I knew Minnie's heart was in the right place. Within a week, by mid-January, Big Liu had documented more than 400 cases, with 723 men and boys taken by the Japanese, mostly around mid-December. Among them 390 were businessmen; 123 were farmers, coolies, and gardeners; 193 were artisans, tailors, carpenters, masons, weavers, and cooks; 7 were policemen; and 1 was a fireman. There were also 9 boys, thirteen to sixteen years old. Day after day more women came to Big Liu to have their cases filed.

Big Liu's hair had grayed considerably, and even his thick shoulders looked hunched when he sat at his desk. He was cheerful and gregarious by nature, but lately he was aloof and taciturn and often lost his temper. He said he had a toothache. When he wasn't busy, he would absently gaze up at the ceiling and let out deep sighs. I pretended to know nothing about his trouble and didn't explain to Minnie when she wondered aloud about what was bothering him. I didn't tell her that his daughter Meiyan was on his mind.

One afternoon, the moment Minnie and I stepped into the main office, Big Liu tossed *The New Shen Bao,* a major Shanghai newspaper, on the coffee table and said, "Heavens, even the Chinese help the Japanese lie to the world!"

"I saw that piece," Minnie said. "Hideous."

I picked up the paper and saw three photographs of Nanjing attached to an article about the Imperial Army's benevolent deeds here. People looked happy and festive in the pictures, because the capital finally had been liberated from "Chiang Kai-shek's oppressive regime." In one photo hundreds of civilians, mostly women and children, knelt in front of Japanese troops to express their gratitude for the bread, cookies, and candies that the soldiers were handing out. The beneficiaries claimed they had never tasted anything so delicious. Beyond them a line of Red Cross flags was flapping, strings of tiny lanterns were bobbing, and an officer was conversing with a shop owner over steaming tea. Another photo showed gentle-faced army doctors curing some old men and women of their blindness, and the patients shouting, "Long Live the Emperor!," all believing it was His Majesty who had restored their sight. The third photo gave a view of an amusement park, in which a bunch of children and two handsome Japanese soldiers with toddlers in their laps were going down a slide together, all laughing with abandon.

Minnie said to Big Liu, "Come, let's go out for some fresh air." But he didn't budge, saying he had a migraine.

So Minnie and I went for a walk outside the campus. She was wearing a thick velvet hat and a woolen cloak while I had on blue cotton-padded jacket and pants, with a purple scarf around my neck. Her calf-high boots were the pair she'd bought in Moscow six years before. It was warm for a winter day, and the sun was sinking beyond the ridge of the hill ahead of us. Rooks were circling in the air and shrieking like crazy, while a pair of white-bellied magpies fluttered their feathers and cackled in the top of an old acacia. Along the road most of the houses were deserted. Some were roofless, destroyed by fire, and some no longer had doors or windows. All the pigsties and sheep pens were empty too. At the foot of the hill perched a small village that showed no trace of life, though it was time for cooking supper. As the two of us walked along, an old peasant, with a wisp of beard and only three or four teeth left in his mouth, appeared, lumbering over from the opposite direction. He carried a bundle of branches as firewood.

"Good day, Principal," the old man said to Minnie, and came to a stop.

"How are you doing?" she asked, apparently knowing him by sight, as did I.

"No good, just getting by."

"How's your family?"

"My wife went away with my son and daughter-in-law to the north of the river. I miss my grandkids terribly."

"When will they come back?" I asked.

"As long as the Japs are here, they won't come back. Matter of fact, most of our neighbors lit out too. Only a bunch of old folks stayed in the village to look after the homes."

"That means the families will come back sooner or later," Minnie said.

"Hope so."

The old man left, and we continued west. A few minutes later we entered a small valley, where we came upon a pond two acres wide, around which were many bodies. The water was still pinkish in spite of the recent rain and a creek feeding the marshy pond. More than a dozen corpses floated in it, puffed like logs. I realized this was an execution site.

Most of the dead were men, though there were some women and children too, all with bullet or bayonet wounds. Many of the men had their pants stripped down and their hands bound with iron wire; a few had their necks slashed. One woman, still wearing suede boots wrinkled at the ankles, had a breast cut off and a cartridge case stuck in each nostril. A small boy, stabbed in the tummy and his head smashed in from the side, still held a squashed bamboo basket. Beyond him lay a middle-aged man, perhaps his father, shot in the face and his hands tied with gaiters; his right hand had a sixth finger.

"The Japanese are savages!" I said.

"We should count how many were killed here," Minnie suggested.

"All right."

Together we began counting, walking clockwise along the waterside. Minnie used a stick to part the reeds and pampas grass that obscured some corpses, while I recorded our count in my small notebook. Now and then I pinched my nose shut because of the overpowering stench. Minnie wore a surgical mask, which she carried in her pocket whenever she went out nowadays. In total, we found 142 bodies, among them 38 women and 12 children. There might have been more under the water, but it was too muddy to see through.

"A monument should be put up here," Minnie said.

"There are execution sites everywhere. This one is nothing by comparison," I replied.

"Still, this should be remembered."

"Most people are good at forgetting. That's a way of survival, I guess."

We fell silent. Then she said, "History should be recorded as it happened so it can be remembered with little room for doubt and controversy."

I didn't respond, knowing that in her heart she resented the Chinese fashion of forgetfulness based on the understanding that nothing mattered eventually, since everything would turn into dust or smoke—even memories would fade away. Such an idea might be insightful, but one could also argue that many Chinese seemed to exploit forgetfulness as an excuse for shirking responsibility and avoiding strife. This was probably due to the influence of Daoism, which to Minnie was more like a secular cult. By contrast, she respected Confucianism—instead of indulging in escapism, Confucius advocated order, personal duty, and diligence. Yet to her, Confucianism, Daoism, and Buddhism were all secular religions. What this country needed was Christianity, she often told me, and I shared her belief.

Suddenly a large silver carp surfaced with a splash and swam away, its back cleaving the water with an expanding V. I said, "Fish must be getting fat in here."

"And the grass will grow thicker. What a crime!" Minnie said.

Originally we had planned to go all the way up to the ridge of the hill and from there to catch a full view of Mochou Lake beyond the city wall, but now we were in no mood for that anymore. We turned back. On our way down, we discussed how to present the petition to the Japanese authorities and the newly established puppet municipality. I wouldn't say a negative word about this matter anymore, since it was already under way. We were both against publishing the petition in a newspaper, afraid of incensing the Japanese unnecessarily. In the distance, a squadron of heavy bombers emerged like a school of whales in the waves of clouds, heading back for base after dropping bombs on the Chinese lines in the northwest, where a battle was in full swing.

Minnie said, "I wish the Christians in Japan knew what their countrymen have been doing here."

"Even if they knew, they might not do anything to stop them," I said, wondering how my son, Haowen, might have felt when he saw the Japanese euphoria. He must have encountered public gatherings and parades in celebration of the Imperial Army's victory. Was he heartbroken or crazed by them? Was he worried about us? Did he miss home? Could he still concentrate on his studies? Then I curbed my woolgathering and told Minnie, "I read in newspapers that all of Tokyo had turned out to celebrate the fall of Nanjing. Even small boys tossed their caps into the air, and women wore slogans across their chests, sang and danced in the streets, fluttering the sun-disk flags. Our calamities are their good fortunes."

"That's because they were ignorant of the truth." She'd also heard about the celebrations all over Japan, and that was why she couldn't stop imagining ways to deflate their jubilation. She had once suggested to the Safety Zone Committee that they rent a plane and drop a ton of truth-bearing pamphlets over Japan. That had brought out peals of laughter from the other foreigners. Lewis even joked that if Minnie could find a plane in Nanjing, he'd fly the mission, and Searle volunteered to be an airborne leafleter.

We stood for a while on the hill slope. From there we could see the Yangtze glittering like lava in the northwest, against the crimson sunset. On the waterway a handful of sampans were sailing upstream almost motionlessly.

15

For a week Minnie had been working on a report to Jinling's board of founders in New York. She was required to keep an official diary that would be mailed to our headquarters in New York at the end of each semester. In addition, she needed to send in a monthly report, so toward the end of each month she would work on the lengthy piece of writing. I wouldn't trade places with her even if they paid me twice her salary, though I could write and even kept a personal diary. In recent weeks Minnie often showed me her writings, and I could see that she couldn't be completely candid about what was happening. Besides the politics within our college, the Japanese monitored the international mail. She knew that other eyes, some hostile, would read the pages.

She used carbon paper to make an extra copy of the report for Dr. Wu, though without her address we didn't know where to send it yet. Minnie reviewed the major happenings before and after the fall of the city, including our efforts to help the refugees, the measures we'd taken to protect the school's properties, the conditions of the neighborhood, and the systematic destruction of lives and homes by the Japanese. She listed some arrests, rapes, robberies, and instances of arson—but they were too numerous to include all of them. Besides, she couldn't mention too many atrocities in case the Japanese confiscated the letter. She included the abduction of the twelve girls on December 17, but emphasized that six of them had come back unharmed the next morning. She wrote: "We deem that this miracle was wrought by our prayers."

I thought about telling her my doubts about the six girls' claim that the Japanese had not molested them, but I had no evidence to back up my conjecture, so I refrained.

Minnie talked with me about the twenty-one "prostitutes." Should we report that as well? If we did, what should we say? Would the board members in New York understand the situation? I could tell that Minnie was worried about Mrs. Dennison, because the old woman was in New York at the moment, fund-raising for our college, and she had always kept a close watch on Jinling. Mrs. Dennison might make a big fuss about this incident and even publicize it as a scandal, as we could not describe the circumstances in detail without putting ourselves at greater risk with the Japanese authorities.

After we had deliberated, Minnie said to me, "If it's a mistake on my part, I'll bear the guilt alone and do more good deeds to atone for it. God is greater than our hearts and knows everything."

I didn't fully understand her last sentence and asked, "You mean your conscience is clear?"

"Well, I wouldn't say that. But for now I prefer to keep this matter between God and me."

"If you're at fault, I'm part of it too. Don't worry about it. Nobody will say you're responsible for losing those women. We all know that the Japanese would have seized them one way or another that day."

Somehow we both felt that some of the abducted women might come back, that it might be too early to fully gauge the weight of the incident. What's more, we were certain that among the twenty-one women there'd been at least two or three former prostitutes. Deep down, though, we both knew that most of the women were unmarried and innocent. If only we had some information on them. If only we could find a way to bring some of them back. Those young lives had been ruined. No matter how we tried to reason away our responsibility, we were somewhat implicated, since by now everyone knew that Minnie had granted the Japanese permission. I made a mental note to write to Dr. Wu about this incident once I heard from her.

The more Minnie ruminated on this, the more remorseful and distressed she became. I urged her to stop thinking about it. There was so much to worry about at the moment that we mustn't let our sense of guilt paralyze us.

We decided to focus on the first eleven days of the Japanese occupation, up to December 23, so that Minnie wouldn't have to mention what had transpired on the twenty-fourth. When the next report was due, she could start from Christmas. Besides her inability to clearly explain her responsibility for the abduction, she was afraid of giving Mrs. Dennison a weapon to use against her. We knew that the only person who cared to scrutinize her report was the old woman, who seemed to hover over Minnie's shoulder all the time. To appease Mrs. Dennison, Minnie stressed that the refugee camp here was only temporary, that we would try to reinstate the college as soon as possible after the refugees left.

Having written about a few more rape cases and several such attempts that had been stopped in time, Minnie concluded: "I wish we could have prevented all the tragedies, but compared to most of the other camps, our record is exceedingly good." That was true, yet it didn't ease her mind.

One of the accomplishments she wrote about was teaching the refugees to line up for food. For weeks the women and girls had crowded the porridge stands, jostling to reach the cauldrons. The lawn had been trampled into puddles of mud, and even the cypress hedges were crushed in places. How marvelous it was to see the women standing in orderly lines at mealtimes now. Minnie also reported that many refugees complained that the porridge was too watery. Obviously there was theft going on in the porridge plant, but as yet we hadn't been able to find out where. The graft angered Minnie, and she assigned Luhai to keep a close watch on the cooks, but he couldn't detect the cause. Minnie vowed to get to the bottom of it and questioned the headman of the kitchen personally. The pockmarked man named Boom Chen hemmed and hawed, saying he'd do everything in his power to thicken the porridge, but so far nothing had changed and the refugees kept griping.

Several times our college had offered to run the porridge plant ourselves, yet the local Red Cross people would not let us. Minnie couldn't understand why they still had profit in mind under such circumstances. If only there was a way to nab the crooks.

The report was at last completed. How should she send it? Minnie said she would ask a fellow missionary going to Shanghai to mail it from there.

16

THE JAPANESE TROOPS grew less violent after the New Year, and some refugees felt things were stable enough that they no longer needed to stay in our camp. By mid-January, we still had seven thousand refugees. Many women believed that only through Minnie's intervention could they get their menfolk back, so they stuck with us. In late January Minnie and Big Liu presented the petition to the Japanese embassy, where an attaché named Fukuda accepted it and said that some office would give it full consideration. At the same time the puppet municipality, the so-called Autonomous City Government, composed of some bureaucrats and local gentry who had Japanese connections, ordered that all the refugee camps close down by February 9, which in a way eased Minnie's mind a little because she knew that Mrs. Dennison would hate to see the college remain a refugee camp.

We began persuading the older women among the refugees to go home. Some left, but they came back within two or three days. Many of the refugees had no place to live anymore, for nothing was left of their homes. One woman in her early forties was dragged away by four soldiers; they molested her for a whole night and did not release her until the next afternoon. She came back and begged Minnie never to make her go home again. A woman of sixty-three went back and was caught by two soldiers. She told them she must be as old as their grandmothers; all the same, they knocked her down, raped her, and stomped on her bound feet. She limped back to Jinling the next day, still shaken, and couldn't stop her tears. Some of the women, shocked and humiliated, wouldn't speak to anyone after they were back in our camp.

Their stories upset us, and we realized that we could not close the camp in a hurry. Even if we tried hard, there was no way to meet the deadline, which was just a week away. One thing we were clear about now—no matter what, we must never force any woman to leave. We ignored the deadline, giving the excuse that most of the refugees were homeless.

THE DEADLINE had passed, but not a single camp closed down. John Rabe insisted to the officials that there was no way to send the women home without exposing them to molestation by the soldiers, so the matter was dropped. Meanwhile, the Autonomous City Government had been registering all the citizens and refugees, and declared that anyone older than fifteen without an ID certificate would be arrested and jailed. Frightened, people lined up at various camps to go through the registration process. Some living outside the Safety Zone even came a day before and, bundled in overcoats or wrapped in blankets, waited a whole night to get registered. A lot of men feared that this might be another ruse to ensnare the so-called former soldiers and have more of them "mopped up." Indeed, in the past three weeks the Japanese had seized more than twenty thousand men from various registration sites. Promised leniency and well-paid jobs, those men had stepped out, hoping to make some money for their families, but the Japanese apprehended them all. About three thousand of them were forced into convict labor while the rest were led to execution grounds.

Hundreds of men were coming to our camp, wanting to get registered here, because if they were accused of being former soldiers, some brave women, as instructed by me, would step forward and vouch for them, saying that the men were their husbands or sons. As a result, the officials would be likely to let them pass and give them the ID papers, a one-page document, five by three inches, folded down the middle, stamped with a scarlet seal, and printed with the characters *Good Citizen Certificate*. On the inside was information about the carrier and also his or her mug shot. The Japanese had been in charge of the registration originally, but it got more and more confusing, and it was hard, almost impossible, for them to tell who was a former soldier, so they left the whole matter in their puppets' hands. The Safety Zone Committee urged all the refugee camps to participate in the registration as a gesture of "cooperation" with the new municipality. In addition, John Rabe and his colleagues all believed that it would be safer for the refugees to register in the foreigners' presence, and therefore they told people to get the ID papers now.

Siemens had decided to close its Nanjing office by the end of February, so Rabe would be returning to Germany. His imminent departure caused quite a stir among the camps. He had been nicknamed the Living Buddha and was revered by the refugees. Some people called him Mayor Rabe, but he forbade them to do that, not wanting to antagonize the Autonomous City Government, which was eager to replace both the Safety Zone Committee and the International Red Cross Committee. For days Minnie and I had been thinking about giving him a farewell dinner, but it was impossible to get fresh meat and fish, so we decided to give a tea party instead.

It was like spring on February 17, balmy and cloudless. The refugees at Jinling hung their bedding in the sun while some girls mopped the floors and wiped the windows and doors of the buildings. The whole campus looked lively and colorful—laundered clothes and diapers were spread on evergreen hedges, making the place resemble a thickly settled village. The unkempt sight made me wonder how long the refugee camp would last. If Mrs. Dennison saw this, she might have a stroke.

I made a kind of fruitcake, using minced candied fruit, for the tea party in Rabe's honor. We also opened the last box of chocolates in our pantry and placed it next to a tray of peeled tangerines and a bowl of canned pineapple. Rabe brought along two stout sausages, which we cut and placed next to a platter of cured duck. In addition to three German businessmen and eight American missionaries, John Allison, the second secretary at the reopened U.S. embassy, attended too. He'd done diplomatic service for five years in Tokyo and Kobe and spoke Japanese. Allison now functioned as the top American diplomat in Nanjing. Oddly, today he was escorted by a Japanese guard, a hulk of a soldier, as if he were under arrest. This was probably because a sentry had manhandled him a fortnight before and several newspapers in the West had reported the incident. Allison had returned to Nanjing six weeks earlier and was still shaken by the horrific condition of the city, particularly by the corpses scattered on the streets, some partly eaten by dogs and birds. He couldn't understand why the Imperial Army, noted for its discipline, would kill so indiscriminately. The Germans in Nanjing—Rabe, Rosen, Sperling, and a few others—often made fun of his shock, calling him Allison in Wonderland.

On the round table sat a bowl of vegetable salad mixed with cellophane noodles and peanut butter, which all the guests liked. Most of them stood around chatting, with plates and forks in their hands. Big Liu proposed a toast, raising a cup of oolong tea and announcing with a smile: "Even if the Chinese are totally deprived, we still have fine tea."

People raised their cups and drank to Rabe's health and good fortune back in Germany. To my knowledge, Rabe wasn't doing well in spite of his hardy appearance. He always carried a vial of insulin and a syringe in his pocket for his diabetes. Because he often had to climb out of bed in the dead of night to repel soldiers who attempted to break into his home or into the small compound of the German school, he'd feel sleepy during the day and nod off at times. Rabe was going to Shanghai first and from there sailing to Genoa, which would take more than four weeks; then he'd head to Berlin by rail. He had no idea what was in store for him back home. He told Minnie and Holly, "I'll collapse by the time I join my children."

Minnie apologized to Rabe for such a shabby party, without cheese or wine. We all knew he loved cheese and nowadays often groused to his cook about a cheeseless table. He even missed potatoes.

"This is wonderful and memorable," Rabe said. "Thank you, Miss Vautrin."

He had grown thinner lately, but still sported a small paunch. Holly often joked about him in private, "If he was single, I'd chase him to the end of the globe." I'd say to her, "Oh, come now, he's too old for you, not a good catch." Rabe was fifty-five, older than Holly by a good fifteen years.

He and Lewis were quite close, having worked together on a daily basis since November. Lewis admired his large heart, his common sense, and his ability to get things done, while Rabe liked Lewis for his energy and unflagging enthusiasm for whatever he undertook. But the two of them wouldn't stop chaffing each other. Lewis would call Rabe Rockefeller on account of the grand house, the headquarters of the Safety Zone Committee, where he stayed during the daytime. Whenever his loyal assistants, Han or Cheng, came in to hand Rabe a telegram, Lewis would quip, "From Hitler?"

Now, teacup in hand, Lewis came over and smiled quizzically, crunching popcorn. Rabe swatted him on the shoulder and said, "I know what you're going to say: Hilter summoned me back. Right?"

"He must have a big job waiting for you," Lewis said, his face straight. We chuckled, knowing Rabe was a leader of the Nazi Party in Nanjing.

"As a matter of fact, the Führer may not want to see me. Chancellor Scharffenberg was in the embassy the other day and summoned me. He chastised me, urging me to stop tangling with the Japanese. He stressed that what the Japanese were doing here should not concern us Germans, because he believed that the Chinese, once left alone to cope with the Japanese, would cooperate with them. I guess by now even Hitler might be tired of me."

Minnie raised her teacup and said to Rabe, "John, regardless of your political persuasion, you're a man I look up to."

We touched cups with him and each took a mouthful. Then Robert Wilson came over, his balding crown pinkish, and rested his hand on Eduard Sperling's shoulder. "John, I have something for you," Bob said. Because the Japanese would let few medical personnel come into the city, for almost six weeks Bob had been the only surgeon in town. He actually lived at the University Hospital so he could work around the clock. His face creased a little as he smiled; he looked frazzled as a result of having to operate on patients day and night. Sometimes his hands got swollen from overwork, yet he had to continue.

"What's that?" Rabe asked. "I hope it's not another house. I cannot bring any real estate back to Germany, you know." There'd been so many houses "given" to him recently that he was sick of them, because the owners also meant to have the properties protected by him, knowing he'd have to leave them behind when his stint here was over.

Bob touched a canvas satchel under the table with the side of his boot. "I have one hundred ampoules of insulin for you—don't you want them?"

"Good Lord, I'm delighted," Rabe said. "But don't you need them for other patients?"

"We only treat people with gunshot and bayonet wounds. I feel like a butcher, doing nothing but cutting and stitching bodies." He lifted the satchel of insulin, put it on the table, and told Rabe, "Use them soon—they'll expire in a year."

"I will. Thanks very much," Rabe said.

While people were talking, Searle Bates dozed off in a chair in a corner, his veiny hand still holding a teacup. His bumpy Adam's apple jigged from time to time. Usually he was the most convivial one among the Americans, thanks to his sharp wit and vast learning, but this afternoon he was too exhausted to remain on his feet. These days, besides managing the camps at Nanjing University, he drove a truck to deliver rice and firewood and coal to porridge plants within the Safety Zone, which fed more than two hundred thousand refugees. Because only foreigners could transport the rations without being robbed, Searle and several others had to do the driving. Now none of us disturbed him.

When the party was about to end, Minnie suggested that Allison leave first because he had a Japanese guard in tow, so the diplomat left before the others. Then Rulian came in and, her almond-shaped eyes smiling, whispered to me that some women gathering outside wanted to say farewell to Rabe.

I went up to him and said, "Mr. Rabe, some women in our camp want to say good-bye to you. Can you spare a minute?"

"Okay, I'm coming." He drained his cup, then followed us to the door. The others were also coming out.

What we saw in front of the Science Building staggered us. More than three thousand women and girls were kneeling on the ground, wailing and begging, "Please don't go! Please don't abandon us!"

"Don't leave us in the lurch!" a voice rang out.

"Don't stop protecting us!" shouted another.

Rabe was flustered. He approached the front row of the crowd and said, "Please get up."

But none of the women budged. He bent down a little and said a few more words in English to them; still nobody moved. Then he bowed three times to the crowd in the Chinese fashion. He straightened up and waved at the women and girls, some of whom were crying louder now. He asked Minnie, "What should I do?"

"Say something to them."

"What can I say? There's no way I can justify my leaving. If only I could stay like you." He swallowed, a film of sweat on his broad forehead. Unable to speak Chinese, he turned to the crowd and made another three deep bows.

Still, the crowd wouldn't get up and many kept crying. Rabe said to Minnie, "I'd better go."

"Okay, this way. You can use the side gate," said Minnie.

I beckoned Luhai over and told him to open that small exit for Rabe. Rabe followed him along the roofed path and went out of the yard through a moon gate, leaving his car behind. He had to walk all the way home, as did the other guests.

Afterward Minnie talked about the crowd with me. "I didn't expect they'd have such deep feelings for John Rabe."

"Yes, they're more than grateful," I said. "Also, they must be scared and want to be protected."

To many of the women and girls, Rabe must have been like a protective father who had never hesitated to confront the soldiers and even risk his own life. He was more than a hero to the refugees.

ONE AFTERNOON in late February, a fortyish refugee woman named Sufen came to the president's office and said she had spotted her fifteen-year-old son in a labor gang in the Model Prison downtown. Surprised, Minnie asked her, "Are you sure he was your son?"

"Absolutely, he called me Ma and hollered he missed home. Principal Vautrin, please help me—help get him out of jail."

"Relax. Tell us more about that place."

That stumped Sufen, who turned tongue-tied.

"How many men are in there?" I asked her, having stepped out of the other inner room, which was my office.

"Hundreds, some wearing burlap sacks like rain ponchos. Some are just teenage boys like my son." As she spoke, Sufen's large eyes shone with excitement and her sunburned nose quivered. I knew she had filed her petition with Big Liu.

"What else did your son tell you?" Minnie went on.

"Nothing more. Two guards took them away before he could say another word. I'm gonna wait for him there tomorrow morning."

"Try to find out something about the other men too."

"Sure I will."

"Don't tell others you saw your son there yet. We must figure out what to do before we spread the word."

"I'll do whatever you say."

I admired Minnie's discretion. If we broke the news at once, we might bring about a chaos among the petitioners that Big Liu and his team would not be able to handle.

Sufen dragged herself out of the office, her shoulders bent and her knees knocking a little as she walked. I remembered speaking with her weeks ago, and knew that she had come with a group of refugees from Danyang and that her husband was a chef in the Nationalist army, though the man was somewhere in the southwest of China now. That made me feel closer to her because my son-in-law was also in the army. Sufen told me that a shell had landed in her back-yard and killed her mother-in-law, who had been feeding a milk goat there. The moment Sufen and her son carried the old woman indoors and covered her with a sheet, word came that the Japanese were approaching. So she and the boy took flight with the other vil-lagers. But before reaching the road that led to a nearby town, they were intercepted by a company of soldiers, who detained all the able-bodied men among them, saying that the Imperial Army needed "many, many hands" and would give them good food and pay them handsomely. Sufen begged an officer to spare her son. He was just a kid, not even fifteen yet, skinny like a starved chicken. "Please, please don't take him away!" she pleaded, holding both hands together before her chest. But the heavyset officer kicked her and threatened to cut off her ear if she made any more noise. She was too frightened to say another word, and all she could do was give the boy the biscuits and water she carried.

Now the information about her son in the Model Prison, a stan-dard penitentiary built by the Nationalist government but used as a military jail by the Japanese, cast a ray of hope on the petition. It also made me see the reason for Minnie's insistence on the endeavor. If my son were behind bars, I'd have done anything to get him out. I thought that I ought to be more involved in helping those poor moth-ers and wives.

Minnie and I wondered if the jail also held other men and boys belonging to some petitioners' families. She called together Big Liu, Holly, and me and floated the idea of sending scores of women to the Model Prison to see if they could find their menfolk as well. Both Big Liu and Holly thought that this might be too rash and might endan-ger the women.

I believed that we could make the petition a much stronger case if more men and boys were found in that jail. Maybe we could send over just three or four plain-looking women? I suggested. They all seconded my suggestion.

With the help of Lewis Smythe, Minnie got in touch with Dr. Chu, who had his clinic in the center of downtown and was well connected and eager to help the women get their menfolk back. Most of the foreigners thought highly of this man, though I had mixed feelings about him. He had earned his medical degree from the University of Leipzig and spoke fluent German but very little English. Reverend Magee said Dr. Chu was warm and trustworthy—unlike most Chinese, he never minced his words and always cut to the chase. Despite working for the Autonomous City Government, he had a decent reputation among the locals, partly because he held no official title and spent most of his time seeing patients. Magee had recommended him to several Americans as a family physician. On a windy afternoon in early March, Minnie and I arrived at his office downtown, carrying the six hundred signatures and thumbprints of the petitioners.

To our surprise, Dr. Chu had met with Big Liu two days before and was familiar with the case. He was in his late thirties, with urbane manners. His three-piece suit was baggy on him, though his boots were shiny. He spoke while drumming his long fingers on the glass desktop as if tapping out a telegram. "I went to the Model Prison yesterday and chatted with an officer," he told us in a low-timbred voice. "The man said that fifteen hundred prisoners were held there as forced labor. Many of them are civilians, and more than forty are young boys. But the officer wouldn't let me speak to any of them. He feared that his Japanese superior might suspect him of leaking information."

"Do you think there might be a way we can get some of them released?" Minnie asked. I was amazed that he was already involved.

"That's possible. Try to get more women to participate and send the petition to Shanghai if the Japanese here ignore you. There must be a way to push them."

"We'll do that."

"The prisoners are underfed and malnourished. Some were too ill to work. Maybe you should have some rice and salted vegetables delivered to those recognized by the petitioners."

"So far only one boy was spotted by his mother," I told him.

"I'm pretty sure more will be found."

"We'll try our best," Minnie said.

"I'll do everything I can to help." He sighed, his eyes dimmed, and his patchy brows drooped.

Dr. Chu was one of the best doctors of Western medicine here, and even some Japanese officers had gone to him for treatment since he had come back to Nanjing a month before. With his help, we hoped that our petition might produce some results.

18

ONE AFTERNOON in mid-March, Minnie and I headed for the garden in the back of campus to look at the double daffodils that were about to unfold. She'd brought the bulbs back from America a decade before and Old Liao had helped to cultivate them. She was fond of flowers, particularly those that bloomed in fall and winter. Passing the small pond, we saw some goldfish, each about a foot long, lying belly-up in the water, and realized they must have been poisoned by soapsuds and night soil. A broken washboard was floating among them. Many women would scrub toilet buckets in the pond. In the beginning we had urged them not to do that, but so many people kept doing it that by now it had become a common practice. The refugees also laundered clothes and diapers in the water. There were three other ponds on campus—one behind the library, another near Ninghai Road and south of the Faculty Residence, and the third before the Practice Hall. But those three were much bigger than this one, and therefore not as polluted.

Although there were 3,328 refugees in the camp now, the 7,000 who were gone had left behind a good amount of garbage and waste. Feces were strewn in the grass and along some hedges, and a group of refugee girls had been collecting them with wicker baskets and small dung forks and piling them behind some buildings. As the weather was getting warmer day by day, the excrement had to be disposed of without further delay or an epidemic might break out. The girls had been digging pits to bury the waste they had collected, but we knew that even this was not a permanent solution. We needed lime, tons of it, to cover the feces and kill the germs, but to date we hadn't been able to come by any.

"Phew, what a smell," said Minnie.

"We'd better clean up this place soon," I said.

"Yes, we must get hold of some lime."

Without going farther west to see the daffodils, Minnie and I veered back toward the business manager's office. She wanted to send Luhai to the Safety Zone Committee to ask Plumer, who had succeeded Rabe as its chairman, about the lime they had promised to help us procure.

Rulian turned up as we walked along. The second she saw us she said, "A girl killed herself."

"Where?" Minnie asked.

"In the Central Building." That was in Rulian's charge now, because Holly had been hospitalized for tonsillitis and exhaustion. When I went to see Holly two days earlier, she had wanted to come back to Jinling, saying the hospital was too clamorous, but Dr. Wilson insisted that she stay there for another week. He knew she wouldn't rest in bed once she returned to the camp.

Together Minnie, Rulian, and I headed for the Central Building. The fragrance of fruit blossoms made the air a little sweetish. Some refugees lazed around in the quad, where the two blind girls brought over by Cola, the young Russian, three months ago, and joined by another two blind ones, piped flutes and sawed away at the two-stringed *erhus*, learning to play snatches of the local Kun opera.

A crowd had gathered on the second floor of the Central Building. We entered a classroom that held more than sixty women. The room had a strong smell that brought to mind a chicken coop, but I was already accustomed to this odor. Rulian took us to the far end, which was shielded by a sky-blue screen. Minnie and I bent down to look at the dead girl closely—she was in her late teens, a tad homely but with soft skin and abundant hair. She looked pallid; her eyes were closed, her lips dark and parted, and through them I could see sticky blood in her mouth. Her round cheeks were grayish, but her expression was relaxed, as though she were about to yawn. Her short-fingered hand was resting on her chest, which seemed to be still heaving. Next to her clothes bundle, which served as a pillow, was an empty ratsbane bottle; she must have found it in one of the defunct kitchens. A frayed blanket covered the girl's abdomen, but her legs stuck out, one foot wearing a scarlet woolen sock and the other bare. Although she looked familiar, I didn't recognize her right away.

"Who is she?" Minnie asked.

"Her name is Wanju Yu," Rulian answered.

At that, I remembered the girl, who'd been among the twelve taken by the Japanese on December 17, but I didn't know how to tell Minnie about her in the presence of this crowd.

"Why did she do this to herself?" Minnie went on.

"I've no idea," Rulian said.

"Any of you know why she took her life?" Minnie asked the women standing around.

They all shook their heads. A moment later one said the girl had cried a lot at night, and another added that she had often skipped meals, just sitting cross-legged in the corner like a statue and studying the floor. A thirtyish woman, suckling a baby in her arms, guessed that the dead girl must have been a student because she had often read a thick book alone and also crooned movie songs to herself. Since the first day these women had wondered if she had a cog loose.

I tugged at Minnie's sleeve and said, "Let's get out of here."

We left the room, followed by Rulian. In the hallway I told Minnie, "The girl was pregnant and went to the infirmary a couple of days ago. She wanted an abortion. We told her we couldn't do that for her because we had no doctor here. We should've given her more help, but we couldn't kill a baby. The nurse and I really don't know how to abort a fetus."

"Who was the father of the baby?" Minnie asked.

"Some Japanese bastard."

"I don't get it. How did it happen?"

"Remember when the Japs grabbed twelve girls one evening last December?"

"Yes. And six of them came back the next morning."

"Well, the dead girl was one of the six."

"But they all said they were unharmed."

"That's just what they claimed. How could they admit they'd been raped? How could any of them find a husband if they were known as having been violated by the Eastern devils? Neither they nor their families could bear the shame."

Stunned, Minnie swayed a little. She put her hand on Rulian's shoulder, sputtering to me, "Why didn't you breathe a word about this? Those girls should at least have received medical attention."

"This isn't something people would talk about. I thought I'd let you know one of these days, but for a long time I had no evidence to back up my guess. Who could've imagined the girl would kill herself?" I lowered my eyes and wished I had informed Minnie after Wanju showed up at the infirmary.

"Where are the other five girls?"

"I don't think they're still here except for Meiyan, Big Liu's daughter."

Without another word Minnie spun around and clumped down the stairs. She went out alone.

Meanwhile, I called in the janitor Hu and Old Liao. They carried the body to a flatbed cart and hauled it away. Minnie turned up, and we followed the men to the hillside beyond a small orchard. We picked a spot on the slope of a ravine and set about digging.

Hu and Liao dug by turns, and I helped them a little, not being strong enough to dig with a shovel for longer than three minutes. When the grave was almost a foot deep, tubby Hu, his sparse hair stuck to his flat forehead, had started gasping "umph" at every thrust with the shovel. Minnie took over the job. She worked with all her strength, leaning the weight of her body on her right foot on top of the scoop and drawing herself up halfway when tossing out the dirt. She swung the shovel with a rhythm, and her supple movement impressed us. I knew she had grown up in a farm village and done all kinds of work in her childhood. She had also been a basketball player at the University of Illinois at Urbana-Champaign, where she got her BA, so she was "sturdy as a Clyde," in her own words. Soon she began breathing audibly, yet she applied herself harder. From time to time tears welled out of her eyes and mixed with the perspiration on her cheeks. She was huffing and puffing, while her nose seemed blocked.

"If only we could give her a coffin," Minnie said a few minutes later, handing the shovel to Old Liao.

"I wish we knew where her folks are," I said, "so they could take her home."

Crows wheeled around in the limpid sky, letting out grating cries.

Two feral dogs, both spattered with mud, stood nearby, pawing at the ground and touching it with their noses, as though they were planning to dig out the interred girl once nobody was around. This reminded us that we must bury the dead at least two feet deep. Old Liao regretted not having brought along a reed mat in which we could roll up the body.

"Wanju, please forgive us," Minnie said, as the men laid the girl in the grave. They began shoveling the dirt back into it. I took the shovel when they needed a breather.

After burying her, we stood in silence before the pile of earth for a while. Minnie said, as if to promise the dead, "I will never let this kind of crime happen in our camp again. I'll do everything I can to protect the girls and women. If I have to fight the soldiers, I will fight. I won't be a coward anymore."

I said, "Rest in peace now, Wanju, and forget about this unjust world. I'll come tomorrow and burn a bunch of joss sticks for you."

Then Minnie crouched down, no longer able to suppress her emotion. She wailed, "It was also my fault, Wanju. I should have stayed in the compound to stop the Japanese from snatching you away. After you came back, we should have given you more help." Minnie paused, then continued, "Rest assured, those beasts will be brought to justice. God will deal with them on your behalf."

I felt so sad that I began weeping too.

Old Liao and Hu helped Minnie up, and together we headed back to campus. Hu was pulling the cart with a leather strap around his shoulder.

We washed our faces in the ladies' room, then went down the hallway to the president's office. Big Liu was in there, seated on a sofa and absentmindedly leafing through his small textbook. When we stepped in, he lifted his eyes and peered at Minnie wordlessly.

She sat down and told him about the suicide. He responded calmly, "I heard about it."

"I'm such an idiot," she said.

"Don't blame yourself, Minnie. It was the Japanese who killed her." His voice was somehow devoid of any emotion.

"I cannot do our Chinese lesson today—my mind is too full."

"I understand," he said.

"Don't go, Anling," Minnie urged me.

So I stayed, and together we discussed the progress of the petition. Sufen had just reported to Big Liu that she'd seen her son four times now. The boy had told her that the prisoners were sent to tear down houses and build a bridge outside the city, though many of them were too ill to work anymore. They were each given two bowls of boiled sorghum a day, plus a few pieces of salted turnip or rutabaga. Once a week they could have rice. He begged his mother to find a way to get him out soon or he would perish in there. She promised to do that, though she had no idea how. He also asked her to bring him some food, which she couldn't come by either.

By now more women had participated in the petition: in total 704 had filed. We decided to take the list to Dr. Chu and hoped he would present it to the office in charge of such a matter.

19

MINNIE AND I SET OUT to see Fukuda at the Japanese embassy with the petition. The moment we turned onto Shanghai Road, we saw that numerous ramshackle stores, mostly built of used plywood and corrugated iron, had emerged on both sides of the street. Many of them were just small stalls manned by one person. There were all sorts of things for sale and barter: door planks, windows, lamps, cast-iron stoves, furniture, stone hand mills, utensils, musical instruments, clothing, used books, and magazines. As for food, there were baked wheaten cakes, fried twists, tofu, vegetables, eggs, pork, and pig offal, all five or six times more expensive than before the occupation. I bought a smoked chicken for seven yuan for Liya, who had been weak after her miscarriage, often coughing and sweating profusely even without exerting herself. "This is like eating silver," an old woman kept saying, watching the vendor wrapping up my purchase in a piece of oil paper. I made no reply and felt that money might get more devalued anyway, so it was better to spend it now.

The city was strictly guarded, and whoever was without a *mingto*, the ID certificate, would be arrested. The soldiers would strip people of whatever was valuable on them—a pack of cigarettes, a fountain pen, a pocket harmonica, even a brass button from a coat. They also examined men who looked like potential fighters, making them stand at roadsides, shed their jackets and shirts, and spread their arms; if a man had a vaccination mark, they would detain him, believing it was a shrapnel scar. The Japanese seemed apprehensive, especially troubled by the guerrillas, who attacked their sentry posts in the countryside and blocked their transportation routes. Lately so many trains had been derailed that the railroad service had become erratic, and sometimes there was no train to Shanghai three days in a row. What was more troublesome was that the guerrillas fought outside the

norms of conventional warfare, harassing small Japanese units day
and night, blowing up isolated fortresses, and ambushing convoys.
Once in a while artillery bombardments could be heard in the early-
morning hours and within five or six miles of the city, as if another
siege was impending. Meanwhile, the new regulations allowed few
foreigners, much less Chinese, to leave Nanjing, though more Western diplomats had returned.

Near the Japanese embassy an opium den flaunted a banner that
read OFFICIAL EARTH. Narcotics used to be banned here, but now
anything was legal for sale. Evidently the majority of the goods were
loot from outside the Safety Zone. After the soldiers had plundered
the houses, the civilians would go in and gut them, taking whatever
was useful or salable. For many people, looting had become a way of
life, because there were no jobs. The Safety Zone was relatively safe
for doing business, so most vendors brought their goods here.

Fukuda received us cordially, but explained that he still couldn't
locate any of the men and boys on the list Minnie had presented to
him in late January. A young Japanese woman wearing a flowered
kimono and wooden clogs came in, carrying a clay teapot and three
cups on a tray. After tea was served, Minnie said to Fukuda, "We've
just learned that there are many civilians in the Model Prison."

"Are you sure?" He looked incredulous, his eyebrows locked
together.

"Positive." Minnie went on to speak about Sufen's son. "He's her
only child and was taken on December fifth. He told her there were
many young boys in there."

Fukuda heaved a feeble sigh, tapping his cigarette over an ashtray
in the shape of a flatfish. He said in halting English, "I thought that
place was holding only soldiers. Well, we shall investigate. Try to give
more physical descriptions of this boy. If he is there, I shall try to help
him come out of prison."

"I'll let his mother know. Thank you."

"Miss Vautrin," Fukuda said with some feeling, his bony face
flushing, "I mean to help. I hope you can believe I have been doing
my best."

"Of course I can."

I knew Minnie didn't completely trust him. He might be sympathetic to the poor women, but he couldn't act himself, given his role as
an attaché. Besides, there must be a military office in charge of such a
matter, but he had just said he was unclear about that when Minnie
asked him. Maybe he simply didn't want to bother or offend the army
with our petition. This could also mean he wasn't deeply involved.

We thanked him again and left the embassy. I was impressed by
Fukuda's courtesy, though Minnie and I were now less convinced
that he would bring our petition to his superiors. He was always very
officious, as if wearing an impenetrable mask, and seemed unable to
feel anything. Never having seen his face fully at ease, I couldn't even
place his age—maybe he was in his late twenties, but he could also be
pushing forty.

We headed south along Tianjin Road. Although the area was within
the Safety Zone, many houses had been reduced to rubble, and some
stood but did not have roofs. Even a good number of electric and telephone poles were gone. Several buildings were no more than skeletal
hulks. At the corner of Hankou Road, we saw a rickshaw carrying two
soldiers. One of them stopped the vehicle and asked the puller to do
something, shouting, "*Hao guniang, duo duo you!*" At first I didn't
catch it, then I realized he meant: "Good girls, many many there are!"
The Chinese man shook his sweaty face and waved, saying he didn't
know where to find girls. Hearing that, one of the soldiers jumped off
and began punching him in the chest. "Ow! Ow!" the man wailed. "I
just don't know how to find them! Even if you beat me to death, I
won't be able to say where there're girls. They're all gone."

Minnie strode up to them and I followed her. The instant the
other Japanese saw us, he gave a cry, which made his comrade stop
short and get back on the rickshaw. Then they both motioned for the
puller to proceed. In a flash the vehicle rounded a street corner and
vanished.

We continued west. Approaching our campus, from a distance
we caught sight of John Magee—his jeep stood beside the front entrance. We hurried up to him. At the sound of our footsteps, he
turned around, his fedora cocked. "Hi, Minnie and Anling," he said.
"I brought over some powdered milk and a barrel of cod-liver oil."

"Thanks," we both said.

Luhai was busy unloading the car. He said, "This is what we need for the kids."

Minnie told Magee, "The porridge plant has been a small disaster for us. Most of the children here were undernourished, so the dried milk and the cod-liver oil will do them good."

"We just got a truckload," Magee said. "I'll give you some more if there're still leftovers after we distribute them."

"Please do. Thanks in advance."

The reverend drove away, leaving behind a haze of dust and an odor of exhaust. He was driving a new jeep now, bought from a Japanese officer for merely 160 yuan after some soldiers had stolen his old Dodge. We still had the clunker Magee had given us, but it was already dead, not worth fixing anymore, according to Minnie.

Minnie turned to Luhai. "Is there any progress in your investigation?"

"No. I've watched the cooks pour rice into the cauldrons every time they cook, but still the porridge is as thin as it was."

"Don't we have some beans?"

"Yes, thirty sacks."

"Add some beans to the rice. That will make the food richer."

"Good idea. I'll get them to start doing that tomorrow."

We had just received the mung beans and navy beans from the Safety Zone Committee. Because of the dropsy caused by malnutrition among some refugees, Plumer Mills had repeatedly asked for the beans and obtained sixty tons from Shanghai. We were pleased with the beans, as well as with Magee's new contribution. But Minnie wouldn't let Luhai distribute the powdered milk and the cod-liver oil, perhaps afraid he might give them to his relatives and friends, so she let me handle them, which I was glad to do.

Within a few days most women had stopped complaining about the porridge, since the beans had thickened it to a degree. Still, Minnie couldn't put the graft in the porridge plant out of her mind, and just the mention of it would make her bristle. If only we could stop the theft.

20

THE NEXT AFTERNOON Dr. Chu came to see us. That morning two women had spotted their husbands in the Model Prison as the men were being herded onto the trucks that took them to work. But the lanky doctor couldn't offer any heartening news. He crossed his thin legs and said, "I personally delivered the petition to the Autonomous City Government, together with the stack of paperwork, but they said the information was too vague and they couldn't do a thing."

"What else do they need?" Minnie asked.

"They want more descriptions of every man." He blew away the tea leaves in his cup.

"What kind of descriptions?" asked Big Liu.

"Physical features, like height and weight."

"That's ridiculous," I said. "How on earth can the women know how much their husbands and sons weigh now?"

"Just give as many physical descriptions as you can."

"That means we'll have to start all over again," Minnie said.

"Probably it will be worth it, considering more women have sighted their menfolk in the jail. I know those officials might want to dodge this case, but you shouldn't give up so easily."

After Dr. Chu had left, the three of us decided to redo the petition. This would take the four people in Big Liu's team more than a week, but the effort would pay off even if we could save only one life.

Minnie let a dozen or so older women go to the Model Prison every morning to see if they could find more of their menfolk in the labor gang. She had an official letter written for them, saying that these women would make no trouble and wanted only to catch a glimpse of their husbands and sons. Following Minnie's instructions, the three women who had spotted their menfolk also went to the

Defense Commissioner's Office to report their discovery and plead for help, but so far there was no official response.

THE CAMPUS, no longer guarded by the Japanese police, was now pretty with blooming flowers—lilacs, magnolias, crocuses, white spirea—and birds kept singing, as if determined to burst their throats with grief. There were so many flowers that once a young Japanese officer came to ask for a bouquet, and Minnie was pleased to get Old Liao to cut a mixed bunch for him. Every day some soldiers would turn up in twos or threes, but few were violent now. They were impressed by our classroom buildings, which combined the Chinese and the Western architectural styles, with high-columned front portals, flying eaves, and gargoyles on the edges and ridges of the roofs. I treated them with courtesy in the hope that one of them might help me find my son in Tokyo. We hadn't heard from Haowen for ten months and couldn't stop wondering if he was still alive, but I never went so far as to ask any of the soldiers to help look for him. I hadn't met one I might trust.

Some of the men admitted to us that the war was a mistake—China was too enormous for Japan to occupy. They had all learned about this country in history textbooks—about its big apples and pears, its vast soybean fields, its rich minerals, and its pretty girls, but they had not imagined that it was such an immense land; it was also much poorer than they'd thought. Many of them had believed that once Nanjing was captured, the war would be over and they could go home; that was why they'd fought with such a blind vengeance. Everyone had wanted to finish off the enemies at the first chance, but now they could no longer envision the end of the war. One man even said that Japan should have been content with the Korean Peninsula and Manchukuo and should have stopped its aggression there. "We swallowed more than we could digest. We got too greedy," he told us with a toothy grin. A lieutenant, a Christian, had come twice to deliver soap, towels, and biscuits for the refugees. Once we took two junior officers to the camp's kindergarten, where toddlers were playing noisily, and Minnie told them that these children no longer had fathers. The two men murmured, "We're sorry, really sorry for them."

On my way back from the infirmary one afternoon, I bumped into Luhai, who came from the opposite direction, limping a little and wearing an octagonal cap, a herringbone blazer, and scuffed oxfords. He stopped, and we talked about some matters in the camp. Our staff had given tickets for free meals to most of the thirty-three hundred refugees, but Luhai still couldn't find the leak in the porridge plant. The headman blamed the cooks for pilfering small quantities of rice at every meal, while a few of them pointed at him as the number one thief. To Luhai, every one of them seemed bent on stealing from the mouths of the poor women and undernourished children. This bad news made my blood boil again. If only there were a way to nab the crooks!

I believed that Boom Chen, the headman, must be guilty of the theft, because the man lived like a spendthrift, smoking Big Gate cigarettes and wearing a spiffy woolen jacket, which was unnecessary for the warm springtime. Whenever I bumped into this beefy swaggerer, he would greet me loudly in a tobacco-roughened voice, as if we had known each other for years, as if I ought to appreciate what he'd been doing for us. Minnie had once asked him to submit to her a thorough report on how the rations were used, but he'd claimed that he was illiterate, rolling his bovine eyes and simpering as though to insinuate that he need not receive instructions from her. Yet every once in a while I would see him lounging around reading a newspaper or a chivalric novel, so I was convinced he must be a fraud.

Luhai and I discussed a girl who had been snatched by the Japanese from the front gate three days before. Minnie had been away from campus and Holly wasn't around when it happened either, so nobody had dared to stop the two soldiers. Later, Minnie lodged a protest with the military headquarters in Nanjing, but there was no trace of the girl, who we all knew was unlikely to come back. Minnie had admonished the whole camp time and again about loitering at the front entrance, but some of the younger girls had ignored or forgotten her admonition and went there to chitchat with new arrivals and passersby. A few even donned colorful clothes. Worse, Meiyan also went to the front entrance, with large scissors beneath her jacket. When we discovered that, we let Big Liu know immediately. He'd kept her home ever since. Two girls had already been carried off from the front gate. If anyone hung around there again, Minnie declared, she would expel them from the camp. That at last stopped them.

While Luhai and I were talking, a commotion broke out beyond the sports ground, and a crowd assembled outside the sprawling porridge plant. What was going on? We went over to have a look.

As we walked, I heard a female voice yell, "Parade her!"

"Yeah, take her through the streets," a man cried.

"Tie a placard about her neck."

"Cut her hair too."

A ragged voice begged, "Sisters and brothers, please let me go! I won't do it again."

I recognized Sufen's voice and quickened my steps. Then I saw the poor woman, her face pinched, standing in the middle of the crowd, her eyes watery and her hair mussed. She hung her head low like a criminal, quaking a little. Now and again she lifted her hand to wipe her dripping nose. Luhai went up to them and asked, "What's going on?"

Tilting his pockmarked face, Boom Chen answered, "We finally caught a thief. This woman volunteered to do kitchen duty today, but she stole rice."

"The evidence is there." A fiftyish man pointed at a green mug on a stool, filled with the unpolished grain.

"No wonder our porridge has been so watery," a woman said.

"We mustn't let her get away with this!" rasped a sharp female voice.

"Denounce her publicly now, then parade her," a small woman added, wielding her fist.

"Please, sisters and brothers!" Sufen wailed. "Don't hurt me. I never did this before. My son's in jail. He's starving and begged me to bring him some grub. I have no money and no clue where to get it."

"Liar!"

"We all know no matter how hungry we are, we must never stoop to theft," a stout woman said.

"She must've stolen other stuff too."

"Don't just wag your tongues and waste your breath. Let's haul her to the front yard."

"Whoa, hold on," Boom Chen broke in. "We shouldn't take this matter into our own hands. Why not send her to the camp's leaders?"

"No, we must teach her a lesson," another female voice insisted. "We must stop the leak in the kitchen or our meals will get thinner and thinner."

As I was about to intervene, though uncertain if I could save Sufen from their hands, Minnie appeared suddenly and said loudly, "Stop acting like a mob. You ought to be ashamed of yourselves."

At once the crowd quieted down. Minnie continued, "This poor woman, Sufen Yan, has a fifteen-year-old son in the Model Prison. That's a fact I know. He has begged her time and again for food. She told me that, but we have no extra rations to spare and can't help him. Some of you here are mothers. Can you eat your two meals a day in peace while your children are starving?"

"No, I cannot," I said.

Nobody else answered, and some dropped their eyes. Minnie went on, "Sufen, tell me, did you take the rice?"

"I did, Principal Vautrin. I am sorry."

Minnie turned to the crowd. "She was wrong to steal from the kitchen, but you all should use your brains to think about the thin porridge. Could it be possible for her alone, with that little mug, to make so many cauldrons watery? There must be a big thief somewhere in the kitchen. We mustn't blame it on this poor mother who just filched a morsel for her hungry child."

Sufen started sobbing wretchedly, and people looked at one another as if to see who among them was a big-time thief. I glanced at Boom Chen, who smirked at no one in particular.

"Sufen," Minnie continued, "I'll let you have that mug of rice this time, but you must promise never to steal again."

"Principal Vautrin, if I do it again, let a hundred thunderbolts strike me dead!"

"Hee hee hee hee!" somebody tittered. Then the whole crowd erupted into laughter.

A few women went up to Minnie, saying she was absolutely right—there must be a big rat in the porridge plant.

After the crowd had dispersed, Luhai suggested to us that Sufen stop doing kitchen duty in case someone might use her to muddle the investigation. Minnie agreed and decided to send her to the feces-collecting team if she still wanted to do volunteer work.

21

IN RECENT MONTHS the local Red Swastika Society, "the Society of Dao and Virtue," had been active in relief work. A Chinese private charity organization formed in the early 1920s and grounded in Daoism and Buddhism, it now had millions of members all over the world. The society's philanthropic efforts had reached the Soviet Union and Japan (after earthquakes), and it had offices in Tokyo, London, and Paris. It urged its members to learn Esperanto. Lately its Nanjing branch had become a main workforce coordinated by the International Relief Committee, which had been established to replace the Safety Zone Committee in mid-March. The local Red Swastika had admitted hundreds of new members and was occupied with burial work. Every member of the society wore a large swastika at the center of his chest when doing his job. The emblem was a Buddhist symbol, the arms of its cross bent left instead of right, and it had nothing to do with the Nazis, but some Japanese soldiers seemed to associate it with Germany and treated these Chinese workers with a little courtesy. To endure the overpowering stench of decaying bodies, many of the men drank cheap liquor before they set about their detail, usually four or five as a team. If possible, they would burn a sheaf of sacrificial paper, donated by some temples, for the dead, especially for the old. In most cases the workers just covered the corpses with lime and a layer of earth in mass graves. According to its records, which Minnie and I had seen on our visit to the main office, from the middle of January to the end of March, the Red Swastika had buried 32,104 bodies, at least a third of them civilians. The men of the Advance Benevolence Society (Chong Shan Tang) had also been interring the dead. Up to early April, they had buried more than 60,000 corpses in the city and its outskirts, about twenty percent of whom were women and children. Some other organizations were also engaged in the burial work. Every week new mass graves were dug as the existent ones filled up. Yet by far the largest burial ground was the Yangtze, into which the Japanese had dumped tens of thousands of bodies.

Several times Minnie had asked the Red Swastika men to bury the dead at the pond west of our campus, but they said they were too busy picking up corpses in the city and at the major execution sites to worry about those scattered in the suburbs. Two weeks ago they'd been given permission to inter twenty thousand bodies in Hsia Gwan, and that job alone would take them more than a month, since they could bury at most seven hundred a day, bringing the corpses together and laying them away in mass graves. So not until late April did a group of workers go to the pond in the valley, collect the dead, fish some bodies out of the water, and clear that area.

At Jinling some of the young women refugees were also busy burying, not human remains but human feces—they'd been gathering all the excrement, putting it in ditches and pits, and covering it with lime. I could detect the decrease of the foul odor in the air, and the camp felt cleaner every day. I was very pleased about their work. One bright morning toward the end of April, when I ran into the leader of the feces-collecting team, a tall twentyish woman with a pair of long braids, I told her, "Take it easy. As long as you girls can bury everything in two weeks, it will be fine."

"We want our campus to be clean and beautiful," she replied in a clear voice.

I appreciated the possessive adjective she used—"our"—and said to her, "At the end of the day, all the girls on your team can take a shower."

"That's great. Thank you, Mrs. Gao." Her eyes gleamed.

We had just put up a shower house for the refugees, who hadn't washed for months. It was Minnie who had insisted on installing these facilities despite some opposition among the staffers. The women and girls here loved the shack, in which there were twenty-six spray nozzles along the walls. Some of them were amazed that they could adjust the temperature of the water by themselves. Yet due to the large number of refugees, one could use the facility only once every other week.

A FEW NIGHTS LATER Boom Chen, the headman of the porridge plant, was killed by bandits. His extravagant lifestyle must have convinced them that he'd stolen a large amount of the refugees' rations, so they demanded that he share his goods with them. He denied that he had appropriated any rice and offered to help them steal our car instead. But when they snuck onto campus at night and got into the rattletrap, they couldn't start the thing however hard they tried. They smashed the windshield and called Boom Chen names, saying he'd pay for this. They broke into his home and searched around for rice, but didn't find any. They tied him to a chair and grilled him. He confessed he'd just sold his cache and remitted the money to his parents in Tianjin City. He promised to get two thousand pounds of rice for the bandits in the near future, but they ran out of patience and one of them plunged a knife into his chest.

That was what his wife had told us. The woman was somewhat silly and let the whole thing slip.

The camp had just received some wheat and barley, so the rice porridge, mixed with beans and the other grains, was finally thick enough for a pair of chopsticks to stand in a bowl of it, which was the conventional standard of quality porridge. Nobody griped about the meals anymore. Luhai swore up and down that it was the hand of Providence that had helped us get rid of the big rat, but for Minnie the denouement had come too late. She also said that the penalty was way too severe, because she didn't believe in capital punishment.

In mid-May the Autonomous City Government ordered that all the refugee camps close down by the end of the month. At the same time, the Japanese embassy invited the foreigners working in the camps to dinner. At first Minnie was reluctant to go, but on second thought, she felt it might be an opportunity to exchange views with the officials and earn their sympathy. She brought a copy of the petition to the dinner in hopes of presenting it to the top diplomat there.

Consul-General Okazaki didn't show up at the banquet, which was hosted by Tanaka and Fukuda and attended by John Allison and some American missionaries, including Minnie and Holly. Tanaka spoke about the necessity of shutting down the camps and praised the foreigners for what they'd been doing for the refugees. Minnie presented the petition to the vice-consul, who riffled through the paperwork and agreed to look into the matter. His promise was welcomed by a round of loud applause from the guests. All the camp workers among them agreed to close down the refugee camps. Minnie was grateful for her colleagues' support, which could be viewed as a favor in return for Tanaka's promise.

Three days later we heard from Tanaka. He said that Sufen's son and four of the eight men identified by the women would be released from jail within a week, but the other four men, according to the prison's files, were associated with the Chinese army and had to remain in prison. Minnie countered, "Look, our information shows that those men are completely innocent."

"Miss Vautrin," Tanaka said, "I've done my best. The prison agreed to let your women come and see whether their husbands and sons are there. I believe that more of them will be liberated."

Minnie didn't press him further and instead fixed a time for the women to visit the prison. Hanging up, she looked elated. I was delighted too. We hugged for half a minute.

After five months' struggle, at last there was some progress. We hoped this might lead to the release of hundreds of men and boys. Minnie looked into Big Liu's office to tell him the good news, but he was not there. Together we went out and strolled around campus for a while.

When we returned half an hour later, we found Big Liu smoking in the hallway. He told us, "Someone from the Quaker Mission came and said there was a mad girl in their hospital. He said she was from our college."

"What's her name?" asked Minnie.

"No idea."

"What should we do?" she asked me.

"Maybe we should go have a look," I said.

"All right, let's go."

The two of us hailed a rickshaw and set out for the small hospital in the south, outside the former Safety Zone, which had been terminated a fortnight before. As we rode along Paolou Lane, four Chinese planes suddenly appeared, flying east to bomb the airfield near Jurong. Immediately antiaircraft guns started shooting at them, drawing blazing arcs. The Japanese flak artillery was weaker than our army's, though their planes were much more effective at intercepting Chinese bombers. This was the third time our planes had flown over Nanjing since last December. Some people watched them glide away with beaming faces, but no one made any celebratory sounds.

"Hope they'll destroy some Japanese aircraft," I said.

"I only hope they'll return to base safely after their mission," responded Minnie.

Our air force, small though it was, must have been emboldened by the recent success in the Xuzhou area, where our army had thwarted the Imperial Army's offensive and forced it to retreat. Newspapers in Nanjing had reported the regional defeat as "a regrouping" of the troops, but we had learned the facts from the radio—the Chinese army had sent sixty-four divisions into battle, too large a force for the Japanese to fight.

The Quaker Mission's hospital was in an abandoned school building, which looked boxy but neat, giving an impression of being half deserted. On arrival, we were taken to the second floor. The deranged woman, wearing a flannel shirt and a black silk skirt, was kept in a small room with a south-facing window. She was skinny and in her early twenties, with bedraggled hair, a wide forehead, and a thin-lipped mouth. At the sight of us, she rolled her elongated eyes and chanted, "Here come the American spies."

"What's her name?" Minnie whispered to a nurse.

"She told us different names—sometimes she's Aiyu Tan and sometimes she's Manyu Fu. Last week she said she was from Manchuria, but this week she claims to be a local girl."

"Then how could you believe she was from our school?" I asked.

"She often mentions Principal Vautrin."

"What did she say about me?" asked Minnie.

"You don't want to hear it." The nurse shook her graying head.

"She looks familiar, though," I said.

"She does," Minnie agreed. "I think I've met her. She might have been one of the twelve girls taken by the soldiers last December."

"Yes, I remember her," I said. "But I don't think she was one of the six who came back. She must be from this area—her accent shows. Miss Lou introduced her to me, and I saw her making origami creatures. She was good at it. Her name is something like Yulan."

At that, the madwoman stopped mumbling, then snickered and touched her small chin with her fingertips. She cried out, "I'm not Yulan. Yulan's dead, sold by the American missionaries and murdered by the officers."

"What officers are you talking about?" I asked.

"Japanese colonels."

The madwoman went on muttering something unintelligible. What should we do? Should we bring her back to Jinling? Minnie and I stepped aside and talked it over. We decided to wait and contact Miss Lou; we should identify the demented woman first and then see what to do. Nowadays there were so many unhinged people that you couldn't possibly take care of every one of them.

We told the nurse to keep a good watch on Yulan and that we would return to see her soon.

MISS LOU CAME the next evening and confirmed that Yulan was from a local neighborhood. Her father, a widower, had been an electrician and had joined the group assembled by John Rabe five months ago to restore the city's power service; later, when the job was done, the Japanese shot the man together with forty-two others. A few days before the arrival of the Japanese, at a neighbor's suggestion, Yulan's father had sent her to our camp and even dropped off a bag of rice—fifty pounds—and a jar of fish paste as rations for the girl. Miss Lou was certain that Yulan had been taken on December 24 last year, among the twenty-one "prostitutes." The young woman had been helping a refugee family wad a quilt with used cotton in the Arts Building when the soldiers burst in and grabbed her.

Astonished, we regretted not having brought the madwoman back. The following afternoon Minnie and I went to the Quaker Mission's hospital again, but to our dismay, Yulan was no longer there. The medical personnel said she'd snuck out but left word with a patient that she was going to see her cousins in Wuhu. That didn't make much sense, because that city was already occupied by the Japanese and her relatives might no longer be there.

"Please notify us if she surfaces again. She's from our school," Minnie said to the gray-haired nurse.

"We'll do that, Principal Vautrin."

"By the way, she called me names, right?"

"Yes."

"What did she say? Tell me. I won't mind."

"She said you'd sold her to the Japanese for two hundred yuan. Don't take it to heart. We all know that was drivel."

Minnie's face stiffened and she didn't utter another word. I said to the nurse, "Let us know if you hear anything about her."

Without further delay we left the hospital. Minnie kept quiet the whole way as if lost in thought.

DURING THE FOLLOWING DAYS we were occupied with disbanding the camp and persuading the refugees to go home. Many women, especially those with small children, had left. On the other hand, owing to the disappearance of the other camps, some young girls came to our college begging to be admitted. We accepted them temporarily, so there were still more than one thousand refugees on campus. Many of those women expected their menfolk to return and so didn't leave, and some went to the Model Prison every morning to plead with the officer in charge.

One afternoon in late May, Mr. Tanaka came in person and told us that some thirty men and boys would be released from the prison. We were dubious because the four men and the boy he had promised would be released before were still in jail.

"How can I believe you?" Minnie asked him. "The women are frustrated and angry. The boy's mother comes to my office every day to see why he's still there. I'm afraid some of the women might call me a liar behind my back."

"Why should I lie to you?" Tanaka said, his dyspeptic face puckering. "This time the prison will let them out. It's final, period."

He sounded so sincere that we were convinced. Minnie thanked him, bowing a little. He added in a toneless voice that he wished there were more civilians qualified for release.

We shared the good news with Big Liu, Holly, Rulian, and Miss Lou, and everybody was thrilled, although we didn't spread the word further right away, not wanting to get the women's hopes up again and because we had no list of the names. Minnie reminded us that we shouldn't celebrate too soon. I exhaled a sigh of relief, saying, "Thirty lives saved is worth any effort. Minnie, you were right about the petition from the outset."

My tone of voice was so earnest that it cracked everybody up. Big Liu said, "Anling, you owe me a good dinner."

"I'll keep that in mind," I replied.

That night I mentioned Tanaka's visit to Yaoping. My husband knew the vice-consul personally and said the man was reliable and would make good on his promise. In fact, we'd all heard that last December Tanaka was almost attacked by some Japanese soldiers who threatened to burn their embassy, because Tanaka had reported their brutalities to Tokyo.

22

IT WAS ALREADY beastly hot by the end of May, the air muggy and stagnant. The sun beat down on everything relentlessly, fueling the internal fire in every creature. Sometimes I saw the soldiers on the streets sweating so much that their uniforms were dappled with wet patches. Some of them, heat-raddled, would unconsciously scratch their throats as they walked, as if they were having difficulty breathing. I hoped it would get hotter and hotter so the semitropical heat Nanjing was famous for might drive them away. The Japanese didn't know what they had bargained for and would have to live in this "furnace" for many years before they could acclimate themselves. I bet a lot of them would have heatstroke and sweat rash this summer. Surely the heat would get rid of some of them just as it had killed thousands of Mongols centuries before.

The hot weather, however, made the children in our camp comfortable, especially small boys who scampered around barefoot—some didn't have even a stitch on, not in the least bothered by the mosquitoes that were becoming ubiquitous. As Minnie and I were standing outside the Faculty House, a clamor went up on the side of the pond behind the Central Building. A naked boy, six or seven, had been caught by a group of women who were attempting to force him into a new pair of pants. "I won't, I won't!" he hollered, kicking and struggling to break loose. Around them, people were laughing, some whooping and clapping their hands. His mother yelled at him, "Don't you feel ashamed? You're too big to run around like a wild animal! If your dad were here, he'd spank the pee out of you." But the boy kept bawling and resisting and finally managed to get away, still buck naked.

"Goodness, that boy has lots of lung power," a woman said.

"He should join a church choir," another told his mother.

Minnie had just presented nine pairs of children's shoes to some mothers who were about to leave the camp. They'd definitely have a hard time breaking their kids of going around barefoot. Or perhaps they shouldn't trouble themselves about that at all. When the cold weather set in, the children would automatically wear shoes. I didn't mind seeing the boys barefoot, but I thought they ought to wear something to cover up their weenies. I said to Minnie, "There should be a law forbidding anyone older than six to go naked in public."

Rulian, smiling and clucking her tongue, came and joined us, followed by a puff of midges that began circling around our heads. We talked about the men and boys promised to be released. Would Tanaka have lied to us? Minnie was certain that he'd been in earnest; otherwise he wouldn't have come in person to deliver the news. We also discussed how to help those refugees who had no home anymore, and those who did but couldn't support themselves and their children. Our college had received some small funds recently, and Minnie had been giving them away to a few women who didn't have any means of livelihood. She gave each person five or six yuan with which they might start a small business, like a little laundry, or a tea stand, or a stall selling fans, soaps, incense, pencils, and candles.

There was so much to talk about that we decided to go to the main office and resume conferring there. Seated at the president's desk and on straight-back chairs, we began reviewing the cases of the women and girls in need of support. A few days earlier, Minnie had proposed to the International Relief Committee the plan for a summer school for one hundred "students," a kind of professional training program, which would be called the Homecraft School, the same as the one we used to run for the local peasant girls whose parents were too poor to give them a formal education. Minnie had kept the proposal on a small scale because she didn't want the campus to continue resembling a refugee camp, but now evidently there were many more who had nowhere to go and therefore our plan had to be expanded to include them. After considering some cases, we figured that there'd be more than two hundred refugees remaining here. For them, some educational program would have to be formed to justify their presence at Jinling.

In addition, Minnie had agreed to take in eighty young women from the Dafang camp, which was shutting down. All together there would be about three hundred refugees on campus, though they'd be called "students."

"Well," Minnie said, "it looks like we'll have to reinstate our Homecraft School, in combination with a kind of folk school."

Rulian and I agreed, because we also wanted to help the refugee women achieve literacy. By "folk school," Minnie had in mind something like the public education programs popular in northern Europe, which she had visited in the summer of 1931. She'd been impressed by the folk schools in Denmark, Sweden, and Norway, where people would attend the adult classes a few months a year, studying sciences, literature, arts, and practical skills without the burden of earning grades or taking exams. In those small countries people went to that type of school just to improve themselves and enrich their lives. Since that trip, Minnie had often talked about how to adopt that model in our country, where only fifteen percent of the populace could read. Ironically, now we had an opportunity.

The next day the camp was closing, and most of the women and girls were leaving. Some slung their bedrolls over their backs, and some carried their belongings with shoulder poles. I admired the husky ones among them, who would become good farmhands back in their villages. Many of them came to thank us for their six months' stay at Jinling, which was an experience they cherished. Around ten a.m., a large crowd assembled before the Central Building to say good-bye to Minnie. She hurried out to meet them.

At the sight of her, the four hundred women and girls sitting on the ground in a semicircle rose to their knees. Rulian stood up and shouted in a strong voice, "The first knock!"

The crowd kowtowed, their heads touching the ground.

"The second knock!" Rulian cried out again, and the crowd repeated the same act. Unlike them, Rulian, our Lady Fowler, was on faculty, but she acted as if she too were leaving.

"Get up, get up, please!" Minnie shouted, standing in the middle of the semicircle and gesticulating, her palms upward and her fingers wiggling, but nobody listened to her. Holly stepped aside and joined me. I was watching with my hands crossed on my abdomen, wondering how in the world Rulian had become their leader.

"The third knock," she chanted, and the crowd kowtowed again.

"Rulian, tell them to get up!" Minnie pleaded.

By now the crowd had begun crying in mixed voices, "Good-bye, the Goddess of Mercy!"

"Long live our savior, Principal Vautrin!" a voice called out.

The crowd repeated in unison, some swaying their heads from side to side.

"Long live our Goddess of Mercy!" the same voice went on.

All of them shouted together again.

Dumbfounded, Minnie didn't know what to do. I saw Luhai standing in the back of the crowd and smiling, a cigarette tucked behind his ear. He seemed to be relishing this sight.

Minnie took a deep breath and addressed the crowd loudly: "All right, get to your feet now. I have something to say."

They began picking themselves up, some rubbing their knees and some lifting their bedrolls. "Although you are leaving today," Minnie began, "you have all stayed here for several months and have become part of the Jinling family. Remember our motto: 'Abundant Life.' From now on, wherever you go and whatever you do, you must carry on the Jinling spirit to cherish and nurture life and to help the needy and the underprivileged. You must also remember that you are Chinese and the fate of your country rests on the shoulders of every one of you. As long as you do not despair, as long as you all do your share to serve China, this country will survive all misfortunes and will grow strong again.

"When you have an opportunity, do come back to see us. The gate of Jinling will always be open to you." She had to stop because a rush of emotion choked her.

I stepped forward and cried to them, "Now, you all go home to be loving mothers, devoted wives, and filial daughters. Good-bye, everyone, God bless you all."

As the crowd was dissolving, Minnie grabbed hold of Rulian, whose face was filmed with perspiration. "Why did you let them do that?" Minnie asked her.

"They made me lead them—they wanted to express their grati-tude. What else could I do?"

Holly and I went up to them. "Minnie, it's over," Holly said. "You handled it perfectly."

"They made me uncomfortable, as though they turned me into an idol."

"Come now," I spoke up, "we all know they love and respect you."

"But they should show that kind of love and respect only to God," Minnie said thoughtfully.

"God's spirit is embodied in humans," I continued sincerely.

Holly giggled and slapped Minnie on the shoulder, saying, "Our Goddess of Mercy, what a wonderful title. I wouldn't mind if they dubbed me that. I'd do my darnedest to live up to it."

Minnie reached out and gave Holly's ear a tweak. "Ouch!" Holly let out.

"I hate to see them confuse humanity with divinity," Minnie said. "It's not right to be called a goddess while I'm doing mission work."

The previous week Miss Lou had told us that a woman of eighty-seven in the neighborhood, blind as a bat, would at night sit in the lotus pose and pray to Minnie's photograph, wishing the American principal a hundred years of life so that she could help and protect more poor women and girls. Many Chinese cannot think of divinity divorced from humanity. Indeed, for them anyone could grow good and better and eventually into a god or goddess.

23

THE NEWS that thirty-four men and boys had been released from the Model Prison was carried by two papers run by the Autonomous City Government, which hoped to show the Chinese that it was making every effort to protect the citizens. Most of the reunited families were about to head back for the countryside, where their homes used to be. We thought about throwing a tea party for them, but then the anxious faces of those women, more than six hundred of them, whose menfolk remained unaccounted for, got the best of us.

The next morning Sufen and her son came to say good-bye. The scrawny boy, short for fifteen, had a man's face, which was sallow and scabbed in places, a little knot of wrinkles on his forehead. He just repeated what his mother told him to say—"Thank you, Principal Vautrin, for saving me." He seemed still in shock, unable to speak a full sentence on his own. His eyes were dull and kept blinking as if he couldn't see clearly. Even when others around him smiled or laughed, his face showed no response. He wore a white collarless shirt that had short sleeves and several holes, and long mud-colored shorts, which displayed his calves, thin like broomsticks. Seeing his big toes peeking out of his tattered canvas sneakers, Minnie gave him a pair of new cloth shoes that looked like they would fit his feet. He took them with both hands and, on his mother's instructions, mumbled, "Thank you very much." I felt sad for him, knowing it would take a long time for him to recuperate. Mother and son were going back to their home village near Danyang, though Sufen wasn't sure if their house was still there.

By early June all the refugee camps had been closed, and some foreigners were leaving. John Magee was returning to the United States by way of Shanghai after twenty-eight years of service in China. His Nanjing International Red Cross Committee had been dissolved months earlier, and most of its members were gone. The reverend was anxious to leave because the Japanese military hated him, particularly for the hospital he had managed—a number of foreign reporters had visited it and published photos of victims of the war atrocities in newspapers in the West. What the authorities didn't know was that Magee owned a 16mm movie camera and had shot some footage of the Japanese atrocities last December. The eight reels of films had been sewn into an overcoat by us and smuggled out of Nanjing by his fellow missionary George Fitch in late February, when he left for the States. Magee would have been detained, even killed, if the Japanese military had known about the films. In early June he left with Mr. Tanaka in the same railroad car, so no police bothered him.

HOLLY TOO WAS LEAVING. She came to say good-bye. I had never suspected that we'd part company so soon. My husband was napping in the inner room while Liya was out with Fanfan. When we sat down, Holly said, "I'll leave early next week."

"Why?" I asked in surprise, sipping chrysanthemum tea. "What makes you want to go? Did someone mistreat you?"

"The camp is shut down and I'm no longer needed here."

"Nonsense, you can teach for us in the fall. We don't have a music teacher yet, and I'm sure you're the most qualified person. When the college reopens, they'll let you continue teaching here."

"I don't want to make trouble for Minnie—the ex-president will be mad at her if she finds me here."

"Even though Mrs. Dennison doesn't like you, she's smart enough to see that you're useful, indispensable, to Jinling. She won't let her personal feelings interfere with the college's business. She'll do anything to make this school stronger. Does Minnie know you're leaving?"

"I told her last night, and we argued a bit."

"About what?"

"About how to live in China. Minnie takes Nanjing as her hometown now and can hardly imagine living elsewhere. She loves this city and this college. But for me home can be anyplace and I don't need a hometown. To be honest, I no longer hate the soldiers who burned my house. I'm leaving for Hankou in four days."

"You're crazy! Isn't a battle about to break out there?"

"That's why I'm going." She tilted her head, which glistened with luxuriant ginger hair, and smiled with her mouth widened. Her eyes were shiny and bold.

"You don't like Nanjing anymore?" I asked.

"After I lost my house, I realized that my life was entwined with the Chinese, whether I like it or not. This is my adopted country and I'll serve where I'm needed most."

"I admire your large heart, Holly."

"The admiration is mutual."

"Write to me when you have time." I wanted to say more, but an upsurge of emotion overcame me.

"I will," she said.

Liya came back with my grandson in her arms, panting a little. I took Fanfan and put him on my lap. He was still sleeping, his lips parted. I told my daughter to cook noodles with leeks for Holly and me. The two of us started to chat again, over a bowl of mulberries.

THREE

All the Madness

24

IN EARLY AUGUST we finally got a letter from our son, Haowen. After reading it, my husband fell silent. His eyes fixed on the table, though his lids were jumping a little. He gave a long sigh.

"What is it, Yaoping?" I asked.

"You don't need to read this now." He folded the two sheets and put them back into the envelope.

"Let me see it," I said. Before he could hide the letter, I snatched it from his hand and began reading.

Haowen informed us that he was in the Japanese army now, garrisoned outside Suzhou, serving in a field hospital as an assistant doctor. He'd left the medical school half a year ago and married a girl in Tokyo. Then the army forced him to join up or his bride and in-laws would suffer, so he had come back to China a month ago.

He wrote:

I am miserable here but dare not complain. They told me that I would serve for only two years, but it looks like that, insofar as the war continues, they won't let me go home. I also feel ashamed of my current role. How could I work for China's enemy fighting my own people? But I love Mitsuko and cannot do anything that might endanger her and her family. In other words, I cannot afford to desert. Please forgive me for marrying her without your permission. I wrote you three times but never heard from you. I guess that the war must have disrupted the mail service in China and my letters went astray. Mitsuko is a good girl and absolutely loyal to me. I don't think I could marry a better woman who unites all the positive qualities I want to find in my wife. Someday you will meet her and see if I told you the truth. Do pray for me and for the war to end soon.

Haowen's letter devastated us. I flung myself on the bed and buried my face in a pillow, crying wretchedly. Grief came over me fit after fit. I'd always hated those Chinese who served in the Japanese army, but now my own son had become "a running dog," "a half Eastern devil." It was proper for him not to endanger his in-laws, but he had disgraced us and put us in potential danger. He must have been madly in love with that girl and not been able to think straight. Yet I mustn't blame him too much, since he couldn't possibly have foreseen that he would be forced into the service. Still, why did he have to marry her in a hurry? Something must have been wrong with him. I brooded on his life in Tokyo but couldn't make any sense of this. His marriage seemed to have doomed him.

Yaoping tried to comfort me, saying that our son must have been isolated and lonely in Japan, that maybe he had found a first-rate daughter-in-law for us, so it was too early to tell whether this was a good fortune or a misfortune. I wouldn't buy any of his conjectures and screamed at him, "Don't you see that our son is ruined? He might never become a normal man again."

That shut Yaoping up. I couldn't eat supper that evening and lay in bed, weeping and dozing alternately. If only I could figure out a way to bring Haowen home.

The next day at work Minnie noticed my grief-stricken face and asked me what was wrong. I had recently confided to her that my son was a medical student in Tokyo. Now, since there was no one else in the office, I told her about Haowen's plight. She was astounded and massaged her temples with both thumbs while murmuring, "This is terrible, Anling, terrible."

"If only I could do something."

"Are you sure you can work today? You should take a few days off."

"That would make me more heartsick—when I'm alone, I can't stop crying." I averted my hot eyes.

Calming down some, I asked her not to divulge my family's trouble to anyone. "If people know of this, I won't be able to work here anymore," I said, believing that the secret was a scandal that, if disclosed, might jeopardize my family.

"I'll keep my mouth sealed," she promised.

Minnie was the only person on campus to whom I could speak my heart, and she would also share her thoughts with me. Sometimes I could guess what she was thinking even before she let on.

IN SEPTEMBER we started another program in addition to the Homecraft School—a middle school for local girls. Despite the original plan for admitting no more than three hundred adult students, almost twice as many had enrolled in the homecraft program. The large number of poor women made the campus still seem like a refugee camp of sorts, and we depended on donations to keep them here. Among the 143 students in the middle school, only a third could afford the full fees: forty-six yuan a semester—twenty for tuition, twenty for board and lodging, and six for miscellaneous expenses. The rest of the girls were on partial or full scholarships provided through work-study arrangements.

A recent Jinling graduate named Shanna Yin had returned to the college. She was capable and had taken many classes in Jinling's former Homecraft School, so Minnie put her in charge of that program. Donna Thayer, a young biology teacher who had come back, was now the dean of the middle school, but she didn't know Chinese and Minnie had to help her with some of the administrative work. Minnie had also hired Alice Thompson, an English teacher, together with a dozen or so Chinese faculty, who were part-timers. Alice had taught at girls' schools in China and also in Japan for a year, and belonged to our denomination, the Disciples of Christ. Shanna and Donna worked well together and had created a routine so the schools could run more or less on their own.

As for the lodging and board on campus, I was in charge of them. I had four kitchens built in the expanse between the Faculty House and the northwest dormitory, and these cookhouses were run by the students in the Homecraft School, some of whom had been learning how to cook professionally. The women students also took courses in tailoring, weaving, shopkeeping, fabric dyeing, and child guidance. Above all, we urged the illiterate ones among them to attend the literacy class.

One afternoon in mid-September, Miss Lou came and told us, "Yulan, the mad girl, is in town again."

"Where is she?" Minnie asked in surprise.

"In Tianhua Orphanage."

"Can we go see her?"

"Of course, that's why I came to tell you."

The orphanage was just beyond the southern border of the former Safety Zone, less than a mile away, so we set out on foot. The city seemed to be bustling with life again, though many houses still lay in ruins, grass growing on the crumbling walls and shards of terra-cotta tiles everywhere. We saw some Japanese civilians and even a couple of Koreans, but there were fewer troops than a month ago because many of them had left for the front. The previous day martial law had been declared to prevent any unofficial rallies on September 18, the seventh anniversary of the Mukden Incident, which had started the Japanese occupation of Manchuria. A balloon, which held a man and a radio set, was hovering in the air to monitor troop movements in the surrounding areas, mainly those of the guerrillas. Rumors were that our army was coming back to retake Nanjing (Chinese soldiers were said to have been spotted inside the city walls), and a lot of people believed that this was about to happen, so most of the Japanese flags disappeared from the houses and buildings that used to fly them. There was even talk of attacking the Japanese embassy and nabbing those puppet officials when the Nationalist troops marched in. Yet whenever the Chinese raised this topic, most foreigners would disabuse them of such hopes, saying that only the guerrillas posed a minor threat to the Japanese here. Unlike the other Americans, Minnie would keep mum about this and let the locals indulge in the fantasy.

We turned onto Hanzhong Road and headed east. At the doors of some restaurants stood girls and young women in blue dresses and gingham aprons, with little flowers in their hair, smiling at potential customers who passed by. This was something new. Were they not afraid of the soldiers? Why did their menfolk let them run such a risk? People had to do anything to survive, I guessed.

When we arrived at the orphanage, Monica Buckley, the American nun in charge of the place, received us. She looked exhausted, her cheeks hollow but her hazel eyes vivid and bright. I'd met her before and knew she was from Pennsylvania and part of the Episcopal mission here, formerly led by John Magee. When we asked about Yulan, Monica said there was indeed a madwoman in the back, but they were not sure of her name.

We went to the backyard, fenced but open to a street through a door fastened with a bolt and a lumpy padlock. There Yulan stood among a cluster of small boys, jabbering and puffing on a cigarette. At the sight of us she chanted, "Here come the missionary bastards."

A barefoot boy said to her, "Show us how a rooster cries."

The madwoman bunched her lips and stretched her thin neck. She let out, "Cock-a-doodle-do, cock-a-doodle-do!"

"That's nice," the same boy said.

Another one asked, "How about a duck?"

Yulan screwed up her mouth and shrieked, "Qua, qua, qua—ka ka ka ka!"

That cracked up all the boys. I noticed that one of Yulan's teeth was missing. Despite that, she was still somewhat attractive, with a heart-shaped face, long hair, clear skin, and a small waist.

"That sounds more like a goose, too loud and too slow," the tallest boy said. "Let's see how a pig does it."

The madwoman lifted her face to the sky and squealed, "Oink, oink, oink!"

"That's not how a piggy cries," said another boy.

Miss Lou shouted at them, "Stop it! Don't tease her anymore!"

Yulan turned to the little woman, flapping her long eyelashes. "Nice to see you, Aunt Lou. How're you doing?"

"Come with us, Yulan," I begged.

"No, you have a big-nosed spy with you. I'm not going with you and her." She pointed at Minnie.

"Yulan," Minnie said, "you know I'd never hurt you."

"Liar. All you foreign devils are liars."

That made Minnie tongue-tied. She and I stood by as Miss Lou tried to persuade the deranged woman. By now most of the boys had left; only two were still around, one holding a soccer ball under his arm and the other wearing a bamboo whistle around his neck. As Miss Lou patted Yulan's shoulder and murmured something to her, the madwoman burst into sobs, nodding continuously.

A few minutes later she left with us. She was quiet now, though her eyes still radiated a fierce light. Minnie told Monica that we were taking Yulan back to Jinling. The nun rubbed her hands together and said, "Oh, that's good. Something ought to be done for her, poor thing."

Minnie flagged down a two-seater rickshaw and let Miss Lou and Yulan take it, saying that we preferred to walk. She also told the little woman to leave Yulan with Shanna when they arrived at Jinling. The rickshaw rolled away and disappeared beyond a crossroads.

Minnie and I headed west. My left shoulder was sore again, and we both grew pensive. In my mind's eye arose the scene of willowy Yanying embracing the foreleg of the stone lion while a Japanese soldier punched her in the gut and her little sister, Yanping, bawled.

"If only we had acted bravely," Minnie said. "We might've saved some of the women."

I knew she was thinking of the same event, but I kept silent.

We began talking about how to help Yulan. I asked, "What should we do about her?"

"Any suggestions?" Minnie said.

"We'd better find out whether she still has some relatives here."

"She's an orphan now, Miss Lou told me. Jinling should at least shelter her and take care of her needs."

Minnie's tone of voice allowed no argument, so I didn't go further. For the time being this might be the only solution.

But I had my reservations because our hands were already full. The madwoman might stir up disturbances and frighten the students, so I kept wondering if there might be a better arrangement. Minnie seemed to have gone out of her way to accommodate Yulan, who was not our responsibility, strictly speaking. Everyone knew that the Japanese had deceived Minnie and would have seized those "prostitutes" one way or another. To care for the demented woman might be to ask for trouble.

Uneasy about those thoughts, I didn't let them out. We went to see

Shanna when we arrived back at the college. Minnie asked her to put Yulan in a homecraft class, stressing that the woman used to be a refugee at Jinling and ought to remain in our care. To our relief, Shanna gladly accepted Yulan as a student.

"You did me a huge favor," Minnie told the young dean.

"No big deal. I hope she's a quick learner." Shanna twisted the end of her glossy braid, in which she seemed to take great pride. She was quite a beauty, with silken skin, a sunny face, and a dancer's figure, though her eyes were spaced wide apart, which gave her a nonchalant look. Somehow I didn't like her that much. She seemed vain and capricious, wearing powder all the time, and could be a bad model for some girls and young women.

Yulan turned out to be good at weaving. She was also literate, knowing enough characters to read newspapers. If she were not insane, Minnie might have let her teach a literacy class. Among the thirty-nine students in the weaving course, she soon excelled as one of the best. She was especially skilled at making stockings and scarves. Once in a while she'd still lose it, yelling at others or wailing without cause, but people thought she was innocuous as long as she wasn't provoked. Some older women were even fond of her.

25

LOCAL AUTHORITIES, uprooted by the war, no longer existed in many areas. According to what refugees told us, guerrillas had caused a good deal of trouble in the country. Villagers were being ground on the millstone, pressed hard from the top and the bottom. If the guerrillas blew up a section of a road, the Japanese would come and order the villagers to repair it within a short period of time. Meanwhile, the guerrillas would warn them that if they did the work, some of them would be executed, so the only thing left for the villagers to do was to pull up stakes and leave, but many of them didn't have the supplies or funds for travel.

Most of the guerrillas were backed by the Communists, but some were also remnants of the Nationalist army. They plagued the Japanese occupiers incessantly, doing things like attacking their sentry posts at night and cutting the transport lines to Nanjing. They would also punish farmers who sold rice and other grains to the enemy. The Japanese would occasionally bribe the guerrillas so foodstuffs could be shipped into our city. Every now and then the local newspapers announced that twenty-five thousand yuan had just been paid to the guerrillas, who had agreed to keep all the roads open, so the citizens shouldn't worry about the supply of rice for months to come. Still, the price of rice kept rising, and I couldn't make up my mind whether to buy more for the two schools now or to wait for the price to drop.

Fuel was another problem. We had difficulty getting coal for the winter because only one hundred tons were allowed each dealer. Worse yet, the price was doubled now—forty yuan a ton for the soft and fifty for the hard. We decided to try to get forty tons from a mine near Wuhan for twenty yuan per ton, though we were unsure if the Japanese would let it enter the city. The good news was that the U.S. embassy approved of our plan and agreed to help us bring the coal in.

Minnie had hired another nurse, so I didn't have to do anything for the infirmary anymore. I was pleased, though I still had my hands full, supervising the servants and the cooks. Somehow I tended to be at odds with the younger women on the faculty. Many of them complained about my bossiness, and Shanna and Rulian even nicknamed me the Ancient One. Ban, the messenger boy, told me that.

I often complained to Minnie that the madwoman, in addition to the four blind girls, was too much of a burden to us. I suggested sending Yulan to the mental asylum funded by the puppet municipality. "The Japanese destroyed her mind," I said, "so their lackeys should take care of her." But Minnie wouldn't listen.

One afternoon Ban complained to me about the madwoman, and I took him to the president's office. I said to Minnie, "Yulan is making trouble again."

"What happened?" she asked.

"Tell her," I urged Ban.

The boy, two inches taller than he had been the previous winter but still slight like a rake, said in disgust, "That crazy bitch follows me wherever I go and calls me 'Little Jap.' "

Minnie looked bemused. "You shouldn't let this trouble you so much. She won't hurt you."

"She scares me."

"Now, come on, she's thin and small. How can she hurt you?"

"She calls him a Jap," I said, "because she has confused him with some soldier."

Ban continued, "She always shouts at me, 'Strike down Little Jap! Go back to your tiny home island.' "

"Try to avoid her," Minnie suggested.

"That won't help. She tells others I did lots of bad things to girls. She also calls me a brazen pimp."

I told Minnie, "Some people don't know her mind was damaged by the Japanese, so they take Ban for a hoodlum."

"She's ruining my reputation!" the boy wailed. "I can't figure out how I offended her. She threatens me at every turn."

"She sees enemies everywhere," I added.

"She bullies me," Ban sniveled.

"Yes, he's a convenient scapegoat for her," I said.

At last Minnie seemed to consider this seriously. She asked me, "What do you think we should do?"

"Send her to the mental home."

"If that place was decent, we might do that. But you know what the lunatic asylum is like. It's like a prison—it's being used as a jail. We can't just throw her into it. I'll never let that happen."

"But we cannot keep Yulan on campus forever. She gives us too much extra work and makes everybody tense."

"I will speak to Shanna about this."

"She's another loony."

"Come on, Anling, we can't just dump Yulan. You know that will go against the grain with me."

I exhaled a deep sigh, my cheeks hot. "You're incorrigible—hopelessly softhearted," I told her.

I took Ban away, feeling unhappy because Minnie would speak to Shanna before making any decision about Yulan, as though this were an academic matter. On the other hand, I admired Minnie for sticking to her principles.

To everyone's surprise, Shanna also felt uneasy about the madwoman's presence on campus now, saying that a lot of students had become unnerved by Yulan, that some were teasing her, inciting her to spew obscenities.

Minnie asked Miss Lou to take responsibility for the crazy girl. The evangelical worker had known Yulan's mother, who'd died of cirrhosis two years before. Miss Lou agreed to keep Yulan as a helper in relief work since she was dexterous and could sew and knit. As long as she was not provoked, she'd be a fine worker.

Our college gave food and clothes to the destitute in the neighborhood every season, and the donations would be distributed through Miss Lou, who knew which people were in desperate need, so there should be no problem about Yulan's keep. We felt relieved and also grateful to Miss Lou.

26

ONE MORNING in early October I found Luhai waiting in my office. He looked anxious but was well dressed as usual, wearing a checkered necktie and leather shoes. He took a folded sheet of paper out of his pants pocket and said to me, "I came across this yesterday evening."

I skimmed the article. It was a short piece printed on a flyer titled "White Devils, Go Home!" I'd seen similar, though less insulting, writings in recent newspapers—apparently some locals, maybe backed by different political factions, had been campaigning against the foreigners. I put the sheet on the desk and said to Luhai, "Thanks for sharing this."

"I'm afraid there might be secret moves against our friends," Luhai said, his high Adam's apple bobbing.

"Yes, we should let them know. I'll pass this on to Searle Bates." I knew that most Americans in town frequented the professor's house.

Luhai was also worried about how to come by coal for the winter. He had just gotten Minnie's permission to take down some trees in case the coal from Wuhan didn't arrive and we had to heat classrooms on the coldest days. The trees on the border of our college's grounds could be felled by thieves at any time.

Luhai left half an hour later. I liked him better than I had before. I used to think that he was a little callow, probably on account of his young age—twenty-six—but in the past months he seemed to have grown more mature and less talkative. Teachers and students thought well of him, especially the girls, some of whom even had a crush on him, despite his little limp and the fact that he was married and had two small children. Once in a while he spoke at the chapel and taught people hymns. He still talked about how he hated the Japanese. Who could fault him? He'd lost relatives outside Dalian City the previous fall. His cousin, a kung fu master, had defeated a Japanese officer at a sports meet and was celebrated as a local hero. But the next day a platoon of Japanese soldiers went to his home, caught him and his only child, tied them to a tree with iron wire, poured a can of kerosene on father and son, and set them aflame.

The article left by Luhai attacked the foreign men on the former Safety Zone Committee, claiming that they had conspired with the Japanese to oppress and persecute the Chinese, so the neutral zone had never been neutral. The author cited several examples of the Westerners' collaboration with the invaders, such as disarming the Chinese soldiers and then handing them over to the Imperial Army, attending its celebratory ceremonies and concerts, and teaching Japanese in Christian schools. The article claimed that some of these foreigners often visited the Japanese embassy and even feasted there while making evil plans against China, and that, more outrageously, they'd made a huge profit from selling food to the refugees despite the free rations they had obtained from the former municipality. It was a fact that a white face could serve as a pass and a guarantee of personal safety here. The article singled out Lewis Smythe as a key collaborator, claiming that he'd met with the Japanese officials as often as twice a day. It also highlighted an incident at the police academy when 450 cadets were "betrayed" by the white men. "Those young officers were well equipped with German-made rifles (not handguns), and even their uniforms, helmets, and brass-buckled belts were German in style," the author wrote. "We all knew how strong and well trained those men were. If they had put up a fight, they could at least have resisted the enemy to earn the precious time for the Chinese army to withdraw fully, or for more of them to break away. But the American missionaries lied to those men and said that the Japanese had granted them clemency, so they all laid down their weapons and capitulated. Later, we saw the Japanese take them through the streets. Most of them were stronger and better fight- ers than their captors, but they were disarmed and roped together, given the illusion of safety. All had their hands up in the air, and they were marched to the riverside and mowed down by machine guns so that the Japanese could dump them into the water without bothering to bury them. Fellow compatriots, who should be blamed for their stupid deaths and for our tragedy? The American missionaries, who are not our friends but a gang of double-crossers."

I wondered whether the Communists were behind this article, since they were also eager to see the Americans leave.

When I showed Minnie the flyer, she was not disturbed, having seen this type of attack before. That evening she called on Searle. I accompanied her because I wanted to thank him personally for saving my husband's life. Yaoping had been depressed ever since we received our son's letter, and I had urged him to go out and meet some people to ease his mind, so he'd begun frequenting Nanjing University and had even resumed teaching a course in Manchu history there. A week ago, as soon as his class was over, a group of Japanese soldiers arrived and grabbed hold of him, saying he could speak their language and must serve as a part-time interpreter. Obviously someone had ratted on him. As they were dragging him away, Searle appeared and blocked the door, insisting that Yaoping was on the faculty, so as the provisional head of the History Department, he could not release the lecturer to anyone. The leader of the group cursed Searle, but he wouldn't give in. Finally the Japanese became so angry that they pushed both Searle and Yaoping down the stairs. Seeing the two men lying on the landing, Searle groaning and Yaoping unconscious, they left without him. These days my husband stayed home, too frightened to go to the university again, though he promised he would resume teaching in a week or so.

When Minnie and I arrived at Searle's, we found both Lewis Smythe and Bob Wilson in the historian's spacious study, which was full of the fragrance of incense but topsy-turvy, books and framed photographs scattered around and the walls bare. The previous day the Japanese police had ransacked Searle's home because they suspected that he had contributed to a book just published in London about the war atrocities in Nanjing and other southern cities. Minnie had disclosed to me that Searle did write under a pseudonym a portion of *What War Means: The Japanese Terror in China*. The police found few of the documents and eyewitness statements they were seeking, because Searle had deposited the materials in the U.S. embassy.

"So they didn't take anything?" I asked him.

"They took some of my books and the calligraphy scrolls," he said with a grimace, his chin slightly cleft. "I should've sold them. They also confiscated my son's toy popgun. He'll be mad at me."

I knew he had owned some rare books, which must also be gone. He had filed a protest with the police headquarters, but it would be of no use.

He was still wearing a sling for a dislocated shoulder. I handed him a bag of pork buns and thanked him for rescuing my husband.

"This is great," he said. "Thank you for these buns, Anling, but there's no need to bring me these. Yaoping and I are friends and I ought to help."

He placed the bag on the coffee table strewn with soda bottles. As Lewis and Bob reached out for the buns, Searle said, "No, no, this is for me only. You just wiped out my pumpkin stew." He hugged the bag and then put it under the table. These grass widowers had sent their families away and ate irregularly nowadays, wherever they could find a meal. The three of them had aged quite a bit lately, and Bob, merely thirty-two, had lost nearly all his hair.

I sat down near a window while Minnie showed them the flyer, which they had heard about. But when he read it, Lewis looked quite shaken, became pale, and his eyes flickered, moist. He frowned and said, "I knew something like this might happen, but I didn't expect to be labeled as a major collaborator. I went to the Japanese embassy every day to file protests. It's true I walked with Tanaka on the streets from time to time, but that was just to show him what the soldiers had done."

He covered his face with one hand and fought to maintain his composure. "This hurts, really hurts. It gets me right here," he moaned, and his left hand touched his heart.

Silence fell in the study. Minnie went into the bathroom, brought back a clean hand towel, and gave it to him. "I know this is awful, Lewis," she said. "But don't let this rattle you. That's what they're hoping for."

"Yes, we must take heart, Lewis," Searle said. "We've done nothing we should feel ashamed of and can hold our heads high."

"Thanks, thanks, I'll be okay," Lewis mumbled, and wiped his face with the towel.

A moment later Bob said, "I saw this sort of propaganda crap in Shanghai too, in the newspapers."

"Do you think the Communists have something to do with this article?" Minnie asked.

"The puppet municipality is more likely behind it," Searle said.

"But only the Reds dare to condemn the Japanese and the Americans like this author," Bob went on.

Minnie agreed. "This does sound like Communist propaganda."

"I'm not that sure," Searle said. "There's no way we can identify the author or authors—anyone can use a pseudonym."

Lewis told us that the Autonomous City Government had been trying to break up the International Relief Committee, because the IRC had too much local power, organizing more than fourteen hundred members to do charity work. The puppet officials didn't want to take over the task of helping the needy, but they were eager to get hold of the resources that the IRC had inherited from the former Safety Zone Committee. Some of the puppet officials had been reaping huge profits from one kind of monopoly or another. For example, those in charge of the city's housing had seized vacant homes and other buildings and had rented them out. For every thousand yuan they collected, the Japanese allowed them to keep four hundred, so the officials had grown unscrupulous in possessing properties. Similar monopolies occurred in other trades as well, such as foodstuffs, medicines, alcohol, and fuel.

The four Americans fell to talking about the brand-new cars that were appearing in the city these days, mostly German-made Fords, Mercedes-Benzes, and Buicks. All of a sudden Nanjing seemed full of officials, who all had chauffeurs and servants. To me, those bigwigs looked more like opium addicts and ne'er-do-wells from wealthy families. Minnie said, "I don't understand why so many Chinese are willing to serve their national enemy."

"The rich must find a way to protect their wealth," Lewis explained, "so their sons must control the government."

"That must be true," Bob agreed. "The other day I ran into one of those sons in the city hall. His dad presented a fighter-bomber to Chiang Kai-shek on his birthday two years ago."

"To be fair," Searle said, "some of the officials in the puppet municipality are not necessarily bad. They may have been disillusioned by the Nationalist regime. I know a man in charge of cultural affairs. He graduated from Rikkyo University, a very fine man who knows Greek and Latin and writes beautiful essays. He doesn't like his current role, but he has to survive."

"That's true," Bob said, waving his large hand. "If I had eight mouths to feed, I'd work for whoever paid me. The belly cries louder than principles."

We all laughed.

Before we left, Searle told his fellow Americans to take precautions and avoid mixing too much with the puppet officials lest the Japanese attack them through the hands of their Chinese stooges and then blame it on the Communists. As Americans, they needed to appear neutral. Searle gave Bob and Lewis each three of the pork buns I'd brought him. He then offered to accompany Minnie and me back to Jinling, but we wouldn't let him, saying it wasn't nine o'clock yet and it was all right to walk back by ourselves. Besides, Minnie had a long flashlight.

We said good night to them and stepped out onto the dark street littered with sycamore leaves. Two pairs of searchlights like four giant rapiers went on stabbing into the depths of the moonlit sky, although no Chinese planes had come for more than a month. I wondered why the Japanese seemed fearful and on the defensive—perhaps because there were not enough troops to defend Nanjing at this time. As we walked along, Minnie talked about the situation in Europe, where she felt a holocaust had just been averted by the Munich Conference. She said, "I'm so glad that a lot of young men's lives have been spared and many cities and towns have escaped destruction."

"Everyone hates war, I guess," I said.

"Even politicians?" she asked.

"Sure, few people are really hungry for blood."

"How about the Japanese?"

"I'm still thinking whether I can take them as human beings."

"Come on, Anling. You shouldn't let hatred rule your life."

Along Hankou Road not a single house had a light on. It seemed as if no one were living here, though from time to time a child's cry would rise from somewhere. This small street used to be a sort of promenade for lovers, especially for university students in this area. Young couples would come here at night, strolling hand in hand or arm in arm or nestling with each other on the benches under the parasol trees. Sometimes they'd sing love songs in low voices. Now, most of the benches were gone, and we did not encounter a single soul here. I couldn't help wondering if this place would ever be the same again. That seemed unlikely. Most things can't stop changing once they have been changed.

As we were approaching Ninghai Road, two Japanese soldiers appeared, cackling with gusto. One was squat and the other skinny. They wobbled up to us and blocked our way. "Girls, purty girls," the scrawny one shouted in Mandarin.

Minnie shone her flashlight on them. Neither carried a gun, but each wore a three-foot-long saber on his waist. The squat one shoved Minnie in the chest and snatched the flashlight from her while the other man stepped closer and put his hand on my shoulder. As the bar of light was scraping our faces, I began trembling, too petrified to say a word. They both looked drunk, and the alcohol on their breath mixed with the smell of raw turnip and boiled peanuts. The thin man burped resoundingly, then lowered his hand to my chest, fondling me. I was too transfixed to make any noise and tried to step aside, but his comrade rushed up and clutched my arm.

"Purty girl." The squat one patted my backside and pinched me there.

"Stop!" Minnie said, and wedged herself between them and me. "Look, she has gray hair." She pointed at me. "She isn't a girl, she's a grandmother."

"Chinese women must serve Emperor's soldiers," the dumpy man said, still holding my wrist.

His comrade gripped my other arm again. "Yes, we need her service. She can do laundry for us."

I was struggling to get out of their clutches but in vain. Minnie pushed the scrawny man, who attempted to kiss me, and shouted, "Damn it, you can't harass women on the street. I'm going to report you to your higher-ups tomorrow morning."

They both looked amazed but continued dragging me away. Minnie began yelling at the top of her lungs, "Help, help! Police, come and stop these hoodlums!"

The stocky man slapped her on the face while the other one took out a pack of unused Old Sword cigarettes and handed it to me, saying, "We pay for your service, lots lots."

I was still in shock and just kept shaking my head speechlessly, my heartbeat rattling in my throat. Minnie went on shouting, "She's working for me, all right? She's an employee of the U.S. embassy."

"Embassy," the squat man stammered while the other one let go of me.

"Yes, she's our interpreter."

"Interpreter, eh?" the skinny man asked.

"Yes, I work for Americans." At last I found my words in English. "Please let me go, officers."

They could tell that I was speaking a foreign tongue, which suddenly worked magic. They looked at each other and bowed a little at us. "Working at embassy?" the stocky man mumbled while nodding his head. "Good, good, smart woman." His index and middle fingers cranked at his temple.

"If you don't leave her alone," Minnie went on, "I am going to report you to Mr. Tanaka first thing tomorrow morning."

"Okay, okay, we know Tanaka. No trouble, no more trouble." The squat man bowed and pulled his comrade away. They both had bowlegs. Perhaps they were cavalrymen stationed nearby.

I hugged Minnie and burst into tears. "It's over, Anling. It's all right now," she murmured, patting my back.

Leaning against her shoulder, I followed her and headed back toward Jinling. Now and again I cried and giggled uncontrollably. I was kind of hysterical and kept trembling. My right calf had cramps, which forced us to stop twice on the way.

"Damn those bandits, they took my flashlight," Minnie muttered when we reached campus.

27

THANKS to the increased number of new cars in the city, Cola's auto-repair business was booming. The Russian man had a Korean partner, who managed the garage and the four Chinese mechanics for him while Cola went out to meet people for business every day. He came to Jinling one morning in mid-October and brought along a little hunchbacked girl, who was blind and frail like a bird, wearing a threadbare sweat suit with the cuffs of the shirt and pants all rolled up. He'd found her begging on the streets, he told us, so he'd taken her in.

"Can you keep her here?" he asked Minnie, smiling engagingly. He always smiled like that.

"My, you've been collecting blind girls," she said.

"I hate to see her running around. Any of the soldiers and gangsters can hurt her, you know."

So we accepted the girl and had her sent to my daughter in the main dormitory. The girl joined the other four blind ones, whom Liya looked after. Cola didn't stay for tea in spite of Minnie's invitation. He was busy, having an appointment with some Japanese logistics officers. Apparently he was on good terms with them. I knew that this yellow-eyed fellow liked the Japanese and looked down on us Chinese. He felt that we had little sense of order, didn't abide by rules and contracts, lacked consistency, and on the whole were unpredictable. He used to tell other foreigners, "You can't take the Chinese seriously."

Before leaving, Cola asked for a bunch of marigolds, which Old Liao gladly went to cut for him. Unlike in the years prior to the occupation, our college no longer held its annual show of a thousand pots of chrysanthemums, an event that both Minnie and the old gardener used to work together passionately to arrange. Now we had plenty of surplus flowers.

As we were waiting for Old Liao in the quadrangle, Yulan appeared, wearing rubber boots and a canary rain cape with a hood in spite of the cloudless sky. At the sight of Cola, she stopped midstride, then shouted at the top of her voice, "Bestial Jap, go back to your tiny home island!" She stabbed her fist in the air while stamping her foot. "Wild beast, get out of here!"

Startled, Big Liu and I ran over to her. Before we could reach her, Miss Lou emerged, grabbed the madwoman by the arm, and dragged her away. Yulan, her eyes blazing with hatred, kept yelling, "Motherless Japs, get out of China!" while the little evangelical worker raised her hand to muffle that furious voice. Together they scrambled away toward the front gate. I was amazed by Miss Lou's strength—she was hauling Yulan away with one hand.

Big Liu and I returned to Minnie and Cola, who knew Chinese and must have sensed Yulan's hostility. He asked us what that was about. Boiling with anger, I spat out, "That young woman was raped by the Japs and lost her mind."

"She took me to be Japanese?" Cola asked.

"Apparently so," Minnie said.

"Good heavens, I'm a Western devil, not an Eastern devil." He laughed out loud, but none of us responded. Indeed, he was tall and blond, and even his eyebrows were yellow, as were the tiny tufts of hair in his ears.

While waiting for Old Liao, we gave Cola a brief tour through a homecraft class in which the women were weaving blankets. He was impressed and touched the looms and the wool time and again, saying that his mother and aunts in Siberia had done this kind of work too, though they used smaller looms. He got so excited that he stepped on the treadle of an idle machine to see how easily the beams revolved. He also spoke to a few women in Mandarin, asking their opinions on the war looming over Europe. None of them had thought of that; in fact, some of them didn't even know where Europe was. When we came out of the building, Old Liao was waiting with a bunch of marigolds. He handed it to Cola. Together we headed for the front gate.

We stopped at the nursery, where toddlers were playing a game called Dropping a Hanky. A little girl was running around a circle of kids, holding an orange handkerchief and laughing, while the others were clapping their hands and chorusing a song.

As we were watching the children, Minnie told Cola, "Most of these kids have no fathers anymore."

"I have to say you've been doing a saint's work," he said. Then to our amazement, he bowed deeply to her with the golden flowers held before his chest.

"Gosh, what are you doing, proposing to me?" Minnie joked.

"Why not?" he said. "Principal Vaultrin, would you marry me?"

"No, you're too young for this woman," Minnie replied.

We all broke up.

Cola went out of the gate, got into his Mercedes with chrome lights and bumpers, and drove away.

After seeing him off, Minnie and I discussed what to do about the five blind girls. I liked them, for they were all cheerful and three of them could knit gloves and hats, and yet I felt they were becoming a burden. Up to now, my daughter had been taking care of them, but Liya might not be able to do this all by herself for long. I said to Minnie, "They'll be better off if they go to a special school for the blind. We should find a permanent home for them."

"I'll write to Shanghai," she agreed, "to see if they can find a school for the girls."

"I'm sure there is a place that would like to have them. The girls are quick learners and can earn their own keep."

Intuitively we both knew we'd better send the blind girls away soon, because if Mrs. Dennison came back, their presence would irritate her. She always emphasized that Jinling must educate the brightest girls in China. We had "to set the bar high for entry" if we wanted to become a preeminent college, ideally China's Wellesley. The following day Minnie wrote to Ruth Chester, the head of the Chemistry Department who was in charge of the Jinling group in Shanghai, to ask her to look for a school for the five girls.

We felt lucky that we had established the two programs on campus; otherwise the Japanese would have seized the unoccupied classroom buildings and dormitories for military use, as they'd done to some deserted schools in town. On the other hand, we couldn't help feeling anxious, unable to envision how long the present chaos would last and how the college could ever get back on its feet. Everything seemed to depend on when the Japanese left, which might never happen. They must have meant to make the seized land part of Japan eventually, since the whole purpose of this war was to expand Japanese territory. Was our college gone for good? We were unsure, and the uncertainty tormented us.

Recently more money had been donated by Jinling's alumnae for setting up a program similar to the Homecraft School, but there was no way Minnie could find more teachers, as most of the educated people had not returned to Nanjing. Minnie said she was glad about the freedom Jinling enjoyed from any government's restrictions and from the academic rigor of a first-rate college—our two programs could tailor their curricula to suit their own needs. The officials in charge of education in the puppet municipality were supposed to supervise all the schools, but some of them were too ashamed to come and instead would send their minions to do perfunctory inspections. Once in a while, an official or two did show up, but they were all quite lenient and flexible. A few were glad that their daughters had taken the entrance test last fall and been enrolled in our middle school.

IN LATE NOVEMBER the weather turned freezing. The naked branches were coated with hoarfrost in the morning, though water would drip from the trees in the rising sun. The cold weather made it hard for the students, who had to take class in unheated rooms. The coal from Wuhan had arrived two weeks before, but to everyone's dismay, it wouldn't burn to give heat. I didn't know what to do with it and often condemned the dealer representing the coal mine, saying, "He'll have enough heat in hell."

"Can't we get a little good coal from a local seller?" Minnie once asked me.

"There's no coal for sale anymore, no matter how much we're willing to pay."

Every day I wore a pair of woolen pants underneath cotton-padded pants; still, I was chilled to the bone, simply because there was no place and no time I could ever get warm. I'd never felt this cold before. Minnie was also cold all the time. She would warm her fingers around a mug of hot water. Even so, she couldn't sit in the office for longer than an hour at a stretch. The students suffered more, and some had chilblains on their hands and feet. In class they all crossed their arms, each hand sheathed inside the other sleeve to keep warm. When they wrote, they'd keep breathing on their fingers. We didn't heat the classrooms yet, having to save the firewood from the felled trees for the coldest days in January. Nowadays the students envied those women in the Homecraft School who could do kitchen duties or take lessons in the four cookhouses, where it was warm.

Minnie would urge me to go out with her, walking as often as possible to quicken the circulation. One morning, as she and I were strolling around, a ruckus broke out at the front gate, and we went over to take a look. "Stop bugging me!" Ban yelled, his shoulder leaning against a stone pillar.

Outside the gate stood Yulan, her arms akimbo, her face smeared with rouge, and her hair combed back into an enormous bun that made her look seven or eight years older. She'd been living with Miss Lou and had snuck back to campus again. "Shame, shame on you, Little Jap. Come out and face justice!" she cried, licking her chapped lips. A crocheted saffron shawl was draped over her shoulders.

"Stinking slut!" Ban cursed.

Minnie went up to the sixteen-year-old boy and said, "You mustn't let her disturb you like this."

"She calls me all kinds of names whenever she sees me. Please, Principal Vautrin, give me something else to do so I won't have to go off campus. I'm scared of her—she waits for me out there all the while." He then turned to yell at Yulan, "Buzz off, psychopath!"

"Come out, shameless scum!" she shouted, jabbing her forefinger at him while squishing up her face.

"Go fuck yourself!"

"Stop deflowering girls!"

"Go to hell!"

"Monster! You'll be fried in hell, in a big cauldron of oil!"

"Leave me alone!"

Minnie shook Ban by the shoulder. "You shouldn't exchange words with her like this. You're only kicking up a row."

At this point Miss Lou appeared and pulled Yulan away, while the madwoman went on calling Ban "a pancake-faced Jap." Hu, a gateman now, asked Minnie whether he should let Yulan in if she came to campus again. "Don't stop her if she comes for meals," Minnie told him.

Hu nodded his balding head without another word.

Later Minnie assigned an elderly man to step in for Ban and sent the boy to Shanna to work as a custodian for the Homecraft School, but the trouble with him was far from over. He often clashed with others, wouldn't listen to Shanna, and even called her a "Japan worshiper" because she used a Japanese facial cream. He seemed particularly fond of fighting with girl students and wouldn't mend his ways in spite of Shanna's repeated warnings. As her patience was wearing thin, Shanna declared she'd have him fired sooner or later.

As I mentioned before, I didn't like Shanna that much; she always called me "Anling," though I'd told her time and again that she should call me Mrs. Gao. I might be even older than her mother. What's more, Shanna often wore flowered clothes as if she were a teenager, and she'd hum silly popular songs, such as "I Want You" and "A Boat of Happiness." As a young lady from Shanghai, she had no idea what a hell Nanjing had gone through last winter.

28

IN EARLY DECEMBER, without informing us beforehand, my son, Haowen, came to see us. He slipped through Jinling's front gate, wearing civvies—a bowler hat, a peacoat, and suede shoes. He looked slightly taller than he had five years before, perhaps because he was much thinner and more muscular. He walked with a straight back, more like a man, yet his face was no longer bright. He was twenty-seven but looked like he was in his mid-thirties. His dad, sister, and I were all shocked but elated to see him home. At first I was somewhat unnerved, assuming that he had deserted. Then I thought that it was high time for him to quit the Imperial Army, whether it was by desertion or discharge, as long as he was back home. But he said that his hospital unit was on its way to Luoyang, that they let him off at Nanjing to deliver some documents at the army's headquarters and also to see his parents. Tomorrow he'd have to head north to catch up with his unit.

I told Liya to sit at the front door with Fanfan in case someone barged in. Yaoping took Haowen into the inner room while I let down all the window curtains.

It was already twilight and the marketplace had closed; there was no way I could get groceries for a decent meal. I hurried to the poultry center and bought five eggs from Rulian, saying I had an important guest and needed her to do me a favor, since the eggs were not for sale. For dinner I steamed some salted dace on top of rice, fried a bowl of peanuts, sautéed napa cabbage with dried anchovies, and scrambled the eggs with scallions. Yaoping had begun restocking his liquor cabinet since he resumed teaching, though most of his wines and liquors were fake. When the table was set, I told Liya to bolt the door, and then we all sat down to the best meal I had cooked since the fall of the city.

Haowen poured rice wine for everyone and said, "Dad and Mom, forgive me for causing you so much pain and anxiety. I came home just to see if you're well. At present, there's no way I can do anything to make your life comfortable, but when the war is over, I'll do my best to be a dutiful son."

Waving his narrow hand, his father said, "No need to talk like that. Let's just enjoy a quiet meal."

"I'm so happy to see you home, son," I said, with tears in my eyes. "We can't give you a better dinner, but we will when you come back next time."

"Brother, let's touch cups," Liya proposed.

We all took a drink of the wine, which tasted thin and watery. Haowen dipped a chopstick into his cup and gave Fanfan a drop of the wine. The child liked it and wanted more. That made us chuckle. Liya told her brother, "Don't give him any more. You'll make him drunk."

So I poured some water into a wine cup and dropped in a tiny lump of crystal sugar. Whenever Fanfan wanted another drink, Haowen would give him a drop of the sweet water in place of the dark stuff we'd been drinking. The boy cried out, "White wine, more." That made us laugh again.

My husband and son went on talking about the war as we ate. Now and again I would put in a word. Yaoping felt that China, poor and backward, couldn't possibly win this war, but Haowen thought differently.

"In fact, the morale is very low among the Japanese troops," he said.

"Why so? Haven't they already occupied half of China?" his dad asked.

"But Japan doesn't have the manpower to control all the territory it has seized. What's worse, its army has suffered horrendous casualties and cannot replenish the reduced units. The Japanese did not expect China to resist so stubbornly."

"You mean they cannot find enough soldiers?" I asked.

"Yes. They've been recruiting men from Korea, Taiwan, and other places, but those are not experienced troops. The army is much weaker now." Haowen's eyes sparkled as he spoke, reminding me of the boy he used to be. He put a shriveled peanut into his mouth and continued, "Originally they planned to finish the war in three or four months, but now they don't even know how to bring it to an end. China is like a vast swamp into which they've been sinking deeper and deeper, though they've kept winning battles. The longer they fight, the harder it will be for them to pull out. The soldiers miss home and complain nonstop. It's difficult for the officers to keep discipline. As a matter of fact, Japan might turn out to be a loser if this war drags on for too long. The politicians and top generals in Tokyo simply don't have a clue how to make an end of it."

"They should have made plans for all the possible ways to end it before they started it," Yaoping said. "That's common sense."

"Human beings can be stupider than animals, which are never afflicted with megalomania," Haowen added.

"Brother, what will you do after the war?" Liya asked, her cheeks glowing with a red sheen raised by the wine.

"I haven't completed my degree yet. Maybe I will return to medical school."

I knew he meant to rejoin his wife, but I made no comment. Yaoping sighed and said, "The Imperial Army is too savage. I'm afraid the two countries will remain enemies for a long time."

After dinner, we sat at the tea table and resumed talking. Haowen was holding Fanfan and made him laugh now and again. The boy was as happy as if he had known his uncle for ages. Haowen tickled him and raised him above his head, and the three-year-old also straddled his neck for a horse ride. I could see that Haowen would be an indulgent father when he had his own children. Even before his teens, he would say he wanted to have a wife and three kids when he grew up. He had been born to become a family man and must love Mitsuko dearly.

When Fanfan fell asleep and Liya carried him to the other room, Haowen took something wrapped in a piece of tissue paper out of his inner breast pocket. "Mom," he said, "I had nothing to bring you. Here's a little keepsake."

I opened the paper and found a gold bangle, smooth and solid. "You don't need to do this," I told him.

"Dad," he said, turning to Yaoping, "I'm sorry I don't have anything for you."

"Forget about that. I'm happy just to see you safe and well. Bring Mitsuko home next time."

"I will."

As I was observing the bangle, I saw a tiny character, *Diao*, engraved on the inner side of the bracelet. My heart sank. I dropped the thing on the table with a clunk and asked, "Haowen, did you steal this from someone?"

"No, how . . . how can you say that?"

"It must belong to a Chinese with the family name Diao. Did you also join the Japanese in looting?" I got angrier as I spoke.

"Mom, you misjudge me. I only treat patients. There's no way I could loot homes and rob my own people." His face went misshapen as if something were stinging him.

"Then how come this bangle has the word 'Diao' engraved on it?"

"Let me take a look." He picked it up and observed it, amazed by the character that he obviously hadn't noticed before. He put it down. "I don't know where it was from originally. It was an interpreter who gave it to me."

"Is he Chinese?" his father said.

"Yes, the fellow had malaria and I took good care of him. You know the Japanese—they'd get rid of him like trash if he couldn't get up from the sickbed within a couple of days."

"What's his surname?" I asked.

"Meng."

"See, this bangle must've belonged to someone else," I said.

"Meng gave it to me as a token of gratitude because I saved his life. I have no idea where he got it."

"This might be ill-gotten," I continued.

He looked tearful, then closed his eyes. "I'm cursed, cursed," he muttered, his upper lip curled a little. "Even my mother rejects my present." He sighed, lowered his head, and covered his forehead with his palm.

Pity and love stirred in my chest. I said, "All right, Haowen, I'll keep this. But you must promise me that you'll never rob anyone or steal from the civilians."

"Do you think I could act freely like the Japanese? Heavens, the Japs treat me as a Chink, they don't trust me. I'm cursed, cursed! I'm a pariah no matter where I go." He stood up and went into the kitchen to wash his face at the sink. He blew his nose loudly.

Yaoping pursed his lips, then said to me, "Let's treat him as our child, our only son. Can't you see he's miserable?"

I remained speechless and put the gold bangle away. Beyond any question, Haowen was good-natured and ill-used by the Japanese, but I didn't want him to take advantage of his own people. Before I turned in, I said to him, "Keep in mind you're a Christian. God will make us answer for what we did in this life."

"I'll remember that, Mom."

That night he and his dad stayed in the inner room while I joined Liya and Fanfan in the other room. Haowen left before daybreak to catch the train.

29

ALTHOUGH THE MAIL was slower nowadays—sometimes it took several weeks to receive a letter sent within China—still its delivery was reliable. The Japanese had left the postal system in the southern provinces in Chinese hands, because it operated at a huge deficit, 120,000 yuan a month according to Minnie. In her official report to our New York board, Minnie said she was full of respect for the Chinese postal workers because we still received domestic mail every day.

I'd been in touch with Holly. She always sounded cheerful and had moved around, doing relief work. At present she was in Henan Province, where millions of people had become homeless because a dike along the Yellow River had been breached by the Nationalist army as a means to deter the advance of the Japanese forces. I had also been in correspondence with Dr. Wu and briefed her once a month about what was going on here. She was in Chengdu now, leading a large group of Jinling's staff, students, and faculty. Once in a while she wrote to Minnie, who would share the letters with me. In the most recent one President Wu expressed her gratitude to Minnie for keeping the two programs in operation, but she wondered about the possibility of reopening the college in the fall.

The president wrote about the homecraft program and the middle school:

I understand that under the circumstances these two programs are the only possible arrangements. In fact, I am pleased that at least the Homecraft School, a fraction of our college, is still in place. But the middle school you are running should be only a temporary operation, and eventually it will have to be replaced by something like our former college. Mrs. Dennison wrote the other day that she was painfully concerned about the disintegration of our college and hoped we would make every effort to bring it back. In principle, I agree with her that the restoration of the college must be our goal, on which we should concentrate our effort. At the same time, I am also aware that as long as the Japanese occupy Nanjing, it will be unlikely we can realize such a goal. Damn the Imperial Army, they have destroyed everything and thrown us back to square one. These days I have often dreamed of our campus and Nanjing. How I wish I were with you again.

Dr. Wu also wrote Minnie that Mrs. Dennison would return from her yearlong furlough in the States, so we were pretty certain that the old woman would come back to Jinling. Had she been here the winter before, she might have remained behind like Minnie and opposed setting up the two current programs on campus: she'd always maintained that Jinling must grow into a top women's college, well known internationally, so as to attract more funding.

Minnie and I agreed with President Wu that the middle school should be closed in due course, but for the time being it met the locals' needs and there was no reason to dissolve it. More than four hundred girls had sat for the entrance test the previous fall and only a third of them were admitted, placed in four grades. For that and for the quality courses we offered, Jinling still commanded a fine reputation in Nanjing.

In her reply to President Wu, Minnie gave two reasons why restarting the college in the near future would not be feasible. First, we wouldn't have enough freshmen, because in times like these few families would send their girls to Nanjing for college. Second, we would need a stronger faculty with college teaching experience, which again was unavailable. Minnie even asked Dr. Wu to encourage some of Jinling's faculty members to return to Nanjing. Recently some foreigners, mostly American academics and missionaries, had arrived, but after speaking with our students and looking around, none of them had any desire to stay. Minnie added in her letter: "It was so easy for them to talk without committing themselves, and I have no choice but to depend on the Chinese faculty I assembled from the highways and byways. They are good enough for our current programs but will be inadequate for college teaching." I totally agreed with her.

The Homecraft School had Dr. Wu's blessing, though we had started it not long ago, in 1934, as a two-year program. Mrs. Dennison must have groused to Dr. Wu about our two ongoing programs and insisted that Jinling must excel in higher education again. Before taking her furlough the previous year, the old woman had even talked about starting some master's programs here. Minnie had been lukewarm about that, though she'd never objected to it.

She had her letter to Dr. Wu delivered to Bob Wilson and asked him to mail it from Shanghai, where he'd go that Saturday. After the messenger left, Minnie resumed working on the accounts. Somehow, hard as she tried, she couldn't balance the books for October. A twenty-six-yuan difference was still there. If only we could hire a bookkeeper, but that was impossible. The capital used to have all types of professionals, and yet nowadays you couldn't find a decent accountant. Small wonder that even the Japanese complained that they didn't have enough capable Chinese to run the government. Big Liu often said he wished his daughter, Meiyan, had studied accounting.

The messenger returned at noon and said that some people belonging to the International Relief Committee had been apprehended. Minnie telephoned Searle and Lewis and found out that the arrests were prompted by a murder at the Japanese embassy. Someone had slipped poison into a samovar there the day before; two guards died and several people were hospitalized, including a diplomat. The police rounded up some Chinese employees and interrogated them. Then they went to the IRC and arrested six of the leaders, all of them Chinese, on the grounds that they had participated in anti-Japanese activities. Now the police declared that these men were involved in the murder. Lewis and Searle were certain that none of them had had anything to do with it and that the Japanese were just exploiting the case as a pretext to disband the relief organization. One of the six IRC men was a part-time math teacher here, and three of them had their daughters in our middle school. The girls begged Minnie to intercede for their fathers.

Minnie spoke with Lewis, who helped her compose a letter of protest demanding the immediate release of the six men. The next day she delivered it to Vice-Consul Tanaka at the Japanese embassy, where she learned that the six men were being kept in the prison downtown. Even though they'd been tortured and their feet had been shackled, they still refused to admit any wrongdoing.

30

THE FIRST ANNIVERSARY of Nanjing's fall was approaching, and the city was under martial law again. People were warned not to assemble in public during the next few days except for celebration; at Jinling, the students, especially the middle schoolers, had been talking about how to commemorate the shameful day.

On the evening before the anniversary, Minnie gathered the girls in the auditorium in the Central Building. She urged them not to endanger themselves and the school. Instead they should study hard and help others, especially the destitute. That was the best way to serve China, which needed capable and rational people, not mobs. Besides, they mustn't let hatred run their lives.

The girls listened quietly, all of them staring at Minnie; none dared speak against her. Even when she was done and invited them to voice their opinions, nobody let out a peep, but I could feel the tension in the hall. We'd thought of having a special service to commemorate the day, but, afraid that it might stir up the students' emotions, we decided against it. Minnie told Luhai to make sure the front gate was guarded strictly.

The next morning, many girls wore black armbands. Both Donna and Alice reported that their students did the same. To Minnie's dismay, Shanna also had on a crape. "You shouldn't be such a leader," Minnie reproached her.

"I might wear this even if they didn't," Shanna said, touching the black cloth safety-pinned to her sleeve.

Surprised, Minnie went on, "I understand your feelings, but it's too risky to do this. Some turncoats might snitch on us."

"I'm also Chinese."

At that moment I loved the girl for saying those words, though I didn't wear a black armband mainly because I wouldn't create more trouble for Minnie. I was worried about the students' safety besides.

Fortunately, Luhai and the gatemen did a good job of preventing the girls from going out—however loudly they chorused patriotic songs and whatever slogans they chanted, they were kept on campus. We felt somewhat relieved. If the officials demanded an explanation, we could say that the school had taken measures to discourage hostility toward Japan, but many students had lost family members and mourned their losses spontaneously.

Some girls also fasted that day, and Meiyan fought with another student whose father served in the puppet municipality.

Miss Lou came early that afternoon and said that Yulan had disappeared. For several days the madwoman had wanted to go downtown, saying she must protest the Japanese occupation on the first anniversary of the city's fall. Massaging her forehead with her claw-like fingers, Miss Lou said, "I stopped her a couple of times, but she slipped out this morning."

"Any idea where she might be?" Minnie asked.

"She must've gone downtown. When she heard about the martial law, she couldn't stop spouting curses. She said she would run away to join the guerrillas, but I didn't take that seriously and thought she couldn't possibly figure out where the Reds were. It was my fault—I should've been more vigilant and shouldn't have let her visit my neighbors."

Minnie had a number of people called in and asked everyone to go out and look for Yulan. I said, "That mad girl is our curse. We should've washed our hands of her long ago."

"Anling, that's rubbish," Miss Lou said. "Now's not the time to speak like that." I glowered at the evangelical worker but couldn't find a word to counter her.

Big Liu said, "I hope the girl won't fall into Japanese hands again."

In spite of her insanity, Yulan was somewhat good-looking, so we feared she might get hurt. We set out to look for her.

Minnie and I walked east along Zhujiang Road. The minute we passed the half-burned building that had housed the Justice Ministry a year before, we saw that most houses had disappeared, and where they'd stood were piles of bricks and stones. The Japanese had been tearing down homes to get the materials for building roads. For each house they paid two yuan as compensation; whether the owner accepted it or not, he had to move out and surrender the property. We'd heard about that operation but hadn't expected to see such large-scale demolition.

It was a sullen wintry day, the gray clouds threatening snow. The sycamore and oak trees along the street were swaying and whistling as gusts of wind swept through them. A rusty sheet of corrugated iron tumbled across the street and fell into a roadside ditch. Here and there scummy puddles, like giant festering sores, were encrusted with ice on the edges. In the distance firecrackers were exploding while drums rolled, *suona* horns blared, and an array of Japanese flags flitted across the thoroughfare—a celebration of the occupation was in full swing. About a thousand Chinese, including some school pupils, were waving tiny flags and shouting slogans in support of the Japanese rule. Some even chanted "Banzai, banzai!" while a procession of men and women was performing a dance on stilts, wearing green and vermilion gowns and waving fans. The cacophonous music jarred the ears like shrieks and screams. On the sidewalk ahead stood a truck, from which a photographer pointed a bulky camera at the celebrators, the black cloth over his head and shoulders. I panted, "I hope those traitors will be rounded up and sentenced to death when our army takes this city back."

The second I said that, I remembered my son, Haowen. A piercing pang gripped my heart and made me speechless.

Minnie shook her head in silence. As we turned a corner near the former Central Hospital, a crowd gathered ahead of us. We caught sight of Yulan and hastened our steps.

The madwoman stood in the middle of a semicircle of people, holding a small triangular flag that bore these words: WIPE OUT JAPANESE DEVILS! She was addressing the crowd, some of whom cheered her on.

Minnie and I jostled through the spectators and reached her. "Give me the flag," Minnie said.

Yulan stared at her for a moment, then snorted, "No. Don't you see I'm using it?"

"Come, let's go home." I reached out for her arm.

The madwoman stepped aside and said, "You're just a lackey of the foreigners. You go with her, but leave me alone." She jerked her thumb at Minnie.

"Please, Yulan. It's dangerous here," Minnie begged. "Come home with us."

"I have no home anymore. Everything was burned by the Japs."

"Don't you respect Miss Lou? She was very upset when she found out you were gone."

"I don't want to live with that Bible freak anymore. She's obsessed with Jesus Christ and says we're all his slaves. Every day she made me memorize poems from the Old Testament. I'm sick of it. I want to be a free woman."

"All right, you can stay with us," Minnie offered, "and take any class you want to. We won't force anything on you, I promise."

"Go chase yourself, evil American!"

I grabbed Yulan's wrist to wrench the flag from her hand, but the madwoman shoved me and cursed me loudly.

People whooped and guffawed, and some egged her on. Minnie said to them, "Don't you feel ashamed to mislead a sick woman? She was molested by the Japanese and lost her mind. You all know what kind of risk she's running to stand here raving aloud. If you care about your compatriots, you should go away or help us bring her back."

Some people dropped their eyes and a few started away. Minnie tugged at Yulan's sleeve and begged, "Please, let's go home."

"No! Where's my home? You sold my parents to the Japs. I hate those Eastern devils. I'll settle up with them one of these days."

As if on cue, three Japanese policemen arrived, each wearing a peaked cap with a tiny rising-sun flag printed on the right side. Their appearance scattered the crowd. Even Yulan clammed up in terror.

"You come with us," one of the police, a glassy-eyed man, ordered her in stiff Mandarin.

The madwoman let out a groan and turned to Minnie and me. "Officer," Minnie explained, "she's out of her mind. We're taking her back to our school and won't let her out again."

"No, she attempted to incite a riot and must come with us. She's an activist against Japan, and we shall question her before we decide what to do about her."

"Where are you taking her?"

"That's our business."

"Can we come with you?"

"No, you cannot."

"You have no right to detain her."

"Don't poke your nose into our work."

By now the other two policemen had caught hold of Yulan, who was screaming helplessly, her legs bent to hold her ground. Minnie glanced sideways at me, and I felt my left cheek twitching. She rushed forward and reached out for Yulan, but the officer stretched out his arms and blocked her. Then he waved for the other policemen to drag the madwoman away. He turned to follow them.

"Let go of my hands!" Yulan yelled, struggling to break loose. "You smell like a stinky fish shop. Damn it, let your grandma go. Help, help, help me!"

"Shut up, rotten cunt!" The officer slapped her across the face, and instantly she went quiet.

Minnie set off following them, but I clutched her arm and pulled her to a stop. "It's no use, Minnie. We'd better go back now."

The officer spun around, having sensed Minnie's attempt, and spread his arms again. Struggling out of my grip, Minnie lunged at him with all her might. The man dodged and punched her on the jaw. She fell and gave a cry of pain but scrambled to her feet instantly. "I won't let you take her away!" she shouted, and plunged forward again, blood trickling out of the corner of her mouth.

A middle-aged Chinese man held her by the waist from behind, saying, "Please, Principal Vautrin, don't follow them!" Another few people stepped over to restrain her. A woman began wiping the blood off Minnie's face with a silk handkerchief.

Minnie stamped her feet, tears flowing down her cheeks while her nose quivered. "Damn you! Damn you, bastards!" she screamed at the backs of the receding policemen.

For days Minnie called various offices and visited her friends and acquaintances to find out Yulan's whereabouts, but nobody could tell her.

Then Lewis, who'd been leading his students in surveying the damage and losses in Nanjing and its surrounding counties, telephoned one morning and said he'd heard that Yulan was in a stopgap hospital near Tianhua Orphanage. Minnie put aside the next semester's academic calendar she'd been working on and set out for the hospital. She asked me to come along.

The hospital was a decrepit three-story building behind a cinderblock wall topped with four lines of barbwire. It was used by the Japanese military mainly for treating tuberculosis and venereal diseases among the soldiers and prostitutes. Some of the sex workers were so-called comfort women, taken from far away, mostly from Korea and a few from Southeast Asia. We were horrified that Yulan was confined in such a place.

A baby-faced Chinese guard stopped us and demanded, "Pass, please."

"We want to see a student of Jinling Women's College," Minnie said.

"You can't go in without a pass. This is an army hospital. If I let you in, I'll be in big trouble."

"Can I speak to your superior, then?"

"He's not here right now."

"Please, let us in," I begged. "The girl was molested by the Japanese and lost her mind. We want to take her back."

He shook his head no.

Then we caught sight of Dr. Chu stepping out of the building and heading toward a car. Minnie called to him, and he came over, delighted to see us. He was wearing a cashmere coat and a Homburg with a curled brim and was holding a copper-tipped walking stick. Today he looked more like a rich businessman than a doctor. Minnie explained why we were there.

Dr. Chu whispered to the sentry and slipped a single-yuan bill into his palm. The guard said to us with a fawning smile, "You can go in now."

Without thanking him, Minnie turned to Dr. Chu and shouted, "Come see us! We owe you one."

I waved at him too. He took off his felt hat. "Bye now," he cried. He strolled away with a measured, flat-footed gait, the ends of the long muffler around his neck flapping.

The interior of the building reeked of Lysol and carrion. My breathing instinctively went shallow, but I forced myself to relax, inhaling and exhaling to get used to the foul air. A nurse in a white gown and cap was on her way upstairs; she led us to the second floor and pointed at a door, saying, "Yulan Tan is in there. I can't let you in, but you can meet her at the small window. You have ten minutes."

Minnie looked through the square opening on the door and called out, "Yulan, are you in there?"

There was no sound inside. I peered in but didn't see anyone either. I closed my eyes to adjust to the gloom, then opened them. This time I saw the madwoman cowering in a corner, her knees tucked under her chin. She was alone in the room. I called to her.

Slowly Yulan rose and came over. "What's this?" she grunted.

I stepped aside to let Minnie speak. "How are you, Yulan?" she asked.

"I'm hungry and cold. Give me a meat pie or a pork bun. I know you have chocolates. Don't you?"

"I'm sorry I didn't bring any. I'll remember next time."

"Get me out of here, please. If you don't help get me out of prison I'll die in a day or two."

"We'll try our best." Minnie took off her light woolen coat with its gray fur collar. "Here, you have this for now, all right?" She rolled it up and pushed it through the opening.

I put my head closer to the window to observe the madwoman,

who threw the coat around her shoulders. She kept staring at Minnie, her pupils contracting. She wiped her dripping nose with the back of her hand. Then she grinned pathetically and said, "Get me out of here, please!"

"I will. But try to be patient for the time being, all right?" Minnie said.

"You don't know how they torture me."

"What do you mean?"

"They beat me if I don't obey them."

"Listen to them, then. Just don't let them hurt you."

"I don't want to open my pants for every Jap. They burned my buttocks with cigarettes. D'you want to see it?"

"Sure."

The madwoman dropped the coat on the cement floor, undid her belt, and turned around. On her behind were some twenty bloody burns; they looked like red beans and peanuts. Minnie closed her eyes, two big tears coursing down her right cheek.

"Beasts!" I said under my breath.

We left the hospital. Heading back to Jinling, we ran into two boys, seven or eight years old, whipping a top on the side of Canton Road. The toy jumped about while spinning and leaning sideways. As we were passing by, one of the boys lifted his scarred face and taunted Minnie, "Foreign devil! Foreign devil!"

We were surprised but didn't respond. The other boy stopped driving the top and said to his pal, "Why call her that? She's Miss Hua Chuan."

"That's right," I spoke up. "Your mother ought to teach you some manners."

Minnie was shivering a little from the chilly wind, holding the collar of her jacket with her hand. The scar-faced boy stared at her, then turned to his pal. "You mean she's the American principal?"

"You bet."

Then they both started chanting, "Principal Hua, the Goddess of Mercy! The Goddess of Mercy!"

"Shush, don't call me that!" she told them.

But they went on shouting "The Goddess of Mercy!" as they scurried away with the top, slashing the air to make loud cracks with their leather-tipped hemp whips.

Minnie shook her head. Dried leaves were scuttling ahead of us like a swarm of mice, mixed with candy wrappers and banknotes no longer in circulation.

MINNIE SPOKE to Plumer Mills, the chairman of the semidisbanded International Relief Committee, to plead with him for help. But Yulan was just an individual; she did not belong to any organization, and her detention would not impair the relationship between Japan and any social or religious group, so Plumer couldn't figure out a way to rescue her. Dr. Chu was the only person who might be able to help us. He didn't work at the hospital but might have connections there.

Minnie invited Dr. Chu to dinner at Jinling, and gave me thirty yuan for the party—not much, but enough to make the occasion festive. I prepared the food in my home and had several Chinese over besides the two American teachers, Donna and Alice.

Minnie was amazed by the dinner, saying she'd never thought it would be so lavish. She wondered if I had spent some of my own money. I had, though just a few extra yuan. I joked that we Chinese were obsessed with food and face, so even in a time of distress like now, we'd still make the best use of the pleasure life could offer, turning a meal into a small feast. There was roast chicken, a large fried bass, smoked duck, and braised pork cubes. Yaoping took out his only bottle of Five Grain Sap and some apricot wine.

Minnie thanked Dr. Chu and proposed a toast on behalf of the college and the women whose menfolk had gotten out of jail in June. We all clinked cups and drank. Alice and Donna wouldn't touch alcohol, so they chose tea instead, but Minnie had to drink some to please the guest of honor and the host, my husband, who didn't speak much but smiled continually. At last he could enjoy himself a little. Meanwhile, I was busy making sure that every dish was served properly.

Dr. Chu was wearing a conventional quilted robe, which made him resemble a country gentleman, with his hair parted down the middle. "Tell me, Mr. Gao," he said to Yaoping, putting down his cup after another swig, "how much did you pay for this Five Grain Sap?"

"Four yuan a bottle."

"No way can you get the genuine stuff here for that price."

Yaoping chortled, "I can taste it's fake too, but this is the best available on the black market."

"This is good enough—it tastes like it's brewed only from sorghum. It brings back happy memories, though."

"Yes, we can drink this as One Grain Sap," Yaoping said flatly.

Rulian translated their exchange for Alice and Donna, who both giggled.

When Minnie mentioned Yulan, Dr. Chu told her, "I don't know if I can help get Yulan out of the hospital, but for the time being I can get you a pass so you can visit her."

"Thanks," Minnie said.

I knew he was a sincere man, and if he could have done more, he would have. Dr. Chu talked about the situation in Zhenjiang, his hometown. The Japanese had taken that city a week before Nanjing the previous winter and destroyed a good part of it. "It was worse than here," Dr. Chu said. "They killed a lot of people and the town is still rather empty. My parents' house has become an officers' club, a cabaret of sorts."

Somehow everyone at the table spoke in a calm voice despite the sad topic. Donna shook her head, a mass of tawny curls, rolled her long-lashed eyes, and said, "Don't you Chinese hate the Japanese?"

"I hate the traitors more," Shanna replied.

Rulian said, "If the Chinese keep selling our country, we deserve to be enslaved."

I shot her a dirty look, but she continued, "I mean, China can be conquered only from within."

Batting her gray-blue eyes, Alice seemed to understand their conversation merely in part and said, "When I was in Japan, most people there were polite and gentle. Certainly they believed the war was good for their country, but very few of them were vicious and violent. To be honest, I felt quite safe there."

Minnie translated her words for the guest of honor and my husband. That made the table silent for a moment. Then Dr. Chu said, "In war, victory justifies all sorts of violence. A complete victory means to have finished off the enemy. In fact, I believe that the Japanese committed all the atrocities as a celebration of their victory, as a kind of reward and gratification. That's why they acted with so much bravado and even beheaded people as a sport."

"That must be true," Minnie agreed. "On the other hand, some of the soldiers who came to our campus later on were polite and well behaved, totally different from those brutes who were here last winter."

"I just hate every one of them," I joined in.

"Oh, come on," Yaoping said, "you're supposed to love your enemies."

That had the table in stitches. In the other room, Fanfan prattled in his sleep while Liya was humming a lullaby, her voice sweet and childlike.

Dr. Chu stood, raised his cup, and proposed a toast with so much emotion that his mouth went a little askew. "Let's drink to this great woman." He pointed at Minnie. "She not only sheltered ten thousand women and children from harm's way but is also devoted to educating the weak and the impoverished. Let me say this: she's a real man— superior to any man in this city. China doesn't lack clever people— we Chinese are way too smart and too pragmatic. This country needs people with sincere hearts willing to serve and take pains."

Minnie got up, but before she could speak, we had already let out "Cheers!" and touched cups.

She sipped her apricot wine and said, "Please consider what we've been doing as our Christian duty. Any one of us, given the same circumstances, would do the same. The other day I came across this aphorism in the Quaker calendar Mrs. Dennison sent me, and I want to share it with you: 'Doing what can't be done is the glory of living.' "

Big Liu proposed, "Yes, let's drink to the impossible task ahead."

Some of us laughed, and we drained the last drops in our cups.

For dessert, we had walnuts, honey oranges, roasted chestnuts, and jasmine tea. I brought out a small basket of spiced pumpkin seeds, which we cracked while conversing.

The fake Five Grain Sap went to Dr. Chu's head and loosened him up. Now tipsy, he kept saying he felt ashamed of being a man. For him, the cause of Nanjing's tragedy was clear and simple, and no one but the Chinese men should be held responsible—because they couldn't fight back the invaders, their women and children were subjected to abuse and killing, so a foreign woman like Minnie had to step up to save lives and to do superhuman work. He even wept for a few moments, insisting that he wasn't a man either and wished he hadn't rushed back from Germany, driven by his youthful aspiration of saving his beloved China. This country was a hopeless quagmire and an endless nightmare. "It's an eternal heartache!" he declared. He should have gone to Italy or Switzerland or to an eastern European country, since with a medical degree from a top German university he could practice anywhere. In short, he claimed that he was a weakling, plus an idiot, who had put himself at the enemy's disposal. No wonder some people viewed him as a traitor.

His ravings pained my heart because I was reminded of my son. Haowen must have moments of despair like this; he might even feel worse, for he was actually serving in the Japanese army. Soon Dr. Chu calmed down and resumed speaking with the others in an amiable voice. When dinner was over, he refused to let Big Liu accompany him home. He said, "No Japs in town dare stop me."

32

IN LATE DECEMBER we heard from Haowen again. A photograph enclosed in the letter showed that Mitsuko had given birth to a baby, so we now had a grandson who carried our family's name. I had mixed feelings, though Yaoping was happy and even reminisced about his student days in Japan, of which he still had fond memories. He used to say that a Japanese woman could make a good wife. I had nothing against our daughter-in-law, who seemed to be a fine girl, but I was unsure if she and Haowen, now plus a baby, would have a happy life together. The hostility between the two countries would cast a long shadow on their marriage.

On the back of the photo my son had inscribed "Mitsuko and Shin." The baby had Haowen's round eyes and wide nose, not his mother's smooth cheeks and tapered eyes. Mitsuko's egg-shaped face had the calm and mild expression of an older woman, someone who already had a bunch of children. As I was observing her, her mouth seemed to be moving, saying something I couldn't understand. I put down the picture, my eyes misty.

Yaoping and I talked about whether to ask Haowen for Mitsuko's address so we could write to her, but we decided not to contact her directly while the war was still going on. That might get our family, and perhaps hers as well, into hot water. Someday we might go to Japan to see our grandson if he and his mother couldn't come to visit us. Ideally, Haowen would be able to bring his wife and son back to China. But for the time being we kept the matter secret. If people knew of it, our family would be disgraced.

I showed the photograph to nobody but Minnie. "What a nice picture," she said. "Mother and son look so content. What does Mitsuko do for a living?"

"She teaches primary school."

"If I were you, I'd go see them right away."

"Minnie, you're American, but few Chinese can do that while the war is going on. Please don't reveal my family's Japanese relations to anyone, okay?"

"Sure, I'll keep my lips zipped."

We went on to talk about the three teenage girls—Meiyan and two classmates of hers—who had just run away, claiming that they wanted to join the resistance force in some interior region. Our staffers intercepted them at the train station in Hsia Gwan, because they didn't have the travel papers necessary for purchasing tickets and were stranded there. I reprimanded the girls and wanted to make them do kitchen duty for a week, which Big Liu supported, but Minnie intervened, saying they had to take the finals they had missed. She gave them a few days to review their lessons.

Meiyan came to our home to see Liya that evening, to return the ten yuan she had borrowed from her for the secret journey. They were friends now, but Meiyan would remain reticent in my presence, so I stayed in the kitchen feeding Fanfan while listening in on the two of them in the sitting room.

"Sorry I didn't tell you my plan," Meiyan said. "I was afraid your mom would let my dad know."

"No big deal," Liya replied. "If I didn't have a child, I might run away too."

"Where would you like to go? To join your husband?"

"I have no clue where he is. I just want to join our army."

"Which one—the Nationalists or the Communists?"

"It makes no difference as long as I can fight the Japanese. They killed my baby, and I still see my daughter now and then." Liya believed that the lost baby had been a girl, perhaps because she'd never had morning sickness during the pregnancy.

"I'm glad you're not mad at me."

"Where were you three headed?"

"We just planned to go upriver. We really didn't have a concrete destination in mind."

"Didn't you want to join the resistance force?" asked Liya.

"We did, but to be honest, I wouldn't mind settling down in a peaceful place where nobody knows me. I want to live a quiet life too."

"Where can you find a place like that now?"

"That's the problem—the only option left is to join the resistance. If there were a convent that's intact, I wouldn't mind going there."

"Come on, don't you want to find a good man and have a family?"

"Not until we drive the Japanese out of our country."

I mulled over their conversation, which changed my impression of Meiyan somewhat. I used to think she was just a hothead, but now I could see that she was also longing for a normal life.

SOON AFTER CHRISTMAS, a former schoolmate of Yaoping's back in Japan came to see him. The man was tall and well turned out, wearing a business suit and patent-leather shoes. He looked like a middle-aged dandy, his hair pomaded shiny and his face somewhat bloated, but he was agreeable, spoke amiably with a northeastern accent, and called me sister-in-law. He used a long umbrella as a walking stick. Yaoping took him into our inner room, where they talked over tea and spiced sunflower seeds for hours, deep into the night. Now and then I went in with the teakettle and refilled the pot for them. I didn't go to bed but instead drifted off in a chair in the sitting room. Their voices rose and fell; at times they seemed to be arguing.

After the man left, my husband became restless, pacing the floor and smoking his pipe. He let out a long sigh and shook his head.

"What did he want?" I asked Yaoping about the visitor.

"They're preparing to establish a new national government, and he asked me to join them."

"So they offered you a job?"

"Yes."

"In what office?"

"The Ministry of Culture or the Ministry of Education."

"Doing what?"

"A vice minister."

"That's big!"

"I know. Obviously they've run out of candidates for the top jobs.

Under normal circumstances no one would think of me for a position like that. But I mustn't serve in a puppet government. That would be treason and no one would forgive me for that. Imagine what would happen to me if China wins the war."

"Do you believe we will win?"

"I'm not sure, but the uncertainty doesn't justify any official role in a puppet government. I cannot ruin our family's name that way. Besides, our son's already in the Japanese clutches."

"I agree. Did you decline the offer?"

"Of course not. I couldn't turn it down flatly. That would be suicidal, so I told him I would seriously consider the offer. The man talked at length about saving our country by taking a roundabout path."

"What does that mean?"

"He said we should cooperate with the Japanese so that we could at least prevent some parts of China from being totally destroyed and annexed. I couldn't contradict him."

"That kind of talk is based on the assumption that Japan will win the war."

"True, but what should I do?"

"When are you supposed to give him an answer?"

"In three days."

"Can't you hide somewhere? Say, go to Searle's or Lewis's?"

"Well, the national puppet government will be established here, so if they find out I'm still in town, they'll never leave me alone. Heavens, it looks like I can't stay here anymore."

I was glad Yaoping wasn't swayed by the temptation, though he used to talk a lot about how he liked Japan, even Japanese things (he had once owned a Seiko pocket watch with a compass on the inner side of the copper lid). But this wasn't just a matter of his personal integrity or preserving our family's name. If he served in the prospective puppet government, he might be killed by the underground partisans. Even if they didn't finish him off, he would eventually be punished by the Nationalists or the Communists. He would become a public enemy and our family would suffer on his account.

Having talked for hours, we decided that he should leave for

Sichuan to join his university there. We considered whether all of us should go with him, but thought that this would attract too much attention. Besides, I could not abandon my job here. I urged him to set off without delay.

The next evening he left for Cow's Head Hill in the south, where he could stay with a friend temporarily. He took along a handbag and a duffel stuffed with half a dozen books and two changes of clothes. Having no travel permit, he would walk and hitchhike to get out of the areas occupied by the Japanese, and then eventually take a boat or train inland. I gave him all the cash we had, about eighty yuan, and told him not to drink too much tea, which might aggravate his arthritis. Before getting on the rickshaw, he hugged me, Liya, and Fanfan, saying he would miss us terribly. Then he climbed into the vehicle, waving at us. We watched his lean face blurring in the dark until it vanished.

33

RUTH CHESTER WROTE BACK, saying they'd found a place in Shanghai for the five blind girls. We were delighted, and Minnie asked Rulian to send the girls there. The blind girls were reluctant to leave, but we assured them that they'd be better educated and better cared for in the specialized school. Better yet, Shanghai was safer than Nanjing. Minnie gave them each three yuan; the cash had been donated by a Japanese officer, Major Toshikawa, who had visited Jinling twice and was moved by the classes, saying that his daughter was going to a Christian school in Kobe. We didn't tell the girls, or anyone else, where the money was from, but the five recipients were happy.

On the afternoon of January 4, we set out for the Hsia Gwan station in a large car Minnie had borrowed from Lewis. She was at the wheel. I always admired her ability to do things most Chinese women couldn't do: driving, cycling, playing ball games, keeping a dog, hiking. When we had pulled onto Ninghai Road, I reminded Minnie, "Remember when you said you'd teach me to drive?"

"I haven't forgotten. Of course I'll do that. When the war's over, I'll build my own house here and buy myself a little car."

I was pleased to hear that. If only I could be as capable as she. A lot of people here regarded her as "a real man," respecting her stately physique and her ability as a leader.

When we had passed Fujian Road and were approaching Yijiang Gate, we saw more houses leveled—the area was more desolate than it had been the previous winter. The site of the former Communications Ministry was now an immense compound fenced by barbwire, in which more than a dozen huge shacks stood as storehouses for military supplies. Along the way most of the deserted buildings had been torn down, the bricks and wood piled up ready to be shipped away. But the area near the train station was alive with people. Peddlers were hawking goods, while small shops lined the streets, offering soft drinks, fruit, snacks, cigarettes, and liquor. A handful of scalpers hung around the station, a three-story white building topped with a cupola and a spire, and were waving tickets at passersby.

All the trains ran on Tokyo time now, an hour behind China time. Inside the hall of the station, people were standing in two lines for tickets. One was short and only for Japanese passengers, while the other was long, with more than one hundred Chinese people waiting. At its end was Rulian. But the wicket at the head of the long line remained shut, and only the short line was moving. Near us stood a slim Japanese clerk in a blue uniform and a cap with a shiny black peak. We worried that Rulian and the girls might miss the train. Minnie went up to the man and said, "See those words?" She pointed at the slogan pasted above the front door, which declared in big characters: WE MUST UNITE TO BUILD A PROSPEROUS EAST ASIA!

The clerk nodded without speaking. Minnie continued, "Don't you think the way you're treating these Chinese passengers may contravene Japan's policy and undermine the union of East Asia?"

He grinned knowingly, showing his tobacco-stained teeth, but he still said nothing. Then he slowly sauntered back into the office, and a minute later the other wicket opened, selling tickets to the Chinese in line.

Outside the windows a train pulled in, shuddering a little as it came to a stop and disgorged hundreds of passengers. The new arrivals didn't have to wash their hands in Lysol or rinse their mouths with disinfectant anymore, and the guards frisked only two young men as they exited. Life was returning to normal, though the police still checked everyone's papers.

Rulian came back with six train tickets and two platform tickets, and together we led the blind girls out of the hall. After checking in their baggage, we reached track 2; at the west end of the platform, about four hundred Japanese soldiers were lounging around, some

lying on stretchers and some sitting on the ground paved with concrete slabs. A few men flailed their arms, groaning and shouting.
Twenty or so young Japanese women—some in their late teens—
moved among them, handing out rice cakes and water in canteens. A
few fed the soldiers who were all bandaged up. Beyond them stood a
sleeping car, in which some wounded officers were smoking and
drinking tea, while others played cards. The windows of the car were
partly fogged—it must be warm in there. Although the wounded
men on the platform were cared for, to me they still looked like bundles of garbage scattered around in the glaring sunlight. The scene
reminded me of the wounded Chinese soldiers I'd seen here just
over a year ago. What a different sight this was. Yet these men were
in some fashion similar to those Chinese men abandoned by their
generals. Every one of them looked miserable, wasted, and aged.

Ahead of the sleeper for the officers stood three flatcars loaded
with vehicles—trucks, sedans, ambulances, steamrollers, jeeps—
waiting to be shipped to Japan. Now I understood why the Japanese
confiscated automobiles driven by the Chinese.

The train to Shanghai came, and Rulian and the five blind girls got
onto the third car. A window went up, through which they waved at
us. Minnie stepped closer and said to them, "Take good care."

"We'll miss you," one of the girls said, a catch in her voice.

I stepped over and touched their hands too. A locomotive whistled, panting heavily and crawling into the station on the other track.
Before we could say more, a conductor shut the door and latched it
with a clank; their train let out a long guttural hiss and a puff of vapor,
then pulled away. Four hands, three small and one larger, reached
out the window, waving. Minnie blew a kiss to them and I followed
suit.

On our way back, we were drawn aside at Yijiang Gate because
Minnie didn't have her cholera certificate; without the papers, newcomers were not allowed to enter the city. An officer took her to a
cabin nearby and ordered her to receive an inoculation. She protested, insisting that she was not a new arrival and had accidentally
left her medical papers at her home inside the city. "Look," she said

to the man with a pimpled face, "I don't have any baggage in my car. I'm living here, a resident of Nanjing." After she argued for five minutes or so, he let her go without receiving the injection. He warned her that from now on she must carry all her vaccination certificates when she passed the city gates.

34

THE MIDDLE SCHOOLERS had left campus for the winter break. Now our staff and faculty could relax a little. Donna and Alice had gone to Shanghai for vacation. Plumer Mills left Nanjing a week after the New Year. With the International Relief Committee disbanded, he felt he was no longer needed here. Plumer had told us that in Shanghai he would look for a way to get the six IRC men out of prison. Minnie asked him to include Yulan in the group as well, and he agreed, though he said he was still unsure how to make her fit in. Every day Minnie checked the mail, hoping Plumer had made progress. She had confided to me that from now on she would lump Yulan with the six IRC men whenever we appealed to the Japanese for their release. I thought this might be a productive move to get the madwoman out of incarceration. Despite lack of word from Plumer, we were positive that he'd been working hard on the case. He was a fine man, honest and trustworthy.

Again the full moon was waning, the sky getting darker night by night. In the third week of January Mrs. Dennison's Christmas gifts for the staff and faculty arrived, in a large parcel weighing more than eighty pounds. Every year the old woman would spend at least one hundred yuan on presents for the employees on campus—every one of us would get something from her, including the cooks and janitors. Like Minnie, she spoke fluent Mandarin, understood us Chinese, and even observed our customs. Both women had lived in China for decades, long enough for some Chineseness to have entered their bones. Yet unlike the founding president, Minnie would give presents only to a few friends at the Spring Festival. She meant to avoid competing with the old woman, knowing that too many gifts from the school leaders might raise expectations too high among the employees. She had asked me what present I'd like, and I said I wanted her to join my family for dinner on the Spring Festival's Eve, as my husband and son were away. She agreed to come.

Two days after Mrs. Dennison's presents arrived, the staff and faculty gathered at the South Hill Residence in the evening, and Minnie gave us a party at which she handed out the gifts. There were tins of gunpowder tea, bags of raisins and pistachios, zippered Bibles in a bilingual edition, cigarillos, candied fruits, dried pork floss, and even packs of firecrackers for some people's children and grandchildren, but the two fresh mangoes for Minnie were already black and no longer edible. Yet she was pleased to receive a Quaker calendar again.

"What a pity. I've never tasted a mango," said Luhai, who got a paisley tie.

Minnie smiled and told him, "I'll remember to get you some one of these days."

I received a sweater and also a flowered neckerchief for Liya and a pack of sesame toffee for Fanfan. Mrs. Dennison had written the recipients' names on most of the gifts, so it was easy for us to distribute them. The old president was always precise about everything, especially about small favors.

Big Liu raised a double-bang firecracker and said, "Good heavens, who dares to set off this rascal nowadays? The Japanese would come and search for firearms for sure."

That cracked people up. Everyone was happy, and the room grew noisy and hazy with tobacco smoke.

Minnie read Mrs. Dennison's letter to us. The former president feared that the presents might arrive late, so we should take them as gifts for both Christmas and the Spring Festival, which would fall on February 19, still a month away. These presents embodied her thanks to every one of us who had worked so hard at Jinling. She also said she would join us soon.

FOUR

The Grief Everlasting

35

MRS. DENNISON CAME BACK to Jinling in mid-March 1939. With her was Aifeng Yang, who served as her assistant and had taught extensively at the college, including horticulture, children's education, and domestic hygiene. Minnie gave them a welcome-home party, attended by all the faculty and staff. People were excited to see Mrs. Dennison again.

Officially the old woman was just an adviser at our college, but she thought of the college as hers. Already sixty-nine, she was healthy and in good shape despite her grizzled flaxen hair and a little stoop due to chronic back pain. She looked much thinner than before. When she spoke to you at length, she'd gesticulate unceasingly, her longish face would begin adopting an expression between smiling and crying, and her tawny eyes would turn fiery. Yet most of the time she looked miserable, as if something unfortunate had just happened to her. She told us that many wealthy families in the States that used to donate to Jinling had become reluctant to give on account of our school's uncertain future, so she was resolved to restore the college and to attract American donations again.

The next morning I took her around campus. We went to the poultry center, where Rulian enthusiastically greeted Mrs. Dennison, who had once taught her. The old woman was satisfied to see that Rulian still conducted experiments and to hear that some hens could lay two eggs a day. Imagine what an extraordinary contribution this project would make to China's larder if a third of the hens in our country were that productive! Suddenly a chicken broke out cackling. "That must be Matchmaker," Rulian said, rolling her almond-shaped eyes, and went into the shack of coops. She had named every bird in her charge. Matchmaker, a black pullet, often brought other young hens to roosters.

In a flash Rulian came back with a huge brown egg. "See, this hen often lays a double-yolk thing." She showed it to Mrs. Dennison.

The old woman held it with both hands. "Oh dear, it's still warm."

"You can have it," Rulian said.

"Are you sure?"

"Absolutely, a double-yolk egg can't hatch."

Mrs. Dennison took out a linen handkerchief and wrapped it around the egg. Rulian found a pastry box and handed it to her. "This is good," the old woman said, putting the bundle into the small paperboard container.

We went to the gardens in the back of campus, where the damage left by the refugees was still visible, although the trees were all leafing and some shrubs were fluffy with wet blossoms. After looking through various parts of the college, the old woman was not pleased, except with the two-hundred-yard macadam road that ran through the expanse between the front gate and the quadrangle—Minnie had gotten it paved for only one-third of the regular price.

"This still looks like a refugee camp," Mrs. Dennison said, furrowing her brow.

I didn't reply, knowing she must dislike the large number of poor students in the Homecraft School. We were standing on the short bridge over the creek that meandered from the pond behind the Library Building to the pond beside Ninghai Road, near the Faculty Residence. Below us a flock of white ducks paddled by, all in silence. In the bushes nearby, orioles were twittering merrily as if crazed with spring joy, but in the south a squadron of bombers was droning, now visible and now lost in the clouds billowing above a wooded hill. Some city, such as Ningbo or Fuzhou, would be bombed today.

"We must bring the college back," Mrs. Dennison said, and shook her head. Her face was slightly gray while her eyes glazed with pain and anger.

"Yes, we must," I echoed.

"Damn the Japanese—they destroyed everything."

"Do you think they'll let us restore the college, given their anti-Christian policy?"

She gave a deep sigh. "I don't care. I just want Jinling to be what it was."

Minnie had assigned Mrs. Dennison the large provost's office. For the time being, the old woman and Aifeng lived at the South Hill Residence, in a five-room apartment on the first floor. They both liked the arrangement. Mrs. Dennison didn't teach, but Aifeng started a course in child guidance in the Homecraft School. Many students who were mothers wondered how this unmarried woman with a lithe figure, a flat belly, and smiling eyes could teach them childcare and child welfare, but after a few classes they were all eager to listen to her, amazed that she knew so much about the subject. I liked Aifeng, who was easygoing and didn't gossip.

Minnie sent Alice to the U.S. embassy to fetch Mrs. Dennison's wedding silver. The large portmanteau, recovered by a Russian diver from the sunken *Panay*, was misshapen and the silver pieces were tarnished, but the old woman wasn't upset and merely said, "I'll sell the whole set if someone offers a good price. Our college needs funds anyway."

I admired her largesse. Mrs. Dennison praised Minnie for having our college's most important documents duplicated before sending them away, particularly those that were ruined in the water-damaged portmanteau. I was glad that the two women seemed to be getting along.

Then, a week later, the old woman came down with an illness no doctor could diagnose. I was worried that she might have had a stroke, for she suffered some kind of emotional incontinence: she was unable to control her tears and laughter even in front of visitors. According to Aifeng, Mrs. Dennison was heartbroken about the condition of our college, and when alone, she couldn't help sighing and often wept. She confessed to Aifeng, "Even when my husband died, I didn't feel so sad. It's like my life is over." She lay in bed most of the time and took her meals in her bedroom. We all knew she had always wanted Jinling to be the number one women's college in China. From the outset she had emphasized, "We aspire to become China's Wellesley." That had pleased Madame Chiang, who had graduated from Wellesley, so much that the first lady, together with her two sisters and in memory of their mother, donated the funds for a dormitory building and the Practice Hall, both of which were built under Minnie's supervision.

Meanwhile, Minnie received word from Plumer Mills that the six IRC men might be released from prison soon, though there was no progress in Yulan's case. In his letter Plumer wrote that the madwoman was classified as a mental patient, so the Japanese would not consider releasing her on the basis that she might disrupt public order. Plumer said farewell to us, as he was about to leave for the States.

Minnie and I went to see Yulan again. The young woman looked sickly and six or seven years older than her age; evidently they wouldn't let her out for fresh air and sunlight. She was now kept in a small room with a teenage girl, who was also demented. They each had a cot, and with permission, visitors could go in and see them. Minnie handed Yulan a bag of dried persimmons, which the madwoman tore open with her teeth. She took a bite of the sugar-frosted fruit, and said, "Wow, this is amazing! I haven't tasted anything like this in ages." Her elongated eyes glittered, and her chin moved from side to side as she munched. In spite of the warm weather, she still wore Minnie's light woolen coat, though its fur collar was gone. What happened to the jacket we brought her last time? I wondered, but didn't let the question out.

"I'm glad you like it," Minnie said about the fruit, seated on the only stool in the room while I was sitting on the other girl's cot.

Yulan asked her ward mate, "Little Catty, d'you want some?"

"No, I eat fresh fruit only," the teenager muttered, and kept picking her ear with a long matchstick.

"Actually she only eats rice, not even vegetables," Yulan told Minnie. "Sometimes she won't eat for two or three days in a row, so they have to tie her up and force-feed her."

"What happened to her?" Minnie asked.

"She's a mental case. The Japs killed her folks in front of her and stabbed her in the neck." Indeed, on the girl's nape was a purple scar that still looked raw.

Minnie asked Little Catty, "Do you want me to bring you something when I come next time?"

"Bring me a knife, a long sharp knife," the girl said through her teeth, her eyes glinting.

"See, see, she's a crackpot," Yulan cried. "But I also could use a big knife so no man will dare to come close to me."

After promising Yulan that we would come to see her again and bring her another jacket and a dress, we left. Stepping out of the doorway, for some reason Minnie said, "I wish we could set this building on fire so in the middle of the mayhem, we could smuggle Yulan and Little Catty out of here."

"That's a great idea," I said.

She grinned and the corners of her mouth crinkled a bit.

We stopped by Tianhua Orphanage to see Monica, who welcomed us effusively, but her cheeks were flushed, her blond hair thinner than before and the rings under her eyes darker. She confessed that she had tuberculosis; yet she smiled, saying, "If God wants me back, I'm ready—I'm willing to go anytime." She spoke as though longing for relief, dabbing her mouth with a hand towel whenever she coughed.

I wondered whether it was appropriate for Monica to stay with the children. Wouldn't she spread the germs and give them the disease? The Japanese were obsessed with sanitation and hygiene—why wouldn't they intervene in this case? Well, to them, these babies must be no more than bastards.

We didn't touch the tea a nurse had poured for us, but chatted with Monica for a good while. The orphanage kept fewer children now, seventeen in total; eleven of them couldn't walk or talk yet. They all looked undernourished, and some stared at the grown-ups with dumb, unblinking eyes. I couldn't help but wonder if they were retarded.

"This boy's father is Japanese," Monica told us, pointing at a bony baby whose face was a little shriveled.

"You mean his mother threw him away?" Minnie asked in surprise.

"Yes, some Chinese women, especially the unmarried ones, are too ashamed to keep babies fathered by Japanese soldiers."

"I don't blame them, but it's a sin to abandon innocent children."

Monica heaved a sigh. "We have eight babies of mixed blood."

"I can't tell a Chinese baby from a Japanese baby," Minnie said.

"Neither can I," I put in.

"It's hard to differentiate them indeed," Monica told us. "Five of them were given to us by their mothers, and three were brought over by a Chinese policeman, who picked them up at the doorstep of a temple."

"What happened to those older orphans?" Minnie asked.

"You mean those six- and seven-year-olds?"

"Yes."

"They were sent to our mission school in Changsha."

Minnie's face brightened. "Monica, you've been doing an angel's work."

"You think I don't know what you've been up to?" The nun smiled, her deep-set eyes gleamed, and her gaunt face wrinkled a bit but was calm. "Be careful. The Japanese and their flunkies hate you. They don't want Christianity to take root and flourish in China."

"I'll try not to be afraid," Minnie said.

"Right, to be afraid is not a way of living. If the soul lives forever, death is no more than a stage of life and we have nothing to fear."

"You're right."

I was impressed by Monica's remarks. The nun was in her late thirties at most but exuded so much serenity that the orphanage, shabby as it was, reminded me of an oasis in tumbling waves.

Back on campus, I filled a glass jar with cod-liver oil. I was in charge of two large barrels of it, given to us by John Magee long ago, and every student at Jinling had been taking a teaspoon of the oil a day since last winter, as Robert Wilson had instructed after he'd examined some of the girls. Minnie dispatched Ban to deliver the cod-liver oil to Monica with a note saying she needed to take it every day.

36

MY HUSBAND HAD WRITTEN me that he had left Sichuan for Kunming and joined the faculty of the National Southwest Associated University. He couldn't write regularly, because he was afraid those who wanted him to serve in the puppet government might find out his whereabouts and mistreat us here. As long as he was safe, Liya and I could feel at ease. My son-in-law, Wanmu, also wrote. He'd been moving around a lot with his intelligence unit but was well and devoted to fighting the Japanese. He missed his wife and son but couldn't possibly come back to see them. Liya sometimes got depressed and cried at night, though during the day she always looked normal and did what she was supposed to do. She once confessed to me that she had often dreamed of Wanmu and was worried that they might never be together again. What if he hit it off with another woman? she asked me. Nowadays the servicemen tended to live an unrestrained life, grasping at every small pleasure that came their way, because they might be killed at any time. I told Liya to scrap such silly thoughts. Wanmu was a dependable man, though I had never liked him that much. He was capable but somewhat nondescript, with a curved scar beside his nose. Liya could have done better than accepting his proposal. Yet I was certain he'd take good care of his family; that's why I agreed to her marrying him.

To my astonishment, I received a letter from Mitsuko in late March. It contained a photograph and a piece of paper stamped with a baby's handprints and footprints in black ink. Those must be Shin's. Apparently Mitsuko didn't know enough Chinese to write a note. The photo showed Shin smiling, with his eyes glittering a little and his mouth widening. He looked happy and healthy. On the back of the picture his mother penned: "Shin, 100 days." Seeing those words, I couldn't help my tears. If only I could hold him.

At night after Fanfan went to sleep, Liya and I sat in our large bed

leaning against each other and talked about Mitsuko and Shin. I wondered if we should write to them. "Mom, Mitsuko probably can't read
Chinese," Liya said. "Maybe we should send her something instead."

"But what can we send?" I thought aloud. Besides the difficulty in
coming by something nice, I wasn't sure that the international mail
was reliable.

We stuck to our former decision not to write Mitsuko, because we
still had to keep our Japanese relations secret here. If people knew
about Haowen's Japanese wife and child, they might find out where
he was and then condemn us as a traitor's family. As long as the war
was going on, we'd better not exchange letters with Mitsuko. On the
other hand, I felt uneasy just ignoring her.

"Do you think you can accept Mitsuko as a member of our family?" I asked Liya.

"She's Shin's mother, so we may not have a choice."

I liked her answer. Liya had her father's head, acute and rational.
"Plus Haowen loves her," I said.

"I hope I can have a Chinese sister-in-law, though." Her pointy
chin jutted aside while her short nose twitched.

"You mean Haowen should have a second wife?" I had never liked
the custom of polygamy, which was still practiced.

Liya smiled, displaying an eyetooth. "I don't know. We're in the
middle of a war and anything can happen." She drew the toweling
coverlet up to Fanfan's chin and then pulled the string to turn off the
light.

"Sleep tight," I said.

Outside the latticed window an owl was hooting. I thought about
Liya's words. What she'd said about a Chinese sister-in-law could be
a possibility, but that should be up to Haowen and Mitsuko. According to what I knew about her, she was a good girl and a loving mother.
If only I could get to know her. I would try to persuade her to come
to live here after the war.

I SHARED my grandson's new photograph with Minnie. She observed him carefully and told me, "He has your mouth."

"Liya said the same."

"If I were you, I'd go to Tokyo this summer."

"I can't get travel papers," I said, without telling her that I couldn't afford such a trip either. We used to have a few valuable paintings, but the Japanese soldiers had made off with them, and there was nothing else I could sell to raise the money.

"What are you going to do, then?" She put her elbow on the glass desktop and looked me in the face, her eyes clear and warm.

"I've no idea." I sighed.

"Can't you write to Mitsuko?"

"She doesn't know Chinese, Haowen told me. If my husband were home, he could write to her in Japanese, but I don't think it's safe to get in touch with her at this time."

"Why not? She's your family, isn't she?"

"You know how crazy people could get here if they knew we have Japanese relations. We have to be very cautious."

"Oh, I see. Everything becomes complicated when it happens in China. But if you're afraid of using your own address, you can use mine and let Mitsuko send her letters to my care. I'll pass them on to you."

"That's a wonderful idea. It's so kind of you, Minnie. When Yao-ping's back, we might need your help with the letters that way. Thank you in advance."

"No problem. Anything I can do, just let me know."

I dared not write to Mitsuko in Chinese, because she'd have to ask someone to translate such a letter and then our family's connection with Japan would become known. After that conversation with Minnie, I felt even closer to her. I knew that Mrs. Dennison disapproved of her, but I'd do anything to help my friend.

37

TWO WEEKS LATER, Mrs. Dennison, having recuperated, offered to keep the books for Jinling. Minnie was pleased, because no matter how hard she tried, she couldn't balance the accounts. Mrs. Dennison was far better at managing money than Minnie. Yet I grew somewhat apprehensive and wondered why the old woman was so eager to take over the treasury. This could be a step toward her taking full control of the college. As a matter of fact, she had always been the real power here, because the donations we got from the States came by and large through her hands. In addition, most of the deans and department heads of our college had been her students.

I offered to take Mrs. Dennison downtown, as ever since she'd gotten back she'd been saying that she would love such a trip. She welcomed my idea but preferred a walk to a rickshaw. We set out for the Confucius Temple in the former amusement district in the southern part of the city, each carrying a shoulder bag printed with JINLING WOMEN'S COLLEGE. She was wearing a long silk dress, her arms spattered with freckles. I was amazed that she was in summer clothes because it wasn't that warm yet. I had on a vest and poplin slacks. The moment we stepped out the front gate, we came face-to-face with a crowd—more than one hundred women were kneeling there, all poor and underfed. Minnie was standing in front of them. They were crying out, "The Goddess of Mercy, help us! Help us, please!"

"Please get up," Minnie shouted. "Get up, all of you."

"Take pity on us, the Goddess of Mercy!"

"Give us some work to do!"

"Help us, please!"

"Get up, all of you get up!" Minnie shouted again.

None of them obeyed and all kept begging her, a few even kowtowing.

"Please get to your feet so we can talk," she said loudly, "or I'll go back to my office."

At last some of them rose and a few stepped closer. "What's this about?" Mrs. Dennison asked.

"I don't have the foggiest idea," I answered.

Minnie said to the women at the front of the crowd, "Why are you doing this?"

"Principal Vautrin, aren't you gonna open a shoe factory?" asked a middle-aged woman wearing puttees.

"Who told you that? We can hardly continue with our current programs."

"Please hire some of us, Principal," a small woman begged. "We all have hungry kids to feed."

"There's no principal here," Mrs. Dennison said. "We're a college that has only a president."

The women looked baffled, having no idea about the difference between a president and a principal. Minnie told them, "Mrs. Dennison is right. Don't call me that again. Just call me Miss Hua, all right? We have no plan for any factory. What you heard is a rumor."

Seeing that they were still unconvinced, Minnie added, "If a factory opens here in the near future, you all can call me a liar. We're a college. We're not supposed to run a factory. Understood?"

Some of the women turned, starting to move away. Several came over to say hello to Minnie, while Mrs. Dennison stood at a distance from them. She kept glancing their way with a frown, her face colored in blotches.

Mrs. Dennison and I continued on to Ninghai Road, which the locals called Christian Way for its superb quality. We were very proud of this road, which the city had built especially for our college in 1921, when Jinling was under construction. The private contractor for the campus buildings, Ah Hong, had distrusted the official team of engineers and workmen, afraid that the foundation they were to lay for this street might not be firm enough for his trucks, so he turned to Minnie. She read every word on road construction in the *Encyclopaedia Britannica* and gave detailed directives, from the type of gravel to the use of a steamroller instead of stone rollers pulled by men. As a result, this road, costing about ten times as much as the one originally planned, was still intact, whereas other roads built at around the same time had fallen apart within two or three years and had had to be repaved.

Mrs. Dennison and I headed south toward the Zhan Yuan Garden area, where the Confucius Temple stood. She seemed unhappy about the incident that had just taken place at Jinling's front entrance, which showed that the Homecraft School might have given these women the wrong impression, since it produced soaps, candles, towels, and umbrellas. The old woman remained silent, which made me uncomfortable. I knew Minnie must have felt embarrassed by the poor women calling her the Goddess of Mercy. To Mrs. Dennison, that must have smacked of idolatry.

As we walked along Zhongzheng Road, the old woman said finally, "Minnie is outrageous. She shouldn't have indulged in that kind of personality cult."

"I'm sure she doesn't like it at all," I ventured. "Those women embarrassed her."

"She ought to feel abashed. Nobody alive should be dubbed a goddess." Her upper lip puckered as she spoke.

I didn't know how to continue and turned reticent again, feeling uneasy because I hadn't told Minnie about this downtown trip with Mrs. Dennison. Along the street I noticed that some Japanese stores had closed, perhaps because business was bad—their goods were too expensive and couldn't be shipped out to the countryside. I'd heard that some Japanese shop owners and restaurateurs had left Nanjing. Many who remained followed the practice common in Manchuria of joining some Chinese as business partners or acting as their protectors or liaisons so as to profit without investing any capital.

We saw a lot of peddlers and small stores, some even selling looted objets d'art—paintings, calligraphy scrolls, marble sculptures, antique bronzes. Mrs. Dennison could not believe her ears when a vendor asked only two yuan for a pair of small Ming vases. She examined the vessels for a long time, turning them this way and that, but finally put them down, perhaps reluctant to let me see her buy purloined things. I told her, "Nowadays only food is expensive." Indeed, a bony capon sold for two yuan as well.

The area around the Confucius Temple had again become a marketplace, bustling with people, wheelbarrows, panniered donkeys, and carts drawn by animals. On both sides of the streets a number of buildings remained roofless, some with the top stories gone, but shops were open on the ground floors. There were restaurants, grocery stores, teahouses, opium dens, barbershops, pet stores full of birdcages and aquariums, herbal pharmacies, pawnshops, and even a bathhouse. Anywhere you turned, vendors would shout their wares in singsongy voices. At a street corner a clutch of people stood before a wide bulletin board; today's newspapers had been tacked to it for those who couldn't afford to buy one. Beyond the board, the narrow Chinhuai River flowed almost invisibly, its greenish water wrinkled a little by a breeze. On the opposite bank, a few middle-aged women were beating laundry on flat rocks with wooden paddles. A redroofed boat came through a bridge arch, and on it two gentlemen were playing chess while a teenage boy at the stern rowed with a scull.

In a small alley, its entrance decked with two strings of tiny sundisk flags, I noticed a number of brothels, all on the top floors with balconies, some of which, as the photos on their windows showed, employed women from Japan as well. The Japanese prostitutes, though mostly in their thirties and forties, charged twice as much as the Chinese women doing the same work and fifty percent more than the Korean prostitutes. I'd heard of such places but had not expected to see them here. It was Jimmy Pan, the most active official in the puppet municipality, who'd been instrumental in setting up these bordellos. In private the Chinese often argued about his role in this matter, some saying that Jimmy had done the city a service by finding a way to protect the good honest women, while others maintained that he'd sold his soul to the devil and become the number one traitor here. Personally, I believed he should be punished for helping to set up the brothels. A poster once appeared on the city wall announcing that he would be beheaded as soon as our army came back and retook Nanjing. Jimmy Pan had also been a board member of the former International Relief Committee and was actively involved in charity work. He was one of the few officials whom the foreigners could trust. To be fair, he was at most a small-time traitor, similar to many of the officials in the municipality; the major traitors were those who had been collaborating with the Japanese to form a national puppet government, which was still in the making. Yet however a traitor, minor or major, might try to justify himself, the Nationalists had issued a clear, indisputable definition of treason: insofar as the enemy's army occupies the land of China, whoever works for them is a traitor.

By now Mrs. Dennison had recovered from the scene she had witnessed with Minnie, saying, "Amazing, you Chinese can survive anything."

"Just a year ago," I said, "everything here lay in ruins. Every house was gutted and had lost its roof, and many were burned down. Who could have imagined that this district would come back to life so soon?" As I was speaking, anger again surged in me. I had lived in Nanjing long enough to consider it my new hometown.

"I guess," Mrs. Dennison went on, "this city was destroyed time and again in history, so people here must be accustomed to all sorts of devastations."

"True, that may explain why we can survive a catastrophe like this Japanese occupation."

The Confucius Temple had been repainted crimson, and even the huge stone lions in front of it and the placards hanging beside its doors had been washed clean. The gateway, with its flying eaves and colored tiles, was decorated with two rows of lanterns, each printed with the character HAPPINESS, below which people hustled to and fro. The Japanese seemed to mean to preserve this shrine and restore its popularity.

We entered a stationery store on the waterside to see if there was something we could buy for the college. The owner, a fleshy-faced man with a hairy mole on the wing of his broad nose, said delightedly, "Welcome to this hovel. President Dennison, I'm so happy to see you back." He nodded at her, beaming.

"Nanjing's home," she said. "I've nowhere else to go."

She was so pleased by his words that she bought a pack of Dearer Than Gold ink sticks.

I knew she couldn't use a writing brush, so she had probably purchased them as a present.

We took a rickshaw back. When we arrived at Jinling, dinner was already over at the dining hall, so we had chicken noodles at my home. After the meal, we drank pu-erh tea while Liya, who knew English, since she had attended a missionary school, read an article in the *North China Daily News* out loud. It reported that the Japanese army had just captured Guling, a hill-encircled resort town in Jiangxi Province, where foreigners and Chinese officials used to flock to escape the summer heat, though it was unclear how many men our army had lost this time. The Japanese claimed that they had eliminated all five thousand defenders, but that was unlikely, because the Nationalist troops were already familiar with the Japanese tactics and knew how to avoid annihilation.

Mrs. Dennison thanked me for a wonderful afternoon and evening. I was glad but unsure if this meant she would now treat me better. If Dr. Wu were around, she could mediate between the old president and Minnie, whom she was fond of, but I was only a forewoman and couldn't possibly perform that function. I just wanted to be on decent terms with Mrs. Dennison. Not only did I need to make sure my family could stay in its safe haven; I also hoped I could calm the old woman if she became upset or angry.

38

FIVE OF THE SIX IRC men were released from jail on April 27, thanks to an amnesty in honor of Emperor Hirohito, whose thirty-eighth birthday was two days away. Our part-time math teacher was among those released, though one student's father was still in jail. The returned men had all been instructed not to talk about their ordeal in prison, or else they would be brought in again. One of them had a broken wrist, and another, his face partially paralyzed, could no longer speak coherently. Yet none of them would disclose what had happened to them, and each one just said he was lucky to come back alive.

In private, one told me that the torturers had often tied him to a bench, then stacked bricks on his feet and filled him with water mixed with chili powder until his stomach was about to burst. At first he denied all of the charges, but later he confessed to whatever crime they said he'd committed. He even said that he had helped John Magee and Holly Thornton embezzle relief funds and had single-handedly stolen a military truck, though he didn't know how to drive. "I just didn't want to be killed by those savages," he said, and shook his head, which was afflicted with favus and reminded me of a molting bird.

"Did they believe what you told them?" I asked him.

"Perhaps not. They once said I lied to them, so they punched and kicked me till I passed out."

"Who beat you, Japanese or Chinese?"

"Some Chinese running dogs man the torture chamber. Every now and then one or two Japanese officers showed up too."

No rally would be allowed on the emperor's birthday except for those organized officially. To keep the girls preoccupied, Minnie declared April 29 a big cleaning day. Then the Autonomous City Government demanded that we send one hundred people downtown to take part in the celebration of the emperor's birthday. They didn't specify that the participants from our campus must be young students, so Minnie believed we should pick a hundred women from the Homecraft School. Mrs. Dennison objected, saying they were not students and must not represent Jinling College. She insisted on sending middle schoolers instead.

We discussed this, and everyone, including the American teachers, supported Minnie's idea, because we knew some of the girls were loose cannons and might take the public celebration as an insult. If some of them started an anti-Japanese chant or song, it would get us into deep water. What's more, Alice and Donna had informed us that some young girls were planning to demonstrate against the Japanese occupation. We didn't want to kindle their anger by sending them to the official rally, so we chose the women from the Homecraft School.

As we were setting out the next morning, bearing a large banner that displayed the characters JINLING WOMEN'S COLLEGE, Mrs. Dennison blocked the procession outside the front gate. She said to Minnie, "I won't let you bear our flag, because these are not students of our college."

Minnie grimaced but caved in. "Okay, we won't carry it, then."

So we continued downtown without the flag, while Mrs. Dennison held it with both hands, standing there alone and watching us march away. The white silk flapped a little, shielding a part of her thin shoulder. It was almost midmorning, the sun already high and hot. The women all knew we were going to demonstrate in honor of Emperor Hirohito, so they looked dejected and walked silently, some hanging their heads low.

In the city, martial law was already in force to prevent protests and to control drunken soldiers. We stood in the plaza before the city hall, each given a tiny sun-disk flag made of paper. The celebration started with a review of Japanese troops—one thousand cavalry, three columns of mountain guns, and a regiment of infantry marched past the platform near the templelike building with three tiers of flying eaves. Every officer raised a gleaming sword, its back against his collarbone, to lead his unit forward. The band was blasting out

"Japan's Army." As the troops passed the platform, they shouted, "Long live the emperor!" and "Japan must conquer Asia!" and "Wipe out our enemies!" On the platform stood two Japanese generals in high boots and some Chinese officials, including Jimmy Pan, a tall, intelligent-looking man despite his slightly lopsided eyes. Pan always claimed that he'd taken the office of vice mayor because it was the only way he could help protect the local citizens' interests, but the Nationalist government had already set the price of two thousand yuan on his head. Some of the puppet officials on the stage kept their eyes on the floor throughout the ceremony, though they applauded from time to time.

One such official, Yinmin Feng, a scraggy man with jug ears who had earned a master's in archaeology from Tokyo University, gave a short speech, which, despite its brevity, was empty prattle. He praised the Japanese authorities for their efforts to restore order and normalcy in the city. He also insisted that all Chinese support "the New Order of East Asia." He stepped down from the rostrum in less than ten minutes, after shouting "Heaven bless the emperor!" and "Long live the cooperation between Japan and China!" Then the Nanjing garrison commander, Major General Amaya, delivered a speech through an interpreter, in which he listed several causes for the suffering the Chinese here had gone through. Among them two were primary. First, the Chinese forces were responsible for the devastation of Nanjing, because they had resisted the Imperial Army, which was renowned for its bravery and invincibility. And once defeated, the Chinese soldiers had disappeared among the civilians, exploiting women and children as camouflage. That was very unprofessional. Also, Chiang Kai-shek had instilled in the entire population so much hatred for the great Japanese nation that most civilians became hostile to the Imperial Army, refusing to cooperate or give provisions. Worse yet, there were snipers everywhere, who mainly targeted Japanese officers; consequently, many commanders had to wear the uniforms of the rank and file to disguise themselves. When Nanjing was taken, the army had no alternative but to "mop up" all the stragglers and deserted soldiers. The second cause was that some foreigners from a certain country—namely the United States—

remained here, and their presence emboldened the Chinese to oppose the victorious troops. Those foreigners actually provoked the Japanese soldiers to break rules and vent their frustration on civilians, so the Westerners were the real troublemakers for China and should be repatriated.

The pudgy general wore circular glasses and two rows of ribbons on his chest. As he was reading from the written speech, his eyes were so close to the paper and the microphone that the audience could hardly catch a glimpse of his doughy face. What's worse, his voice was drowned out by the interpreter, a young dandy with slick hair and powdered cheeks, whose delivery in Mandarin was much more impressive.

After the speeches there was a large demonstration against communism, which the women from our school didn't join. We just stood there as spectators. Even Chiang Kai-shek was labeled an arch-Communist who'd taken up the hammer and sickle of the Russians, and some placards with his portrait crossed out in red ink were raised among the civilians who lined up in front of the platform.

As soon as the celebration was over, Minnie and I led our students back to campus. John Allison from the U.S. embassy telephoned Jinling and urged the American women to be vigilant and to avoid the downtown area for a few days.

We wouldn't let any students go there either, and instead held a service late in the afternoon. More than three hundred people gathered in the chapel, and some of them were girls from the middle school. The service started with the hymn "He Leadeth Me." Next was a prayer led by Minnie—for peace in Asia and Europe and for the reduction of the suffering inflicted on the Chinese. Then Lewis Smythe preached his last sermon here, as he was leaving for Chengdu in two days. He wore a gray tunic, which made the narrowness of his shoulders more pronounced. He read out Matthew 5:11–12 and spoke about slander against the righteous as an indication of their virtue. He declared in a cadenced voice, "True Christians should rejoice when evildoers vilify them, for the Lord says that you shall be hated by men for his name's sake. The vilification is proof that you have been doing something right. In fact, all the wicked tongues cannot really discredit you. What they can accomplish is just an emphatic verification of your righteousness. Let the vilifiers wag their tongues and waste their breath while we do our work with a clear conscience." He went on to speak about God as the only qualified judge for the upstanding who would always make fair judgments.

I could tell he was still troubled by the malicious rumors about his collaboration with the Japanese. He had worked so hard for the benefit of the needy and the weak that he deserved to be honored, not slandered. He had recently completed his survey of the damage to our city and its suburbs and secretly published the results in a booklet with the small Mercury Press in Shanghai.

The service ended with the hymn "I'm a Pilgrim." Afterward Mrs. Dennison invited Lewis to a wonton dinner, which Minnie, I, and four others also attended.

That evening the middle-school girls got restless. A few wore black armbands, and some sang patriotic songs in the open. In the south, salvos rumbled while fireworks cascaded over ragged clouds, bringing to mind towering willow crowns and dangling bean sprouts. The racket of the official celebration outraged the girls. A group of them, led by Meiyan, began singing "The Big Sword March," which had been a battle song popular among the troops defending Shanghai twenty months before. Arm in arm, the girls stood in rows, swaying from side to side while belting out: "Big swords chop off the devils' heads. / All the patriotic compatriots, / Now's the time to fight the Japanese invaders!" As they were chorusing, tears bathed their faces and their voices grew shrill. Meiyan was the loudest among them and even kept time with a tiny national flag. She was half a head taller than most of the other participants.

We observed them from the windows of the dining room. After the battle song, Meiyan shouted, "Topple the puppet municipality!"

The crowd, more than a hundred strong, repeated the slogan together, all thrusting their fists into the air. Luhai stood beyond them, massaging his nape with his hand, as if he couldn't decide whether to join in. I could see that he was excited, but why did he just lurk around watching? Did he have a hand in this?

"Repay blood debts in blood!" Meiyan cried again.

All the voices shouted after her in unison.

"Drive the invaders out of China!" she went on.

Again the others followed her in one voice.

Mrs. Dennison said about Meiyan, "I like that girl. She's full of fire and can become a fine leader."

"She's Big Liu's daughter, very hot-blooded," Minnie told her.

"Yes, I saw her and two other girls cursing a Japanese woman on the street the other day," Mrs. Dennison continued. "I've always admired Chinese women more than Chinese men."

"We should stop them," Minnie said. Without waiting for the old woman to respond, she set out. Some of us followed her.

Minnie went up to the girls and said, "All right, enough for today. You all go back to your dorms."

Meiyan, her face burning with passion, stepped forward and blasted, "Why are you so scared of the Eastern devils?"

Taken aback, Minnie said, "I have only your safety in mind. If the Japanese find out about this, they'll start an investigation, and you all will get into trouble."

"Let them come. Who cares?"

"Don't boast like that," Minnie warned.

"Stop it, Meiyan!" I said almost in a cry.

Mrs. Dennison came over and intervened. "Girls, don't do anything rash. Listen to Dean Vautrin. It's for your own good—she just wants to keep you out of harm's way."

"There're no spies here," another girl said.

"You never know," Minnie went on.

The girls looked around to see whether some of the puppet officials' daughters were still among them. None of those rich students was around, though a few had been here half an hour ago, clapping their hands while watching the gorgeous fireworks. One of them had even mocked the demonstrators by sliding her index finger across her throat. Now the girls seemed swayed by Minnie's words; some even took off their black armbands, and some turned, leaving for the dormitories and the classroom buildings. Although the crowd was dwindling, Meiyan and about thirty others continued chanting patriotic songs.

I left with Minnie and Mrs. Dennison, and as we neared the front entrance, we saw a company of cavalry passing by on the street. We stopped to watch the tall horses galloping away and fading into the dark while their hooves clattered on the asphalt. Then we continued toward the south of campus, the two American women's long shadows mingling on the ground bleached by the moonlight.

39

I NOTICED that the students liked Alice very much, not because of their fondness for English but because of the way she conducted her classes. Although thirty-seven, Alice was so youthful and vivacious that if viewed from the rear and with a kerchief over her cornsilk hair, you could easily take her for a student, especially when she was among the girls. She often taught them hymns and American folk songs, staged miniature scenes of American life—shopping, asking for directions, visiting the post office, canvassing—and even showed them how to make lemonade, cakes, and fruit pies. One evening in early May, Minnie, Alice, and I took a stroll through campus while talking about how to monitor the students, particularly the few firebrands, so that they wouldn't run away again or endanger themselves. Alice agreed to often engage them in small talk to follow their concerns. As the three of us were approaching the south dormitory, we saw a crowd in front of the building.

"Yeah, smash her mug!" someone urged. I recognized Meiyan's rasping voice.

We hurried over and saw two students rolling on the ground. One was a tall girl named Yuting, whose father had been among the six IRC men arrested by the Japanese and had died in prison recently. The other was the mousy girl who'd slid her forefinger across her throat on the night of the emperor's birthday, mocking the singers of patriotic songs. "Damn you," Yuting gasped, pulling the girl's hair. "Tell your dad we'll get rid of him sooner or later."

The small girl kicked her assailant aside, rolled away, and scrambled to her feet. "He had nothing to do with your father's death, all right? You're going out of your mind."

"Rip her tongue out of her trap!" Meiyan told Yuting.

The runty girl turned to the crowd. "My dad just designs boats. He only supervises twelve people in his institute. You've blamed the wrong man."

"He builds patrol boats for the Japs," someone said.

"Yeah, your dad is a stooge," added another.

"But he has to work to support our family," the girl wailed, her nose bleeding. "He has no direct contact with the Japs."

"I'm gonna to finish you off right here!" Yuting yelled, and rushed toward her again.

All of a sudden, the cloudless night became darker, the moon fading away. The whitish boles of the ginkgos and aspens around us disappeared. A handful of yellowish stars blinked faintly, as if the invisible chains connecting them had all at once snapped, scattering them across the sky. Everybody turned silent, awestruck. It took me a while to realize that a full eclipse was under way. Dogs began barking, and a tremendous din rose from the neighborhood in the southwest. Then came the sounds of people beating pots, pans, and basins while firecrackers exploded and horns blared. Every household in the area seemed to be engaged in the great commotion, which threw the girls into a panic. They all stood there listening; some moved their heads this way and that, totally confused. I felt embarrassed by the racket, which showed how backward we Chinese were in understanding this natural phenomenon.

"What's going on?" Alice asked in a guarded whisper.

"It's an eclipse," Minnie said.

"That I know."

"People believe that some animal in the sky is swallowing the moon, so they're making all that noise to scare it away."

Indeed, this was the locals' way of driving off the mystical creatures, a dragon or a divine hound, who was attempting to eat up the moon. If they'd still had firearms, I was sure they'd have fired volleys of bullets and pellets into the sky. There was simply no way to convince them that the moon's momentary disappearance was merely due to Earth's passing between the moon and the sun.

Alice told the girls in her stern contralto voice, "You all see that the Lord of Heaven doesn't approve of your fighting like wild animals. Now, go back to your dorms."

Meiyan, who knew English better than the others, told the girls what the teacher meant. At once the crowd dispersed, disappearing into the dark or into the nearby dormitories. A few scraps of paper were fluttering on the ground in the dim light shed through several windows.

Once the girls were out of earshot, we couldn't help laughing. "You scared the heck out of them," Minnie told Alice.

"We had to break up the fight. The eclipse came in handy."

"You'd better explain to them that it's just a natural phenomenon—that there's no such thing as a dragon or divine dog."

"Okay, I'll speak about it in class tomorrow."

A couple of minutes later, the moon came out again, bright and golden like a huge mango. In the distance a line of electric poles reappeared with the wires glistening, and the distant din subsided. We headed back to Minnie's quarters. Alice told us, "I once saw an eclipse in Kyoto, but nobody made a fuss about it. People just went out and watched."

"That's why I sometimes wonder how a backward country like China could fight Japan," Minnie said.

"Do you believe China will win this war?" Alice asked.

"Only in the long run and with international help."

"I'm sure we'll win eventually," I said.

We entered the flower garden encircled by a white picket fence that Minnie had designed a decade before. The air was intense with the scent of lilacs, sweetish and slightly heady. Alice was worried about her job here. Her former girls' school, sponsored by our denomination, had shut down, and she felt that Mrs. Dennison was always lukewarm about her, probably because it was Minnie who had hired her. Minnie assured her that Jinling needed English teachers and she'd be in demand for a long time, so there was no reason to worry.

"She's such a pain in the ass," Minnie said about Mrs. Dennison. "I'm wondering if she's the empress dowager reincarnated."

We all cracked up. I said, "Minnie, you must avoid clashing with her. Keep in mind that she's pushing seventy and will retire soon."

"I don't think she'll ever leave China," said Alice.

"That's true," I agreed, "but she'll be too senile to interfere with the college's affairs."

"Sometimes it's so hard to control my temper," Minnie admitted.

"Remember our Chinese saying—a bride will become a mother-in-law one day?"

"I may never have that kind of patience," Minnie said.

"There's no way to remove Dennison," I went on. "All you can do is outlive her. Just don't provoke that crone."

Minnie turned to Alice. "Someday I'll become your crazy mother-in-law and kick you around. Will you still put up with me?"

"Only if you find me a husband first," Alice replied, poker-faced. "Do you have a grown-up son somewhere?"

We all laughed.

40

MRS. DENNISON and Minnie were discussing how to use the funds at hand. I happened to be in the provost's office, and the old president wanted me to join their discussion. Jinling had just received four thousand yuan, which the donor specified should be spent on education programs for the poor. I listened to the two American women without expressing my opinion. Mrs. Dennison talked excitedly, as she always enjoyed making financial plans and was particularly fond of the Chinese saying "Money is like bastards—the more you get rid of, the more will come."

The old woman had been supervising renovation and construction projects on campus. She wanted to have the half-finished apartment house near East Court completed and all the buildings repaired. In addition, she'd have the four ponds cleansed of weeds and algae. All the lotuses and water hyacinths would be eradicated too. She just wanted limpid ponds with some goldfish in them. Because people needed jobs and labor was cheap, she was eager to get the work done without delay.

Minnie sipped the green tea I had poured for her, and said, "What we really need is a neighborhood school for children."

"How are we going to staff it?" Mrs. Dennison asked.

"We don't need to hire any faculty. We can let some students teach the classes. It won't cost much."

"Who will run it?"

"How about letting Meiyan head the school?" Minnie suggested. "It will train the girl to be a leader."

"How old is she?"

"Seventeen."

"Well, I don't know," the old woman said. "I don't think we should have a neighborhood school at the moment. We must make every effort to bring our college back."

"As long as our faculty's away, we can do nothing about that."

"But we can prepare for them to return. I'm sure they will in the near future."

I worried that the old woman would want to hear my opinion. I felt we should start a school for the poor kids in the neighborhood, some of whom had been running wild, since most of the primary schools were gone. On the other hand, I dreaded offending the former president. Luckily, she didn't ask me.

Mrs. Dennison thought that if we renovated the faculty's houses and apartments, we would have an incentive to draw the teachers back. The renovation would include all the classroom buildings as well so as to justify the use of the funds specified for educational purposes. I also missed the former college, particularly the regular schedules and the peaceful academic life, which were so different from the current disorder. I could see why Mrs. Dennison had always emphasized that leisure was essential for the faculty's intellectual and professional growth. Minnie seemed to share that belief and agreed to shelve the plan for the children's school.

Nevertheless, Minnie and I felt uneasy about the renovation, because the future of the college was still uncertain and it might never pay off to bank so much on such an effort.

THREE YEARS AGO our college had decided to build a bungalow for Minnie so that she could meet with faculty and students in small groups in her own home, but because funds were in short supply after the war had broken out, she'd offered to suspend the project. Several faculty members already had houses for their personal use, including Eva Spicer, a professor of history and religion who was a graduate of Oxford. At present, she was teaching in Wuchang and couldn't come back. Her bungalow had been damaged by the three hundred refugees who had sheltered in it for half a year. At Eva's request, Mrs. Dennison decided to have it repaired. The decision pleased Minnie, since Eva was her friend, used to send Minnie bird-feed via British gunboats, and had written that Minnie could borrow her house for the summer. Minnie had told me several times that she was tired of living in the dormitory with more than eighty students, listening to all the noise they made and the wake-up bell at six a.m.

A team of workers came to renovate Eva's bungalow, replacing the broken terra-cotta tiles on the roof, refinishing parts of the floors, fixing the leaky pipes, resealing some panes of glass with putty, and repainting the interior and exterior of the house. A week later it was like new again. Minnie was excited and packed everything, ready to move. She wouldn't mind the sour smell of the paint and couldn't wait to sleep in Eva's queen-size bed. But early in the afternoon, when she was about to ship the first batch of her belongings, Luhai came and told me that Mrs. Dennison had just moved into the bungalow, together with Aifeng. I hurried to Minnie's to brief her about that. She was nonplussed, and also outraged.

There had been shelling in the south, where even the skyline seemed to be jumping with ruddy-edged clouds. Fighting had been going on outside the city since the previous day. It was said that the New Fourth Army, the Communist force liked by the country people because of its strong discipline, was active within ten miles of Nanjing and had been exchanging fire with the Japanese. That afternoon three truckloads of wounded soldiers had been brought back into the city. We'd also heard that many Japanese women and children were leaving Nanjing, which might herald something ominous for the occupiers. Rumor had it that the Japanese military was about to abandon the city, but none of us believed that this would happen.

That evening we visited Mrs. Dennison. We found her in a buoyant mood, and she received us warmly. Seated on a leather sofa, I looked around, admiring the bright, spacious living room. There was carved furniture, and a tall Ming vase stood beside the door. The floor was glossy, just waxed, and the built-in bookshelves, freshly painted, still held hundreds of Eva's books. What a splendid place for entertaining friends. Mrs. Dennison was so lucky. I glanced at Minnie, who must have been nettled by envy. She avoided eye contact with the old woman.

I wondered if Mrs. Dennison had planned to move in all along.

Had Eva said she could use this house as well? Unlikely. A careful person, Eva wouldn't have made such a blunder. Should I tell the old woman that Eva had promised the bungalow to Minnie? What was the good of that? Minnie couldn't possibly chase Mrs. Dennison and Aifeng out. God willing, I hoped they might soon find this place lonesome and too far from everything and might move back to their apartment. Nothing could be done for now.

Minnie remained quiet for the whole visit, while the old woman talked at length about the Rockefeller family. Despite the lethargic stock market in the States, they had just promised to donate more to our college once the war was over. But when would that be?

Mrs. Dennison was so pleased with her new residence that she began to host dinners a few times a week and always invited Minnie. Minnie was grateful at first, but soon she told me that the old woman might be utilizing her popularity to draw visitors. No wonder Mrs. Dennison appeared so friendly to her in front of the guests. The old woman's dinners began to feel more and more onerous to Minnie, who was increasingly chafing under Mrs. Dennison's continual interventions.

In early June Mr. Morrison of the United Christian Missionary Society approached Minnie and proposed that she return to the States to serve as the vice president of their organization, in charge of education.

"What do you think I should do?" she asked me.

"I would accept it if I were you."

"It's hard for me to leave."

"A boat missed may never come again."

She gave it serious thought for some days—it was an opportunity to disentangle herself from the mess here. Though she would still supervise a good number of missionary schools in China, she feared that it would distance her from Jinling. The previous summer another job had been offered her as well—to work on Jinling's executive committee in New York, and although she'd declined, her friend Rebecca Griest had written that the position wasn't filled yet. So New York could be another option for Minnie. She would love to use the libraries at Columbia again, for which she still had an alumni card. She had earned her master's in school administration from that university's Teachers College.

After long consideration, she decided to stay, saying she couldn't possibly abandon Jinling, especially the six hundred poor women in the Homecraft School who regarded her as their protector. Jinling had become her home and China her adopted homeland. She wrote back to Mr. Morrison, stating that she didn't have the training and experience for such a consequential position; that her departure from Jinling would put more burden on Dr. Wu's shoulders, which she would never allow to happen; that a younger and more energetic person would likely be more suitable for the job, since the society needed new blood; and that, above all, she ought to remain here in China's hour of trials. In short, she simply couldn't cut her losses and leave. She showed me her letter and also the reply from Mr. Morrison, who wrote that he understood Minnie's decision and was full of admiration.

As the summer vacation was approaching, some faculty members planned to go elsewhere to escape the sweltering heat. From Aifeng, we learned that she and Mrs. Dennison were leaving for Shanghai soon, and from there they would travel north by ship to a beach resort on Bohai Bay. This news gladdened Minnie, because she believed that once they left, she'd be able to live in Eva's bungalow for the rest of the summer.

It rained on and off for a whole night—enough to revive the withered shrubs and flowers on campus, but not enough to flood the paddies so rice seedlings could be planted, which should have been done two months before. Farmers had been having a tough time this spring. Besides the drought, the turmoil of the war still persisted. During the day many Japanese planes flew by to drop bombs outside the city. It was said that the guerrillas had been active in the vicinity of Nanjing, but the Japanese were determined to keep them away. For a whole week gunfire could be heard in the south.

Mrs. Dennison and Aifeng left a few days later, together with Ban. The boy had never been to Shanghai, so Mrs. Dennison, who was childless, wanted him to visit the metropolis. She was fond of him, having seen him grow up.

On the same day they left, Minnie moved into Eva's bungalow. She was excited to have the entire house to herself now, but when I went to see her the next evening, she said the place felt somewhat isolated. She wasn't sure she would like it.

41

To our astonishment, Mrs. Dennison came back with Ban a week later. Her return embarrassed Minnie, and yet it would be humiliating to move out of the bungalow right away.

Though flustered, Minnie decided to stay in the house with Mrs. Dennison in Aifeng's absence. Aifeng had gone alone to the beach resort in the north to meet her fiancé there. Mrs. Dennison showed no sign of resentment and only told us, "There's so much to do here that I'd better not leave—I won't have a summer vacation anymore. I'm used to the heat here anyway." She still had her personal possessions in the bungalow and hardly needed to unpack.

Minnie soon realized that she couldn't possibly live under the same roof with the old woman for the whole summer, sharing breakfast and supper with her every day, so Minnie applied for a permit from the city's travel office.

The permit arrived the following week. Minnie decided to go to Tsingtao by way of Shanghai, because it would be easier to travel by boat from there. We all were surprised by her sudden decision to spend the summer elsewhere. Rulian decided to give her a picnic send-off at the poultry center and invited seven other young faculty members and me. The main course was *zongzi,* pyramid-shaped dumplings made of glutinous rice, dates, peanuts, and ham. There were also steamed shrimp, sautéed vegetables, and fresh dates. Minnie loved *zongzi* and peeled away the reed leaves, which were wrapped around the rice to give it an herby aroma, but she wouldn't dip it into a plate of brown sugar as we did. She said she liked the natural flavor better. In the center of the table stood a glass jar holding daisies mixed with young dog-tail grass. The flowers were delicate and fluffy, each displaying a disk of white petals that surrounded a golden heart, and they gave off a faint fragrance. Rulian had thoughtfully asked Old Liao to cut a bunch.

It had rained heavily the night before; the air was washed clean and shimmering a little. A few gnats were flickering around. Rulian had not invited Mrs. Dennison. Minnie enjoyed socializing with the young faculty. If Mrs. Dennison were here, Minnie wouldn't have had a peaceful meal. These days, whenever the two of them ran into each other, the old woman would smirk, probably relishing her small victory in chasing Minnie out of the bungalow. I also noticed that Mrs. Dennison would speak louder, with forced cheerfulness, whenever Minnie happened to be within hearing, as if everybody were her friend. I knew the crone meant to provoke her.

THE WEEK AFTER Minnie left, I again heard from Holly. To my surprise, she was in the Zhenjiang area now, working at a refugee relief center. She invited me to visit, saying she lived outside Gaozi, a suburban town that had a train station. Not having seen her for more than a year, I was eager to visit, so I set out a few days later, taking the train early in the morning. It was just a thirty-mile trip to the east, and I brought two pounds of barley taffy along with an umbrella, as it was cloudy.

The refugee relief center was easy to find, in a village outside the town of Gaozi. Holly was ecstatic to see me. She hugged me for half a minute, as if afraid I might disappear the instant she released me. She took me to a ramshackle cottage, into a room she shared with a young woman named Siuchin, whom Holly had mentioned in her letters as her friend. Siuchin turned up a moment later, fetched a thermos of boiled water, and began brewing tea in a porcelain pot. She was tall and had a squarish face, in her mid-twenties. Untying the thin paper string, Holly opened the package I'd brought and poured some of the barley taffy, each piece covered with sesame seeds, onto an enamel plate. I observed her closely and found her aged a bit but in full health, her eyes brighter and her broad face more vivid, though it showed more wrinkles when she smiled. Siuchin had to leave to finish wrapping some iodine tablets, so after telling Holly she would arrange lunch, she went out with a fistful of the taffy.

It was already past midmorning, and Holly and I were reminiscing about people we both knew while munching the sticky candy. I usually don't like sweets that much, but, affected by my friend's great relish, I kept chewing one piece after another. Holly remembered Minnie fondly for her big kind heart and straightforwardness, and she also praised Rulian as a fine young woman, mild and gracious. I saw Holly's violin in its sky-blue case hanging on the wall; a Bible sat below the instrument on her bed, which was just a sheet spread over a blanket and a straw mattress on some boards supported by three small trestles. The Bible, bound in morocco, was the only book in the room. It was the American Standard Version, which I hadn't read yet, since I always used the King James version. Amazed, I asked, "You belong to a denomination now?"

"No, I'm still on my own." Holly smiled, the same old nonchalance on her heavy-boned face. "So far I've always attached myself to a mission group for protection."

"But you dip into the Scriptures."

"Sometimes I enjoy reading them."

"Then why not join the church?"

"Do I need an institution to communicate with God?"

I closed my eyes and announced: "I am the way, the truth, and the life. No one comes to the Father except through me." I paused and opened my eyes to look at her.

"Gosh, you sound like a priest."

"For the nonce I am a bishop." I chuckled, then went on, "Even if you don't need the church, you still need Christ, don't you?"

"That's why I've been looking for him."

"So you've been wandering around in search of the Lord?"

"I also look for him in my heart."

"You're a strange woman, Holly."

"That I won't deny. It was an irony that the Japanese burned my house and set me free."

"How do you mean?"

"Without my old home anymore, I can go anywhere I want to and live a different life."

I'd heard her say that before, so I shifted the subject a little. "I admire your devotion to our people. You've become one of us."

"Not really. I belong to myself only."

"But you're a Chinese citizen, aren't you?"

"Citizenship is just a piece of paper. I belong neither to China nor to America. Like I said, I'm on my own."

"Still, you've been helping us in our cause."

"That's because I believe it's the right thing to do. I've followed only my heart."

"Come on, Holly, you're living a hard life, and so is your friend Siuchin. You cannot say you two haven't made sacrifices for this country."

"We've been doing the work only because we believe it's worth our effort. One doesn't have to love a country to do what's right."

"So you like this kind of life and will live as a widow forever?"

She laughed. "I know what it was like to live with a man I loved. It's enough to love once in a lifetime."

"You still miss your husband?"

"Yes, I do. My husband, Harry, was a poet, although he didn't publish many poems. He was a good man and we enjoyed each other so much that we'd like to be a couple again if we meet after this life."

I chuckled, amused by that quaint notion, as if she were a Buddhist. "So after he died you never found a better man?"

"No. I dated a few, but they were nothing compared to Harry. So my heart gradually shut itself to men."

"How about your friend Siuchin? Doesn't she want to marry and have a family? She's still so young."

"Her late fiancé must've been a splendid fellow or she wouldn't live this way."

"You told me about her loss." I knew Siuchin's fiancé had been an officer, killed in battle by the Japanese.

"She's often said she would've been happy to die for him. She loved him that much. I urged her to settle down somewhere, but she likes wandering around and doing mission work. She feels safer this way."

Siuchin stepped in and announced that it was time for lunch. She had asked the cook to prepare a pork dish, which we should eat before lunchtime; otherwise we might make others crave meat and cause trouble for the kitchen. I followed them out to the shed that served as a dining room.

A small basin of rice and two dishes—one of sautéed tofu mixed with scallions and baby bok choy and the other of pork cubes stewed with pole beans—sat on a makeshift table constructed of two naked boards nailed onto the tops of six short wooden poles. The pork tasted so-so, but I liked the tofu dish and put some of it on my rice and mixed it with chopsticks. Holly used a spoon instead, chewing the meat with relish. I could see that this was a treat for her and Siuchin.

The air smelled of cow dung and freshly sickled grass. In the distance a pond spread beyond rice paddies, dotted with a couple of white geese. As we were eating and chatting, a knot of children appeared, all skin and bones, watching us with hunger-sharpened eyes. Yet none of the kids made a peep or stepped closer. A girl, six or seven years old, with one bare foot on top of the other, opened her mouth halfway, saliva dripping from its corner. As I wondered if I should give them some food, Holly and Siuchin glanced at each other. Then the young woman stood and turned to the five children, saying, "You all go get bowls and chopsticks, and come back in a few minutes. We'll leave you some. But everybody must promise that you won't fight over the food, all right?"

They nodded and raced away. Hurriedly we finished the rice in our bowls and left the benches. Siuchin covered the rest of the rice with a towel and the dishes with a bamboo basket to shield them from the bluebottles droning around. A few of the flies, stripped of their wings, were crawling about on the table. Holly told the cook to keep an eye on the food for the children. "Fine," the man said. "What can I say if you mean to spoil them again?"

"Make sure they share everything."

"I will." The cook's palm was cupped behind his ear as he spoke; he appeared to be slightly hard of hearing.

Holly and Siuchin would have to work in the afternoon as some refugees had just arrived from Anhui, so I stayed another hour and then headed back to the train station. It had begun sprinkling, fat raindrops spattering on treetops, roofs, and my striped umbrella. All the way home, I pondered the two women's lives. I admired them but couldn't say that their way of living was better than mine or Minnie's. Even if we had wanted to live like they did, we were no longer free to do so. In Minnie's case, on her shoulders was the responsibility for those underprivileged women and girls at Jinling, who viewed her as their protector.

42

THE SUMMER MOVED ON almost uneventfully until early July, when a letter arrived from Luoyang. It contained a handwritten note and a newspaper clipping that had my son's snapshot on it. The title of the brief article announced: "Traitor Killed by the Partisans." I read the contents while my heart began thumping so violently that I had to sit down. The article stated that Haowen had been murdered outside a theater in that city. "We are glad that another traitor got his comeuppance," the author declared.

Liya read out the note, written in pencil, which said: "Aunt Gao, your son, Haowen, was killed. He was a good man and they stabbed him when he went out to see a civilian patient in the suburbs. This was probably because a Chinese colonel, a POW, had died in his care. Haowen really did his best for the man, but he had been wounded fatally in the stomach. I am very sorry about your loss." Strangely, the sender of the letter hadn't signed his name, but the fluid handwriting indicated that he must be Chinese, probably a comrade of Haowen's who also served in the Japanese army and therefore was afraid to identify himself.

Both Liya and I burst out weeping. This scared Fanfan, who started bawling too. Liya held him up, her hand covering his mouth. "Don't cry, don't cry, Fanfan. Mom has goodies for you," she said, and took him to the sitting room. When she threw him a half-empty pack of toffee, he stopped blubbering.

Our world was turned upside down, but we dared not make too much noise. We locked the doors and closed the window curtains. Then Liya and I collapsed on the bed, sobbing our hearts out. Our heads touched each other and our hair mingled, wet with tears. "Mom, why did this happen to us? Why?" she went on wailing.

Similar questions were rising in my mind as well, but I was too distraught to say anything coherent. By instinct we knew we must not let our neighbors hear us, so we continued weeping in a subdued way, muffling our voices with our palms.

It would be hard for Liya and me to conceal our grief. I already felt half dead and might not be able to go to work the following day. What should we tell others about the death in our family? We could not say that Haowen had been assassinated by the partisans. That would amount to admitting that he'd been a traitor and deserved the punishment. But wasn't his death already known to lots of people? True, yet it might be known only in Henan Province. Here no one but Minnie knew he had been a doctor in the Japanese army. We might be able to guard the secret of his identity, even if others saw us mourn his death. Liya and I decided to tell people that Haowen had been killed by the Japanese on his way back to China. It was a lie, but it might protect us and also keep his name clean.

We wouldn't be able to do anything about bringing Haowen's body home, and would have to leave him somewhere like a nameless ghost wandering in the wilderness. The Japanese didn't ship their dead soldiers back to Japan. At most they would cut off a finger from a body, burn it with other dead men's fingers, and then send a bit of the ash to each family. The thought of my son's body not being interred properly suddenly seized my heart with a piercing pang, and I cried again.

That night, after Fanfan had gone to sleep, Liya and I talked about Haowen's wife and son in Tokyo. The more we thought about their future, the more hopeless we felt. For the time being, there was no way we could help Mitsuko and Shin. As a matter of fact, as long as the war continued, we dared not even acknowledge their existence publicly. We believed that the Japanese army must already have notified Mitsuko of her husband's death. I couldn't help but imagine the miserable widowhood awaiting her. From now on Shin would have no father and might be treated as a Chinese bastard by other children, who might ridicule and bully him. As though several hands were twisting my insides, I tossed in bed, sobbing again.

The next day I stayed in bed, my limbs so weak that I felt partly paralyzed. Liya cooked rice porridge and brought it to the bedside, but I couldn't eat, choked by a hot lump in my throat. Mrs. Dennison came late in the afternoon and was apparently perturbed by my sickness. I told her that my son had just been killed by the Japanese on his way back to see us, so I needed a couple of days to grieve and recuperate. She was surprised to hear that Haowen had been in Japan, but knowing he'd been my only son, she could see that the loss was colossal to our family. She sighed and cursed the Japanese, saying she'd have wiped out Tokyo if she could.

"Rest well, Anling," Mrs. Dennison said. "I'll ask Rulian to step into your shoes for a while."

I insisted that I'd be up and about soon. In the meantime, I could have Liya act in my stead, since my job didn't need much expertise and I could tell her what to do. The old woman thought about my suggestion, then said, "That's true. You could manage things even if you're in bed. Let Liya be your deputy for a few days."

For a week I lay in bed. In my diary I just mentioned Haowen's death as a crime committed by the Japanese and that Yaoping and I were sonless now. I was afraid that someone might read what I'd written, which was always a possibility. I woolgathered a lot, indulging in memories of the old days. I remembered that twenty years before, in the fall, we'd gone often to Purple Mountain to look for mushrooms. At that time the grand mausoleum in honor of Sun Yat-sen wasn't there yet, as he was still alive. We'd bring along a small hamper of food, fruits, and bottles of drink and would picnic at the lakeside or under the huge stone animals and the immense maples in the royal park. The weather always seemed to be gorgeous and the sky blue and high, while warm breezes shook the grass and leaves from time to time. We'd also go to the Yangtze for boating. Yaoping was so happy on those outings that he often played a bamboo flute while I sat at the stern of a rented dinghy, applying an oar noiselessly. Meanwhile, Haowen and Liya would dive and float in the shallows. The boy invented a swim style he called frog-paddle, which combined the arm movement of the breaststroke with the kicking of the butterfly. He tried to teach Liya how to do it, but she couldn't synchronize her limbs that way. Joyful occasions like those felt as remote as if they had belonged to another life.

I also recalled the times we'd gone to fly kites on the embankment. Yaoping was good with his hands and made various types of large creatures, like a hawk, a multicolored butterfly, a phoenix, a centipede. People would enviously watch him flying them. Haowen was always excited about those trips. Once he came down with a raging fever for two days afterward, thanks to running in the summer's heat for hours. Now he was dead, and we had no idea where his body was. Even if he were alive, I suspected he could never be a happy man again.

Had he not been a family man, he could have abandoned his wife by deserting the Imperial Army soon after he'd landed in China. He might have joined the resistance force and survived. People might even have respected him as "a real man" who put his country above his family, devoting himself to fighting our national enemy. But he'd been doomed by his nature as a good, faithful, average man.

43

A WEEK LATER I returned to work. Neither Liya nor I wore a black armband lest we draw attention to our situation. I put on the gold bangle Haowen had given me and no longer cared whether it had been ill-gotten. Now it became something my son had left me, something precious, so I'd wear it all the time, though I'd keep it under my sleeve.

One morning toward the end of July Mrs. Dennison summoned me to her office. She had been occupied with the housing renovation, and by now the half-built apartment house was finished but not yet inhabited. The second I sat down by her mahogany desk, she said, "Anling, I want you to help us reduce the enrollment in the Homecraft School."

"Why?" I asked in surprise.

"The next stage of our development will be reinstating our college."

"But where will those poor women go?"

"That's not our problem. We cannot remain a refugee camp forever."

"Does Minnie know of this?" I said.

"She has no say in this matter. It's already been decided by our board in New York. They wrote to me and agreed to our school's proposal."

"What proposal?" I played the fool and tried to put on a blank face.

Her jaw fell, as if she were holding something hard to swallow. "Stop beating around the bush. Anling, I know you—you're smart and understand everything. I need your help."

I was speechless, although my mind raced. The old woman could have me fired if I refused to cooperate. For some reason, Minnie hadn't sent me a word after she'd left. Now what should I say to Mrs. Dennison?

"Anling," she continued, "you've been with us for more than ten years and I'd hate to see you leave. But this time you must help us put our college back on its feet." While speaking, she turned teary, her eyes fierce.

"I'll do my best," I mumbled.

She went on to explain that we'd have a much smaller budget for the Homecraft School, and therefore we must persuade some of the women to leave. She wanted me to announce that the work-study arrangements would no longer be available for most of them, so they needed to go elsewhere. I had no choice but to agree to participate in this plan.

I talked with Big Liu about Mrs. Dennison's instructions in hopes that he might have Minnie's address in Tsingtao, but he hadn't heard from her either. We didn't know how to resist the old president's move.

When I told the students about the enrollment cut in the fall, they were stunned. Some begged me not to drive them away. I told them, "Look, I'm just a forewoman here and have no say in such a matter. I merely passed the decision from above on to you. Sisters, I cannot help you. You should gripe to Mrs. Dennison, who has direct contact with New York."

While speaking, I tried to remain emotionless, but I felt awful and hated to see them so desperate. I knew that none of them would dare to make a peep in front of the old president, who wouldn't even bother to listen to them. Within a week some women began leaving Jinling. Gnawed by guilt, I'd give them a towel or a bar of soap as a little keepsake, but some wouldn't touch the presents or speak to me. They must have viewed me as a bogeywoman.

To make matters worse, Shanna reported that a good number of the middle schoolers had dropped out, because the schools in the city funded by the puppet municipality were free and had lured our students away, especially those who couldn't afford the forty-yuan annual tuition. I still had no idea how to communicate all the changes to Minnie.

MINNIE DID NOT RETURN until mid-August. I arranged a car to pick her up and went to the train station myself. She looked tanned and thinner—she must have swum quite a bit during her stay in the coastal city. Her suitcase contained two thousand yuan and a hundred tubes of toothpaste. She was fearful that the guards might discover the money and confiscate it, but no one asked her to open the bag when we exited the Hsia Gwan station. Most of the cash had been donated by Jinling's alumnae in Tsingtao and Shanghai, whereas the toothpaste had been given by the five blind girls, who were all well but said they missed Nanjing. Three hundred yuan of the money was from the sale of Mrs. Dennison's wedding silver, also donated to our college. At Yijiang Gate, however, an officer pulled Minnie aside, because her typhoid papers had expired. He took her to a nearby cabin, where a nurse was to give her an inoculation. Several Chinese were already in there waiting for injections. The nurse jabbed the same needle into everyone's arm, and each time wiped it only with a cotton ball soaked with rubbing alcohol. The sight of the same needle being used again and again made Minnie cringe, but she took the injection without a murmur.

Minnie handed the two thousand yuan to Mrs. Dennison, who was delighted and said that Jinling's strength lay in the fact that we could always find donors for projects, and that with enough funding, the college should regain its eminence in the near future.

Minnie sensed the reduction of the student enrollment at the two schools. She asked me, "Why do we have fewer students now?"

"Mrs. Dennison said we wouldn't have financial aid for many of the women anymore, so they'd have to leave."

"How about the girls in the middle school?"

"Some dropped out because the schools in town are free."

"I'm not worried about the girls who can have an education anyway. But what will happen to those poor women who are gone? Some of them have small children."

"I feel sorry for them too."

"How many do we still have in the Homecraft School?"

"Less than half, two hundred seventy-three."

"What a betrayal. I take this personally, as an insult." She glared at me, her eyes flashing.

I was embarrassed but countered, "Look, Minnie, you didn't send me a single word. Big Liu and I were both worried about this but couldn't find a way to contact you. How could I oppose Mrs. Dennison alone? She could've laid me off without a second thought."

That quieted Minnie. Lowering her eyes, she said, "I'm sorry, Anling. I was sick in bed for weeks and couldn't write."

"What was the trouble?" I asked.

"I was depressed, listless, and couldn't get out of bed, but I'm well now after swimming for two weeks."

"What should we do?" I went on, hoping we could find some remedies for the reduction of the enrollment in both schools.

"I'll speak to Mrs. Dennison and demand an answer."

"No, you'd better not. She said she received permission from the board of founders. Plus there's no way we can bring those poor women back."

"What a mess! I hate myself for this," Minnie said. "I feel so trivial. How could I care so much about my personal feelings and bolt to Tsingtao? Just because I couldn't use that damned bungalow for the summer, I left the two schools open to dismantling."

"Don't reproach yourself," I said. "You're not made of iron and needed a vacation. Nobody should blame you. What's done is done. Let's keep calm and figure out what to do."

"We must be more careful from now on."

I told her about my son's death. She hugged me and then wiped away her tears. "Anling," she said, "you're a tough woman, steady like a statue. If only I could be like you."

I didn't know how to respond in words and cried too. From then on I felt we were closer than ever. When she was depressed or frustrated, she often disclosed her feelings to me. I promised her that I'd write to Dr. Wu to apprise her of the developments here. We were both certain that the president would not align herself with Mrs. Dennison, though the old woman had once been her mentor. If we had Dr. Wu's understanding and support, we should be able to manage Mrs. Dennison.

Before the fall semester started, Minnie and I decided to visit Yulan. To our horror, the hospital was gone. The building was under construction, encaged in bamboo scaffolding and being converted into a hotel for the military. Minnie asked a foreman what had happened to the patients and the staff of the hospital. The man shook his shaved head and said, "I heard they all left."

"Do you know where they went?" she said.

"I've no clue, ma'am. They all might've gone home. You know the Japanese—they change plans every month."

I tugged at Minnie's sleeve. "Let's go."

Many of the medical personnel had been Japanese and couldn't possibly repatriate in the midst of the war, not to mention the Chinese patients who no longer had a home to return to.

We left the construction site and stopped at Tianhua Orphanage in hopes that Monica might know something about the disappearance of the hospital, but the nun, paler than ever, had no idea either. In fact, she hadn't even heard it was gone and kept apologizing. "Don't blame yourself, please," Minnie said. She left a box of walnut cookies— intended for Yulan—with Monica and told her to be more careful about her health. The woman looked even more consumptive, with sunken cheeks and feverish eyes; yet she was in good humor, so glad to see us that she couldn't stop beaming. I was afraid she might not be able to work much longer.

Back on campus, Minnie telephoned Dr. Chu and asked him what had happened to the hospital. "Can you help me find out where the patients are?" she asked.

He agreed to look into it, and Minnie invited him to have tea with us.

Dr. Chu came the next afternoon. He seemed under the weather, his eyes dull and his face drawn to the point of being emaciated. I poured oolong tea for him and placed a dish of small dough twists on the coffee table. He said he had looked into the dissolution of the hospital but didn't know for sure where all the staff had gone. Seated on an old canvas sofa in the main office, he went on, "They might have merged with other hospitals."

"How about the patients?" Minnie asked.

"There weren't many to begin with."

"I want to know where Yulan is."

"What can I say?" He sighed and put his teacup down. "I heard they had shipped some patients to Manchuria."

"Why there?"

"A unit specializing in germ warfare needed human guinea pigs."

" 'Germ warfare'? That's horrible. Is the place they were sent to like an experiment center?" Minnie asked. That was the first time I'd heard the term "germ warfare."

"I don't know much about it," he replied, "but I'm told there's a Japanese army unit somewhere in the northeast that uses people for testing bacteria and viruses. They've been collecting *marutas*, human logs, for experiments."

"So whoever ends up there won't come out alive?" Minnie asked him.

"I'm sorry. In a way, the sooner Yulan and the other mad girl die, the better for them."

"That's an awful thing to say!"

"They were both afflicted with venereal diseases—very severe cases, to my knowledge. The girls were actually kept as sex slaves. What kind of life was that? I'm not like most Chinese who believe that the worst life is better than the best death. If life is insufferable, one had better end it. If I were them, I must say, I'd have killed myself long ago." He gazed at me as if to see whether I wanted to challenge him. I had to say I agreed.

"But both of them were no longer clearheaded," said Minnie.

Dr. Chu didn't respond. He laced his fingers together on his lap and averted his melancholy eyes as though ashamed of what he had said.

Minnie continued, "I have a favor to ask you. Can you find out that unit's name and its whereabouts?"

"You mean the one doing germ experiments?"

"Yes, please do this for me."

"I'll try my best."

The conversation threw Minnie into a depression. For several days she kept wondering whether she might have been able to rescue Yulan if she had returned sooner from her summer vacation. She believed that what had happened to Yulan from the start was partly due to her negligence. If only she had spent her summer here. She could have returned to her apartment so she wouldn't have to rub shoulders with Mrs. Dennison every day. Minnie rebuked herself for caring too much about her personal feelings and about losing face. How could she let petty personal disputes stand in the way of more important matters, such as saving a woman's life and protecting the two schools? She could at least have written to Big Liu or me to stay informed of any development here. She couldn't escape feeling small-minded. How could she make amends? The more she thought about her faults, the more disappointed she was in herself.

Her laments got on my nerves. However hard I tried to dissuade her from reproaching herself, she wouldn't stop talking about Yulan and the students we'd lost. I felt Minnie was somewhat obsessed and told her that even if she'd been here, she might not have been able to save Yulan. Why would the Japanese military let an American woman interfere with their plan?

I knew Minnie was close to Big Liu and might have talked to him about these problems as well. He still taught her classical Chinese twice a week. But these days he had his hands full, because Meiyan again wanted to flee Nanjing, either to Sichuan to join the National-ists or to Yan'an, the Communists' base in the north. Meiyan hated everything here, even the air, the water, the grass, and the trees, let alone the people. She called Jinling a rathole. She had stopped going to church and had thrown away her Bible, claiming she was con-vinced that God was indifferent to human suffering. She'd told Liya that she no longer believed in Christianity, which in her opinion tended to cripple people's will to fight. Big Liu used to have high hopes for his daughter, whose mind was as sharp as a blade, but now she had become his heartache. Worse yet, it was whispered that she'd begun carrying on with Luhai and wouldn't come home until the small hours. Mrs. Dennison had spoken to Luhai, who promised to stop seeing Meiyan and claimed that there was absolutely nothing going on between them; yet people still saw them sneak off campus together.

44

O N SEPTEMBER 18, John Allison invited Minnie to the U.S. embassy for tiffin. She asked if she could bring me along, and he welcomed me. When we arrived, Allison was still at a meeting but had us sent into the dining room, which had wide windows, a swirled stucco ceiling, brass revolving fans, and two pots of cacti in the corners. A moment later he joined us.

A few minutes after we had started eating creamed spinach and macaroni mixed with seafood, the host opened his briefcase, took out a small brocade box, and placed it in front of Minnie. "I'm supposed to present you with this," Allison said, and spread his palm toward it, a chased ring on his fourth finger.

"For me?" she asked.

"Yes. Open it."

She did. Inside the box's silk interior, a gold medallion was perched like a sunflower, its center inlaid with lambent blue jade. "How many of us got a medal like this?" she asked Allison, pointing at the gold corolla.

"Only you and John Rabe, the Living Buddha."

"I wish Holly Thornton got one too."

Allison grinned, revealing his strong teeth. "Maybe Holly will be among the next batch of recipients. To my mind, Lewis Smythe also deserves such an award."

"John Magee should get one too," Minnie added.

I picked up the medallion, turned it over, and saw Minnie's name engraved on its back. Together with the medal was a certificate inside a leather-covered booklet. I opened it and saw the citation saying that the Chinese Nationalist government had awarded her this prize for saving ten thousand lives in Nanjing. "It's gorgeous," I said.

Allison smiled and put down his fork, his domed forehead shiny.

"This is called the Order of the Jade, the highest honor the Chinese government can bestow on a foreigner."

"What does this mean?" I asked him.

"It means that the recipient is China's honorable friend and is welcome to live anywhere in this country."

I said to Minnie, "Congratulations!"

"I just did what I was supposed to do. Any one of us would do the same given the circumstances."

Allison continued, "I want both of you to be quiet about this award. The public mustn't know of it until the war is over."

"Sure, I won't let it slip," I said.

"You feel the war will be over soon?" she asked him.

"I don't think so. The Russians have just invaded Poland. The situation in Europe looks dire and a war might break out there."

This was the first time we had heard about the Russian invasion, although we knew that the Germans had already occupied western Poland. We were so dumbfounded that we both could only gasp.

Beyond the window screen the hissing of cicadas was swelling and ebbing. A donkey brayed on the street, shaking its harness bell fitfully. "People seem to have lost their minds," Minnie said with a sigh.

"Why does evil always get the upper hand?" I said.

"We prayed for peace every day," she went on. "Evidently the prayers didn't help."

"No one in Europe is prepared to stop Hitler," Allison said. "I'm afraid there'll be a world war."

"How about Stalin?" asked Minnie.

"He looks in cahoots with Hitler."

For the rest of the lunch we talked about the situation in China, where the Japanese invasion seemed to have bogged down, but a peaceful solution was unlikely. The Communist troops kept harassing the Nationalist army, and that forced Chiang Kai-shek to fight the Reds as well. The generalissimo was also bedeviled by the scandal that resulted when the Nationalist army had breached the dike along the Yellow River at Huayuankou the previous year to stymie the advancing Japanese forces. According to newly revealed statistics,

eight hundred thousand civilians had perished in the flood—no military strategy could justify that. In addition, the Nationalist government had levied too much from the poor farmers in the northern
provinces who had been struck by droughts and famine. It was
reported that some people in the countryside, unable to pay the heavy
taxes, had begun to support the Japanese.

When lunch was over, Allison hugged us and climbed the carpeted
stairs to the third floor for a meeting. We walked back to Jinling, talking about the ominous future of Europe, foreshadowed by the German and Russian invasions of Poland. We knew Mrs. Dennison
planned to visit Germany the next summer and might have to cancel
her trip to Dresden, Vienna, and Prague. I teased Minnie, saying
she'd better find a safe place for her medallion or someone might
steal it.

"I would sell it if I could," she said. "If Mrs. Dennison hears of
this, she'll get madly jealous."

"That's true. We must keep it secret."

This topic discomfited Minnie, so she changed the subject, talking about some projects we had to undertake in the fall, such as
storing enough rice and fuel for the two schools and providing
shoes and winter clothes for some children of poor families in the
neighborhood.

Before the first frost we'd need to buy a lot of vegetables for the
women in the Homecraft School to pickle. We would also organize
them to make quilts and cotton-padded clothes. I'd have to get
more coal, because Mrs. Dennison had instructed that no more
trees be felled—we would hire people to guard them against thieves
if need be. She said it took just a few minutes to cut down a tree that
had resulted from many years of growth, so we'd better protect
them.

I had tried to buy coal from some mines but without success,
because the Japanese, besides controlling the supply, shipped a good
amount of the product directly to Japan. The coal dealers I had spoken with all told me they would only retail it, selling two or three
hundred pounds at a time. I guessed that must be more profitable for
them.

Finally, about a month later, I managed to get twelve tons of anthracite. This meant that at least the offices would be heated in the winter.

DR. CHU WROTE to Minnie that the Japanese germ warfare program, codenamed Unit 731, was headed by General Shiro Ishii, known as "the Doctor General." It was located in the Pingfang area south of Harbin City. Some foreigners—Russians and Koreans—were also confined there, being used as test subjects. Since the research project was top secret, Dr. Chu had the note carried by Ban directly to Jinling and instructed that the messenger boy must destroy it, either by swallowing it or tearing it to bits, if he was detained by the Japanese on the way. He also urged Minnie to burn the note after reading it and not to divulge its contents to anyone. She read it twice, then shared it with me because she wanted to hear my opinion. After I read it, she struck a match and set it afire.

For days she'd been thinking about going to the northeast, fantasizing that her visit might help get Yulan out of that place. Minnie revealed her thoughts to nobody but me.

I vehemently objected to her plan. "Look, this is insane," I told her. "Why run such a risk? Your very presence there will endanger yourself and others."

"How so?"

"The Japanese will jail you too and won't let you go until you tell them how you came to know about their secret program. In fact, they might even kill you to eliminate an eyewitness."

"I don't care what happens to me. It's in God's hands—if I'm supposed to die, I'll die. But do you think my being there might help Yulan get out?"

I shook my head and sighed. "To be quite honest, you're too obsessed. We don't even know if Yulan is still alive. The truth is that once they put her in there, she'll never be able to come out."

"So I should just give up?"

"What else can you do? Also, you must consider the repercussions of such a trip. Your absence from campus will cause a sensation, and all sorts of rumors will fly. What's worse, Mrs. Dennison will take you to task if you're lucky enough to come back. Your trip will just give rise to a scandal."

Finally Minnie saw the logic of my argument, so she agreed to drop the plan. Yet thoughts about Yulan kept eating away at her. She couldn't help but imagine other possibilities of rescuing her and often discussed them with me. "Don't be so obsessed," I reminded her. "Sometimes we must learn to forget so that we can keep on going."

All the same, she remained tormented and couldn't stop talking about Yulan when we were alone.

45

AIFENG YANG had not returned from her summer vacation yet, though the fall semester was already in its third month. Nobody had heard from her since July. According to the information provided by the U.S. embassy, she'd gotten involved in some resistance activities and was apprehended by the Japanese. In early November Mrs. Dennison finally received a letter from Aifeng, which said she was well but her fiancé, a journalist based in Beijing, was imprisoned in Tianjin, accused of espionage by the Japanese police. She said he wasn't a spy at all and that there must have been a miscommunication, or misunderstanding, or backstabbing by some Chinese. For the time being she had to stay there trying to rescue him, but she promised to come back to Nanjing as soon as he was released. Mrs. Dennison shook her head of flaxen hair and said to us, "Aifeng is smart and resourceful and she'll be all right." Because of our reduced enrollment, she wasn't needed for teaching.

A week later we heard from Dr. Wu, who was pleased by the smaller size of the Homecraft School now—she must have assumed that this was a step closer to restoring the college.

Ever since she returned from her summer vacation, Minnie got frazzled easily. Sometimes she nodded off at her desk, and once she missed an appointment with a reporter from the *Chicago Tribune*. Every Monday morning she would give Big Liu her weekly schedule so he could remind her of the important matters and arrangements every day.

More Japanese came to visit our campus. Most of them were civilians, some were Christians, and one even brought his children with him. Among the visitors was a fortyish man named Yoguchi, slightly hunched and beaky-faced, whose eyes would disappear when he smiled, as if afraid of light. He came often and would converse with us whenever he could. He spoke Mandarin with a sharp accent, having lived in Manchuria for more than a decade. In the beginning Yoguchi would not believe what we told him about the atrocities the soldiers had committed, but Minnie took him to some women in the Homecraft School and let him interview them. They told him their stories, which gradually convinced him. He even bowed to some of them apologetically when they collapsed, sobbing, unable to speak anymore.

One afternoon Yoguchi said to us, "The army has taken measures to control its men and make sure they're better supplied. I'm quite certain that no orgy of burning, rape, and bloodshed will happen again."

"What do you mean?" Minnie asked.

"An officer told me that since last winter, the army has been sending the military police ahead of the troops whenever they are about to take a city. And also, officers have been ordered to treat their men like brothers so they won't vent their spleen on civilians like they did here two years ago. You see, the army has been trying to prevent brutalities."

That sounded stupid; Yoguchi was a civilian but still attempted to defend the Imperial Army.

Minnie said, "Do you think they can simply slam the brakes on violence?" Seeing him flummoxed and with two vertical lines furrowing his forehead, she added, "The atrocities will continue to take place in the victims' minds for many years. They're not something that can be put behind easily. Hatred begets hatred as love begets love."

Silence ensued while Yoguchi's face reddened. Then he said, "I'm sorry. I never thought of it that way."

He didn't raise the topic again. He ordered three cotton-padded robes from the tailoring class at the Homecraft School as Christmas presents for his children. I arranged the order for him but didn't tell the seamstresses anything about the customer, afraid that they might refuse to work on the garments if they knew they were making them for a Japanese family.

Minnie and I were glad to see the change in Yoguchi, which further convinced her that only through the fully informed Christians in Japan could the people of that country be persuaded to see that the war was wrong and make peace. Yoguchi brought other Japanese Christians to Jinling, and some of them were impressed by the classroom buildings, the library, and the gardens. Minnie would tell them, "Come again in the spring—our campus will be like a beautiful park. In fact, that was what I wanted it to become when I joined the faculty here."

Yoguchi suggested that Jinling send some people to Japan to speak to the Christians there about what had happened in Nanjing. This could be a good step toward mutual understanding between the Chinese and the Japanese. The suggestion amazed us, but Minnie didn't respond right away. After Yoguchi left, we talked about it. I admitted, "If my grandson and daughter-in-law were not there, you'd have to cut off my legs before you could make me step foot in that country."

"You mean you don't want to go?" Minnie asked.

"Of course I'd like to go. I want to see Mitsuko and Shin if I can locate them."

"Then we'll make you the head of our delegation."

Minnie also spoke to Alice to see if it would be safe for Chinese people to travel to Japan. "That shouldn't be a problem," Alice assured her. "The Japanese there are not the same as the soldiers here."

Heartened by Alice's support, Minnie talked with Searle Bates. He had spent a summer in Japan three years ago and liked the country, though he was still documenting the Japanese war crimes and exposing their manipulation of the narcotics trade as a way to weaken the Chinese mentally and physically. He worked as an official of Nanjing University now, in charge of the school's properties, because as a foreigner he could deal with the Japanese in person. Searle thought that the trip was a good idea and added that it would be more productive if some Chinese could speak at seminaries and colleges in Japan, but he was unsure if we could get the travel papers. The Japanese military meant to keep the truth of the Nanjing atrocities from spreading internationally and might deny citizens here entry to Japan, where the war was being propagated as *seisen*, "sacred war," waged against communism and Western colonialism and led by the emperor himself.

To Minnie's amazement, the young Chinese faculty members received the idea of the reconciliatory trip warmly. Both Shanna and Rulian were happy at the prospect of visiting Japan. They each spoke English well and were appropriate candidates to accompany me. Minnie and I discussed the matter with Yoguchi on his next visit. The man smiled and said, "Don't worry about the travel permits. We'll try to get them. We have some pull at the embassy. You know Mr. Tanaka?"

"Yes, he's better than the other officials," Minnie replied, though we hadn't seen him for months.

"Tanaka is a Christian. This is just between us." Yoguchi put his bony hand on a large package sent to Jinling's nursery by the kindergarten of a church in Nagasaki. He had come to deliver the gifts today.

"Oh, no wonder Tanaka was so helpful," I said. "We won't breathe a word about him, of course."

We then talked about how to fund the trip. Yoguchi said he could get some money from a Christian association, but it might not be enough to cover all the expenses. Minnie told him that she would look for funds too. "For the time being," she said, "let's split the cost fifty-fifty."

"That's fine. I hope we can work this one out."

We thought that Jinling should sponsor the trip, since we had quite a bit of cash at the moment. But when we broached this subject without mentioning me as part of it, Mrs. Dennison said, "No, we won't give a penny. If Shanna and Rulian want to visit Japan, they should pay for the trip out of their own pockets, or the Japanese side should pick up the bill. We must spend every yuan on restoring our college."

"I want to go with them too," I blurted out.

The old woman looked amazed. "Why do you want to be part of this? What's in it for you?"

"I want to see what that country's like," I mumbled. "To know the enemy is a necessary step toward victory."

"But you're not an officer."

Minnie said, "Rulian and Shanna were your students, Mrs. Dennison." She must have assumed that the old woman resented her friendly relations with the young faculty members.

"That's why I won't play favorites," the old woman responded.

"We have a good amount of cash now, and I cannot see why we shouldn't sponsor the trip," Minnie said.

"Remember we've both agreed to devote all our efforts and resources to rebuilding the college."

"Their visit to Japan will help improve the communication and mutual understanding between the Japanese and the Chinese. That's more meaningful and necessary—I mean, to make peace. Besides, our delegates will find ways to form relations with the churches there, and our direct contact with Japan will strengthen our college's position here in the long run. In other words, this trip would also help to rebuild Jinling."

"I just don't want to deal with the Japanese. They've done enough damage. I would also warn you not to mix too much with them."

"What do you mean?" Minnie asked.

"The Japanese are the enemy of the Chinese. If you get too chummy with them, you will arouse animosity among our employees and make us vulnerable. You need to be more careful about receiving Japanese visitors."

"That's ludicrous." Minnie flung up her hand. "The Chinese know I love China and work only in their interest."

"Then you should concentrate on restoring our college. This is the best we can do for this country."

"You're too obsessed with the restoration."

"To be frank, obsession is what you lack. You always want to be praised by everybody, but you don't understand that no human being can please everybody. Worse still, you don't get much done—you're just busy all the time."

"Do you mean I'm not efficient?"

"Also inadequate." The old woman's eyes flared while her face remained wooden.

At this point Ban poked his head in the door. "Yes, what do you want?" Mrs. Dennison asked him.

"Mr. Yoguchi wants to see Miss Vautrin."

Minnie glanced at the old woman's smirking face, then stood and went out to see the visitor. I wondered if I should follow her, but resisted. Mrs. Dennison seemed to have known of our travel plans beforehand and was intent on thwarting them. She had been to Japan before the war and been deeply impressed by it. It was "clean, charming, and well ordered," in her own words. What's more, she believed in the exchange of ideas and information. That was why she had always encouraged faculty members to visit foreign countries during the summer and even had funds earmarked for that purpose when she was in office. Why this sea change in her attitude? Why had she become so hostile to the trip? She seemed determined to scuttle whatever Minnie attempted to accomplish.

Disappointed, I just sat there without saying a word. How I wished I could go see my grandson Shin.

Finally Mrs. Dennison said, "We cannot keep Minnie Vautrin here anymore. She has become an obstacle."

Those words astounded me. When I later told Minnie what the ex-president had said, she frowned and wondered aloud, "What's next? What do you think she might do?"

"I've no clue," I said. "But don't provoke her. Remember what I told you? Wait patiently till the day the bride becomes the mother-in-law."

"Okay, I'll try to keep cool."

Despite her frustration, Minnie attempted to be conciliatory toward Mrs. Dennison. For better or worse, the two of them would have to work together until Dr. Wu came back from Chengdu; our college could not afford to be polarized by their conflict. Minnie also said it felt like it was beneath her to quarrel with the old woman. Indeed, in people's eyes Minnie was like a saint, the Goddess of Mercy, and she must not diminish herself with petty squabbles.

We did not discourage Yoguchi from getting the travel papers for Rulian, Shanna, and me. Minnie said she would raise funds for us if necessary. For the time being, there was too much to do before Christmas. If we went to Japan, it would not be until the summer.

46

ON SUNDAY, the day before Christmas, Big Liu came to the president's office and flopped into a chair. "Meiyan and Luhai ran away," he croaked. "I didn't mean to spoil your holiday mood, Minnie, but I thought you should know so you could find someone for the job left by Luhai."

"Heavens, you mean they just eloped?" Minnie asked.

"I don't know if they're close like a couple. Apparently Luhai has been a bad influence and misled her. The girl has been in terrible shape ever since she was taken by the Japanese."

"She must've been traumatized."

"She's hatred itself and kept saying China needed a revolution if we wanted to defeat Japan." Big Liu's face contorted as if he were suppressing a hiccup caused by heartburn.

"Do you think she's really fond of Luhai?" I asked.

"I can't tell, but she said they were just friends. Luhai must have connections with some resistance force. Who could've imagined he would abandon his family? I just hope he'll treat Meiyan well, but that man has shifty eyes—he's not reliable."

"Are you going to hunt them down?" Minnie said.

"Where would I look? She's grown enough to choose her own way of living."

"Luhai's family must be in a muddle." Minnie turned to me. "Should we do something for his wife and kids?"

"Maybe we should," I said.

The door opened and Donna stepped in, holding a letter. "Minnie," she panted, " this is for you."

"From whom?" Minnie took it.

"A young boy handed it to me and said it was from Ban, who left with Luhai. I was told to give it to you immediately."

"You mean Ban also ran away?" I asked Donna, whose face was flushed.

"Apparently so."

Minnie unfolded the sheet of yellow paper and found that Luhai had written the letter in English. I knew he had often perused the *North China Daily News* and other English papers, but I'd never heard him speak the language, which I'd been unsure he could read. Probably he had composed the letter in English to keep other Chinese from learning its contents. Nonetheless, Minnie read it out loud to us:

Dear Dean Vautrin:

    Meiyan, Ban, and I decide to escape Nanjing. We want to be in the force fighting for our motherland, so we prepare to sacrifice everything, including family. If the country is lost, our home can not be same any more and our individual success mean nothing. Please do not trouble yourself and find us, because we are going very, very far away, under different name. But I have ~~favors~~ a favor to beg you—please give some helps to my wife and children, because I can do nothing for them from today on. One day I shall return like a fighter and a hero. Thank you from bottom of my heart. I shall remember your kindness <u>forever.</u>

Donna burst into laughter. "What kind of nonsense is that?" she snorted. "A man dumped his wife and kids on the pretext of sacrificing for his country."

"The rascal is shameless," Big Liu grunted.

"This is a bizarre letter," Minnie admitted. "But why would Ban flee with them as well?"

"That boy hates the Japanese," I said.

"Where do you think they might go?" Minnie asked.

"I've no idea," Big Liu answered. "I hope they won't head for the Communists' base in Yan'an. Meiyan said she'd join any kind of resistance force as long as she could get out of Nanjing."

"By why did the three of them flee together?" I said.

"Luhai was unhappy about his marriage, because his parents had picked his wife for him," replied Big Liu.

Donna tittered, her face shiny and slightly fleshy. "So to fight an invader is a fine solution to marital trouble."

"Stop it, Donna," Minnie said. "Don't be so sarcastic. I don't think Luhai ran away because he wanted to dump his family. He's not that kind of man."

"That's true," I chimed in. "He wants to fight the Japanese, and so must Meiyan and Ban."

We all agreed that no matter what, we ought to do something for Luhai's wife. So Minnie and I went to see Mrs. Dennison to brief her about the runaways. To our relief, the old woman suggested that Jinling offer Fuwan, Luhai's wife, a hundred yuan and persuade her to return to her folks in the countryside. We both felt this would be a reasonable solution.

"Son of a gun!" Mrs. Dennison said about Ban. "He took off without leaving me a word."

With little difficulty, I convinced Fuwan to leave for her parents' home. The poor woman, her eyes puffy, said that she was tired of city life anyway—if she stayed here, her two small sons might grow up to be bad like their father. In addition, Nanjing was such a horrible place that she was often depressed, so she wouldn't mind returning to the countryside.

But a week later Luhai's father, a trim man with beetle eyebrows, came from Shenyang to fetch his grandsons. He claimed that nobody could separate his grandkids from him and his wife. Fuwan and the boys left with him on the sly. This baffled us, and Mrs. Dennison regretted having given away a hundred yuan too easily.

With the old woman's approval, Minnie offered Big Liu the business manager's job left open by Luhai's departure, but Big Liu wouldn't take it, saying he preferred to teach. He had a good reputation as a teacher and used to be on the faculty of the language school, which had shut down long ago. Since there were more foreign academics and diplomats in town now, he could have earned more than his current salary—fifty yuan a month—by offering Chinese lessons (we all drew eighty percent of our normal pay now). To our relief, he told Minnie a few days later that he would continue working as Jinling's Chinese secretary, because he felt this was more meaningful and also it was safer for his family to stay on campus. Mr. Rong, the assistant manager, was promoted to the position abandoned by Luhai.

AFTER THE NEW YEAR a bullnecked man named Boren, a friend of Luhai's, came to see Mrs. Dennison and Minnie. He lived in the neighborhood and had always been hostile to Jinling and the local missionary groups. He had come to visit Luhai every once in a while. Boren was respected by the locals as a community leader of sorts and had been quite vocal about the missionary work, which he believed had brought about chaos in China. He had disliked Miss Lou and accused her of always toadying to the foreigners. He and I had never been on good terms either. But the moment he sat down in the president's office, he was all smiles and even thanked me as I poured tea for him from a red clay teapot. He told us that the fall of our city had changed him, because Jinling had sheltered his family of seven for four months while he was away in Hunan Province taking care of his bedridden mother. His home, which was three hundred years old, had been burned down by the Japanese, and most of his antique furniture had been fed to the bonfire in the center of his courtyard.

He wanted to sell us a piece of land because he needed cash. His dog had snapped at a Japanese soldier's heel and gotten its master into trouble. The bite was nothing serious, just two tiny punctures on the foot, but the Japanese police had hauled Boren in and beaten him up, despite his promise to kill the dog and let them have its meat.

"I sent everything, including its skin, to those bastards," Boren said, "but they still won't leave me alone. They said I had disabled a soldier and must accept the full consequences."

"What does that mean?" Minnie said.

"I asked a friend of mine. He suggested I spend some money to appease the Japanese. But I don't have any cash on hand. Everybody's hard up for cash these days. My neighbor works in a factory and is paid in pots and ladles because they can't ship their products out of Nanjing anymore. Every evening he has to peddle utensils downtown. If your school can buy a piece of land from me, you'll save my life, and also my family."

This came as a surprise. Both Mrs. Dennison and Minnie were intrigued. When the college was being founded, the old president had tried in vain to purchase land from Boren's father; now this offer could be an opportunity, but Mrs. Dennison and Minnie wanted to look at the property again before deciding.

47

A FEW DAYS LATER we set out for the southwestern end of Jinling's property to see the land Boren was offering. Apple and pear trees were bulky despite their leafless branches, and in the depths of the orchard some rooks were cawing like crazy. Old Liao appeared, trundling a load of bricks in a wheelbarrow. Even on such a wintry day the gardener wouldn't stop working. He seemed ignorant of idleness, a typical peasant. Pointing at a path he'd newly paved with bricks, Mrs. Dennison said, "Nice job." The man smiled without a word, then nodded at Minnie.

The land Boren offered was bumpy and overgrown with brambles, different from what we had expected. It would have to be leveled before it could be used. Also, because it was separated from Jinling's property by a brook, it wouldn't be easy to incorporate the land into the campus unless our college owned a length of the stream as well. Mrs. Dennison puckered her brow while the outer corners of her eyes drooped. I could tell she had misgivings.

"We will discuss this with the trustees and will let you know our answer soon," Mrs. Dennison told Boren.

"Sure, no need to rush," he said.

When the two women talked about the offer again, Mrs. Dennison was against buying it, saying it was just an acre of wasteland. Actually, it was 1.3 acres, at half price—four hundred yuan. Despite its bumpiness and its separation from our campus, Minnie believed we should jump at this opportunity. She said to Mrs. Dennison, "We'll figure out how to use the land eventually. Let's grab it."

"No. At this time we mustn't acquire anything we don't need."

"We have the money."

"We must be frugal. The renovation will cost a fortune. You never know where an extra amount will have to be put up."

"Please, it's just four hundred yuan, a bargain."

"No, I don't want it."

"I'm the dean of this college—my opinion doesn't count at all?"

"Well, I don't have to listen to you."

"Don't you remember how hard you used to haggle with those landowners over tiny parcels of land?"

"That was then. Things have changed and we have to concentrate on the task at hand."

"Since when have you become so shortsighted?"

"I know what I'm doing."

"Can't you see this is a windfall? We'll need a lot of land for future development."

"I don't want to spend the money now."

"It's not your money."

"Neither is it yours. If you love that piece of dirt so much, why not buy it for yourself?"

Mrs. Dennison's last sentence put Minnie in mind of acquiring the land on her own. She talked with me about this. Since she wanted to spend the rest of her life here, she could build her home on that slope beside the babbling brook. From that spot you could see a good part of campus and enjoy peace and quiet. If the college provided her with a bungalow someday, the land still wouldn't be wasted—she could donate it to Jinling or build a small folk school on it. She had been making one hundred yuan a month since the previous winter and had saved about eleven hundred yuan, too little to build her own house. But she would save more and buy the lot first.

Her reasoning made sense, so I encouraged her to buy the land. At such a low price she could sell it and make her money back whenever she wanted. We went to Boren's three days later and wrapped up the purchase. The man was elated and even called Minnie "the goddess of generosity" when she told him she was acquiring the land for herself. This unnerved her. "Please don't call me that," she said, but he merely grinned, showing his square teeth.

48

MONICA BUCKLEY DIED in early February, and the missionary community, regardless of denomination, assembled in the Shigu Road Cathedral for her funeral. The nave had a domed roof and stained-glass windows, which were high and narrow with arched tops, the panes iridescent like peacock feathers. More than two hundred Chinese also attended.

Reverend Wei presided over the ceremony. People stood up and sang the hymn "O Thou Whose Own Vast Temple Stands." Next, Pastor Daniel Kirk read out Psalm 23. Minnie was moved by the solemn, serene poem, which she said she'd never before thought so sublime. Then a few friends of Monica's went to the chancel lined with winter plum blossoms to deliver their eulogies and to reminisce about her. Among them was Alice, who had started her missionary career at the same time as the dead woman back in Anhui, though they belonged to different denominations. She told the audience that Monica had often missed her hometown in rural Pennsylvania but never lost sight of her real home in heaven, in God's mansion, because she believed we were all virtually foreigners or guests on earth. After Alice, a tall American man with graying hair and sagging cheeks spoke. He declared that he'd known Monica for almost two decades, and in spite of her languid appearance, she had a good sense of humor and an extraordinary memory, and she enjoyed telling stories, especially to children. Once he'd told an anecdote from his childhood in which a man got drunk and exchanged his ulster for a puny catfish. A few weeks later he heard Monica telling the same story to a group of small girls but with a more dramatic ending: the man gave away his team of mules and wagon for a salmon, so now he couldn't go home anymore and had to sleep in the open air with snow falling—he almost froze to death and lost two fingers.

What had happened was that Monica had overheard him in the adjacent room when he was telling the anecdote. "Now," the man concluded, "I hope she will entertain angels up there with all the jokes and stories she can make up with such grace and ease."

That brought out laughter among the foreigners, while most Chinese remained quiet, bewildered. Indeed, a funeral was a sorrowful, solemn occasion. How come these foreigners wisecracked and gave belly laughs?

After the reminiscences, Searle, his face freshly shaved and his hair combed back, went to the pulpit and delivered a sermon in honor of Monica titled "The Christian Duties in the Time of War." He spoke in Mandarin about the Japanese annexation of some Asian countries and about their brutalities. I knew that the Japanese kept a watchful eye on him because of his writings about their exploiting the narcotics business, and that they had also demanded that he surrender all the paperwork of the International Relief Committee—including the records of nine hundred cases of murder, rape, and arson within the Safety Zone perpetrated by Japanese soldiers during the first weeks after the fall of Nanjing—but he had told them that Eduard Sperling had taken all the files back to Cologne. Searle talked about the situation in Europe. He said, "Under the threat of a world war, what should we Christians do? First, we must strive to make peace and oppose war. Some of you were here when Nanjing fell two years ago and saw with your own eyes what it was like. Men can be more vicious than beasts of prey if they're put in the extreme situation of war. No rules will be followed, and all kinds of evil will be unleashed. War is simply the most destructive force we human beings can produce, so we must make every effort to prevent it.

"However, if we survey human history, we can see that there were times when war was unavoidable, even necessary. There have been some wars that can be called just wars. For example, if people take up arms against foreign invaders, can we blame them? Should we attempt to dissuade them from fighting their national enemy? Of course not. Therefore, the Christians in those countries should fight like common citizens and should combine their fulfillment of Christian duties with the survival of their nations. As for those Christians whose countries are aggressors, they should do the opposite—work against war and do their utmost to make peace."

After hearing Searle's words, I was sure that the Japanese wouldn't leave him alone from now on, but he must have become accustomed to dealing with them.

Searle concluded, "As for those Christians in countries that are not involved in war, like the Americans among you, we must align ourselves only with the weak and the victims, just as our late Sister Monica did for the orphans in Nanjing. This is the only moral stand we should take. The true Christian position should be standing between humanity and the unregarding force."

The audience liked his sermon, especially the Chinese. The instant Searle had finished, a few people clapped their hands, then stopped short, realizing this wasn't an occasion for applause.

Reverend Wei gave a closing prayer, imploring God to receive Monica's soul and to grant her eternal joy. Then everyone stood and sang "O God of Love, O King of Peace."

After the funeral, Minnie said she hoped that when she died, she could have a similar service, full of warmth and dignity, like the one we had just attended to celebrate the ascent of Monica's soul. The dead woman must be at peace now.

MISS LOU CAME to the main office the next morning, because some families in the neighborhood had run out of food and their children were starving. I stepped out of the inner room and joined the little woman. Seated in her chair with the unfinished paperwork for student scholarships on her desk, Minnie yawned. "Excuse me," she said, covering her mouth with her palm. "I get tired so easily these days that I often drop off. And my eyes throb with double vision." Lately she often joked that she looked sixty and felt eighty.

"You've worked too hard," Miss Lou said. "You need a long vacation."

"Yes, you owe yourself one," I agreed.

"I'm supposed to be on furlough in the summer, but it's unlikely I can do that," Minnie said. "I'll have to stay around to take care of things here. Now, Miss Lou, what should we do for your neighbors without food? We must make sure they will at least have a decent meal on the Spring Festival's Eve."

"That's why I came to see you. I'm also wondering if your college has an extra quilt. A poor woman lost her only quilt yesterday afternoon, stolen by a thief who broke into her home. Her husband disappeared and she's too ill to scratch out a living. Actually, she sewed all her savings, ten yuan in total, into her quilt, so the money is gone too."

Minnie turned to me. "Do we have enough rice to spare some?"

"Sure," I answered. The previous fall I'd bought eleven wagonloads of rice at twenty-five yuan per picul (133.33 pounds), a smart move at two-thirds of the current price, so we could offer some to the destitute. "But we might have given away all the quilts we made last fall," I said. "I'll have to check."

We went to the main dormitory and found no extra quilts. So Minnie turned into her own apartment in the same building and grabbed the one from her bed. "Take this," she said to Miss Lou.

"You have another quilt for yourself?" the little woman asked.

"I have a duvet and a warm blanket."

Miss Lou left happy, having said she would come with a wheelbarrow to pick up the rice the next day.

49

IN MID-MARCH Yoguchi informed us that Mr. Tanaka couldn't get the travel permits for the three of us anymore, because the officer in charge of travel papers, Tanaka's fellow townsman, had left Nanjing. Also, citizens here, especially the Christians, were discouraged from visiting Japan. The cancellation of the trip disappointed me and aggravated my temper, and my antagonism toward Shanna and Rulian flared up again. If they got on my nerves, I didn't hesitate to give them a piece of my mind to let off some steam. I knew they would bad-mouth me behind my back, but I didn't care. Minnie said I sometimes deliberately picked fights with them. That might be true, but she couldn't see the main cause: there was this anger seething in me because the canceled trip had dashed my hopes of going to Japan.

Rulian was tolerable on the whole, but I found Shanna insufferable. She was from a well-to-do family and had the extravagant habit of dining out every weekend. She often boasted about the dishes she ordered in restaurants downtown. One day at recess, I overheard her speaking about the Osaka Terrace to a bunch of women in the Homecraft School. "Believe it or not," she said, "I wanted to puke when I tried sushi for the first time. It tasted like a dead slug in my mouth, especially the tuna. But my friend urged me to go on, and by and by I began to like it. Now I can taste different kinds of sushi. I like the eel most."

"My goodness, even if they paid me I wouldn't eat raw fish," a short woman said.

"It's actually more nutritious," replied Shanna.

"That's wild," said a spindly woman.

"You don't believe me?"

The bell rang, and the women started back for the classrooms. After they were gone, I said to Shanna, "You shouldn't have talked about fancy Japanese food in front of them."

She pulled a long face. "They asked me about it."

"But you're not supposed to be a salesgirl for Japanese restaurants." My gorge was rising as I spoke.

"You know what? That place is owned by two Chinese men who're brothers." Her nose, the shape of a big clove of garlic, quivered, but she avoided looking me in the face.

"Still, you went too far. Lots of people in Nanjing are starving, while you brag about raw seafood."

"It's none of your business."

"It is my business to stop you from making others feel cheap and abject."

"Nuts!" She turned and strode away, her hands in the pockets of her flannel jacket.

Exchanges like that often broke out between us. Whenever she went out of bounds, I would let her have it, though I always spoke to her privately. I simply couldn't tolerate her kind of extravagance and foolishness.

Then one afternoon Shanna came to see Minnie and said she had decided to resign immediately. Minnie was flabbergasted, never having expected that a dean would quit before the semester was over; no matter how she tried to dissuade her, Shanna wouldn't change her mind. From the inner office I overheard her say, "I'm just sick of all this. My family needs me." She claimed that her father was bedridden and wanted to see her back in Shanghai.

Minnie could do nothing. Shanna left two days later, and Minnie had to take over the administrative work of the Homecraft School. Although Donna was the dean of the middle school, she needed a lot of help because she didn't know Chinese and couldn't even figure out the girls' names on paper. With the additional work, Minnie had to put in extra hours every day and often didn't go to bed until early in the morning.

This situation could not continue. If only Aifeng would come back. But her fiancé was still jailed in Tianjin, and she couldn't leave in the midst of all the efforts to rescue him. Mrs. Dennison came and talked with Minnie about how to bring Shanna back. The old woman was also worried, seeing that it was impossible for Minnie alone to handle so many things. Mrs. Dennison had tried to help, but the bookkeeping and the housing renovation were almost more than she could manage. I hardly spoke a word and, cheek on fist, just listened to them. Having considered the pros and cons, the two leaders decided to send Alice to Shanghai on behalf of Jinling to beg Shanna to come back. "We should have trained more leaders," Mrs. Dennison said, and sighed.

In fact, a good number of Jinling's graduates had served as middle school principals throughout China, but none of them would come and work in occupied Nanjing. As soon as Mrs. Dennison left, I burst out at Minnie, "You shouldn't have made that suggestion!"

"What are you talking about?"

"You shouldn't send Alice to Shanghai to get Shanna back. That will make the little bitch more insolent and forget who she is."

"We need her."

"All right. In that case, I'll leave when the semester's over."

"Come on, Anling, I know you're unhappy and frustrated. Everybody here has frayed nerves, but we have to work together to survive the hard times and prevent this place from lapsing into a loony bin."

"I'll leave. Don't say I didn't tell you beforehand." I stood up and made for the door.

Minnie didn't take my threat seriously. She must have understood I couldn't possibly resign, because my family lived on campus and I might not be able to find a safe place elsewhere. She often said I had "an iron mouth but a tofu heart," using the idiom that refers to a person who is harsh only on the outside. She also lamented that China's greatest obstacle was not the war or corruption but the so-called face—everyone was afraid of losing face, unwilling to make concessions; as a result, too much energy and time were wasted on trivial matters. For that Chiang Kai-shek had her sympathy, having to save so much face constantly, for both himself and others.

Four days later Alice came back without Shanna, though she'd met with Dr. Wu in Shanghai. The president was on her way to New Delhi to attend a conference, representing Chinese women. Dr. Wu wrote me a letter, chastising me mildly and urging me to help Minnie keep things together on campus. As for Mrs. Dennison, she wrote that we should just humor her and avoid any confrontation. Minnie went to Rulian and begged her to take over a part of the work left by Shanna for the time being. Rulian agreed and also promised her not to bicker with me again. Both she and Minnie ran the Homecraft School.

I felt sorry about the trouble I'd brought about and told Minnie that I wouldn't lose my temper again.

Mrs. Dennsion was also frustrated by the loss of Shanna. Despite fretting about the Homecraft School, the old woman knew we had to pull the program through the academic year. To calm everybody down, she gave a party at her place, to which all the faculty and many staffers were invited.

Minnie arrived later than the others, having had to accompany a group of visitors through a class that taught how to preserve duck eggs with mud and lime. In the living room of Eva's bungalow hung a long horizontal scroll that read SET THINE HOUSE IN ORDER. This was something new, added by Mrs. Dennison. The Chinese faculty members praised the calligraphy in the scroll. "Sturdy like trees and fluid like floating clouds," one enthused. "August and masterful," another echoed. Most of them assumed that it was a quotation from Confucius, since the sage had also said something about cultivating yourself and putting your household in order as the first step toward governing a state. I knew that those words were from the book of Isaiah, but I made no comment.

Everybody enjoyed the buffet dinner, and I felt conciliatory and spoke with Rulian at length. When we were eating apples and honey dates for dessert, Donna brought out a bunch of letters addressed to Jinling that had just arrived. She opened them one by one and read the contents out loud to the room. Most of the letters were from people interested in the relief work, expressing their admiration and good wishes. A few inquired about China missions. One, however, was written by a high school sophomore in Camden, New Jersey, and it impressed everybody. The writer, Megan Stevens, knew about Minnie Vautrin's deeds and declared that Minnie was her hero. The girl said she would learn stenography and improve her typing skills because she dreamed of becoming Minnie's secretary someday.

"Listen to this." Donna went on in a lilting voice: "'Last month our town's paper published an article on what you did, and the people of our church all know about you. You are a great woman, a model for young girls who want to follow the way of the Lord. We all love you.'"

"My, you're an international celebrity, Minnie," Alice said.

"Come on, don't embarrass me."

In the postscript Megan asked: "Is it true that a missionary woman is not allowed to marry? My parents told me that, but I am not convinced. Besides serving God, I also want to have a family and children."

"That's so sweet," Donna said, and put the letter on the octagonal dining table.

"Maybe we should give her an interview," Minnie quipped. "We could use a secretary like her if she's good."

"We'd better not," Mrs. Dennison snorted to no one in particular. "We mustn't indulge in a personality cult."

Minnie's thick eyebrows shot up. Possessed by a sudden fit of anger, she burst out, "Why don't you say idolatry?"

"It does smack of that. A human being should not aspire to become the Virgin Mary or a bodhisattva." Mrs. Dennison stared Minnie in the face.

"You simply cannot abide anyone who's doing better than you. You're envy personified."

"At least I've never used personal notoriety to keep our college as a refugee camp."

"Who made those poor women come here—me or the Japanese?"

Without waiting for Mrs. Dennison to answer, Minnie walked away. I kept stealing peeks at the old woman, whose face was changing colors, now pink, now chalky, and now yellow, while everybody remained silent. The air was so charged that I felt a bit queasy. Minnie went into the kitchen and stayed there awhile, then slipped out the side door.

50

A VERY QUALIFIED APPLICANT named Yan Ning accepted the dean's position at the Homecraft School and would come to Nanjing in late April. She had a good deal of experience in this kind of adult education in Fujian Province. We felt a bit relieved. As long as we could get through this semester, there'd be a whole summer for us to look for qualified teachers and administrators.

One morning in early April (three days after the national puppet government headed by Jingwei Wang had been installed in Nanjing), I received a note from Mrs. Dennison that said she wanted to see Minnie and me at once. I went to Minnie's place in the main dormitory and then together we headed out to Eva's bungalow. Light fog swayed over the treetops while the warm, moist air dampened the birds' tumultuous songs. A rain frog rattled like a broken bellows. We chatted as we walked, disturbing some warblers, which took off, darting away.

Neither Minnie nor I had any idea why Mrs. Dennison wanted to see us. Had she heard that Minnie had purchased the land from Boren and abandoned the plans for our visit to Japan? If so, Minnie said she ought to appear composed and conciliatory. She wouldn't mind, if necessary, apologizing to the old woman, since it was she, Minnie, who'd lost self-control a few days earlier.

"Yes," I said. "Remember that the bride will become the mother-in-law in due time."

Minnie laughed and swatted me on the shoulder.

Mrs. Dennison looked sullen: without makeup, her face was slack and creased, her neck appeared more freckled than usual, and a small dewlap was noticeable on her throat. The second we sat down, the old woman took out a newspaper, *The Purple Mountain Evening News*, and handed it to Minnie. "Look at the article on the second page," she said. "I'm totally scandalized."

Minnie began reading while I drank tea and glanced at her now and again. Her face darkened, then went pallid, as if she had aged all of a sudden. Meanwhile, Mrs. Dennison scowled and fixed her furious eyes on me. My heart shuddered. Did I do something wrong? I wondered. Why is she staring at me like that?

Finally Minnie sat up. "A pack of lies!" she said, and threw the newspaper on the glass coffee table, glaring at Mrs. Dennison, her eyes smoldering.

The old woman grimaced, which crinkled her upper lip and crimped her droopy brows. She said, "I can see there might be some exaggeration in the article, but you never mentioned the incident in your reports to the board of founders. I was appalled to read that you actually let the Japanese choose one hundred women."

"No, it didn't happen like that."

"Stop dodging. I asked a number of people, and they said you'd made a mistake in believing the Japanese. But to me, it's not a mistake. It's a sin and a crime, unpardonable because you've tried to cover it up all along."

Dumbfounded, Minnie groped for words but couldn't find any. She got up and dragged herself out the door.

I picked up the article. It was titled "The Real Criminals" and attacked the Westerners in Nanjing. It condemned the establishment of the refugee camps in the former Safety Zone, claiming that the camps had gathered women together so it would be easier for the Japanese to "defile them." As a consequence, even Chinese pimps would lead the soldiers to the camps for girls. "This was a sneaky American way of procuring women for the Japanese," the author declared. He then singled out Minnie as a chief collaborator. The writer, who called himself Truth Preserver, recalled the incident on December 24, 1937, and stated: "Minnie Vautrin, the deputy principal of Jinling College, agreed to provide 100 good-looking young women for the Japanese, and on that dark day they abducted 21. Acting like a madam of a brothel, she later kept apologizing to the officers and promised to let them choose the other 79 women. To add insult to injury, she assured them that the school's gate would always be open to them. Small wonder the Jinling camp entertained dozens of Japanese policemen every night with hot tea, meat pies, and roasted peanuts even after they had raped girls there. Brothers and sisters, it's high time to reevaluate the tragedy that happened to our city and to see through the so-called Goddess of Mercy. Minnie Vautrin is actually a trader in human beings and a traitor to the Chinese people. We must expose her and hold her accountable for the numerous women and girls whom she proffered to the soldiers."

Putting down the paper, I told Mrs. Dennison, "This is hogwash! I was at the scene when it happened. Minnie did her best to protect the women and girls."

"I knew she and you were hand in glove in this crime," she said, pointing at my nose. "I did my investigation. As an accomplice, you cannot cover up for her anymore."

I realized there was no way to reason with this madness, so I stood up and strode out of the house.

FOR THREE DAYS Minnie worked without respite. She'd neither eat nor go to bed—she was tormented by insomnia—and yet she kept busy in order to quell her miserable feelings and thoughts. Then, on the fourth day, she collapsed and had to lie down. From then on, she wouldn't come out of her apartment and wore felt slippers and velveteen pajamas all the time. We made chicken soup and yam porridge for her, which Minnie hardly touched. Time and again she tried to work on a schedule for the middle school's class meetings, but her mind couldn't focus. Sometimes she talked about the setbacks and disasters that had befallen Jinling. She was convinced that she was to blame for most of them, especially for those young women taken by the Japanese soldiers. She kept saying to me, "I saw the handwriting on the wall long ago. Now I'm coming to the end of my energy and can't continue anymore. I've failed, failed miserably." Whenever she dozed off, she'd have nightmares.

Big Liu often went to see her and even offered to speak to Mrs. Dennison about the twenty-one "prostitutes" and about the circumstances in which Minnie couldn't have responded otherwise. But she adamantly forbade him to intercede for her, saying Mrs. Dennison had become a maniac and might turn on him. I didn't think it would be wise for him either. The old woman seemed to have lost her mind, unable to listen to reason.

On April 10, Minnie handed in her resignation to Mrs. Dennison. Afterward Minnie refused to see anyone except for Big Liu, Alice, and me. We all tried talking her out of her decision. But to whatever we said, she'd merely reply, "I'm responsible for their deaths. I'll answer to God."

In the evenings she listened to Radio Shanghai and heard the news that Germany had invaded Denmark and Norway and that the British navy and the German fleet were engaged in a fierce battle. "What's the world coming to?" she kept musing aloud. Everything seemed to be crumbling. And she would talk about those countries she'd been to or that she imagined she'd been to, saying lots of people would be killed and many towns and cities would be flattened. Her mind was no longer coherent.

Alice brought in her mail one afternoon in mid-April. A letter from Yan Ning informed Minnie that she had decided to withdraw her acceptance of the dean's position for family reasons. Minnie flung the letter to the floor and shouted, "I'm sick of this, sick of it all!"

Silently Alice set down a bunch of white azaleas in a vase and backed out of the room.

Mrs. Dennison came one morning, but Minnie didn't speak to her. The old woman told her that Aifeng Yang was coming back, her efforts to rescue her fiancé having come to nothing—the man had died in jail. Minnie didn't respond to the news. Afterward the former president and I talked briefly; she told me to spend more time with Minnie and keep watch over her.

Day by day Minnie's condition was deteriorating. We called in an American doctor, who, together with Dr. Chu, diagnosed stress, fatigue, trauma, and malnutrition during menopause as the causes of her breakdown. After receiving a few hormone injections, Minnie refused to continue. She became more depressed, telling us that she was responsible for all the problems Jinling had encountered and for all the suffering the refugee women and girls had gone through; she felt she was a total failure, disgusting even to herself. We tried in vain to convince her that she was more capable than any of us and was a leader we all looked up to. She was our beloved principal.

Mrs. Dennison reported Minnie's illness to both Jinling's board of founders in New York and the United Christian Missionary Committee, based in Indianapolis. Minnie had no close family except for a somewhat estranged brother in Shepherd, Michigan, who still resented that she had not returned to care for their father before the old man died. The plan was for Minnie to go back to the States for treatment, and the two institutions agreed to split her medical bills. Alice was assigned to accompany her back to America, but Minnie refused to leave before the semester was over. Not until Mrs. Dennison promised her that she and Aifeng would keep the Homecraft School and the middle school intact did Minnie agree to go.

The day of her departure was wet and a little chilly, though spring was at its peak—trees all green, flowers in clusters, the ground velvety with sprouting grass, and the air atremble with the trills of birds. About a dozen people gathered at the front gate to see her off, mostly her friends and colleagues. I burst into tears and wailed, "Minnie, you must come back. Remember, you and I planned to spend our last years here together. You promised to teach me how to drive." Beside me stood Donna and Rulian, their tearful eyes fastened on Minnie. Beyond the two young women was Old Liao, staring at her, his neck stretched forward and his bronzed face taut, as if he was trying hard to comprehend what was going on.

"We will wait for you to come back!" Rulian cried.

Minnie didn't reply, but simply smiled vaguely, as though all emotion had seeped out of her. Big Liu watched her in silence, his glasses flashing while his lips twisted. He waved at our friend, but she didn't respond.

Mrs. Dennison placed her hand on the door of the black car and said with a glum face, "Minnie, try to get well soon. Remember you're one of us and Jinling is your home—we'll always take you back."

Minnie gazed at her with a faraway look, the corners of her mouth wrinking a little. She didn't seem to register the meaning of the old woman's words. Then the car rolled away, leaving behind the faint smell of the exhaust and all the waving hands in the powdery rain.

Epilogue

51

ALICE SENT ME REPORTS about Minnie's condition to forward to Dr. Wu. The words that follow are hers.

May 8, 1940 (SHANGHAI)

Our trip to Shanghai was peaceful and pleasant. I was told that the USS *Luzon* used to be the flagship of the Yangtze River Patrol, and Admiral Glassford of the U.S. Asiatic Fleet was on it. He was a kind man and came to our cabin twice to see if we were comfortable or needed anything. Minnie was quiet most of the time, and when she spoke, she would blame herself, saying that she had become such a burden to me and others. She seemed clear-minded about her illness and told me that she would recover soon and return to the work she'd left behind. Minnie looked happy at dinner and we shared the table with the admiral.

June 20, 1940 (IOWA CITY)

Our voyage to the States was quite rough. In fact, we boarded the *Empress of Asia* three weeks ago and sailed first for Victoria, British Columbia. We ran into John Magee, who had gone back to China last year to do relief work and was heading home. Minnie seemed at ease in his presence, but she was seasick, which worsened her condition. She told me that if I hadn't accompanied her, she would have jumped into the ocean. That frightened me, and in some measure she acted suicidal, refusing to eat or drink. Reverend Magee, two other missionary passengers, and I took turns looking after her. We never left her alone.

Yesterday Minnie was admitted to the Psychopathic Hospital

of the State University of Iowa. I am staying at a guesthouse nearby. Minnie is under Dr. Woods's care and has a clean room, which looks out onto a small park, to herself. The doctor diagnosed her case as depression and said that most patients with this condition usually recovered within two months. So we should take heart.

July 9, 1940   (IOWA CITY)

I visit Minnie every day. Together we go out for a walk or call on local churches. We also stroll in a wood, where we do some lovely little devotionals of our own. This afternoon, she asked a nurse to telephone me, saying she wanted me to take her to the train station so we could leave Iowa once and for all. Of course the nurse refused to comply. When I went to see Minnie this evening, she felt ashamed and kept saying, "How could I do such a selfish thing?" I told her that it was over as long as she didn't do it again.

"I must get well and stop being a burden to others," she said.

She has been improving. I hope she will recuperate soon so that I can go to Texas and see my parents, but at present I should stay with my friend here.

I just heard from Rebecca Griest of Jinling's board that they had raised $1,200 for Minnie. This is wonderful. Minnie is constantly worried about spending Jinling's money on herself. I will share the good news with her tomorrow.

August 13, 1940   (IOWA CITY)

Minnie often says, "I built a wrong home in a wrong place— a home that was shattered easily. I should have known that a home doesn't have to be a physical entity." But then she will correct herself, saying, "I mustn't grumble so much. Millions of Chinese have lost not only their homes but also their families in the war. Compared to them, I'm more fortunate."

She wants to get well soon so she can return to Jinling. She has little family in America. Her brother wouldn't come to see her. On the other hand, her hometown, Secor, Illinois, was preparing a big welcome-home reception for her, and they have named August 22 as Minnie Vautrin Day. Minnie knows nothing about this, nor do the folks in Secor know about her nervous breakdown. Dr. Woods thinks that at present it would be too risky for Minnie to return to her hometown, since any excitement might throw her into a deeper depression. I called Secor and explained the situation. The town was disappointed and even wanted to send delegates to Iowa City to see Minnie, but Dr. Woods would not allow that.

August 29, 1940   (IOWA CITY)

Sometimes Minnie is like a normal person, and sometimes she is very depressed. She follows the news of the war closely and is worried about the situations in China and Europe. She asks others to pray for her, saying that she believes in prayers as well as medicine and that she needs to be helped "out of the valley of the shadow." Yesterday she said she should prepare to return to China for the next academic year. I pray for her every night.

September 26, 1940   (BROWN COUNTY
                                             STATE PARK, INDIANA)

At Dr. Woods's suggestion, we came to a state park in Indiana a week ago. He believes that the fresh air and the natural beauty of the surroundings will do Minnie good. She enjoys the peace and quiet here. Every morning we walk along the trails in the forest and also along the side of Ogle Lake, where a lot of waterfowl paddle around—they are not afraid of people and will take bread directly from your hand. Minnie likes feeding them.

The doctor has stopped the Metrazol treatment because it gave Minnie back pain and made her sore shoulders worse.

Without any medical attention at the moment, she seems to continue recuperating.

October 20, 1940   (ALPINE, TEXAS)

We stayed at the Indiana state park for less than a month. Dr. Woods agreed to let me take her to my parents' home in Texas. This is the only way I can keep watch on her while seeing my parents. Minnie likes the warm weather here and started helping my father in the garden. She wants to be "of some use."

She often mentions Yulan, the mad girl in Nanjing, and says, "Who could imagine I too would end up unbalanced?" Sometimes she muses aloud, "I'm wondering how the Japanese will get their retribution for what they did in Nanjing."

December 18, 1940   (ALPINE, TEXAS)

Minnie often claims that she will be confined in a mental hospital for good. She has been preparing gifts for Christmas. She has made a number of friends here, so she wants to surprise them with her gifts. Last week she sold two dozen fancy cards she brought back from China and donated all the proceeds, $12.50, to China Relief. Dr. Woods has instructed that we mustn't give her any responsibility or remind her of the war atrocities.

January 25, 1941   (ALPINE, TEXAS)

Mrs. Robert Doan of the missionary society came to see Minnie. She found Minnie almost normal, she told me, and left two days later. She and Minnie seemed to have hit it off, and they often laughed when they were together. The other day we dined in a Mexican restaurant and Minnie even ordered her own food, which she hadn't been able to do since last summer, as it was hard for her to make up her mind about almost everything. Before Mrs. Doan left, Minnie told us not to worry about her, saying she would get well soon and head back to China.

February 2, 1941   (ALPINE, TEXAS)

I was out of town for two days to see my sister's twins. During my absence Minnie went to an emporium and bought thirty sleeping pills. When I came back, she was in a nasty mood and accused me of abandoning her. I said I had gone to visit my sister for just two days. "See, now I'm back with you," I told her.

But she wouldn't trust me. She took out the sleeping pills and popped them all into her mouth. I was horrified, and no matter how I begged her, she wouldn't spit them out. I had to call for an ambulance to take her to the hospital.

I reported this incident to Dr. Woods immediately, and he urged me to take Minnie to a mental hospital in Indiana. The doctor emphasized that I must not accompany Minnie on the trip alone, so Mrs. Doan will come and together we will head for Indianapolis.

March 5, 1941   (INDIANAPOLIS)

Minnie didn't enter the mental institution because Mrs. Doan found her another physician, Dr. Carter, who examined Minnie and concluded that she was recovering. The doctor resumed giving her hormone injections. Minnie has been staying in Mrs. Doan's apartment downtown. In the morning she goes to Mrs. Doan's office and helps her pack and label parcels to be shipped to China for refugees. In the evening they are together, reading, conversing, and going to the movies. Sometimes I join them. In every way she is getting better.

Mrs. Doan told me this evening that she was going to assign Minnie a more complicated job: selecting and filing articles on missionary education. Minnie likes the idea and feels that this will be a good way to get her mind back completely.

April 20, 1941   (INDIANAPOLIS)

Minnie is confident that she will go back to work at Jinling in
the near future. In her letters to her friends she keeps asking
everyone to pray for her. Dr. Woods and Dr. Carter both believe
that she is recuperating. They are even allowing her to attend
the International Convention of the Disciples of Christ in town.
She is elated and is preparing to speak briefly on behalf of
Jinling.

May 14, 1941   (INDIANAPOLIS)

Today when she was left alone in the apartment of Miss Gene-
vieve Brown, the secretary of the missionary society, Minnie
gassed herself by turning on all the jets on the stove. By the
time I arrived at the hospital, she had passed away. We had her
body shipped to a small church in the suburbs, where the chief
pastor is a friend of Mrs. Doan's. Minnie left a note saying that
she ended her life this way because she was sure that she could
never fully recover. She also mentioned that she had a will in a
safety-deposit box in the bank.

   For months Minnie had been expecting to hear from Jinling
and to be invited back to China. The only letter that she received
was two weeks ago, from her niece in Michigan, who was willing
to take her in and care for her. Evidently someone had made an
agreement with her niece, which Minnie construed as a means
of abandoning her. After reading her niece's letter, Minnie
smirked. She was too proud to become a responsibility to others.

May 16, 1941   (INDIANAPOLIS)

We held a funeral for Minnie yesterday afternoon. Six people
attended. The chief pastor read Psalm 23. No hymn was sung,
since there were just the six of us. Mrs. Doan spoke briefly, saying: "Minnie Vautrin is also a casualty of war atrocities. She

fought courageously and fell as a fighter." I wish Mrs. Doan had said "as a hero."

Minnie's will was opened this morning. She had some savings in a Shanghai bank, 710 yuan in total, which she gave to Jinling as a fund for a scholarship. Also she donated to our college the 1.3 acres of land she bought last year. At the bottom of the will she had penned: "Jinling Forever!"

52

HALF A YEAR after Minnie's death, the Japanese Imperial Navy attacked Pearl Harbor, and the United States went to war with Japan. The Japanese confiscated our college and deported Mrs. Dennison, Donna, and Alice. Our campus became a cavalry barracks for some years.

My family moved to a suburb, and Liya and I did odd jobs to get by. My husband, Yaoping, didn't return until the Japanese were defeated. He'd lost half his teeth. In the meantime, my son-in-law came back once to see his wife and son, but he fled to Taiwan with the Nationalist army before the Communists seized power in 1949. Afterward he sent Liya a letter via Hong Kong and told her to remarry, for he couldn't come back to the mainland anymore. He implied that he would form a new family in Kao-hsiung. "Life would be too short for such an indefinite wait," he wrote. Liya took to her bed for weeks, though two years later she married a shop clerk and has lived an uneventful life since.

Owing to his past connections with the American professors, my husband was classified as an unreliable person by the Communists, but he remained at Nanjing University as a lecturer, unscathed by political shifts. Big Liu was not so lucky. When Searle Bates was leaving China in the spring of 1950, dozens of Chinese saw him off at the side entrance of the university, and Big Liu cried out in front of everyone, "Searle, come back someday. We will miss you!" Those words were reported as evidence of his reactionary outlook, and seven years later he was labeled a rightist who constantly dreamed of the day the American imperialists would take over China. For that he suffered bitterly for decades.

Ban also had rotten luck. He fled Jinling with Luhai and Meiyan and joined the Nationalist army in Hunan Province. He was captured

by the Communists in the civil war and sent back to Nanjing, where
he was made to labor at a brick kiln. I saw him once in the summer of
1951—he was tall but bent like an old man and had a gray widow's
peak, though he was not yet thirty. He called me Auntie and I only
nodded, too sad to say a word. Probably luckier than him, both Luhai
and Meiyan died in the war. He was killed by Japanese artillery, and
she was shot dead by a sniper while she was rescuing a wounded soldier. Although she was named a martyr, her father still had to suffer
by virtue of his closeness with the foreigners.

Times have not affected Miss Lou that much. She worked at the
orphanage left by Monica for a few years and later, after the Communists took over the country, became a kindergarten teacher.

Dr. Wu didn't leave with the Nationalists for Taiwan despite their
repeated urging. For that, she was reinstated by the Communists as
the head of our school, which later became part of Nanjing Normal
College. She was respected as a dignitary, and I resumed working
for her.

After the Japanese surrendered, a portion of my diary was serial-
ized by *Nanjing Daily* as evidence of the Japanese war atrocities. For
that I was known as the Chinese woman who helped Minnie Vautrin
run the Jinling refugee camp. In the summer of 1947, the Nationalist
government interviewed me and then sent me to Tokyo as an eyewitness at the war crimes trials. For the first time I set foot in Japan.

All the hearings were conducted in a large white building, and
each session was attended by more than a thousand people. The Chinese side hadn't made a lot of preparations for the trial, assuming that
as victors we could punish those war criminals at will, whereas the
Japanese side was well prepared. Each defendant had two lawyers
assigned to him, one American and the other Japanese. Most Japanese lawyers didn't raise a peep, but the American lawyers were loud
and arrogant and would even ridicule the witnesses as if we were the
ones on trial. As a result, the judges threw some of them out of court.

One day in mid-August, as I was approaching the courthouse with
a group of Chinese eyewitnesses, a thirtyish woman in a white
kimono appeared with a young boy and bowed to me. Instantly I rec-

ognized her, so I stepped away from my colleagues and took her aside. Mitsuko kept bowing while saying in accented Mandarin, "Mother, here's your grandson."

Tears gushed out of my eyes, but I dared not speak much. She pushed Shin forward and told him, "Say 'Grandma.'"

"Grandma," he mumbled, a little worm of wrinkles on his forehead.

I squatted down and hugged and kissed him. He even smelled like his father. "Do you go to school?" I asked.

"Uh-huh."

"In what grade?"

He didn't get the question, but Mitsuko put in, "Second."

"When's your birthday?"

His mother answered, "December fourth."

"I will remember that, Shin," I said, and kissed him between the eyes.

The hearing was to resume at one thirty, just a few minutes away. A Chinese official came out of the foyer and beckoned me to enter the court. What should I do? By no means could I let others know I was meeting my family members here. I was representing all the Nanjing women brutalized by the Japanese army and couldn't possibly acknowledge Mitsuko and Shin overtly now. That would have amounted to inviting disaster. On the spur of the moment, I took off the gold bangle from my wrist and handed it to Mitsuko. "Haowen wanted you to have this," I said, clasping her hand with both of mine. "Please don't come to this place again. It's not safe."

Without waiting for her response, I veered and headed for the courthouse, my legs shaking. I had no clue where exactly we were staying, because all the Chinese eyewitnesses were semiquarantined, traveling as a group between the courthouse and the hotel, a wooden villa on the Sumida River. Otherwise I would have let Mitsuko know where we might meet again.

Several American missionaries were in Tokyo for the war crimes trials as well: Searle, Reverend Magee, Dr. Wilson, and Holly Thornton. I was happy to see them, though I was gloomy after meeting Mitsuko and Shin.

"What's wrong?" Holly asked me one evening. "You look so blue."

"I'm kind of under the weather," I said. "This humidity really gets to me."

"The hearings must've gotten to you a lot too."

"I can't sleep well these days."

I dared not confide in Holly, whose eyes crinkled up at the corners as she observed me. Unlike Minnie, she might not be that discreet in spite of her good nature.

The Chinese side had little material evidence to support our charges because during the war nobody had expected to face these criminals at such a trial. But thanks to the conscientiousness of the Americans—particularly the Safety Zone Committee's paperwork kept by Searle, the photographs shot by Magee, and the medical records filed by Wilson—and also thanks to some secret reports about the Nanjing atrocities that the German embassy had dispatched to the Nazi government, the court could make a fair assessment of the crimes perpetrated by the Imperial Army. Magee disclosed to me that he'd brought along the footage he'd shot, but the court wouldn't accept the films as evidence. In truth, the U.S. government meant to downplay the trial and avoid antagonizing the Japanese populace so that Japan would become a staunch anticommunist country. Among the twenty-five major war criminals on trial, only seven received the death penalty.

When the judge asked Iwane Matsui whether he was guilty, he muttered that he was not. Still, the moment the death sentence was announced, the top general, skeletal and bespectacled now, sobbed and collapsed in his seat, unable to stand up. His bald head was bobbing. Two tall guards wearing white helmets and "MP" armbands stepped forward, pulled him up, and hauled him out of the courtroom.

We left Tokyo on a balmy morning in late August. As we walked out of the hotel and headed for the sedans that were taking us to the airport, I caught sight of Mitsuko and Shin again. They stood at the side of the gate, she wearing an apple-green cheongsam that set off her curvaceous figure, while he had on a white shirt and navy blue shorts. Behind them was a large bonsai in a stone planter, and beyond them seagulls were sailing above the turquoise river, letting out cries. Mother and son waved at me almost timidly while my colleagues and the officials turned to watch. There was no way I could go up to Mitsuko and Shin, so I just nodded at them. Slowly I climbed into a car. As we pulled away, I covered my face with both hands.

That was the last time I saw them.

This is a work of fiction. For the information, facts, and historical details, I relied on numerous publications and am indebted to their authors, editors, and translators.

In addition to the electronic version of *Minnie Vautrin's Diary (1937–1940)* provided by Yale Divinity School Library, I found the following publications very useful in creating this novel: *Terror in Minnie Vautrin's Nanjing: Diaries and Correspondence, 1937–38* (University of Illinois Press, 2008), and *They Were in Nanjing: The Nanjing Massacre Witnessed by American and British Nationals* (Hong Kong University Press, 2004), both edited by Suping Lu; Hua-ling Hu's *American Goddess at the Rape of Nanking: The Courage of Minnie Vautrin* (Southern Illinois University Press, 2000); *The Good Man of Nanking: The Diaries of John Rabe*, ed. Erwin Wickert (Alfred A. Knopf, 1998); *Eyewitnesses to Massacre: American Missionaries Bear Witness to Japanese Atrocities in Nanjing*, ed. Zhang Kaiyuan (M. E. Sharpe, 2001); Iris Chang's *The Rape of Nanking* (Basic Books, 1997); Honda Katsuichi's *The Nanjing Massacre: A Japanese Journalist Confronts Japan's National Shame*, trans. Karen Sandness and ed. Frank Gibney (M. E. Sharpe, 1999); *Documents on the Rape of Nanking*, ed. Timothy Brook (University of Michigan Press, 1999); Mary Bosworth Treudley's *This Stinging Exultation* (Taipei: The Orient Cultural Service, 1972); *Ginling College*, coauthored by Mrs. Lawrence Thurston and Miss Ruth M. Chester (New York: United Board for Christian Colleges in China, 1955); *The Rape of Nanking: An Undeniable History in Photographs*, coauthored by Shi Young and James Yin (Chicago and San Francisco: Innovative Publishing Group, 1997); *Qin hua rijun nanjing da tusha riji* [*Diaries by the Japanese Soldiers in the Nanjing Massacre*], ed. Guangyi Wu (Beijing: Sociological Documents Press, 2005); Zhaiwei Sun's *Chengqing lishi* [*Clarifying History: Studies and Reflections on the Nanjing Massacre*] (Nanjing: Jiangsu People's Press, 2005); Tamaki Matsuoka's *Nankin-sen tozasareta kioku o tazunete* [*Battle of Nanking: Searching for the Closed Memories—Witnesses of 102 Japanese Soldiers in China*], translated into Chinese by Meiying Quan and Jianyun Li, and edited by Weifan Shen, Zhaoqi Cheng, and Chengsha Zhu (Shanghai Reference Books Press, 2002); *Nanjing da tusha shiliao ji (7: Dongjing shenpan)* [*Historical Materials of Nanjing Massacre (vol. 7: The Tokyo Trials)*], ed. Xiaming Yang

(Nanjing: Jiangsu People's Press, 2005); *Nanjing da tusha shiliao ji (28: lishi tuxiang)* [*Historical Materials of Nanjing Massacre (vol. 28: Historical Photographs and Graphics)*], ed. Bihong Cao et al. (Nanjing: Jiangsu People's Press, 2006); and *In the Name of the Emperor* [documentary], directed by Nancy Tong and Christine Choy (Hong Kong, 1995).

ACKNOWLEDGMENTS

My heartfelt thanks to my editor, Dan Frank, for upholding a rigorous standard; to Deb Garrison for her invaluable comments; to my agent, Lane Zachary, for her patience and unflagging enthusiasm; to Suping Lu for allowing me to reprint the map of Jinling Women's College; to Rong Cai and Changsheng Li for helping me get some details right; to Aimin Chen and Yuen Ying Chan for sending me needed materials; and to Lisha and Wen for their constant love and support.

THE BRIDEGROOM

In the title story, the head of security at a sewing factory is shocked, first when the handsomest worker on the floor proposes marriage to his homely adopted daughter, and again when his new son-in-law is arrested for the "crime" of homosexuality. In "Alive," a man is sent by his employers to collect a debt in a faraway town; when an earthquake induces amnesia, he marries a stranger and begins a new life, only to remember later that he has left a family behind in his native Muji City. And in "After Cowboy Chicken Came to Town," the Chinese workers at an American-style fast-food franchise receive a hilarious crash course in marketing, deep-frying, and that frustrating capitalist dictum, "the customer is always right." In these and nine other unforgettable tales, Ha Jin has triumphed again.

Fiction/Short Stories

THE CRAZED

When the venerable professor Yang, a teacher of literature at a provincial university, has a stroke, his student Jian Wan is assigned to care for him. Since the dutiful Jian plans to marry his mentor's beautiful, icy daughter, the job requires delicacy. Just how much delicacy becomes clear when Yang begins to rave. Are these just the outpourings of a broken mind, or is Yang speaking the truth—about his family, his colleagues, and his life's work? And will bearing witness to the truth end up breaking poor Jian's heart?

Fiction/Literature

A FREE LIFE

In *A Free Life*, Ha Jin follows the Wu family—father Nan, mother Pingping, and son Taotao—as they sever their ties with China and begin a new life in the United States. As Nan takes on a number of menial jobs, eventually operating a restaurant with Pingping, he struggles to adapt to the American way of life and to hold his family together, even as he pines for a woman he loved and lost in his youth. Ha Jin's prodigious talents are in full force as he brilliantly brings to life the struggles and successes of the contemporary immigrant experience.

Fiction/Literature

A GOOD FALL

A lonely composer takes comfort in the antics of his girlfriend's parakeet; young children decide to change their names so they might sound more "American," unaware of how deeply this will hurt their grandparents; a Chinese professor of English attempts to defect with the help of a reluctant former student. All of Ha Jin's characters struggle to remain loyal to their homeland and its traditions while also exploring the freedom that life in a new country offers. In *A Good Fall*, Jin gives us a collection that delves into the experience of Chinese immigrants in America.

Fiction/Short Stories

IN THE POND

Shao Bin is a downtrodden worker at the Harvest Fertilizer Plant by day and an aspiring artist by night. Passed over on the list to receive a decent apartment for his young family while those in favor with the party's leaders are selected ahead of him, Bin chafes at his powerlessness. When he attempts to expose his corrupt superiors by circulating satirical cartoons, he provokes an escalating series of merciless counterattacks that sends ripples beyond his small community. Artfully crafted and suffused with earthy wit, *In the Pond* is a moving tale about humble lives caught up in larger social forces.

Fiction/Literature

OCEAN OF WORDS

The place is the chilly border between Russia and China. The time is the early 1970s, when the two giants were poised on the brink of war. And the characters are Chinese soldiers who must constantly scrutinize the enemy even as they themselves are watched for signs of the fatal disease of bourgeois liberalism. In *Ocean of Words*, Ha Jin explores the predicament of these simple, barely literate men with breathtaking concision and humanity. This thrilling collection of stories is a triumphant volume—poignant, hilarious, and harrowing.

Fiction/Short Stories

WAITING

The demands of human longing contend with the weight of centuries of custom in *Waiting*, a novel of unexpected richness and universal resonance. Every summer Lin Kong, a doctor in the Chinese Army, returns to his village to end his loveless arranged marriage with the humble and touchingly loyal Shuyu. But each time Lin must return to the city to tell Manna Wu, the educated, modern nurse he loves, that they will need to wait another year. Caught between the conflicting claims of these two utterly different women and trapped by a culture in which adultery can ruin lives and careers, Lin has been waiting for eighteen years. This year, he promises, will be different.

Fiction/Literature

WAR TRASH

Ha Jin's masterful novel casts a searchlight into a forgotten corner of modern history, the experience of Chinese soldiers held in U.S. POW camps during the Korean War. In 1951 Yu Yuan, a scholarly and self-effacing clerical officer in Mao's "volunteer" army, is taken prisoner south of the Thirty-Eighth Parallel. Because he speaks English, he soon becomes an intermediary between his compatriots and their American captors. With Yuan as guide, we are ushered into the secret world behind the barbed wire, a world in which kindness alternates with blinding cruelty and one has infinitely more to fear from one's fellow prisoners than from the guards.

Fiction/Literature